Old Lies
by
Linzi Carlisle

In memory of Agatha Christie for inspiring my love for mysteries

Table of Contents

THE MAIN CHARACTERS

Elizabeth Payton, resident of Meadowvale
Judith Bertram, her daughter, and her husband David
Elspeth Parkhurst, resident of Meadowvale
Miriam Smithers, her daughter, and her daughter Lucy
Albert Bird, resident of Meadowvale
Raymond Bird, his son
Davinia and Agatha Lovewell, sisters,
residents of Meadowvale
Howard Norton, resident of Meadowvale
Richard Carding, his nephew, and his wife Moira
Lillian Springer, resident of Meadowvale
Mervyn Springer, her son
Monty Mallowan, resident of Meadowvale
Dorothy Newton, former resident of Meadowvale, deceased
Mrs Goodwin, manager of Meadowvale, and her staff:
Greg, carer
Kirsty, cook
Mary, kitchen assistant/carer
Spencer, carer
Tanya, carer
Willow, activities therapist
Colin Hartley, gardener

PROLOGUE

Extract from a personal diary
She looked so harmless the first time I laid eyes on her. There she was, just a sweet little old lady, dressed up like a small girl in a pink dress, white cardigan, multi-coloured clips in her grey hair, and a bulging handbag over her arm. Oh, and she was wearing her slippers of course, as most of the residents tended to.

Out of everyone at Meadowvale, residents, visitors, and staff, alike, she seemed to have the most fun, always chatting away to herself and giggling, giving us all those funny sidelong glances of hers that I came to recognise. Her head would tilt to the side as she contemplated one of us, her eyes glinting as if she knew all our secrets, and then she'd lean across to an empty chair and have a whispered conversation with a cushion before sitting back, nodding, pleased with herself.

Next would come the grand opening of the handbag. Delving into its capacious depths she would bring out her notebook, followed by her pen, and proceed to make copious notes, all the while eyeing one or other of us, staff member, resident, or visitor, with her strange birdlike eyes. Nodding and chattering away, she would discuss her written notes with the cushions closest to her, these chats sometimes ending in uproarious laughter, before hiding her notebook back in her handbag with a triumphant glance in the direction of one of us.

One time I tried to ask her about it. 'What have you got there, Dorothy? Mind if I take a look?' I reached for her handbag but her shriek was enough to draw attention and I had to withdraw quietly.

'It's a secret!' she'd hissed at me after the member of staff had wandered off. 'Wouldn't you like to know,' she'd taunted.

Well, yes, actually, Dorothy, I would like to know, because if it's my secret that you've got written in your precious notebook then I'd like to destroy it before anyone reads it. Of course, the likelihood of that happening was pretty slim, considering my own lack of success in that department but still, it was a worry.

I began to observe Dorothy whenever the opportunity presented itself, which wasn't overly frequently, Meadowvale being, surprisingly, an extremely busy place. The residents themselves were all fairly able which meant they were inclined to roam the property at all times of the day and night, spending time in the lounge, the library, playing scrabble or monopoly in the games room, and even table tennis. Staff were kept busy every day and might be found anywhere throughout the property, and visitors would make themselves at home, moving freely around Meadowvale and its grounds, in search of one errant relative or another. And then there was carpet boules, a popular activity in which residents, staff, and visitors all joined in, and a game which became increasingly competitive, such was the desire to be heralded as this week's carpet boules champ with one's name and photo up on the board.

Add in the large grounds to the mix and you can see that it would be quite difficult to keep tabs on someone if you so desired. Nonetheless, I managed to spend enough time close to Dorothy to conclude that she was a complete busybody and very much enjoyed knowing everyone's business. Rumour has it that she was the renowned poison pen letter lady whose missives caused untold chaos not so long ago, in the village of Parva Crossing, on the outskirts of which Meadowvale is situated. I must applaud her for that for it must have taken some doing, but still, in the interests of my future, the last thing I needed was Dorothy knowing my business and meddling in such a way that word got out about my own secret.

Dorothy took to making little comments, just loud enough for those of us closest to her at the time to hear. She'd throw out a comment like 'So many words but it only takes two to change things,' or 'Tweet tweet, I'm going to tell her,' or 'Who threw out the baby with the bath water?' Of course, none of it made sense to anyone, or perhaps just to the person concerned, but it was enough to worry me. She'd never look directly at anyone after making one of her comments, just peer around gleefully, giving her little knowing nod, before shuffling off to make more mischief.

It was when she passed a comment that I was sure was directed at me that I knew I must take action before it was too late. And so began my rather more in-depth surveillance of the woman, when circumstances allowed and when suspicion would not be aroused.

I noticed that Dorothy enjoyed spending time in the gardens, often walking off along the paths as she muttered to herself, and always with her handbag over her arm. Of course, I couldn't just follow her every time, for this would have aroused suspicion, but I managed to find enough reasons to take a walk in the garden, as well as using other means at my disposal, to enable me to find out her favourite place. And this was when I formulated my plan to murder her.

NO FUN ANY MORE

'I'm sorry, Eric, but I'm going to Parva Crossing and that's final.' Sasha slammed the bedroom door behind her, sighing at the mess in the lounge. Throwing the balcony doors open, she picked up empty wine bottles and glasses, taking them to the kitchen where last night's dinner plates sat in the sink, their congealed contents emitting an unpleasant odour of sour onions. Loudly scraping the hardening food remains into the bin she rinsed the plates and put them into the dishwasher before returning to the lounge to fetch the overflowing ashtray.

Eric appeared, wrapping his arms around her from behind. 'You know how hot you look doing that in this little tee shirt and knickers?' He nuzzled into her neck as his hands crept down over her hips but she brushed him away irritably.

'Leave it, I've got to clear up, this place is a disaster. You could help, you know?'

'I am helping, I'm relaxing you.' He rubbed her shoulders, turning her to face him. 'Sash, come on, come back to bed.'

'I can't, Eric, I've got stuff to do, I told you.'

Sulkily, Eric leaned against the counter. 'Tell me again why it's so important for you to go back to Parva Crossing – some retirement village in the middle of nowhere. What, you're going to single-handedly solve the murder of some old woman in a care home? Correct me if I'm wrong but they do have their own police to do that don't they? What makes you so special?'

Wiping the dishcloth over the surfaces angrily, Sasha tried to hide her exasperation. 'Firstly, it's not a retirement village, my own sister lives there, in case you've forgotten; secondly, it's a scenic area and popular with tourists; thirdly, no, I don't think I'm going to solve the murder on my own, but the police haven't had any success and I might be able to help; and finally, she's not some old woman, she's someone that I knew, that I had a little understanding of, and even if she'd lost her marbles and caused a lot of trouble in the past, she's been killed, and she didn't deserve that. There's a murderer out there who needs to be caught – that's the most important thing.'

'Is *he* going to be there?' Eric's eyes narrowed.

'Who?'

'You know who. That bloke you were hanging out with last time you were there when your niece went missing.'

Not meeting his eyes, Sasha shrugged her shoulders as she banged cupboard doors, filled the kettle, and shoved bread into the toaster. 'I don't know, maybe, maybe not, that's got nothing to do with anything.'

'Oh, it's got everything to do with everything, babe, seeing as we're engaged. I've got a right to know what you're getting up to and who you're getting up to it with.' Eric's eyes flashed dangerously.

'Oh ho, don't get me started on that, Eric. We've been engaged for what, two weeks? Since we've been back from Paxos I've only seen you two or three times, one of which I caught you chatting up some bird at the pub while you thought I was busy on my phone. No, don't look like that, I saw you, you even gave her your number. I thought you'd changed, you said you were finished with all that crap, and after everything we went through recently–' she stopped to draw breath, exasperated and emotional. 'Eric, you said you'd stop all that, and you said you'd lay off the booze a bit, but the night I was supposed to have dinner at yours, I found you passed out, so I came home – you didn't even remember the next day. Most nights you're too busy to see me but you never say why. I don't get it, why are we even together, let alone engaged?'

'Baby, baby, come on. I'm sorry, okay? I admit it, I've relapsed a bit, okay? This is all new, this being engaged. I've just been blowing off steam a little, hooking up with mates, celebrating. I just need to get used to it all, that's all. We went through a lot with the whole Miles fiasco, I thought I was going to lose you, and now that I've got you and everything's alright, I suppose I just kind of relaxed and slipped back into a few of my old ways. Look, I'm sorry, babe, I'll try harder, I promise. Go. Go to Parva Crossing, it's fine, maybe I can come up for a few days and join you – hopefully it won't be as bad as the last time I did that when you dumped me. You can show me why the village is so special.' His eyes crinkled as he grinned at her.

Sasha felt her shoulders relaxing. 'Alright, I suppose we've both needed to blow off some steam after everything that happened. But I swear, Eric, if you start messing around with other women then it's over, and just, well, maybe try and cut down on the drinking a bit, you've been going crazy.'

'Done.' Eric gave her his puppy dog face as he held his hands out innocently. 'No women, less booze.'

Once Eric had gone Sasha put the washing machine on and went off for her hair appointment with Marlene at Scissors Sisters. It was just a coincidence that she'd be going to Parva Crossing again with her hair freshly cut and highlighted, she told herself. Cal might not even still be there and even if he was, well, she was engaged to Eric now. What Eric had said was true, they had been through a lot, Eric beaten half to death by Miles, Zoe held captive and Sasha herself abducted by him. They had a lot of stuff to work through but they'd get there – wouldn't they?

While she sat in the hair salon, her hair in foils, Sasha messaged back and forth with her best friend, Zoe. They still hadn't talked properly about what Zoe had gone through while held captive by Miles, she seemed to want to keep it locked away in the back of her mind, which was hardly surprising. She now knew that he'd taken photos of her and posted them to Graffic, but apart from glancing at them when Sasha had tried to broach the subject gently, Zoe had determinedly refused to talk about it.

It was with relief that Sasha read Zoe's message telling her that she'd started meeting with a counsellor to talk things over – her friend would heal slowly, and she now had a good man by her side, in James.

Back in her flat, she phoned Jules at The Spotted Dog to confirm her booking and tell her what time she'd be arriving, then she phoned her sister.

'Oh, Sash, we can't wait!' Tessa beamed into the phone. 'Chantelle's so excited, she's planned a pizza night for us tomorrow evening and she's making the pizzas herself. I've not seen her like this for ages, it'll be just like old times, I can't wait.'

Eric was on his best behaviour for their last night together, having booked them a table at The Reading Man, and after an evening of good food, good wine, and honest talking, they returned to her flat where he poured them a night cap, presented her with a gift *to be opened when she got to Parva Crossing* and took her to bed.

Lying beside him later, Sasha thought dreamily that it could all work out okay, and drifted off to sleep with her alarm set for six o'clock.

~

Greg tiptoed along the low-lit corridor checking that everyone was sleeping soundly in their beds. As he passed each window, he made sure it was securely closed, the same with the exterior doors. Ever since Dorothy Newton had been murdered he'd been feeling spooked out when on night shift, and tonight was no exception. Of course, he'd told Richard about how nervous he was, and Richard had done his best to visit him on his night shifts when possible. But tonight he'd had family commitments, whatever that meant, and so was unable to come through. Poor me, thought Greg, as he turned away from the window he'd just checked, only to jump in fright and emit a high-pitched squeal as a ghostly apparition appeared from around the corner.

'Good grief, Elizabeth, you scared me half to death. What on earth are you doing walking around in the dark at night for?' He hurriedly removed his hand from his rapidly beating heart and tried to compose himself.

'Well really, Greg, whatever's the matter with you? When we lived in Rhodesia we certainly didn't let a little darkness scare us, you need to toughen up.' With a pitying look at Greg, Elizabeth Payton walked past him and into her room, leaning heavily on her stick.

'Yes well,' sniped Greg to the empty corridor, 'this isn't Rhodesia, which is now Zimbabwe by the way, Elizabeth, and we happen to have a murderer on the loose.' He hurried on, wanting to get his two-hourly check over with and retreat to the staff room with a calming cup of camomile tea.

He stood looking at Monty Mallowan's open door, feeling exasperated. Where had he disappeared to? This was all he needed, now he'd have to check the lounge, with all its dark corners, as well as the dining room, the library, the games room, the conservatory, and please, not outside, not in the dark.

'Monty,' he hissed, entering the cavernous residents' lounge. 'Are you there?' The dim night lighting threw eerie shadows into the room and created ominously dark shapes from the furniture. Pausing, he sniffed the air – cigarette smoke. Tutting, and feeling braver, Greg marched towards the conservatory, feeling a draught from an open window or door.

The elderly man looked up guiltily as Greg appeared in the conservatory. 'I know, I know, you're going to tell me off aren't you, young Gregory?' He held his hands up. 'I couldn't sleep, keep thinking about poor Dorothy. Who would do that to her? We all knew she was up to mischief half the time but the poor old girl was mad as a hatter and harmless as they come.'

Closing the door and locking it, Greg turned to him, hands on his hips. 'Yes, I know, I understand, I do, but, Monty, you can't go unlocking doors at night and leaving them open, it's not safe. And you should be in bed, it's the middle of the night.'

'Oh, what a drag it is getting old, d'you know, in my youth, we'd be out at parties until the early hours of the morning, thought nothing of it, and now I'm expected to be in bed by nine-thirty. It's no fun anymore, it really isn't.' Stubbing his cigarette out, Monty Mallowan heaved his not inconsiderable size out of the armchair. 'Right, I'm off, don't report me to Matron, will you? I don't want a spanking for being a naughty boy.'

With all his charges safely accounted for, Greg hurried back to the sanctuary of the staff room and switched the kettle on. He'd never relax, he really wouldn't, not until they caught Dorothy's murderer.

~

Jules sat at the bar counter in the silent pub, sipping her wine, wondering if she'd done the right thing in not telling Cal that Sasha was coming. Well, to be fair she'd only known for certain earlier that day and she hadn't seen him since then. Maybe she should just let events happen naturally, she'd interfered enough in telling Sasha about Cal's return, as well as with her blunder over the photos, where she and Cal had stared in disbelief at the photo announcing that Sasha was engaged. No, she'd leave it. Smiling, she thought of how much she was looking forward to seeing Sasha again. She drained her wine glass and switched off the last of the lights, heading through to her flat behind the bar, looking forward to her bed.

HARD STUFF

As much as she loved London, Sasha felt a sense of relief as she headed north towards Parva Crossing. Blasting her tunes, she sang along loudly as the sun rose on a beautiful spring day, and found herself looking forward to her visit immensely, even if the underlying reason was to catch a murderer.

Stopping at a service station for a rest break she ordered herself a toasted egg and bacon sandwich and a cup of tea, before stocking up on a few snacks and drinks for the road.

As she drove, she thought about Dorothy Newton. No doubt the woman had been murdered as a direct result of her endless meddling – but whose lives could she meddle in at a care home, she pondered? And who would have a secret so terrible that they would feel the need to kill a defenceless old lady? Surely the residents were all in their seventies or eighties? It hardly seemed credible that one of them would be capable of murder. But then she reminded herself of how Dorothy had been murdered, conceding that it wouldn't take particular strength or skill and so would be manageable by even the frailest of persons, within reason. There was also the staff, and, she suddenly realised, visitors should also be part of her consideration. She found herself feeling excited about the case – nothing got her blood flowing like having a good mystery to solve.

Mixed emotions fought for space in her head as she pulled into the car park of The Spotted Dog, memories of her last visit engulfing her. But these were put aside as the door opened and Jules, the owner, emerged to welcome her.

When the two women had finished hugging and laughing, they took a bag each and headed into the pub. 'You've got your same room, is that okay, Sash?'

'Perfect, Jules, thank you.' Smiling, Sasha followed Jules up to the top floor, stopping for a moment to glance at the closed door across from hers. 'Is he–?'

Jules nodded. 'He's back, yes, I'll tell you all about it when we get the chance. And I understand congratulations are in order? You're getting married? That's wonderful, Sash, as long as you're sure about it and happy?'

'I am, thanks, babe.' Sasha grinned at her. 'I know Eric probably came across as a total disaster last time you saw him, so I don't blame you for having your doubts, but a lot's happened since then. Let's just say we found out what we mean to each other and are working on the issues that caused us trouble last time.'

'Well, I'm pleased for you, you deserve it after what you went through last year, it must have been awful.'

'You've got that right. Being kidnapped by a psycho wasn't exactly much fun, but I'm still here, that's the main thing.'

'You certainly lead an interesting life, Sash. I'll leave you to unpack and see you in the bar with a glass of wine then?'

'Sounds perfect, thanks.' Giving Jules another quick hug, Sasha unpacked her bags, pausing to try Eric's number again, before heading down the stairs for her wine.

~

'Afternoon, Uncle Howie.' Richard Carding leaned over and kissed his uncle before handing him a box of his favourite chocolates. Still holding the bunch of rather droopy flowers, he glanced around, wondering what to do with them.

'And how's my favourite nephew?' Howard Norton grinned happily.

Richard rolled his eyes exaggeratedly. 'I'm your only nephew.'

'Where did you get those sorry specimens, rob a petrol station shop?'

Groaning indulgently, Richard laughed. 'You need a new repertoire, Uncle Howie. If I can find a vase maybe they'll perk up in some water.' He looked around uncertainly.

The Lovewell sisters jostled with each other as they both offered to take the flowers and put them in a vase.

'I said I'll do it.' Davinia snatched the cellophane-wrapped bunch and picked up her stick.

'Oh, do be careful, Davinia, when did you lose your rubber bit on the bottom, we must ask Mrs Goodwin to sort it out.' Agatha snatched the bunch back and, kaftan flowing, walked briskly off, calling back over her shoulder, 'We can't have you rushing and falling over, and Howie doesn't want to wait until tonight to enjoy his flowers, does he?'

Howard winked at his nephew as Richard murmured, 'I see you've still got your fan club.'

'Well come on then, tell me some news. How's Moira? Not found out you're a fraud and left you yet?' Guffawing, Howard rocked back and forth in his chair as Davinia gurgled fawningly.

'No, she still hasn't found me out.' Richard played along with the familiar routine he and his uncle had enjoyed for what seemed like forever. Sitting back comfortably and crossing his legs, he chatted to his uncle about this and that, throwing in the odd mention of his military memorabilia shop and its struggles.

They stopped chatting, politely, when Agatha returned with the vase of flowers, and Howie thanked her profusely. 'What would I do without you, Agatha? You're an angel, that's what you are.'

'Anything for you, Howie, you know that.' Agatha simpered, casting a triumphant look at her sister who glared in return.

A short while later a bell tinkled and Greg appeared, wheeling in a tea trolley laden with teapot, milk jug, cups and saucers, as well as a Victoria sponge, cake plates and forks.

'Tra La La, who's for tea?' Exaggeratedly wobbling his bottom as he walked, Greg halted, clearing his throat theatrically. 'Good afternoon, everyone. Oh, and hello, Richard, lovely to see you. Now for this afternoon's treat, we have a delicious Victoria sponge courtesy of the wonderful Mary. Ladies?' He turned to Davinia and Agatha Lovewell. 'Can I tempt the two most beautiful women in the room to a slice of cake?'

Giggling happily both women accepted and while Greg served them slices of cake, Howard leaned over and whispered in Richard's ear, 'They're the only two women in the room but let's not spoil their fun.'

'Gentlemen?' Nodding, Howard accepted a slice of cake, but Richard declined.

'Watching your figure, are you?' Greg winked at him before waving his arm at the teapot. 'Shall I be Mum?'

'Oh no, dear, you go off and get on with things, I'll be Mum.' This time Davinia was not going to be upstaged by her sister and she picked up the teapot.

'Well, I'll leave you darlings to it then, toodle pip.'

Howard watched Greg leave the lounge, his eyebrows raised. 'Good job you didn't turn out like that. It's not natural, that's what it's not. We didn't have that kind of thing in my day. When my sister – your mother – and I were growing up in India there'd have been a terrible to do if anyone had behaved like that. It would have been ten years' hard labour, I reckon.' He looked at his nephew approvingly. 'No, you turned out alright, my boy, marrying that good wife of yours as well, although some children would have been nice. Still, you're alright, and a good thing too, otherwise I'd have had to cut you out of my will.' He nudged him sharply in the side, tea sloshing into Richard's saucer, as he slipped a folded banknote into his nephew's pocket.

'Yes, Uncle Howie, oh, you really shouldn't...' Richard smiled tightly, holding in his irritation, before excusing himself for the bathroom.

'You've got a bladder like a woman, boy.' Howard's parting shot had the Lovewell sisters chuckling delightedly as he winked at them.

'In here.' Greg beckoned Richard into the linen room as he left the residents' lounge. The two men embraced as Greg groaned. 'I've missed you.'

'Me too.' Richard held Greg, smiling into his eyes as he let out a long sigh. 'My uncle's been off on his favourite subject, it's as much as I could do to hold my tongue. If he ever found out about us...'

'But he won't will he?'

'No, I've made sure of that, but we must still be careful.'

Greg shivered.' You sound so mysterious. What d'you mean you've made sure of it?'

'Oh, well, I married Moira, didn't I? Now come here.'

A little while later Greg opened the door and peered out. 'All clear.'

'You took your time, your tea's gone cold.' Howard scrutinised his nephew for a moment before declaring, 'Well, the sun's well over the yardarm, how about a sherry? Ladies? That's if Elizabeth hasn't finished it off.'

'Oh, Howie, you are a devil,' Davinia and Agatha declared delightedly, as Elizabeth Payton looked up with a frown, to which Howard mimicked devil's horns, bringing forth more admiring laughter, at which point Richard announced it was time for him to leave.

~

Sasha was on her second glass of wine when she glanced at her watch. 'Look at the time, I'd better call a cab.' Five minutes later she was on her way – tomorrow she'd get down to the business of investigating Dorothy's murder, and first thing in the morning, she'd call the police station and arrange a time to meet with Nick and Jane. Frowning at her phone, she tried calling Eric again, leaving a message when he didn't answer.

With a bottle of wine in each hand, Sasha was enveloped in hugs from Tessa, Chantelle, and Dave, and after an evening of family, laughter, too much booze, and Chantelle's excellent pizza, Sasha fell into a cab back to the pub, feeling nicely sloshed. It had felt so good being with family again, she thought happily. Chantelle had looked a little peaky though, shadows under her eyes, and had she lost weight? Her niece hadn't eaten much, now that she came to think of it, but maybe she was still struggling with the after-effects of her ordeal and the dreadful loss of her friend – which was hardly surprising – it hadn't even been a year yet.

The lights were still on at the pub but customers were leaving. Good, she'd made it just in time for a last drink. Entering the bar, she glimpsed a tall figure about to go through the door to the rooms and, recognising his long hair tied back, she realised it was Cal. About to call out, she closed her mouth as he turned to smile at an attractive, willowy woman behind him, before putting his arm around her and leading her through the door to the rooms.

Something sank inside her. Why was she feeling like that? She was engaged to Eric after all. Pasting a smile onto her face she walked to the bar where Jules was finishing up.

'You're just in time for a nightcap.' Jules grinned at her before noticing her slightly strained expression. 'You just saw him, didn't you?'

'Yes, and he's with someone by the looks of it.'

'Willow. That's her name, I'm not kidding, I mean, she couldn't actually be any taller or slimmer. She's staying here, and she's got a job at Meadowvale, and, well, it looks like she and Cal are becoming quite friendly.' Glancing sympathetically at Sasha, Jules waved a tumbler. 'Hard stuff?'

'Hard stuff,' agreed Sasha. *It didn't take him long, she thought bitterly, one minute a pregnant wife, the next minute some perfect-looking new girlfriend.*

MRS PRINGLE PRONOUNCES JUDGEMENT

Sunlight streamed in through the window, and she lay in her bed for a moment, squinting her eyes – she'd forgotten to close the curtains the night before. The sounds of murmuring voices reached her ears from outside her door, followed by a woman's gentle laughter, the sound of a door closing, and footsteps descending the stairs. Urgh, it was probably willowy Willow, she thought, ungraciously.

Instinctively, she reached for her phone – still no messages from Eric. Sighing, she stepped out of bed, flicked the kettle on and took a quick shower, before wrapping herself in the fluffy towel and calling the police station to arrange an appointment. It was time to get down to the business of solving a murder.

Sipping her tea while she dressed, Sasha found herself checking her watch and calculating how long it had been since she'd woken up. They'd have had their breakfast by now, wouldn't they? Or maybe little miss skinny willow the wisp didn't eat breakfast, and anyway, what the hell, she was hungry, she realised, and if she didn't want to be late for her appointment then she would just have to face the lovebirds downstairs.

'Morning, hun, sleep okay?' Jules's smiling face appeared in the empty breakfast room as Sasha poured herself some fresh juice.

'Morning, Jules, I slept like a log.' She ordered boiled eggs and toast and checked her phone again for messages from Eric – still nothing. Her engagement ring sparkled in the morning sun which reminded her that he'd given her a gift to open when she got here – she'd open it later. Although if Eric thought that sending her off with a gift let him off for not answering any of her calls or messages then he had another think coming.

Her breakfast arrived – the toast sliced into soldiers and thickly buttered – and when she sliced off the top of her egg, the yolk was revealed in all its golden glory, just slightly runny in the centre. *Oh, my word.* On autopilot Sasha picked up her phone and took a photo, sharing it to her Graffic account and selecting The Spotted Dog pub as her location. A chill took hold of her momentarily as she recalled the horrors of the previous year and how Graffic had played its part as lives and lies were shared and lives were lost. It had been a dark time, but it was behind her now, behind all of them, for better or worse, and today was a new day.

~

It was like meeting up with old friends again as they first shook hands and then hugged. 'Detective Sergeant Crossley, I believe, it's so good to see you again. And Sergeant Jane Weaver, you're looking great, being in charge must agree with you.'

Laughing, Jane Weaver guided Sasha into the small meeting room at the back of the police station. 'It's good to see you, Sasha, I'm sorry it's murder-related, maybe one day you'll visit our neck of the woods purely for pleasure. But I suppose this feels a little like unfinished business to you, am I right?'

'That's exactly it, Jane. To have been a part of the whole thing before – Dorothy Newton's poison pen letters, her husband's insanity and the lives he took, let alone my niece's abduction, and finally believing that all the loose ends had been tied up, well, it feels like one of them's unravelled with Dorothy's murder. But the big question is whether her death is related to events in the past or something entirely separate.'

Nick chimed in, nodding, 'Yep, you said it. Jane received the letter from D.S. Tony Palmer, your police contact in London. He can't speak highly enough of you.'

Jane Weaver nodded. 'It seems you've well and truly earned your private investigator's license, you helped take several dangerous criminals off the street, and all while dealing with your own problems. That must have been pretty awful, Sasha, being stalked and abducted – we were all so relieved to hear that you and your friend were okay. Our local news station, Mrs Pringle, did a great job of giving everyone a running commentary as the situation unfolded, no one could enter the chemist without being pounced on – well, except me, of course – ever since I ticked Dolly Pringle off about gossiping out of turn, she's made a point of turning mute the minute I go in there.'

'Poor old Mrs Pringle, you've got to love her.' Sasha laughed. 'She means well, bless her heart. I must pop in and say hello, er, what should I give as my reason for being here? Any suggestions?'

Nick rubbed his chin thoughtfully. 'It won't take much for people to put two and two together, to be honest, you'll have already been spotted coming in here by someone, no doubt, so that'll start the grapevine off. And as soon as you set foot in Meadowvale then all bets are off. But keep it simple – you're giving us a hand with something – Jane will liaise with you as things progress as I'm partly based in Rentham CID so I won't be here all the time. Which reminds me.' Checking his watch, Nick collected his bag and files, 'I've a meeting to get to so I'll leave you both to it.'

Thanking Nick, Sasha turned back to Jane. 'I read about the weed house bust, by the way, that must have been pretty exciting?'

'It was certainly satisfying, that's for sure.' Jane nodded. 'Although Nick and I were kept out of the actual bust. But you should have seen the inside of the house, one huge forest of greenery, right here under our noses, and discovered thanks to Dorothy's letters which you found. Oh, you got a few mentions in the newspapers, did you know? *Sasha Blue, private investigator, uncovered information leading to the drugs house bust, Sasha Blue sniffs out dope house*, stuff like that. I clipped a few articles out and popped them in the box file, remind me to show you sometime.'

'How embarrassing.' Sasha cringed. 'All I did was find Dorothy's letters, the rest of it was down to good police work, mainly yours.'

'Well, that's a matter of opinion, but anyway, talking of good police work, we've got nowhere with investigating Dorothy's death, hence our arrangement to bring you in as a consultant. We'll cover all your costs as well as pay you a consulting fee, as agreed. Hold on a sec. Pav!'

A young police officer appeared in the doorway, smiling enquiringly. 'Yes, Sarge?'

'This is Constable Pavani Datta. Constable Datta, this is Sasha Blue, she'll be assisting us with the Dorothy Newton case at Meadowvale.'

'Call me Pav.' The young woman shook Sasha's hand, flashing her a welcoming smile, before turning back to her boss. 'What can I do for you, Sarge?'

'Can you make copies of the reports, and the interviews that you and Constable Canfield conducted at Meadowvale? Sasha can take them with her and go through them in her own time.'

'Yes, Sarge.'

'New young blood.' Jane grinned. 'Takes me back it does, seeing them starting out, all young and eager beaver like. Now, I'll introduce you to Ross and then I must go, but both officers will assist you if you need anything, and may I suggest that one of them accompanies you on your first visit to Meadowvale? Just to set the ground rules with the residents so you don't come up against any opposition – they're not the easiest bunch to deal with.'

Constable Ross Canfield turned from the reception, holding out his hand to Sasha. 'Pleased to meet you, you're pretty famous in these parts.' His wide grin and sparkling eyes fetched an answering grin from Sasha.

'Ross, either you or Pav are to accompany Sasha Blue on her first visit to Meadowvale, alright? I want the residents to know quite clearly that they are to give her their full co-operation. Let's see if Sasha can get a word of sense out of anyone up there.'

'Good luck with that.' Ross rolled his eyes. 'Bunch of oldies can't seem to remember what they had for breakfast, what day it is, or who said what half the time.'

'Yes, thank you, Constable.' Jane shot Ross a reproving look. 'Ah, here are the copies for you, thanks Pav.' Handing the file to Sasha, Jane guided her towards the door. 'Take these with you, have a read through, and when you're ready, call for one of my officers to meet you at Meadowvale. Ross isn't wrong about the residents – although he could maybe benefit from a little age sensitivity – they're a crotchety bunch, and none of their stories seem to match up or make sense. Someone must have seen something though, an elderly woman can't just be murdered at a residential home and no one sees a thing.'

~

Monty Mallowan yawned. He wasn't tired, not really, just bored. The days seemed to rather run into one another here, no one's fault. He missed Dorothy, missed her mischievous face, her barbed comments which brought looks of concern or flushed faces to one or other of the residents as they reacted to something she'd said. No idea what she'd been on about half the time, but it had brought a little interest to the days. Sighing, he leaned back in his chair and closed his eyes, the simpering tones of Elspeth Parkhurst's voice reaching his ears through the open door of the conservatory.

'Oh, Albert, the garden looks so pretty, doesn't it? And little old me is going to spoil it all dressed up like a bride at my age, whatever am I thinking?'

'Nonsense, you'll be the best bloom of the bunch my girl, I'd pick you every time.' Albert Bird took Elspeth's bejewelled hand, his eyes briefly taking in the large red gem in its golden mounting. 'Watch your step now, just about time for our morning coffee, I reckon.'

A whiff of cheap scent reached Monty's nose as the couple passed in front of him and he watched through half-closed eyelids as the couple headed into the residents' lounge, Elspeth giggling gushingly in a way he could only suppose she thought of as beguiling.

'You'll trip someone up slouched there with your feet sticking out, you know.' The strident voice of Elizabeth Payton jarred him and he sat up a little straighter, glaring at her.

'Did I hear someone mention coffee? Is it that time already? I've got such a day, Judith's coming to discuss the wedding, we've got the seating arrangements to consider – just exactly where *does* one seat the prime minister?' Elizabeth strode off into the lounge and Monty stretched out his legs again.

'Monty, are you joining us for coffee? Kirsty's made ginger biscuits, our Tuesday treat. Oh, Howie, there you are, did you hear about the ginger biscuits? Is there a chair for Monty?' The Lovewell sisters passed Monty and made a beeline for Howard Norton, Davinia moving slower than her sister, as she leaned on her floral walking stick.

'Ginger biscuits? Who needs them when I've got my own two Gingers to my Fred Astaire? How about a quick twirl?' Howard collapsed into laughter and the sound of the two women's gurgling chuckles joined the general air of hubbub.

'Tra La La! Coffee time, girls and boys!' The affected voice of Greg, as he wheeled in the coffee trolley, was the final straw for Monty. If you can't beat 'em join 'em, he decided, heaving himself out of his chair. And ginger biscuits did sound good...

Greg looked around, pleased to see all his ladies and gentlemen convening for morning coffee. They were in for a treat with Kirsty's biscuits, he'd just sampled one fresh from the oven. He noticed Lillian Springer sitting alone in the corner and bustled over. 'How's my lovely Lillian today? Coffee time, my darling, and Greg's got a treat for you, fresh ginger biccies. Come along now.'

Lillian's slightly confused face looked up, her hands busy with pen and paper in her lap. 'I've just got to finish this chapter, I'm on a deadline you see...'

'Yes, yes, my darling, but come and have your coffee, there's a good girl.' Greg's eyes were sympathetic as he helped Lillian from her chair. 'Ah, Monty, mind if Lillian joins your group for coffee?' He expertly steered Lillian to the chair next to the one Monty was lowering himself into.

'Not at all.' Monty waved at the empty chair. 'Take a seat, Lillian, how's the writing going today?'

Greg beamed happily. Everyone present and accounted for, just the way he liked it. He began to pour the coffee as Tanya, a fellow staff worker appeared and began handing around the plate of ginger biscuits to much approval.

~

The bell above the door to the chemist jingled and Mrs Pringle looked up, taking in Sheila's flushed face as she hurried to the counter. 'What's got you all in a bother, Sheila?' She took the box of loose tea and packet of custard creams from the excited woman, her nose quivering with interest.

'Oh, Dolly, you were right, you said she'd be back. I've just seen her, clear as day, walking out of the police station.'

Mrs Pringle smiled knowingly and encouragingly nodded her head. 'Let's get the kettle on and you can start from the beginning. Now, are we talking about our private investigator, Sasha Blue?' At Sheila's nod, Mrs Pringle guided her to her seat behind the counter. 'Was she with anyone? Was she carrying anything? Now, think carefully, Sheila, it's all about the details.'

While Sheila spoke, Mrs Pringle warmed the pot, added four teaspoons of loose tea to the tea infuser, placing it into the teapot, added boiling water, and popped the knitted tea cosy on, all the while nodding encouragingly to Sheila.

Once Sheila had breathlessly recounted her story, Mrs Pringle poured two cups of tea, nodding approvingly as the rich amber liquid filled the cups. The two women sipped their tea and munched on a custard cream as they considered the, admittedly somewhat meagre, details, Sheila's eyes glued on Mrs Pringle as she awaited her expert opinion.

Finally, she pronounced judgement. 'She's here to investigate Dorothy Newton's murder, you mark my words. And she was carrying a file, you say? Well, that settles it, no doubt about it. She'll be staying at The Spotted Dog, like last time, and of course, *he's* back, so that'll cause a few fireworks, you see if it doesn't, and her with a boyfriend in London, as we saw on the television when the poor woman was abducted by her stalker. And I'll tell you now, Sheila, you see if I'm wrong, but *he's* involved with that new girl working up at Meadowvale, the tall one, although what Mrs Goodwin's thinking of employing an activities therapist for, I don't know. She can hardly have the residents cavorting around doing aerobics in the garden at their age, now can she?'

'Oh, no, I don't think it's those kinds of activities, I think it's more like making things, you know, like paper flowers, or–'

'Now, Sheila, it's not for us to be second-guessing things we aren't knowledgeable about, is it dear?' Mrs Pringle spoke reprovingly.

'Oh, no, I'm only saying–'

'Not now, dear.' Mrs Pringle shot Sheila a warning look as the bell jangled, smiling as she adjusted her blouse. 'Constable Datta, good morning to you, and how's your Tuesday going? Just another quiet day in our simple little village, I expect, no criminals running around, no murders to investigate? And we can be grateful for that, of course. Although it's a terrible worry to think someone is walking around who took poor Dorothy Newton's life. Perhaps a private investigator like our dear Sasha could help out, I believe she's visiting...' Her keen eyes fixed on Pavani Datta's face, hoping for a clue from her expression.

But Pavani Datta had been well coached in Mrs Pringle's tactics for eliciting information from the unsuspecting, by her boss, and she kept her expression neutral as she approached the counter. 'Good morning, ladies, lovely day.' She picked up the packet of hair ties from the display, placed them on the counter, and handed over a pound coin.

'Well, she's a cool one,' Mrs Pringle remarked, once the officer had left the chemist. 'Didn't want to give anything away, that one, which only reinforces what I'm saying, there's something going on with the investigation. If she didn't have anything to hide, she wouldn't have been so secretive, now would she? There'll be enough tea in the pot for a second cup.'

Sheila nodded, picking up the teapot, not sure if she followed Mrs Pringle's logic, but knowing better than to contradict her any further.

Pav Datta grinned inwardly as she left the chemist. The sarge had been spot on about those two, and Mrs Pringle was clearly the ringleader and chief interrogator. Still, they were harmless really, and it didn't hurt to have the women keeping an eye on the comings and goings in the village. And Mrs Pringle was right about the murder at Meadowvale – it wasn't great knowing that someone was walking around who'd taken the life of an elderly resident – it would be interesting to see what Sasha Blue made of the whole thing, once she'd read through all their interviews. What had they missed, she wondered, as she walked back to the station...

HOW DID DOROTHY DIE?

Thanking Jules for the sandwich, Sasha gulped some water and looked around for a moment, enjoying the sunshine as she gazed at the river, before spreading the papers out on the table.

First, she took stock of the number of people related to the case – eight residents – nine, of course, if you included Dorothy Newton before her death; seven staff, if you included the manager, Mrs Goodwin – two of them part-time; and what looked like nine relatives listed.

Next, she picked up the coroner's report, studying it with a feeling of sadness at the indignity of Dorothy's last moments. She ate her sandwich as she absorbed the information.

Dorothy Newton had drowned in a garden pond two feet deep – about sixty centimetres. She'd been found with her upper body lying prone in the water, her legs still on the ground. Signs of a struggle had been evident – the grassy earth beside the pond, muddied from her efforts to find a foothold and lift herself up, was scuffed, with pieces of both adhering to her slippers, one of which had been found lying beside her bare foot. Mud from the bottom of the pond had been found underneath her fingernails where she had desperately clawed as she'd tried to push herself out of the water.

She studied the crime scene sketch indicating items found in the area: a hairclip; a damp, stained handkerchief; a peppermint wrapper; and a wet ball of muddy tissues. Next, she turned her attention to the diagram of the body showing areas of bruising – small, circular, bruises around the upper back and neck, some depicted by a cluster of dots, and some appearing to be equidistant – all possibly indicative of a pole or stick – and a single larger bruise in the mid-point of her back. Pond water had been found in her lungs, and her handbag – although found on the grass – had contained pond water.

Feeling saddened, Sasha lit a cigarette and stared out at the Black River flowing past, as she considered what she'd just read. Someone had hit or shoved Dorothy, causing her to fall face forwards into the pond, and had probably used a walking stick to hold her down while she struggled, before using it to retrieve her handbag, no doubt.

Why had someone felt it necessary to murder Dorothy? Why had they wanted to retrieve her handbag? Who walked with the aid of a walking stick at Meadowvale? Surely that last one shouldn't be too difficult to establish, she asked herself? Ha, Sasha derided her naivety – the residents probably all used walking sticks – it was almost an ingenious move by the killer…

~

Cal stood quietly, watching Sasha, trying to decide whether he should go and speak to her. She was completely absorbed in her thoughts and by the looks of the files on the table, had been busy working. He felt a painful tug inside as he took in her familiar appearance, her hair glinting in the sunlight, her shoulders hunched as she leaned her elbows on the table.

Would she even want to speak to him after what she perceived he'd done to her? He let out the breath he hadn't realised he'd been holding. He'd never had the chance to explain how he'd appeared to suddenly have a wife – a pregnant one at that – and what had been the beginning of a relationship full of promise had ended abruptly. They'd gone their separate ways – they'd both moved on – hell, Sasha was engaged to that loser who'd pitched up last time and acted like a total slob – and he was seeing Willow – but they could be civil with each other, couldn't they? Friends even?

Maybe he'd leave it for now, see if they bumped into each other at the bar, that might be easier. He turned and opened the door, walked inside and, heading to the bar, ordered a pint from Jules.

Sasha looked around, but there was no one there. She stubbed her cigarette out and replaced the coroner's report in the file. Leaning her head back she allowed the sun to warm her face for a moment. She should start reading through the notes of the interviews with the residents, but a glass of wine suddenly felt extremely appealing – and she blamed that entirely on the beauty of the scene around her – the sparkling river, the pretty pub garden, and the feeling of peace that being here gave her. A small click disturbed her thoughts and she looked round again.

'Sorry.' The fair-haired man smiled apologetically as he walked towards her, holding up his camera by way of explanation. 'It's such a beautiful setting and you looked so relaxed sitting there. I hope you don't mind? I'm Charles Priestley, by the way.' He held out his hand.

'Sasha Blue.' She shook his hand, not wanting to seem unfriendly, but feeling disconcerted. 'And you're right, it is a beautiful setting. Are you here on holiday, or–?'

'Yes, taking a few days off to indulge in my photography hobby. The wife's gone to her mother with the kids so I've got some time to myself. It looks like I've picked a good place, plenty of scenic areas to enjoy.'

'Well, you'll be spoilt for choice, I'm sure.'

He smiled as he turned to head back around to the car park, 'Maybe I'll see you in the bar later? I'll buy you a drink for taking your photo.'

'Yes, maybe, well it was nice to meet you.' Smiling politely, Sasha began to gather up her files. She didn't want to be roped into chatting with anyone right now, her head was full of Dorothy Newton's cruel murder and she wanted to remain focused. Maybe she'd take a glass of wine up to her room and read through the interview notes there.

~

Gentle snores could be heard as Willow moved quietly through the lounge. She pulled two of the dining tables together, arranging the chairs around them, before laying out the materials for her afternoon activity. It should be fun, she thought, checking that she'd brought enough card, wool, coloured fabric samples, glue, and pens, from the outdoor storeroom. Finally, she wrote the names of the residents on small pieces of paper, folded them, and popped them all into the bowl. Checking her watch, she noted that she still had half an hour until the afternoon activity started, but the residents would need time to stir, and no doubt to use the bathroom. She looked around doubtfully, never quite sure how to go about easing them from their sleepy states, but she needn't have worried.

Greg appeared, a beaming smile on his face as he burst into song, flamboyantly parodying Julie Andrews as he pranced through the lounge, tidying the books and magazines on the coffee tables as eyes began to open. 'Wakey wakey, everyone, Willow's waiting!' He winked at Willow as he plumped cushions.

Bodies began to stir, indignant mutterings coming from some of the armchairs, as the room awoke.

'No rest for the wicked.' Howard Norton rolled his eyes as he surveyed Greg, turning to Elspeth Payton, who giggled as she patted Albert Bird's hand.

Davinia Lovewell reached for her stick, nudging her sister. 'Agatha, the sooner we get moving the sooner Greg will stop torturing us.'

'And you are all my favourite things...' Greg improvised, holding the last note, his arms flung out theatrically as he surveyed the results of his performance. 'And where d'you think you're going, Monty? No sneaking off to the conservatory, now.'

The various residents began extricating themselves from their chairs and Monty Mallowan put his cigarette packet back in his pocket with a sigh, turning towards the tables set out by Willow. Gradually everyone assembled, looking at her expectantly.

'Afternoon, everyone.' Willow smiled as she saw interest begin to flicker in their faces. 'I'm going to pass this bowl around and I want you to take a piece of paper and read the name on it. But keep it a secret. We're going to make a picture of the person whose name is on the paper – even if it's our own – and then we'll all try and guess who they are. And don't forget to sign your name. It'll be fun.'

Blowing a kiss to Willow, who smiled gratefully, Greg exited the lounge, popping into the kitchen to say goodbye to Kirsty. 'I'm off now, darling. What's that you've got cooking for tonight? It smells delicious.'

'Kirsty looked up from her large saucepan, her face flushed from the steam. 'They've got beef stroganoff tonight, let's hope there are no complaints. Rice for a side dish but I've got baked potatoes to prepare for the fussy ones – you never know who's going to decide to be choosy at the last minute. Doing anything special tonight?'

Greg pulled a sad face. 'No, just me on my lonesome with my meal for one and the television. I swear life's more exciting here than it is for me in my little old flat. Ciao ciao, darling.' Greg left and Kirsty turned back to her saucepans.

Tanya wandered into the residents' lounge and joined Willow and her group. 'I'll give you a hand if you like? Not much for me to do right now.'

'Thanks, Tanya, perhaps you can help out where needed?' She smiled as she watched her charges opening up their pieces of paper and begin to reach for the various items set out on the tables.

'No worries.' Tanya seated herself beside Lillian, holding out pieces of card for the woman to choose.

All was quiet as shapes were drawn on card, fabric cut and adhered a little messily, and rather grotesque apparitions began to appear.

'I'm done.' Elizabeth sat back, slapping her creation down on the table and pushing her chair out. 'It shouldn't be hard to guess who this is, so have fun with your guessing games. Now, I'm expecting Judith here at any moment, we've lots to plan.'

'You're rushing off again, just like before.' Lillian nodded, her eyes magnified through her glasses as she stared at Elizabeth, knowingly.

'Can't say I blame her, Lillian, I hardly like to hang around doing this stuff either.' Albert intervened.

Agatha shrieked, putting her hand over her mouth and all eyes turned towards Elizabeth's handiwork. 'It's Monty!'

'Let me see that.' Monty reached his arm across the table, his eyes peering at the crudely drawn character, the large round piece of fabric depicting his stomach, two lengths of red wool replicating his braces, and the piece of pink paper, roughly cut, left blank and hairless as it sat floating slightly above the body.

But Albert had swiped the card and was holding it up as if to compare it to Howard, as Elspeth giggled. 'I don't know, it could be Howie.' He turned to stare at Howard, who pursed his lips and held up his own card.

'That's you, you got your own name!' Davinia took the card from Howard. 'It really looks like you, Howie, with your round glasses and your tie.'

'So, who got Elizabeth?' Elspeth's head bobbed around enquiringly. 'Oh, Monty, you did,' she exclaimed gleefully, her eyes falling on his card where he'd placed it down prominently.

'That's not funny, Monty.' Elizabeth glanced at the thin body with sticklike arms and legs, its head a mass of white wool, with a large bottle-shaped piece of card glued beside it. 'Just because I enjoy a sherry in the evening, it's civilised, if you must know.' She stood up, ready to leave.

'And your stick, oh you are clever, Monty, look, it's even got three little feet,' Elspeth gushed, holding the card up as Elizabeth glowered.

'Who got me?' Lillian looked around, holding up her own offering which Tanya had helped her make.

'I did, sweetheart.' All eyes swivelled to Albert's creation of a figure dressed in pink.

Lillian blushed. 'Can I have it? We can swap.'

'Albert's nose isn't that big.' Elspeth patted his hand. 'Where am I? Let me see?' She looked at the remaining cards on the table. 'Oh, that's very pretty, yes, that must be me, I've got a blouse just like that. And you got my jewels just right.' She snatched up the card, showing it to everyone. 'Who did it? I love it!'

'Isn't it time for our sherry, Tanya?' Elizabeth hovered impatiently, checking her watch. 'Judith will be arriving shortly, there'll be no time if we don't get a move on.'

'We're almost finished, Elizabeth.' Willow raised her eyebrows at Tanya, as Howard interrupted with a grin.

'Thought it was gin with you lot?'

Elizabeth pursed her lips. 'Yes, well, when we–' she was joined by the mimicking voices of Howard and Davinia.

'When we lived in Rhodesia...'

'We know all about your wild partying days, Elizabeth.' Howard winked at Davinia, whose heart did a little flutter as she looked triumphantly at her sister.

'Let's just finish up.' Willow smiled encouragingly. 'Agatha, that's a lovely picture of Elspeth, now, who's left?'

A finger prodded down hard on one of the cards. 'That's Agatha, no one else wears those shapeless dresses.' Elizabeth's eyes glinted at Davinia as she snorted, 'Nothing like sisterly love.'

'The piece of cake in her hand is a nice touch. Well, that just leaves our Davinia, then.' Howard pointed to the last creation. 'Very nicely done, Elspeth.'

'Sorry, Davinia, it's not very colourful, but I gave you a nice pretty walking stick.'

'But why hasn't Monty got any hair?' Lillian's face was confused as she picked up Elizabeth's card that had started all the fuss.

'Oh, come on, everyone knows that Monty wears a–'

'Elizabeth...' Willow's tone was gently reprimanding.

'Why don't we all move into the comfy chairs and I'll fetch the sherry?' Tanya decided it was time to break things up, as Willow began the job of tidying up, after the rather unsuccessful craft activity.

'I'll pop these up on the wall in the games room before I go.' Willow smiled at the cards. 'They're really not that bad.'

~

Yawning, Sasha looked at her watch. Her glass of wine was long finished – she'd freshen up and head down to the bar, she could do with another drink.

Thanking Jules for the wine, she went outside, sitting with her back to the table she'd used earlier, facing the river, and took out a cigarette. It was early evening and still light, although a breeze had picked up and she could see dark clouds in the distance.

'Looks like we might get some rain later.' Cal's voice was gentle in her ear as he held out his lighter and lit her cigarette. 'And I can't believe those are the first words I said to you after all this time.' His eyes twinkled – a mix of amusement and uncertainty. 'It's good to see you, Sash, mind if I join you?'

Trying to appear calm, Sasha smiled and waved at the bench beside her. 'Sure, it's good to see you too, Cal.'

Cal took a mouthful of lager and stretched his long legs out in front of him, leaning his elbows on the table behind them. 'Sash, I never got the chance to explain things to you, there's stuff I wanted to tell you, it was complicated.'

'It's fine, Cal, really, it's all in the past, we've both moved on.' *Why did she allow this man to affect her?*

'I can see that...' His eyes glanced at the ring on her engagement finger as she lifted her wine glass and gulped more than she meant to.

Swallowing desperately, she coughed. 'Wrong pipe,' she spluttered, putting her glass down with a shaking hand, as Cal patted her back.

'Eric's a lucky guy. Jules told me, I guess congratulations are in order.'

'Thanks, yeah, we had our problems but things are working out well now.' *Apart from the fact that she still hadn't heard from Eric, not one word...*

'And you're okay? After everything that happened to you? Must have been terrifying, Sash. I'm glad he was there for you.' Cal turned towards Sasha, his hand still resting on her back. 'Sash, I–'

'There you are, Jules said you were out here. I got back and took a quick shower.' A soft scent reached their nostrils as a woman appeared beside Cal, her long hair still damp from her shower, tendrils falling onto her tanned shoulders beneath the straps of her sun dress, her toenails a pretty shade of pink in their flip flops.

Standing up, Cal guided her to the bench on the other side of the table, taking a seat beside her, as Sasha swivelled round and lifted her legs over the bench, noting her own chipped nail polish. *Perfect.*

'Willow, this is Sasha, an old friend. Sasha, Willow. Willow works up at Meadowvale.'

The two women smiled across the table, assessing each other.

Sasha spoke first. 'Nice to meet you, Willow, how's it going at Meadowvale? What is it that you do there, exactly?'

Willow gave a gently tinkling laugh. 'It's going okay, I've only been there a few weeks. I just had to apply when I saw the position advertised, it was so perfect for me. I'm an activities therapist and trust me, they're not an easy bunch. But they're all good souls underneath, I'm already becoming fond of them and all their funny ways.'

Sasha threw back the rest of her wine. Did the woman have to be so *nice*?

'Yes, well, I'll have to interview you at some point, of course, in my role as a police consultant. I see you were there at the time of Dorothy Newton's murder?' *That was mean.*

'Oh, yes, poor Dorothy, I'd only been there for about a week. It was so sad, such a special lady.' Willow's mouth pulled into a moue, her eyes large with sympathy, as she leaned into Cal's shoulder, his arm wrapping itself around her.

Get. Me. Out. Of. Here. 'Oh, she was certainly special,' Sasha snorted, 'in more ways than one.' She softened her tone, 'But she didn't deserve what happened to her, and I mean to find out who did it.' She tried to pull her eyes away from the movement of Cal's thumb as it rhythmically stroked Willow's bare shoulder.

Willow's eyes locked onto Sasha's. 'You should join us for dinner tonight, you must be lonely all on your own here.' She lifted her face to Cal's, pecking him on the cheek. 'You don't mind, do you, Cal?'

She couldn't stand it, not for another second. Her phone rang – *saved by the bell* – and she extricated herself awkwardly from the wooden bench seat and table as she glanced at the screen and saw Eric's name. *At last.* 'Excuse me.' Walking a few steps closer to the river bank, she answered her call, relief making her a little over-enthusiastic. 'Eric, baby, how are you? I miss you.'

Sitting at the bar of The Woolly Sheep in Covent Garden, Eric raised his eyebrows in surprise, certain he'd been going to get a mouthful from Sasha about his neglect. 'Hi, babe, how's it going? I miss you too, sorry I didn't call before, work's been crazy and I've been so knackered. This is the first chance I've had to call.' A cheer went up beside him as the group of male drinkers banged on the tables and hooted.

He was out partying, she should have known... 'Where are you?' She lowered her voice, not wanting Cal and Willow to hear.

'Just leaving the pub, I popped in for a quick pint before going home for my microwave dinner and an early night.' Eric eyed the women who'd entered the pub and caused all the furore, appreciatively – there was nothing like a hen party to liven up the evening. 'Did you open my gift?' He sucked in his stomach as one of the women glanced in his direction, her eyes travelling slowly over him, and he sat up straighter on his bar stool.

'I haven't opened it, I forgot.' She felt terrible. 'I'm going up to my room right now to open it, sorry, baby, I've been pretty busy.' *They were kissing. Stop staring. She kissed him, didn't she? He was pulling back. He's embarrassed.* 'Eric, let's chat soon, let me know when you're coming up to see me, okay? I love you.'

'I love you too, baby.' *Well, that had been easy.* He turned back to his friends, grinning, 'This round's on me. Ladies? Care to join us?' The music was turned up in the pub and the guys cheered and clapped, eagerly pulling in more bar stools for the hen party.

Needing to retrieve her bag and files, Sasha walked back to the table where Cal and Willow were still seated. 'Sorry, that was Eric, my fiancé. Er, thanks for the dinner invite, Willow, but I've got stuff to do, so I'll see you at Meadowvale for your interview. Cal, good to see you again.' Before either could reply, she'd gone.

Thumping her wine glass down on the bar counter, she slumped onto a bar stool. 'Fill 'er up, please, Jules.'

'Everything okay?' Jules took in Sasha's flushed expression and general air of discomfiture.

'I don't know. Yes. No. Maybe... You know what? Can I get a bottle to take to my room? And one of those pies? I think I should just hide away from the world and see if I can emerge a better person tomorrow.'

Sitting up in her room, munching on her pie, a few minutes later, Sasha relived the exchanges outside. She'd made an idiot of herself, overreacted to little miss perfect, shown Cal her petty side, blurted out what she was doing at Meadowvale – hell, all in all, she'd been a total flipping disaster. Miserably, she picked up the last few pastry crumbs with her finger. Well, at least she hadn't bitten Eric's head off – that was a first.

Her gift – she still hadn't opened it. Washing her hands and pouring herself another glass of wine, she rummaged through the odd bits and pieces in the bottom of her holdall, and pulled out Eric's gift from its crumpled brown paper bag, softening as she looked at the clumsy gift-wrapping.

Pulling on the tape, she opened the wrapper and took out the small box, removing the lid. Lifting the circular pendant on its leather thong, she smiled – she loved that photo of them, it was from when they'd got engaged – her friend Zoe had taken it of them on Paxos. It was gorgeous and so thoughtful of Eric. She needed to trust him more, was always so quick to assume the worst about him. Picking up her phone, she called him, smiling as she took a mouthful of her wine, feeling filled with love. He was probably sitting at home by now, watching TV and eating his dinner for one.

~

The noise in the pub was deafening, the warm spring evening having brought out people in their droves, and drinks were flowing. 'Come and dance!' The two women each pulled on one of Eric's arms and he grinned at his mate over his shoulder as he allowed himself to be enveloped into the mass of warm, inebriated bodies moving to the music. His phone buzzed, unanswered, on the bar counter as he leaned in to hear what one of the women was whispering in his ear.

~

Maybe he'd gone to bed already, he'd said he was tired. Sasha typed out a quick message before switching off her phone. Bed suddenly seemed like a good idea.

SASHA INTERVIEWS ELSPETH PARKHURST

The shriek caused a commotion as a door banged and Elspeth's voice carried along the corridor, 'My ring, it's gone!'

Lights were switched on and Elizabeth hurriedly drained her glass, pushing herself out of the armchair as Albert appeared, tying his dressing gown, his hair tousled.

'What's going on, was that Elspeth?' He glanced at Elizabeth, knowingly, and she scowled.

Mary rushed through from the staff room and shushed everyone. 'We don't want to wake all and sundry, whatever's the matter, Elspeth?'

Elspeth was peering around on the floor where they'd held their crafting activity that afternoon. 'I was lying in bed when I remembered that I'd taken my ring off to make the picture. But it's not here, someone's taken it.'

'Good Lord, not this again.' Elizabeth rolled her eyes as she pushed her tumbler under the cushion and moved away from her chair.

'I demand a search of the premises,' Albert said dramatically as he put his arms around Elspeth. 'We've got a thief in our midst.'

'It wasn't me.'

'No, of course it wasn't, come on back to bed, Agatha.' Davinia steered her sister away with her free hand, leaning on her stick with the other.

Mary stood amid the chaos, her hands on her hips, unsure of what to do first. 'We'll look for it in the morning, Elspeth, let's all go back to our rooms, for now, it's the middle of the night.'

'I saw Elizabeth hiding something under the cushion.' Albert pointed at the chair Elizabeth had vacated as she flushed a dark crimson.

'Nonsense, you need your eyes tested.' She strode off slightly unsteadily as Mary shepherded the others away.

'But it's so valuable, we have to find it.' Elspeth sobbed as she allowed Albert to walk her back to her room. 'You'll find it won't you, Albie?'

'Course I will, don't you worry about that, it can't get far now can it?'

'And you really shouldn't be so mean to Elizabeth.'

'Why not? Can't stand the woman.'

Their voices faded as they moved along the corridor to their rooms.

The rain began to fall noisily and Mary walked about, checking that the windows were securely fastened. On an impulse, she moved to the chair that Albert had pointed at and lifted the cushion, removing the tumbler and sniffing it. Whisky. Oh well, you couldn't blame the old girl. She switched off the overhead lights and made her way back to the staff room and her, now cold, cup of tea.

~

The morning dawned dull and gloomy, and Sasha pushed the bed covers back, shivering slightly. Taking a quick, hot shower, she pulled on her tee shirt and jeans and, as an afterthought, slid her arms into a loose shirt. She needed to focus, she decided, as she entered the breakfast room – no distractions, no thinking about Eric, *or Cal*, or anything else except getting her investigation underway at Meadowvale. While she waited for the toast to pop up, she called the police station and spoke to Pavani Datta, arranging to meet her at Meadowvale a little later.

~

'Thank you, Mary, leave it with me, you go on home now.' Mrs Goodwin smiled at Mary and sat back, pondering the situation. This was the second time – or was it the third? – that Elspeth had declared that pieces of her jewellery had gone missing. And then there was Elizabeth's drinking, not that it was necessarily a problem, just something to keep an eye on. She sighed, breakfast should be starting shortly, then the new girl, Willow, would have everyone doing some kind of activity, and now they had the consultant coming through to begin interviews as well. Sasha something, she checked her notes,

Sasha Blue, the girl who'd been involved in the last fiasco in Parva Crossing. Well, if she found out who Dorothy's killer was that would be a good thing, let them all rest a little easier, although she felt sure that it was a fool's errand, clearly it had been the cruel work of an outsider, someone who'd decided to murder on a whim. If it had actually been murder at all...

~

'Morning, Sasha, a rather miserable one, unfortunately.' Pavani closed her car door, smiling, and looked at the sky, grimacing. 'Looks like there'll be more rain.'

'Hi, Pav, thanks for meeting me. Yes, I think you're right about the weather.' Sasha pulled a face. 'And this idiot only packed a couple of shirts, not even a jumper, I don't know what I was thinking.'

The two women walked into the front door of Meadowvale and were greeted by the manager, Mrs Goodwin. 'Morning Constable Datta, and you must be Sasha – oh, you've been here before, haven't you?'

Sasha nodded, smiling, 'I have, I visited Dorothy Newton last year. I'm so sorry about what happened to her, I'm determined to get to the bottom of it.'

'Yes, well, it was a dreadful time for us all, and we've all felt Dorothy's loss. I'm sure it won't turn out to be anyone associated with Meadowvale in any way. They're just finishing up their morning activity so perhaps you'd like to make yourself comfortable in the dining area for now? There'll be morning coffee once they're done so I'll make introductions then if that's okay? Everyone's in rather a mutinous mood this morning, I'm afraid, we had an incident last night which has left us all rather scratchy.'

'Nothing serious, I hope?'

'Oh no, one of our ladies has misplaced a piece of jewellery and she caused quite the fuss. It'll turn up, of course, the carers are keeping an eye out for it.' She hesitated. 'They're a good bunch overall, our residents, a little cliquey, if you know what I mean. Elizabeth, Davinia, and Albert were thick as thieves for a while, they're the stronger ones of the group, and then there's Monty's little crew – Agatha, Lillian, Howard, and Elspeth. Of course, our little romance complicates things, and they will fall out with each other – friends one minute, enemies the next, like children I suppose, but we manage to tick along. Now, if you'll excuse me.' Mrs Goodwin left them to settle in and Sasha turned to survey the morning activity.

The music stopped abruptly, while the shuffling residents continued to move around aimlessly, the rather overweight, elderly man in brightly coloured braces continuing in the direction of what looked like a conservatory.

'Monty, you're supposed to stand still when the music stops.' Willow clapped her hands. 'Everyone, let's try again, and remember, we're playing musical statues, not musical chairs, Lillian.'

The warmth of the room hit Sasha and she slipped her shirt off. No risk of feeling chilly in a care home, she realised, trying not to feel amused at the antics playing out in front of her. She studied Willow surreptitiously, taking in her slim legs enclosed in dusky pink leggings, her cute little trainers and tight-fitting tee shirt. Damn the girl for looking all sweet and girly with her hair tied back and that big smile on her face. And how old was she, anyway? She barely looked twenty, but must be older... Cal couldn't be going out with someone almost young enough to be his daughter, could he?

A young lad not much older than her niece wheeled a trolley in and parked it beside the dining tables, straightening the cups and saucers before scuttling out of the room.

'It's coffee time. I don't want to do this anymore, we're not children for goodness' sake.' The strident tones of a thin woman, her white hair swept back in a bun, switched Sasha's attention back to the residents.

'I'm a bit puffed I think I'll sit down.' A rather plump, shorter woman, in a flowery blouse, pulled at her collar, her face pink. 'My ankle's hurting.' She pouted, looking sorry for herself, as a dark-haired man with a long nose took her arm.

'Careful, old thing, you've got to watch those ankles, we don't want you having to use a stick again. Elspeth and I are going to sit down, it's feeling rather warm in here.' The man mopped his brow with his handkerchief, a tell-tale trickle of hair dye transferring itself to the cotton.

Willow looked around despondently as the others began to drift away. 'We've still got ten minutes. Come on, Howard, you show them how it's done.'

The small man in the shirt and bowtie pulled a silly pose, winking at the two women standing beside him, who giggled.

The larger of the two, in some kind of brightly patterned, flowing kaftan, looked hopefully towards the coffee trolley. 'Oh good, we've got a biscuit assortment today. Come on, Howie, let's sit down, like Elizabeth said, it's coffee time.'

Giving up, Willow turned and noticed Sasha and the police officer. She clapped her hands. 'Well done, everyone, that was fabulous! You all deserve a rest and a cup of coffee, let's find our seats now.'

Talk about treating them like children, snorted Sasha, inwardly. She fixed a smile on her face but was saved from having to greet Willow by the appearance of Mrs Goodwin, whose presence brought immediate quiet to the room.

'Good morning, everyone, I hope you enjoyed your morning activity. Now, Spencer will serve your coffee and biscuits and I'd like you to welcome Constable Datta and Sasha Blue, who are here regarding the recent loss of Dorothy Newton. Please assist them in any way that you can, Sasha will be spending some time with us over the next few days so you'll get used to seeing her around. Constable?' She looked in Pavani's direction and the young woman stood, clearing her throat.

The young man who had wheeled the trolley in a little earlier, walked quietly into the room and, keeping his head down, began to serve coffee and biscuits. Sasha accepted a cup with a smile and watched the residents' reaction to the police officer's short speech.

All eyes seemed to turn towards her, as Pavani finished up, explaining Sasha's role and asking them to do their best to assist her as much as possible so that the perpetrator could be brought to justice. Thanking Pav, Sasha smiled around at the expectant faces, wondering quite where to begin.

'It was me!' The small man, clearly the joker of the pack, held out his wrists as if for handcuffs, to much amusement from the gathering.

'Howie, you are a one!' The large kaftan-enrobed woman giggled as the man whose stomach bulged between the red braces holding his trousers up, slammed his fist on the table beside him, looking upset.

'It's not funny. Dorothy was murdered, we shouldn't make jokes.'

It was time to intervene. 'You're quite right, it's not funny.' Sasha addressed the man directly. 'And you are?'

'Monty, Monty Mallowan.' He leaned back in his chair, scowling at Howard.

'It's nice to meet you, Monty. Well, as you all know, my name is Sasha Blue, and I've been invited here to assist the police with the investigation into Dorothy Newton's murder. I met Dorothy last year, I visited her here, at Meadowvale. I'll be chatting with each of you so that you can tell me everything that you remember about the day of Dorothy's death. I'm sorry to bring up such an awful time and I'm sure that you'd prefer to forget all about it. I'd also like you to know that no one is under suspicion, we just need to confirm as many details as we can from that day, in the hope that something new crops up and, unless anyone objects, I'll need to have a little look around your rooms, as well as all areas of Meadowvale. Now, I just need to get all your names straight. Let me see, you must be... Howard?' Taking a guess, she looked at the man who'd made the joke.

'That's me, Howard Norton, and these two lovely ladies are Davinia and Agatha.' He waved his arms theatrically in the direction of the two women seated beside him.

'I'm Davinia Lovewell, and this is my sister, Agatha.' The thin woman with straight, silvery hair shaped in a bob, spoke, pointing at the woman in the kaftan. Apart from their identical hair, there was nothing that would have indicated that they were sisters.

'And this beauty is my bride-to-be, Elspeth.' The man with suspiciously dark hair and a long nose, dressed in a tracksuit, patted the knee of the girlishly dressed plump lady beside him, who blushed, bobbing her head so that her white-blonde curls bounced fetchingly.

'Albie, don't make me blush.' She patted a hand to her face, the rings on her fingers a dazzling array of colour. 'I'm Elspeth Parkhurst, and Albie is my fiancé, Albert Bird, we're getting married this summer.' She giggled again, beaming at Sasha.

'Oh, well that just leaves Elizabeth and Lillian. Lillian's a famous author, you know!'

All eyes turned towards the lady with fluffy, white hair and large glasses, who looked up from her hands where they busied themselves with paper and pen. 'Somebody stole my pink pen the day Dorothy died, Agatha, you remember? You helped me look for it in the library.' She turned to look at Willow, who was hovering near the door, ready to leave. 'I can't sign my contract today, Mervyn hasn't brought it back.'

'That's alright, old girl.' Monty intervened as Willow smiled uncertainly. 'No rush, I'm sure.'

The woman who had to be Elizabeth Payton snorted, and Sasha turned to her. 'And you're Elizabeth, then. Well, it's nice to meet you all. Before we meet individually, I thought we could all just chat about that day, three weeks ago, and what stands out in our memories? Perhaps you've remembered something unusual about it? Was it a Wednesday? Did anyone see anything strange or notice anyone hanging around or anything?'

'It can't have been a Wednesday, it was Monday, wasn't it? We had homemade cake for afternoon tea, we always have a cake on Monday afternoon. Don't you remember, Davinia, I brought you a piece but you weren't there?'

Davinia nodded primly to her sister. 'I must have been in the *other* room, Agatha, really, is nothing sacred? The cake was lovely, I'd missed lunch so it was quite welcome.'

'It was lemon drizzle cake.' Elspeth bobbed her head, patting her stomach as she smiled girlishly at Albert. 'I really shouldn't have indulged, I have to watch my waistline.'

Food was obviously an important topic here, thought Sasha, as she observed expressions.

'And a lovely waistline, I'll watch it any time.' Albert grinned, winking at Elspeth, who opened her mouth to speak as Elizabeth interrupted.

'We didn't have any cake, you've got the wrong day, all we had was the tea. We had shortbread with our morning coffee, it was the day you were making a big fuss about something.'

'That's right, my nephew brought the shortbread, Richard, he came to visit. I'm sure you remember, Monty, you had some, good thing too, can't have you wasting away.' Howard grinned as the Lovewell sisters smiled appreciatively.

Monty flushed. 'No call for that, Howie.'

Elspeth finally got a word in. 'I was making a fuss because my bracelet went missing. I remember now, it's the day Miriam took me shopping for a new cardigan.'

'Albert spent quite a while in the garden searching for it, didn't you?' Monty turned to look at him, yawning.

'Raymond helped you, don't you remember? He visited you that day.' Elspeth shuddered. 'To think you could have walked right past the murderer.'

'Yes, but that was in the morning, and there were lots of visitors that day, let's see now, Lillian, your son was here, wasn't he, and, Elizabeth, you had your daughter here.'

'Yes, Judith and I had the wedding to discuss.'

'Oh, was it you with your daughter? Thought it was Davinia for some reason.'

'Howard, dear, I certainly wasn't off walking around the garden, I didn't go outside at all, and certainly not with Judith.'

'Well, who tripped Monty up with their walking stick?' Lillian piped up and all eyes turned to Monty, but he'd nodded off.

'Okay, this is all very helpful, thank you.' Sasha looked down at her scrawled notes, wondering if any of them would make sense to her later. Suggesting the wrong day for Dorothy's death had got them all trying to recall things, but as Constable Canfield had implied, the residents certainly struggled to remember details precisely.

'Mrs Goodwin has offered us the use of the library for our interviews.' She looked around, wondering who to ask to join her first. 'Elspeth, would you be happy to join me for a chat?'

'Yes, alright, do we have to be on our own, can't Albie come with me?'

'It won't take long and I do need to speak to each of you on your own. Is that okay?'

'Scared you'll give yourself away, Elspeth?' The Lovewell sisters giggled appreciatively at Howard's question as he winked at them.

Elspeth pouted. 'No, but maybe I'll give someone else away. Perhaps I'll tell Sasha what I saw that day.'

'Easy, girl, you and your overactive imagination.' Albert laughed, glancing around as Elizabeth snorted.

'You should control your fiancé, Albert, all these flights of fancy can't be good for her.'

'She's alright, aren't you, love?' he patted Elspeth's hand as she stood up and waited for Sasha to say goodbye to Pav.

'I just need to visit the powder room, can I meet you in the library in a moment?'

'Sure, no problem, Elspeth. I'll just pass out my card to you all, that way, if you think of anything at any time, you can give me a call.' With her cards distributed, she gathered her papers, and made her way to the library, frowning at how dark it had become. She looked out of the window at the angry clouds gathering and grimaced as she switched the light on. It was strange that Eric hadn't called her back or sent her a message, maybe she'd give him a quick call while she waited for Elspeth. Smiling, she touched the pendant on its leather thong as she waited for him to answer.

'Hello?' The woman's voice sounded distracted and voices could be heard in the background.

'Er, hi, is this Eric's phone?' *Dumb question.*

'It might be, hold on a sec,' sounds were muffled and Sasha felt a seed of anxiety growing in her stomach. He'd been up to his old games, she knew it... 'Sorry about that, this is The Woolly Sheep. Covent Garden?' Still not getting a response from Sasha, the woman spoke again. 'The pub?'

'Sorry.' Finally Sasha spoke. 'Is he there? Eric, I mean?'

'Oh, no idea, look, someone left this phone behind last night, it was a bit of a crazy one, I thought you might be the owner. It's behind the bar, tell him to ask for Roz. Sorry, I have to go.' The call was disconnected and Sasha stared at her phone as if it might have answers.

'I didn't see anything, I was just annoyed with Howard, the man can be too much sometimes, always making stupid jokes.' Elspeth sat down across the table from Sasha as she tried to pull her mind away from Eric.

'Right, well, it might be best not to go around saying things like that, Elspeth, it might not be safe.'

Elspeth gave a tinkly laugh. 'Why on earth not? You can't seriously think we've got a dangerous murderer lurking in our midst? Oh!' She put her hand to her mouth, her rings glinting, as she realised what she was saying. 'I wasn't thinking, sorry.'

'It's fine, Elspeth, really, but why don't you just tell me everything that you can remember about that day?'

'Alright, well, first of all, it was the day my daughter, Miriam, was going to take me shopping for a new cardigan. I remember thinking what a pity because the weather was awful, miserable and rainy. I was feeling extra glum because someone had stolen my bracelet.' She leaned forward in her chair. 'We've got a thief here, you know. I had a ring stolen yesterday but everyone behaves like I'm just losing things, apart from Albert, my fiancé, he believes me. We had a crafting session yesterday afternoon with Willow, such a sweet girl, and I'd taken my ring off, then in the night I woke up and realised I must have left it on the table but when I went to look it was gone.'

Willow possible jewellery thief? Sasha scribbled over the note she'd just written, but really, *such a sweet girl?*

'Yes, well I'm sorry to hear about that, perhaps something will come to light during my investigation...'

'Oh no, it's no bother.' Elspeth flustered. 'You mustn't waste time trying to find my jewellery. Of course, it'll be long gone by now, they'll have sold it.'

'I'll see what I can do, Elspeth, I certainly will.'

'Please don't.' She looked anxiously at Sasha. 'You're here for Dorothy. Now, I recall that Albert and I took a walk in the garden after breakfast–'

'Wasn't it raining though?' Sasha interrupted.

'Oh, that's right, well, no, maybe it just *felt* rainy, you know what those days are like? Actually, come to think of it, it can't have been raining as there were quite a few taking a walk in the garden.'

This was not getting off to a good start... Sasha nodded encouragingly. 'Go on.'

'Yes, we saw Dorothy, she was walking on her own, she did that quite often, and then there was Elizabeth and her daughter, she was wearing a very bright, red blouse, most unbecoming, far too garish.' Elspeth shuddered, looking down approvingly at her floral blouse and skirt in pastel shades. 'Her name's Judith, Elizabeth's daughter, they were deep in conversation, overtook Albie and me and we weren't walking slowly, they never even greeted us. Elizabeth thinks she's so important, Albie can't abide her. It's not the only wedding being planned, you know.'

Her head reeling, Sasha asked, 'Er, whose wedding would that be?'

'Oh, Elizabeth's granddaughter. Judith's married to David Bertram, a member of parliament, so of course, all they talk about is the big society wedding. Do you know, I'm sure Howie was taking a walk with Agatha – Davinia wouldn't have liked that.' Elspeth giggled. 'They both spend their time vying for his attention, it's quite sad, at their age as well.'

Sasha glanced at her file, noting that Elspeth Parkhurst was seventy-eight years of age – which hardly made her a spring chicken herself.

'This is great, Elspeth, you're doing really well, go on.'

Pleased, Elspeth continued. 'Now, if I remember rightly, Davinia was a bit off that day, I don't think I saw her in the morning at all, oh no, I'm wrong, perhaps at coffee...'

Sasha sighed inwardly.

'Richard brought shortbread – he's Howard's nephew, so we indulged at morning coffee.' Elspeth looked ruefully at her waistline. 'I should watch my figure, but it was so tempting. And then Miriam collected me for our shopping trip. We went to Beedham's, such a nice store in Rentham. Have you been there?'

Without waiting for Sasha to answer, Elspeth carried on speaking. 'Anyway, Miriam bought me a lovely cardigan and then we decided to have lunch there in the restaurant, just a sandwich, but it made a nice change.

'Well, when I got back, they were still busy with afternoon craft with Willow so I just tiptoed past the lounge. Albie wasn't there, it's not manly enough for him, and neither was Agatha, I don't think, because I saw her disappearing off along the path in the garden, in one of those huge, flowing kaftans that she always wears.' Sasha looked up from her notes as Elspeth paused, looking puzzled.

'So, you missed the crafting session. Did you see anyone else? Was there something that you–?'

They were interrupted by the arrival of a young, teenage girl, dressed head to toe in black, with various piercings. 'Oh, there you are, Nan, me and Mum thought we'd call in to see you.' The girl slouched against the doorframe as Elspeth beamed.

'Oh, this is my granddaughter, Lucy. What a lovely surprise! Tell Mum I'm coming.' She turned back to Sasha. 'There isn't anything else, I'm sure.'

Smiling at the young girl, Sasha nodded at Elspeth. 'Perhaps we can just finish off? You were telling me who you saw when you got back from your shopping trip.'

'Oh, yes. No, I don't think I saw anyone else, now let me think quickly, well, I thought I saw a strange man in the garden when I went out to look for Albie – I remember I was calling his name because really, the gardens are quite large – and he appeared out of nowhere. He was surprised to see me arriving back so early, said that he'd been looking for my bracelet, and he said I must have imagined it, seeing that man. It must have been drizzling, poor dear, and with his knee playing up as well, which he tries to hide, he does so hate using his stick.' She flushed becomingly. 'He steered us off in here for a few minutes, it's nice to have somewhere private to spend a little time together. The door to the garden had been left swinging and Albie closed it, he said if that woman did it one more time, he'd report her to Mrs Goodwin.'

'And after you'd, um, spent a little private time together?' Sasha tried to block the mental image of Elspeth and Albert in a romantic clinch beside the bookshelves.

'Well, Albie said he'd worked up quite an appetite, he's such a tease, you know, and anyway, it was time for afternoon tea. Albie told me to save him a seat and I was first in for tea, and we had a treat – Kirsty had made lemon drizzle cake – it's a favourite of mine. Mary usually makes a cake for Monday tea but she'd been off sick so it was quite a nice surprise to have freshly baked cake on a Tuesday, so anyway, I saved a slice for Albie– oh, there, you see? I just remembered which day of the week it was, just like that. Agatha went to look for Davinia because she'd been having a lie-down, but rushed back for her cake – she likes her food, and I told her that Albie was changing on account of the drizzly weather. When Davinia sat down she was really looking quite flushed. Howie made some silly joke about her cheeks matching her blouse and of course that made her blush so her face reddened even more.

'The lemon cake didn't last a second – I'm sure Monty helped himself to two pieces – I was wearing my new cardigan and everyone was so nice with their compliments. Tanya said something about a goose, I think, no, that's not right, a gander, oh, isn't it funny how we confuse words? She said let me have a gander, and I had to give her a twirl, I felt quite the centre of attention. She cleared our tea plates away as fast as we could finish – maybe she was in a hurry to get off work – and then a little bit later Greg came in and cleared our teacups.'

Pausing dramatically, Elspeth's eyes widened. 'And that's when someone noticed that Dorothy was missing...'

'Mum, Lucy said you were in here.' A tired-looking woman poked her head through the doorway. 'I've got your ankle supports, Mrs Pringle called to say they'd arrived so I picked them up, didn't want to miss them as it's half-day closing, and I've got Lucy off sick although I'm not sure there's anything actually wrong with her. They've called me in for two full days at the surgery from tomorrow, Saturday morning as well, so I won't get another chance this week.' Noticing Sasha, she apologised. 'Sorry for interrupting, I'm Miriam, Elspeth's daughter.' She entered the room, kissing her mother on the cheek. 'How's your ankle, Mum, managing without the stick still?'

'Oh yes, dear, and Albie takes good care of little old me. This is Sasha, the lady investigating Dorothy's death.'

'It's nice to meet you. Now, I must go, I'd like to get home before it rains. I'll call you, Mum.'

'Thank you for my ankle supports,' Elspeth called out to her daughter's retreating back, while picking them up and pulling a face at Sasha. 'Ugly things.' She shuddered theatrically.

'Do you often have to use a walking stick, Elspeth?' Sasha fixed a sympathetic expression on her face.

'Oh no, well, not really, it was just when I sprained my ankle, but that was a few weeks ago. Now, if you don't mind, dear, I need to go and freshen up before lunch, they're very punctual here.'

'Yes, of course, thank you, Elspeth, you've been very helpful.' Sasha checked her watch, surprised to see that it was almost one o'clock. The heat in the room felt stifling and her head was pounding. The growl from her stomach sounded loud in the library, as she gathered her files, and she decided to head off and find somewhere for lunch. These interviews were going to take time.

'I remember you! You visited Dorothy with that handsome man of yours – Sasha, isn't it? Mrs Goodwin told us all about you. It's Greg, in case you don't remember. Such an awful thing to happen.' He held his hand to his heart, dramatically. 'I still haven't got over it. Poor Dorothy, such a sweetheart. How's it going, have you found out anything helpful yet? No, I don't expect you can tell me. Are you joining us for lunch? It's fish cakes today.'

'Greg, of course, I remember you, it's nice to see you again, and thanks for the invitation but I think I'll pop out for lunch. I'll come back later and continue with my interviews. Er, what time does lunch usually finish?'

'Well, it's all go, being Wednesday, now let me see, lunch is from one o'clock to two o'clock, then our newest addition, Willow, will be supervising the carpet boules, they usually all join in, it's quite competitive. That will start at half-past two so, let me see, about an hour, then it will be afternoon tea and visitors. Although not sure if anyone will come out in this weather.' They both turned their eyes to the window where rain streaked the window pane, the sky beyond darkening by the second. 'Anyway, I expect you could interview one or two during afternoon tea.'

'Sounds great, I'll do that, thanks, Greg, I'll see you later then.' Grabbing her stuff, Sasha hurried out and made a dash for her car just as the heavens opened in earnest.

Soaked in the time it took to get into her car, Sasha left Meadowvale, peering through the windscreen as her wipers fought a losing battle with the rain. This was great, she was now wet, cold, hungry, and had a headache. And she'd only managed to conduct one interview. Her mind calculated what it was best to do first, as she drove carefully on the narrow, rapidly-flooding lane, a car drawing close behind her, its lights bright in her rearview mirror. She'd stop at Pringle's Chemist first, get some headache tablets, and she needed to buy herself a jumper or something, she was going to freeze. Then she'd pick up a sandwich–

The car moved in a flash of blurry whiteness, one minute it was behind her, the next it shot past and pulled in front of her at speed. She slammed on her brakes as her wheels skidded on the slippery tarmac and, realising her mistake, Sasha watched in dismay as she slid slowly from the road towards a tree, hitting it with an unpleasant crunch. Switching off her engine, Sasha sat, shaken, for a moment, her heart pounding, before she galvanized herself into action.

'Hey!' She shouted angrily at the faint red lights as they disappeared in the distance. Slipping in the mud in her rush to try to catch the registration number, her foot squelched into a puddle and she went down, landing with both knees in the muddy water, her hands spread-eagled on the wet ground on either side of her.

Headlights appeared, coming from the opposite direction and, as a white car pulled up, the driver's window opened and Willow's cheery face appeared as she peered through the still-falling rain. 'Sasha?'

Great, the last person she wanted to see her like this. And now she'd have to be nice to her.

'Hold on, let me move off the road.' Willow moved her car into the lay-by, popped on her hazard lights, grabbed a blanket from the parcel shelf, and rushed across the road. 'Sasha, you poor thing, what happened?' She wrapped the pink blanket around Sasha's shoulders as she helped her up.

SASHA INTERVIEWS LILLIAN SPRINGER

The two women looked up as another car pulled in behind Willow's and a man exited the car, pulling his hood up against the rain.

Did everyone drive a white car around here? Sasha tried to stop herself shivering as she realised the man looked familiar.

'Everything alright, ladies? Can I help?' He joined them under the shelter of the tree.

She felt sure that her attempt at a smile was more of a grimace.

'Sasha! What a way to run into you again. Oh dear, who's had an argument with the tree?' He glanced down at Sasha's mud-covered knees and feet. 'You poor thing. I'm Charles, by the way.' He smiled at Willow, who introduced herself, and then he turned back to Sasha.

'D'you mind if I try moving your car back onto the road for you? Will you be okay to drive?'

'That's very kind of you, but I'm sure I'll be fine.' *She sounded horribly ungrateful. What was wrong with her?*

'No, you've had a shock, let Charles help.' Willow pulled the blanket tightly around Sasha as she felt sudden tears pricking her eyes.

She was falling apart, that couldn't happen, not in front of Willow of all people. Nodding, she stood helplessly as Charles started the engine and expertly reversed the car onto the road, before pulling forward a few metres and parking it in the lay-by.

Grateful for the rain disguising her tears, Sasha wiped her eyes roughly with her hand. *Pull yourself together.* She smiled her thanks to Charles as he returned to them, after checking out the front bumper with a rueful expression.

'Not too bad, could have been worse. Ah, rain's stopped, must be a sign.'

'Thank you, both of you, you've been very kind.' She removed the blanket, noticing the muddy handprints on it. 'I'll get this cleaned for you, Willow, it's the least I can do. No, really.' She smiled at both of them. 'Perhaps I can buy you both a drink in the bar later, to say thank you?'

Finally, they left her alone, but only after she'd started the engine and then pretended to check her phone for messages. Waving at them and nodding firmly, she watched them go before slumping in her seat. Unable to stop herself, she gave in to the tears. She was soaked to the skin, covered in mud, her head was pounding so painfully she couldn't think straight, her car was smashed up, Eric had let her down, and Willow, bloody perfect all skinny and tall, Willow, had been *kind* to her. She'd been... *nice*. No wonder Cal adored her. In frustration, she slammed her hands against the steering wheel before taking a deep breath. *That's it, enough of the self-pity.*

Switching on the car heater, she ran her hands through her wet hair before pulling out of the lay-by. First stop the chemist for painkillers – the state of her would give Mrs Pringle something to gossip about... Sasha, you've turned into a total queen bitch today, she ticked herself off as she headed along the almost deserted village high street and parked outside the chemist. Where was everyone? A comment Elspeth's daughter had made came back to her – it was half-day closing. Did that still happen? *It did in Parva Crossing.*

About to start her car, Sasha's eyes caught a movement through the glassed door of the chemist and she waved back at Mrs Pringle, who was flapping her hands and motioning to her to come to the door, which she had now opened.

'Oh, my goodness, someone's been in the wars. It's Sasha, isn't it, oh dear, what a time you've had lately, we were all so pleased to know that you were safe. Now, you must come in, I was just closing up but a few minutes won't make a difference, the customer comes first I always say. Sheila!' She turned her head towards the counter. 'Bring yesterday's newspaper.' Then back to Sasha. 'That's it, dear, sit yourself down.' She pulled a chair forward and pressed Sasha's shoulders so that she had no choice but to sit and then lift her feet as Sheila appeared, placing the newspaper under her muddy feet.

'I'm sorry, Mrs Pringle, I don't want to be a bother.' Feeling guilty for her uncharitable thoughts a moment earlier – and really, the woman was being so *kind* – everybody was – Sasha smiled at the two hovering women. 'I just needed to buy some painkillers, I've got a dreadful headache. I'm sorry about the mud.' She glanced in despair at her flip-flop clad feet and mud-encrusted toes.

'Now, don't you worry about that. Sheila, some tablets for Sasha, and a glass of water. You can take two now and no need to worry about payment, no arguments.'

Mrs Pringle's excitement levels were through the roof – the very object of their interest was here and in need of help. She took in the damaged bumper of Sasha's car and assessed her bedraggled appearance. 'Tell me all about it, dear, where was the accident? Tea, that's what you need, you're soaked through and shivering, you'll catch your death.' She turned imperiously to Sheila. 'Pop the kettle on before you go, Sheila, there's a love, no need for you to stay.'

She couldn't believe it, she really couldn't, she'd sat in Pringle's chemist, drunk a cup of tea, eaten two custard creams, and bawled her eyes out to Mrs Pringle, telling her everything – she was seriously falling apart. And for her ultimate humiliation, she was now wearing Mrs Pringle's *spare cardigan* – navy blue, with embroidered flowers and ladybirds all over it – finding herself helpless to refuse in the face of Mrs Pringle's kindly insistence – *We can't have you catching a chill and the shops are closed until tomorrow, borrow it for as long as you need.*

Driving off with another wave to Mrs Pringle – *you must call me Dolly* – Sasha squared her shoulders and headed for the pub. She needed a shower and a change of clothing – hopefully, she'd be able to sneak in without anyone seeing her.

~

'Here she is! Oh, look at you, you poor thing.' All eyes in the bar turned towards Sasha. Willow's face was the picture of sympathy as she jumped up from the table and rushed to envelop Sasha in a hug. 'We were just telling Cal all about it.' She gently steered Sasha towards the table where Cal and Charles were sitting, pints of lager in their hands.

So much for sneaking in without being seen.

Cal put his glass down, coughing and choking, as he took in Sasha's horrified expression, his eyes a mixture of sympathy and amusement. 'Nice cardigan.' He winked.

Heat rushed to her cheeks as Sasha forced herself to smile. 'Thanks, Mrs Pringle kindly lent it to me.' She nodded at Charles. 'Thanks again for your help, Charles, you too, Willow, now I must go and shower and get some dry clothes on.'

'And I must be getting back to Meadowvale otherwise I'll be late for carpet boules, I just popped back to dry out and change my shoes, and then I just had to tell Cal all about poor you and your nasty accident.' Willow kissed Cal on the cheek and was gone.

Reaching her door, Sasha fumbled for the key as a hand gently rested on her shoulder and pulled her around.

'Sash, sorry about your accident. I'm glad you're okay.' He held her at arm's length and studied her face. 'You are okay, aren't you? What happened?'

Trying to ignore the feel of his hands on her shoulders, Sasha sighed. 'Someone pretty much ran me off the road. It was pouring with rain, visibility was poor, and suddenly a car came up behind me, lights blazing, overtook me and pulled in right in front of me. If I hadn't hit my brakes, I would've hit them. But I hit a tree instead.' She shrugged, feigning nonchalance. 'One of those things, I was just a bit shaken, that's all. But Willow suddenly appeared and pulled over to see if she could help, then that guy, the photographer, Charles, appeared as well.'

'Stroke of luck, them both turning up. How bad's your car?'

'Just some bumper damage, nothing major. Listen, Cal, I need to shower and change, I have to get back to Meadowvale, I only managed one interview this morning.'

'Sure, no problem, see you in the bar tonight for a drink?' At her nod, Cal dropped his hands from her shoulders before giving her one last amused look. 'And, Sash? That cardigan – you look kind of cute in it.' He winked and was gone.

She went into her room, closing the door behind her. *Was Cal flirting with her?*

~

'Well done, Howie!' The Lovewell sisters clapped their hands as Albert scowled and walked off, rubbing his knee.

'Someone can't keep score,' he fumed, glaring at Elizabeth, who'd been tasked with scorekeeping.

'Take it easy, Dad, d'you need your stick?' Albert's son, Raymond stepped forward to hold his dad's arm as Albert did a wobble.

'I don't need a damn stick, son. You're early, tea hasn't come through yet. Staying long?' The two men moved to the armchairs and joined Elspeth, who'd just sat down, red-faced from the activity.

Raymond leaned down and kissed Elspeth on the cheek. 'You're looking lovely as ever, Elspeth, the old man treating you alright?' He winked and Elspeth giggled delightedly.

'He's wonderful, I'm a lucky girl.'

'And he's a lucky man.' Raymond gave his father a knowing grin, before looking around. 'Your daughter not visiting you? Too busy to see her dear old mum, is she?'

Bristling slightly, Elspeth shifted in her chair. 'Oh, no, she called in for a minute this morning, poor Miriam, she does work hard.'

Albert shot his son a warning glance. 'Now, come on, lad, I'm sure Miriam does her best.'

'All I'm saying is, if you can't spare the time to visit your mum or dad for a cup of tea, then what's it all about, eh?'

Albert nudged his elbow into Raymond's side, exclaiming brightly, 'Sounds like the tea trolley.'

As if on cue, Greg appeared with the trolley and made a show of watching Willow change the carpet boules champ photo from last week's winner – Albert – to Howard. 'Congratulations, Howie, you get the biggest teacake. And is your handsome nephew visiting you this afternoon?'

'If his wife lets him out of her sight, the woman's got him on a tight leash, but she's a good woman, Moira is, and there's not too many of them to be found, present company excepted, of course.' He winked at Agatha before flicking his eyes in Elizabeth's direction and raising his eyebrows. 'Well, almost. And what about you, Greg, about time you found a good woman, isn't it?'

'What, me?' Greg placed his hands on his hips in a camp fashion. 'With all these wonderful women to look after me at Meadowvale?' He shuddered theatrically. 'No, what I need is a good man.'

'That's what I used to say, dear boy, in my younger day. 'Monty sank into an armchair, his stomach bulging between his braces. 'Never thought I'd end up living with a houseful of women.'

'Who are you calling a woman?' Albert looked across at Monty, angrily, as Elspeth touched his arm.

'He's only joking, aren't you, Monty? Those teacakes look nice, Greg, I really shouldn't, of course, but...'

'Well, I'm off, that was a good game, you all did really well, and congratulations, Howard. I'll see you all in the morning for some music activity.' Willow smiled and bounced out of the room as Elizabeth rolled her eyes.

'Good grief, I feel like I'm back at school. She'll have us finger-painting next.'

Sasha watched from her car as Willow drove off, she hadn't felt like facing her again. She was being unfair, she knew she was, but that sweet, cheerful, caring little girl act had to be too good to be true, didn't it? She locked her car and walked across to the front door as it opened and a man in his sixties walked out, limping slightly and leaning heavily on his stick, an irritated expression on his face. Standing aside, Sasha acknowledged his muttered thanks and was about to enter the building when she realised that she'd left her bag in the car with the files in it.

Retrieving it, she wondered about the man. He wasn't a resident then, no, of course not, she'd met them all, he must be someone's relative. She watched him drive off in his car – so it wasn't only residents who needed walking sticks then...

Entering the hallway, Sasha headed to the library to put her files down, smiling at the elderly woman with fluffy white hair, dressed in pink, who looked up at her through large glasses from her chair at the library table. 'Sorry to disturb you, it's Lillian, isn't it? Lillian Springer?'

The woman looked back at Sasha blankly, before straightening her notebook and pen. 'I've told Mervyn, my agent, a thousand times, I refuse to sign my new contract until I've gone through it with my publisher, I told them both. Now, here are my chapters for typing up today, and I'll take a cup of tea, thank you.'

It didn't look like Lillian would be able to give her any helpful information about the day of Dorothy's murder, but as she was already in the library, she may as well start with her. 'You stay right where you are, Lillian, and I'll be back with your tea.'

'Look out, it's the interrogation squad.'

Laughter rang out in the lounge at Howard's comment, and Sasha grinned. 'I'm saving the thumbscrews just for you, Howard.'

'Hi, Sasha, want a cuppa?' Greg wiggled the teapot at her.

'Thanks, Greg, and can I take one for Lillian? She's in the library so I thought I'd just go ahead and interview her, although–' she leaned closer to him, 'Lillian was talking about a contract and her publisher – she doesn't still write, does she?'

'No, poor thing hasn't written a word for years, bless her, but she wrote lots of children's books years ago, we've got most of them in the library, or we did have, a few of them seem to have gone walkies lately, I'll have to track them down – they're first editions so they're pretty valuable, Lillian brought them with her when she moved in. They were very popular, and this past year they've had quite a revival so they've been selling like hotcakes, I'm told. Word is–' Greg whispered to Sasha, 'she still earns a fortune in royalties. If it's true then an obscure children's home will do nicely from it. Strange that she's not leaving it to her son though, I wonder what made her choose the Sisters of Mercy. Of course, it's not my business but I overheard Mervyn speaking on the phone one day, and he didn't sound too happy about it, I can tell you.'

He waved the tongs at Sasha. 'Teacake? Tell you what, you take the tea through and I'll bring you and Lillian your teacakes. Butter?'

Realising that she hadn't eaten lunch, other than the two custard creams with Mrs Pringle, Sasha nodded. 'That sounds good, thanks, Greg.'

~

Eric rushed into The Woolly Sheep and made his way to the bar. He must have left his phone here, it couldn't be anywhere else.

'Yes, love?' The woman behind the bar looked up, stifling a yawn. 'Sorry, late nights are catching up with me. What can I get you?'

'Er, my phone, hopefully. I was in here last night and we had a few drinks.' He held his hands out, shrugging. 'I don't suppose you've found it by any chance?'

'Eric, is it?' At his nod, the woman smiled. 'You're in luck.' Reaching behind her she picked up his phone and passed it to him. 'Someone called you this morning, a woman? And I'm guessing from your expression that's not good.' She grinned. 'Don't suppose you'll forget your phone in a rush again.'

Thanking her, Eric left the pub, frantically bringing up his call history on the screen. *Shit*. Now he had some explaining to do to Sasha. And he hadn't even done anything wrong, well, not really... He clicked on her name and waited for her to answer.

'Sash, before you say anything, let me explain, I–'

'Hold on, Eric.' Smiling at Lillian, Sasha excused herself, trying the library door handle and, finding it unlocked, went out into the garden where she could speak without being overheard. 'What's the excuse this time, Eric? Too much to drink? Someone took your phone by mistake? Did you even go home to your own flat last night? You said you were leaving the pub when we spoke. I actually felt sorry for you, all alone with your dinner for one, and all the time you were out getting hammered – so hammered that you left your phone at the pub.' She'd been walking fast, following one of the paths, and stopped as she came out into a small clearing containing a garden bench, its occupant taking up most of the seat. 'Sorry,' she mouthed to Monty, who waved his cigarette nonchalantly in return. She turned around and took another turn, surprised at the number of pathways winding through the dense bushes in the gardens.

'Sash, baby,' Eric wheedled, 'alright, I told a little white lie, I was with a few mates. It was only going to be a pint, but one thing led to another, you know how it is. I don't even know why I said that to you. Nothing happened, I swear, it was just that it turned into a bit of a party, someone was getting married and there was a bit of fun, that's all.' He'd said too much.

'Who was getting married? One of your friends? A stag night, you mean?' Sasha's eyes narrowed as she awaited his response.

He took a deep breath. 'There was a hen party, music, a bit of mucking around, we just had a bit of a laugh...' he finished lamely.

'I knew it.' Her heart sank, getting engaged to Eric had been a bit of a gamble, he was never going to change the way he was, it was just in his nature. 'Eric, tell me the truth, did you go home with someone last night? Please don't lie.'

'I swear, Sash, I went home alone. Listen, we all had a bit of a dance, a bit too much to drink, and it got late so we shared a cab, that's all.'

'Eric, look down at your feet and tell me which one's got the bullet hole in it.'

'What? Oh, haha, I get it, very funny. Alright, I'm an idiot, I open my mouth and rubbish comes out. But, baby, honestly, we only–'

'I can't do this now, Eric, I've got to go.' She finished the call and walked despondently back to the library. She'd never know when Eric was telling the truth and that was the problem – it would *always* be the problem.

~

Monty heaved himself up from the garden bench, feeling sad. Poor girl obviously had romance troubles, some cad treating her badly by the sound of it, nice girl too. Sighing, he walked slowly along the path towards the pond, pausing to lean on his stick and remember Dorothy as he gazed at the star-shaped flowers of the water lilies resting on their pads. Such a pretty scene and yet it would forever signify death to him now.

~

Zoe answered her phone in the silence of the art gallery, her fingers gently nudging a frame a fraction up on the right. 'Eric, how are you?' She smiled into her phone. 'Are you missing Sash?'

'Well, that's what I wanted to speak to you about, Zo, I've kind of gone and got myself into a bit of a mess. I don't think she's very pleased with me, it's all been a big misunderstanding and–'

'Eric, what have you done now?' Exasperated, Zoe rolled her eyes at the monochrome oil painting of a London street scene.

'Nothing, I swear, well, it's not as bad as Sash thinks, but, look, are you free after work? Can I buy you a drink and explain?

I've got an idea about this weekend, if you think James will spare you?'

'As it goes, he's off on business for a few days tomorrow, so yes, I'm free. But it depends what it is and what you've done, I won't be used to get you off the hook, Eric, not if it involves lying to my best friend.'

'You're a lifesaver, Zo, I'll explain everything later. Meet you outside the gallery at five?'

Shaking her head, Zoe returned to her task, holding up the next painting as she pondered where to hang it.

~

'Sorry about that, Lillian.' Sasha closed the library door, smiled, and took a seat across the table from where Lillian was sitting. 'It's lovely and sunny out now, hard to believe it was raining so hard earlier. What was the weather like the day Dorothy died, can you remember?'

'Poor Emily, my little girl, couldn't visit that day.' Lillian appeared distressed for a moment. 'The poor little thing, I had to choose, you see, you do see, don't you?' Lillian nodded at Sasha. 'My next book is due in three months and my agent brought the new contract in for me to sign, in the morning. I had to choose, you see, and he was such a poorly little thing. I think, perhaps, a little less butter next time, if you don't mind, dear?

Momentarily confused, Sasha looked up from her notes and saw the plate containing the remains of the buttered teacake which Lillian was pushing towards her. 'Right, I'll tell Greg.' She moved the plate aside and smiled encouragingly at Lillian.

'I'd just finished breakfast and I told him I'd discuss it with my publisher – she came to see me in the afternoon but she will talk to everyone. And Mervyn, that's my agent, gets so annoyed with me, he stormed off with the contract and I couldn't discuss it with her in the end. I can't remember her name.' Lillian's puzzled eyes looked at Sasha, magnified by her large glasses.

'Dorothy was disturbing me in the morning, she was on about my word count – I told her that's what it's called – *two words*, she kept laughing, *they want you to write two words*. Oh, that's when Mervyn appeared, he does get upset so easily, but then she came, the nice one, and tried to calm me down, said there was no need to make a fuss.'

Lillian glanced out of the library window. 'What a lovely sunny day, just like that day, once the weather cleared. I excused myself from the afternoon meeting, it had barely started when one of them rushed off, and came in here to look for my missing pink pen. Agatha insisted on coming to help, and we found the door swinging so she closed it as there was a draught. She said the smell of food was making her hungry again, but we're not supposed to eat in here. Then she came back to the meeting with me and insisted on sitting with me, fiddling with beads and making a mess. It wasn't like a meeting at all, and I didn't find my pen.' She looked sadly at Sasha.

Greg swooped in, deftly picking up the teacups and plates. 'Oh, now who didn't finish her teacake?' Pouting sadly at Lillian, Greg stacked the plates and cups and waltzed out, calling behind him, 'Greg's going to make sure you eat all your dinner tonight, my darling, it's savoury mince with mashed potatoes, carrots, and peas.'

'Excuse me a moment, Lillian.' Sasha hurried after Greg.

'Greg, does Lillian have a daughter?'

He leaned into Sasha, conspiratorially. 'She sometimes talks about an Emily in Australia, but with Lillian, you never know when she's off with the fairies.'

'Oh, so she wasn't due to visit Lillian the day that Dorothy died? She called her my little girl?'

'She's never visited, I've certainly never met her,' Greg murmured, raising his eyebrows. 'Like I said, off with the fairies, all in her head probably, our sweetie here has got quite an imagination on her, after all. Strange coincidence – there's a little girl called Emily in her children's books – maybe that's who she's thinking of.'

'Right, and she keeps talking about meetings...?'

Greg shook his head. 'Bless her heart, everything's a meeting, meal times, crafting activities, you name it. Poor thing lives in a terrible muddle.'

Thanking him, Sasha returned to the library.

Smiling vaguely, Lillian tilted her head at Sasha. 'What was it you wanted to know?'

'Er, you were just telling me what you could remember from the day that Dorothy died?' She wasn't going to get anywhere with poor Lillian, she realised sadly.

'Ah, that terrible day, yes, I remember now, I looked out during my meeting and saw the sister heading out, the large one, and there was a man out there, and a bit later Monty was complaining to the thin one when she came in. That walking stick is dangerous with all those feet. And then he rushed in for his cake, it's very romantic, she'd saved him a piece, although he is a very unsavoury man. It was the wrong day for cake though.'

Was this how all her interviews were going to go? Confused jumbles of memories which may or may not relate to the day in question? Sasha's bewildered brain tried to keep up with who was who – or who might me who.

'Do you mean that Monty rushed in?' *But romantic? Who?* 'And you saw a man – do you know who it was?'

'It was the young boy who came in and said, 'I've found Dorothy, she's dead.'

It was pointless to continue. 'Well, thank you, Lillian, you've been most helpful.' Sasha smiled kindly, as she stifled a yawn in the warmth of the room.

ERIC HAS AN IDEA

Detective Inspector Stephanie Wendover sipped her tea as she looked around at her newly refurbished offices. Gone were the grubby fabric partitions, the battered wooden desks, and the peeling wall paint. The walls were now a bright, clean white, with huge whiteboards affixed to them at regular interviews, and her staff sat at shiny new workstations. Best of all, she had her own glass-partitioned office at one end of the office space, through which she could observe her staff at work, as well as any comings or goings.

Feeling refreshed and energised from her two weeks' leave (one of which had been spent with her sister down in Cornwall, the other at home in her flat in Putney, where she'd spent an extremely pleasant few days catching up on her reading – her guilty pleasure being fiction books of the murder mystery genre, which, being a police detective inspector, was something she preferred to keep quiet from her colleagues), D.I. Wendover clicked through her e-mails, making sure not to miss anything of the slightest importance.

Her finger hovered over the keyboard, about to click on the next message, as she re-read the short e-mail from Dr Taylor. The name was familiar, the doctor being one of the police appointed counsellors, and at the mention of Miss Pullman, Steph nodded in recollection – Zoe, of course.

Breaking no patient confidentiality, Dr Taylor, who had been fully apprised of the case of Zoe's abduction and duress at the hands of Miles Bleak, formerly known as Blake Selim, wondered if she could meet with D.I. Wendover to discuss a small concern.

Intrigued, Steph Wendover typed out a short reply, confirming that she'd be happy to meet Dr Taylor at her convenience. She leaned back, wondering what the concern could be. They'd tied the case up nicely, got their man behind bars, and the case was closed. She hoped there wasn't anything hampering Zoe's recovery – as far as she knew the poor woman had managed to move on with her life. Interrupted in her musing by the ringing of her phone, she switched her attention back to the present and a new case.

~

Sasha tidied her papers, wondering if she should find another resident to interview. She'd had no idea that a care home could be so busy, had thought she'd sail through the residents' interviews in no time at all. Her thoughts were interrupted by the appearance of Elizabeth Payton, immaculately turned out with freshly applied makeup.

'I don't expect you learned anything from Lillian, her head's all over the place.' Elizabeth wandered into the library, gently trailing her fingers over the books on the shelves. 'We had a library when we lived in Rhodesia, of course, it was fully stocked with all the proper books, not like this sorry excuse.' Her eyes gazed off into the distance for a moment before she turned back to Sasha. 'So, have you solved it yet?'

Sasha shook her head, smiling. 'It doesn't quite work like that, Elizabeth, I'm purely recording everyone's recollections of the day in question at this point. I could interview you now if you'd like?'

'Oh no, dear, it's gin and tonic time for me – I'm expecting Judith and Gemma, we have so much to talk about, it will be the society wedding of the year, you know. You're welcome to join us for drinks if you'd like? They do their best here, but it's not the same, of course – nothing like the good old days, having our drinks served from the drinks trolley by the servants as we watched the sun go down.'

The gin and tonic sounded tempting but Sasha wasn't sure that she wanted to sit drinking it with the residents. 'Thanks, Elizabeth, but I think I'll be off. I'll see you tomorrow.'

On a whim, Sasha called her sister, Tess. 'Are you home yet, sis? I thought I'd pop in for a drink.'

Arriving at Tessa's, Sasha spent the first ten minutes recounting her day and convincing her sister that she was fine, that her car damage was minor, and that there was no need to involve the police. Pulling a rueful face, she admitted, 'I'm afraid I must have made Mrs Pringle's day though, I still can't believe that I sat in the chemist's drinking tea and pouring out my woes.' She grimaced. 'A moment of weakness on my part.'

Laughing, Tessa opened the fridge and took out a bottle of wine. 'Well, I hope you didn't tell her too much, her heart's in the right place but she does love a gossip. White wine?'

'Actually, have you got any gin? I fancy a gin and tonic – long story... Chants not home from school yet?'

A worried look passed over Tessa's face. 'No, she's taken up with some new friends.' She sighed. 'It's been hard for her, you know, since Britney died, they were joined at the hip. I'm pleased that she's making new friends but she never brings them round. Oh well, she's just growing up, I suppose, remember what we were like at that age?'

Laughing, the two sisters took their drinks through to the lounge as the sound of a car slowing down outside reached their ears. Car doors banged and a male voice called out.

Sasha stepped to the window in time to see Chantelle waving at the driver of the white car as it drove off. *Another white car.*

The front door opened and slammed shut, followed by footsteps climbing the stairs.

'Chants? Sasha's here, come and say hello. How was school?'

The footsteps slowly descended and Chantelle hovered in the doorway for a moment. 'Hi, Sash, hi, Mum. I've gotta go, I need to have a shower, then I'm meeting my mates.'

The two women shrugged at each other as they listened to Chantelle running up the stairs and closing her bedroom door.

'She looks pale, Tess, and what's with all the black makeup?'

'I know, and it's not just the makeup, all she wears is black clothing when she's not at school, Dave calls her his little goth.'

Half an hour later, Sasha kissed her sister goodbye, called out to her niece and, receiving no reply, headed to the pub. She'd promised Willow and Charles a drink this evening to thank them for their help. And Cal had said he'd see her in the bar. *Not that that meant anything, of course.*

She looked down at the engagement ring on her finger, thinking about Eric and wondering what he was doing. Annoyingly, she missed him, but the thought that he might well have cheated on her the night before upset her, angered her, even, and was made worse by the fact that she had the new little happy couple right under her nose at the pub.

Jules looked up from the bar and beckoned Sasha over as she walked in, reaching under the counter for a bag. 'Here's one of my cardies for you to borrow, can't have you wearing Mrs Pringle's, and it's a little chilly. Sorry about your car accident, not a great start to your visit.' Without being asked, she poured Sasha a glass of wine and handed it over.

'Thanks, Jules, you're an angel, I'll pop and buy one tomorrow. Where is everyone?' She looked around, expecting to see Willow bubbling around, the centre of attention. A giggle and sounds of male laughter drew her eyes towards the door to the adjacent room. 'Is it poker night?'

'No, we stopped those after the village murders, the police were a little too interested in the amounts being gambled but turned a blind eye as the players had put themselves on the line to provide your brother-in-law with his alibi. It's just a pool room now, I can't risk losing my licence. They're in there.' She nodded at the door. 'Cal said to tell you to join them, he and Willow seem to be quite friendly with our visiting photographer.'

'Could you organise a round for them please, Jules? I owe Willow and Charles a drink for their help earlier, might as well get one for Cal, too.' Bracing herself for Willow's puppy dog bouncing as she entered the pool room, she was nonetheless caught off guard when Willow *literally* bounced over to her and hugged her.

'Here she is! How are you feeling now, Sasha? Say cheese!' Willow swivelled them both around as Charles aimed his camera and clicked a few photos. 'Cal, come and have your picture taken with us.'

Sasha found herself sandwiched between the two of them, and smiled for the camera, feeling uncomfortable. She felt old and drab in the face of the younger woman's exuberance. Extricating herself, she dropped her bags on a chair. 'Hi, guys, I'll just fetch your drinks, Jules was pouring them for me.'

'No need, here you are.' Jules placed the tray down and put the drinks on a table.

'Let's have another game, girls against boys.' Willow clapped her hands as Cal smiled at her indulgently. 'I'm so useless, but the men have been teaching me.'

Gulping half of her glass of wine in one go, Sasha nodded, *of course they had.* 'Fine, but I'm pretty useless myself.'

~

Zoe and Eric found a table out on the street and sat down with their drinks.

'Start talking.' Zoe gave Eric a stern look, worried about what he was going to tell her. The last thing she wanted was to hear confessions of his cheating on her best friend.

A few minutes later and Eric had finished recounting his story. 'And that's it, I swear, Zo, you know what it's like, a few too many drinks and you're an easy target.'

'Eric, you're telling me that it was all the woman's fault? What, you were powerless to escape her clutches? Come on, I wasn't born yesterday. You might not have gone home with her but you let her put her tongue down your throat. You're blowing your last chance with Sash, you know that, right? You have to tell her.'

'That's why I need your help, I've got an idea, I thought we could surprise her this weekend.' Eric looked pleadingly at Zoe. 'I'll drive us and pay for your room. She won't give me the chance to explain over the phone so I thought if I could talk to her in person, and if you're there as well...' His voice trailed off as he waited for her to say something.

Sighing, Zoe agreed. 'It does sound like fun, but if you think I'm going to stick up for you or anything, you're wrong. You must tell her the truth, she doesn't deserve to be treated like this, Eric. She'll either forgive you or finish things and you've only yourself to blame.'

'I know, and I'll tell the truth, but surely just drunk-snogging some bird is better than ending up in bed with her?'

'You just don't get it, do you?' Zoe shook her head in exasperation.

'He's back there, did she tell you? That bloke she had a bit of a fling with.'

'Who, Cal?' Zoe's eyes flickered in interest, it would certainly be interesting to meet the man who had captured a part of her friend's heart for a while, before hurting it... 'Wait a minute, is this part of the reason you want to surprise her? You can't seriously think Sash would do anything? Are you hoping to catch her out in some way, to get yourself off the hook?'

'No, scout's honour.' Eric held up his crossed fingers as Zoe laughed.

'You were never a scout.'

Eric grinned. 'So, it's settled then? I'll book you a room and drive us up on Friday – let me know what time you can get off work – we'll stay for two nights and drive back on Sunday. Now, tell me what's happening in your life.'

Zoe leaned back. 'Oh, well, James is wonderful, but I think I've said that about a million times. I decided to take the police up on their offer of a counsellor. I'm fine, really, but I knew I'd blocked everything, refused to think about it, and the trouble was that I'd have these odd flashbacks and didn't know what to do with them. Like, I'd wake up in the night, trembling and feeling anxious, and just for a second I'd think I was back there with a chain around my ankle.' She shivered. 'Dr Taylor's been really good, she's encouraged me to talk through each moment that I can remember, what I was feeling, what I sensed...' She frowned. 'There were times when he was taking pictures of me but I didn't know it. I've gradually allowed myself to unlock the memories, but they're disturbing and I'm not quite sure what it all means.' Suddenly Zoe looked up at Eric, her eyes wide. 'There was one time when it felt like someone else was there, but there can't have been, can there? I mean, if there was, then who was it and where is he now?'

Eric placed his hands over Zoe's and smiled gently. 'No, Zo, he did everything all on his lonesome, we know his history now. You must have been pretty disorientated, not being able to see, so it's natural that your memories are going to be muddled. He's safely behind bars and all you need to do is get it all off your chest to the doc and then get on with enjoying life with James.'

'Yes, you're right.' Zoe nodded gratefully. 'And talking of James, I must go, tonight's his last night and I'm cooking us dinner.'

They parted with plans for Eric to pick Zoe up on Friday for their trip to Parva Crossing.

~

Oh, she was good, just the right level of helpless femininity, Sasha thought bitterly, as she tried to pull her eyes from the sight of Willow's slender form draped over the pool table, her top riding up just enough to expose a sliver of bare flesh between the top of her leggings and her hoodie – right where Cal's hand rested gently as he guided her aim.

'Like this?' Willow turned to look at Cal as laughter tinkled from her throat.

'Perfect.' Cal grinned, patting her bottom as she squealed.

Sasha could stand it no more. It wasn't that she was jealous, it was all just too... girly, too perfect. 'More drinks anyone?'

'My turn.' Charles went off to the bar, leaving Sasha stuck.

'I'll come and help carry them,' she called out, hurrying to join him at the bar.

'So, Sasha, word is you're hot on the trail of a killer, is that true? And at a care home, no less?'

The village grapevine was obviously operating excellently if even visitors knew her business. 'I'm an investigator, I've been invited to help the police as I was personally involved with the victim a little while back, that's all. Now, tell me, how's the photography going?'

'It's going well.' Charles passed two glasses of wine to Sasha and picked up the pint glasses.

They placed the drinks on the table in the pool room and he turned to her. 'I've got a bit of an interest in lifestyle portraiture, hoping to improve my capture of facial expressions, that kind of thing. I was wondering if I might offer my services at the care home, for free, of course. Perhaps the residents and staff would like to have their pictures taken, it would mean my hanging around there for a couple of days...'

'That's a fabulous idea, Charles!' Willow clapped her hands together, a habit that Sasha was finding increasingly irritating. 'I'll speak to Mrs Goodwin, I'm sure she'll say yes, she loves new ideas, and anything to help the darlings fill their days will be appreciated. I think they'll find it quite exciting, don't you, Sasha?'

Caught on the spot, Sasha nodded. 'Yes, maybe, but I do need to spend time with them for my interviews...'

'That's settled then.' Charles beamed. 'Willow, take my camera, it's that button on the top, I must have a photo taken with our detective here.'

Pulled into Charles's side, Sasha found herself in yet another uncomfortable situation as she smiled weakly at the camera in Willow's hands.

DINNER TIME

Kirsty finished putting the dishes onto the trolley and paused to sniff the air. Shaking her head, she moved closer to the open window. Someone was smoking something they shouldn't and she'd bet she knew who it was. Turning, she smiled at Tanya. 'That's everything, you can take it through, there's a dear.'

The kitchen door opened and Kirsty frowned at Spencer as he walked in, the smell of marijuana hanging around him. 'You're late and needed in the dining room, Spencer, Tanya will need help serving, but mind you go and wash your hands and face first, you stink of it, and don't think I don't know what I'm talking about. And you can stop encouraging young Lucy to smoke that stuff, Elspeth would be devastated if she knew what you were getting her granddaughter involved in.'

'Yeah, alright, Kirsty, don't go on, and Lucy's not such a little innocent, you know.' Spencer disappeared off, smirking.

'I'll have a glass of red wine, thank you, Greg.' Elizabeth placed her hand over her glass as Greg prepared to pour her a glass of water.

He hesitated, wondering how much she'd had to drink already. Still, they weren't policemen, the residents had every right to enjoy a tipple if they wanted to. 'I'll fetch a bottle, anyone else?'

Monty peered around myopically. 'Why not? I'll have a glass too, thank you, Gregory.'

'If it's a good year then I don't mind if I do. Ladies? Albert?' Howard looked around encouragingly to enthusiastic nods.

'I'll go and check the wine cellar, shall I?' Greg's sarcasm went unnoticed as he waltzed off. They'd end up with a bunch of geriatric alcoholics on their hands at this rate.

'How are the wedding plans coming along, Elspeth?' Agatha scooped up a forkful of savoury mince and mashed potato.

'Well, there's not much to plan, surely, it's hardly a big affair, not like Gemma's.' Elizabeth took a small mouthful of the mince, wrinkling her nose. 'We certainly won't have food like this at Gemma and Alec's wedding, it will be far more sophisticated.'

'Do you always have to be so full of yourself?' Monty looked up from his plate for a second.

'We won't be having food like this either, will we, Albie?'

'Not a chance, but we've got to watch the old budget a bit, your Albert's not made of money you know. You can always sell some of those fancy jewels, I suppose.' Albert guffawed as Elspeth looked worried.

'Yes, well, the main thing is that we get married, isn't it? Mary said that she and Kirsty would make something special for everyone. There's no need to have outside caterers, I'm sure, they're very good cooks, even this dinner is quite delicious, don't you think so, Agatha?'

Agatha nodded, her mouth full, as Davinia spoke for her.

'Agatha does enjoy her food, don't you? Greg, do be sure to thank Kirsty, it's very nice.'

'I certainly will. Now, that's everyone's wine glass filled. Lillian, you're quiet, everything alright, my darling?'

'Who was she?' Lillian looked up from her plate. 'That lady who was talking to me?'

'That's our detective, Lillian, the one busy nosing into our lives. Did you have anything interesting to tell her?' Davinia's eyes were trained intently on Lillian, as Elizabeth interposed.

'Highly unlikely, don't you think? Greg, be a dear, just a little drop more if you don't mind.'

'I told her who I saw going out into the garden. Oh, no, it can't have been, I must have got that wrong, we were in my meeting together the whole time. Then who... I don't understand...' Lillian's voice trailed off for a moment. 'She was very nice, brought me tea, and I told her about Mervyn. I do wish he wouldn't get so upset with me.'

Sounds of general sympathetic murmurings came from around the table, accompanied by the clink of cutlery on the dinner plates, as Tanya moved to Lillian, patting her shoulder. 'Don't you upset yourself, Lillian, you've got yourself all worked up over nothing, Mervyn's just trying to help you, that's all, he's a top bloke, your son.'

'Someone did something they shouldn't.' Lillian's voice sounded loud in the lull in conversation.

Albert looked up sharply. 'No need to go getting anybody into trouble, Lillian, no one likes a tittle-tattle.'

'Guilty conscience, Albert? Or was it someone else? Who's hiding a secret?' Elizabeth threw the last of her wine back.

'Dorothy knew everyone's secrets from our old lives.' Monty placed his knife and fork together precisely in the centre of his empty plate and leaned back, rubbing his stomach. He peered around the table. 'Makes you wonder whose secret was so bad that they'd kill her to keep it from coming out.'

Elspeth shivered. 'Oh, Monty, don't say that, you're scaring me. I'm sure I've got nothing to hide.' She giggled uncertainly.

'Well, now you've got us all wondering, Elspeth. Just what could you have got up to in your younger day, or anyone else for that matter? We can be sure that our old lies will come back to haunt us.' Howard winked conspiratorially at the Lovewell sisters, who, for once, didn't laugh encouragingly.

Davinia fiddled with her hands in her lap and Agatha shifted in her seat, looking around for Greg, calling out, 'I think we've all finished, Greg.'

'As if a bunch of old crocks like us could have anything to hide, I ask you.' Albert shrugged. 'And certainly not my Elspeth. No, if you ask me, our lady detective needs to look into the secret lives of our visitors and the staff, not my Ray, though, of course. Maybe it was one of them who did Dorothy in.'

'That's enough talk of secrets and doing people in.' Greg took the plates from Spencer and indicated to Tanya that she should begin serving the fruit flan. Surreptitiously, he checked his watch, wondering if Richard would still make it tonight.

'Maybe Elspeth's got a secret admirer,' Agatha threw into the conversation. 'I saw the cake earlier, it looked delicious.'

'Oh, Miriam dropped it for me, it was a little gift from Lucy, really such a sweet girl, and she'd look so lovely if only she didn't wear all that black, so dowdy. There was one for Spencer, too, wasn't there, Spencer?'

All eyes turned to Spencer, who grinned. 'Your granddaughter spoils me rotten, Elspeth, she knows I can't resist a bit of cake.'

'Well, aren't you two the sweet couple,' Greg quipped.

'They're from the patisserie in the village,' Elspeth nodded as she informed Agatha. 'Sasha's going to search our rooms, and everywhere in Meadowvale.' Elspeth giggled, 'It's quite exciting, like being criminals.'

'Haven't the police already searched everywhere? Not that I can imagine what anyone hopes to find.' Elizabeth was indignant. 'I hope she's not going to turn the whole place upside down. Greg, I need another glass of wine, these glasses are so small, quite ridiculous.'

'Of course she is, that's why she's here,' Albert said knowingly, 'put us at our ease, then catch us off guard. I don't like it, all this prying around.'

'You sound like you've got experience, Albert.' Agatha's tone was teasing but her eyes were anxious. 'I don't want her going through my things, they're private.'

'He's probably got Elspeth's jewels hidden away, that's what he's worried about.' Howard guffawed as Albert shot him an irritated glance.

'Don't be mean to my Albie.' Elspeth pouted, placing her hand on Albert's arm. 'He didn't mean it, as if you'd take my jewellery when we're going to be married.'

'Have you heard about the bird? He lived in Norwich and ate porridge,' Elizabeth mimicked Dorothy's voice, her eyes glinting cruelly. 'I can clearly hear Dorothy saying that. I wonder what she meant?'

All eyes turned to Elizabeth.

'Elizabeth, would you stop with your incessant stirring?'

'Hear, hear, Monty.' Greg pushed the trolley of dirty crockery away from the table to await the pudding plates.

'Dorothy said a lot of nonsense, we all know that.' Albert laughed a little too loudly. 'I saw him kissing the little dickie bird.' What was that all about? Reckon she had a thing about birds, she liked to say something about the magpie liking shiny things, didn't she?'

'Keys in the pot what have we got?'

'Mum's the word.'

'Nobody likes a thief.'

Comments rang out from around the table as they recalled snippets of Dorothy's taunting remarks.

'All that glitters is not gold.'

'Tanya, don't encourage them.' Greg glanced reprovingly at Tanya.

'Sorry.' Tanya looked embarrassed. 'I can just hear her saying that as if it was yesterday, but we all know none of it meant anything. I'll go and organise the coffee.' She scuttled off to the kitchen, away from Greg's glare.

'Dorothy's favourite was the bald eagle.'

Everyone stared at Lillian.

'She must have liked birds.' Smiling and nodding, Lillian took another mouthful of fruit flan.

Elizabeth snorted. 'Someone comes to mind at the word bald, finally something that makes sense.'

'I'll take my coffee in the conservatory, please, Greg, I'm going to go and smoke a cigarette, if you don't mind.' Leaning on the table, Monty pushed himself up, glowering at Elizabeth.

'None of it made any sense.' Elspeth gave a tinkly laugh as she patted her curls. 'None of it meant anything at all.'

'For once I'm going to agree with you, Elspeth, the woman was dotty, plain and simple. She spewed a lot of rubbish, none of which is going to help find her killer. We should just forget all about Dorothy's little snipes and let our female sleuth work with the facts – which are few and far between. Thank you, everyone, for the scintillating dinner conversation, it's been fun, as always.' Elizabeth left the table, swaying slightly as she made her way to an armchair in the lounge.

'Rude old bag.'

'Albie, don't be so dreadful.'

'Albert's making sense for once, Elizabeth really is quite obnoxious.'

'I thought you were friends, Davinia?'

'How could anyone be friends with that woman?'

~

'All I'm saying is that we must be extra careful,' Greg whispered into his phone, 'Dorothy might be gone but her little taunts seem to have remained with us, I've just had the whole lot of them sitting around the dinner table trying to remember things that she said. I was a bag of nerves when one of them repeated what she said about us. What if someone works out who she meant? Are you still coming to see me tonight? Maybe you should park a bit further away – come through the side entrance – I'll unlock it for you.'

A click from the bushes behind him startled Greg and he looked around, squinting at the tiny red glow. 'Who is it? Who's there?' But whoever it was had moved silently away, leaving a slight whiff of smoke in their wake.

'Greg, are you there?' Richard Carding glanced towards the living room window, noticing that his wife had moved from the sofa. As the front door opened and Moira looked out enquiringly, he spoke hurriedly into his phone, 'I'll come through in a couple of hours, I've got to go.'

Waving his diary at his wife, Richard closed the door of his car. 'Found it.' He stepped back indoors, shutting the front door. 'I've got to pop out a bit later, might be a good one – old chap's died and apparently he was an avid collector of military history.'

Moira tutted. 'Surely it can wait until the morning, Richard? I don't understand the urgency, you're forever having to go out to these old houses late at night these days.'

Richard tapped the side of his nose. 'Ah, well, I've got my sources – that's what gets me ahead of the game – and if I don't get there for first pickings there are plenty of others waiting in the wings.'

'But you're not, are you, Richard?'

'Not what?'

'Ahead of the game. And military history books? Are they so popular?'

'They are to collectors, and it's not just books don't forget, Moira, I picked up an old, World War Two dagger collection the other day which I've got locked away in the safe until I can find a buyer. You never know when I'll come across a real rarity, that's what makes it all so exciting.'

'Exciting would be paying our bills on time and not worrying about where the money's going to come from. Maybe I should look for a job, I could ask at Meadowvale.'

'No.' Richard spoke firmly, 'My wife is not going to spend all her time at Meadowvale. And dear old Uncle Howie's not going to live forever, is he? When he goes everything will be alright.'

'Yes, well, Uncle Howie looks like he's got a good few years in him yet. You're putting a lot of faith in your inheritance – one step wrong and he could change his mind about you... Anyway,' Moira yawned, 'I think I'll take a bath, then make a cup of tea, have a read in bed, and take one of my sleeping tablets.'

'There's nothing for Uncle Howie to change his mind about. Don't wait up, I'll try not to disturb you when I come in.'

'For heaven's sake, how long does it take to look at a few dusty old books?'

~

Glen Cutter wiped the last piece of bread around his plate, mopping up the gravy, and pushed it into his mouth, chewing appreciatively. Swallowing, he leaned back, burping loudly. 'Nice bit of pie that.'

His sister, Sharon, picked up their plates from the coffee table, taking them through to the kitchen.

'Leave the washing up, I'm taking you out for a drink, I've got a surprise for you,' Glen called out.

'You could have told me earlier, Glen, I look a right mess.'

'You look fine, it's only for one drink, come on, I'm paying.' Grabbing his keys, he opened the front door.

'You'll have to, there's not exactly a lot of money around these days, is there?' Sharon slammed the passenger door.

'Oh, things are picking up, I've got quite a few new customers, course, the cut's a lot smaller, but if I do well, they said I can help out at the Rentham house. Once they get out, we'll start our own place again, you'll see.'

Sharon shifted in the passenger seat to face her brother, as he drove. 'Once they get out? They'll be in for years, Glen, you know that. That bloody bitch, I could kill her.'

'Now, now, sis, keep calm or you'll spoil my surprise.' Glen grinned mysteriously as he pulled into the car park of The Spotted Dog.

Looking around as they entered, he pointed to an empty table. 'Go and sit there and I'll be back with the drinks.'

As she sipped her vodka, Sharon looked around. 'So, what's your big surprise then?'

'Recognise anyone?' He held up his hand, warningly. 'Don't make it too obvious. I gave her a little fright earlier, ran her right off the road, pity I couldn't hang around to watch the fun.'

Sensing eyes on her, Sasha turned and surveyed the room, but everyone was busy chatting and drinking. Turning back to her table, she took her last mouthful of salad and chewed slowly. She'd been about to order the chicken and chips when Willow had said she'd have the chickpea spinach salad, and Sasha had, for some obscure reason, announced that it was exactly what she'd been about to order too. It had just been her imagination, surely, that Cal had looked amused.

'That was delicious, so filling,' she lied, picking up her glass to finish the wine, as Cal placed his knife and fork on his plate.

'You can't beat chicken and chips. How was yours, Charles? Our Jules certainly comes up with the goods.' His eyes twinkled as he glanced at Sasha.

'Really good, country cooking at its best.' Charles wiped his mouth with his serviette. 'I must say, my trip is turning out to be thoroughly enjoyable.'

'I think I might finish with some apple pie and cream, anyone else?' Cal looked round at the other three.

'Oh no you don't, Cal, not after chips.' Willow smiled sweetly, patting Cal's stomach. 'We don't want you putting on weight.'

'Oh, come on, it won't hurt. Sasha, fancy some apple pie?'

He was teasing her. She didn't even like apple pie, but it felt incredibly appealing after the rabbit food she'd just forced down.

'No thanks.' She smiled tightly. 'Like I said, I'm full. I'll take these plates to the bar.'

'I'll help.' Willow bounded up and followed Sasha, holding two of the plates.

'How was the food?' Jules smiled her thanks as she popped the plates through the kitchen hatch behind her. 'Any pudding?'

'The salad was scrumptious, Jules, I couldn't eat another thing.' Beaming, Willow placed her hand over her flat stomach. 'Sasha loved it too, didn't you?'

Jules looked at Sasha in surprise. 'I thought you were having chicken and chips.'

'No, that was the guys, just salad for me tonight.' She flushed slightly at Jules's quizzical look.

Taking drinks back to the table, her arm was knocked by a young man, spilling a few drops over her hands. Looking at her without an apology, he pushed past her and sat down at the table next to them.

The woman he was with was older than him, dark roots showing through her bleached hair and, as she lifted her arm to drain her glass, Sasha glimpsed the tattoo on her upper arm. I suppose he must be Drew, thought Sasha subconsciously, putting the drinks down and wiping her hands on her jeans. The woman looked up and stared straight at her, making her feel uncomfortable. The pair certainly didn't look the most savoury of couples.

'I think I'll pop out for a smoke.'

'I'll join you.' Cal jumped up, ignoring Willow's pout. 'Won't be long, you keep Charles company.'

Sasha flashed Willow a smile. *Payback for the chickpea salad*. She and Cal placed their drinks on an outside table and Cal passed her a cigarette.

'Thanks.' She lowered her head to his lighter, inhaling gently.

'This was our table.' Cal was looking at her with an intensity that she couldn't read. 'I can still remember us sitting here the first time we met, can you?'

Cal's with Willow. I'm with Eric. 'Yeah, I think we sat here or was it over there? Hard to remember, you know?' Feigning nonchalance, Sasha waved her arm around.

'Sash, you've got to let us talk eventually, please. You have to hear me out at least.'

'We're talking now, aren't we?'

'You know what I mean, I need to explain to you what happened last time. I know it won't make any difference, we've both moved on with our lives, but—'

'But that's exactly the thing, Cal, we've both moved on and it's all in the past now. Look,' she said, fixing a smile on her face, 'you're happy with Willow, I'm happy with Eric, it's called life, it just happens, it happened to us and here we are now.'

'I miss you.'

'I'm right here, Cal.'

Their eyes locked as a man's voice sounded, clear in the silence.

'So, did you like your surprise then, Shaz?'

'Bloody bitch, I wanted to kill her. Little smug-faced cow, carrying on like everything's fine, but thank you, lady, my life's not fine, is it? It's ruined and all thanks to you.'

Car doors opened. 'Take it easy, sis, you leave it to your little bruv, he's got it all under control. I've got a delivery to make on the way home, it won't take long.'

Distracted from the intensity of the moment, Sasha and Cal watched the man and woman as they got into the car and drove off.

Another white car. Or had she seen that one somewhere before? 'Cal, the accident I had today, I'm sure someone deliberately tried to run me off the road. And that couple, they were giving me strange looks in the pub. Whoever caused my accident was driving a white car,' she paused, 'I dunno, it just all seems a bit weird, that's all...'

'Sash, you can't go jumping to conclusions just because someone drives a white car. They didn't sound particularly pleasant but why on earth would they have tried to force you – a complete stranger – off the road? Hell, you might as well say it was Willow – she drives a white car – or Charles, for that matter – he also drives a white car. Half the village probably drives a white car. Look.' He touched her arm. 'It was bucketing down, you couldn't see, the road was slippery – it could have happened to anyone. The main thing is that you're alright.'

She nodded. Cal was right, but doubts niggled in the back of her mind. 'You're right, I'm just letting my little imagination run away with me, it tends to have a habit of doing that.'

Grinning, Cal opened his mouth to speak as Willow appeared beside him, wrapping her arms around him. In the awkward moment of quiet, Sasha's stomach growled noisily.

'Oh, poor you, you're still hungry, you should have had the chicken and chips, not that tiny little salad.' Willow's eyes were perfectly sympathetic as she gazed at Sasha.

She smiled tightly. 'I think I'll head up to my room, I've got a few notes to go through before tomorrow.

Turning abruptly, Sasha's attention was caught by a flash of movement at one of the windows. Taking large strides, she pulled open the door to the pub and scanned the room. No one was watching her, she was just imagining things.

'Sasha, thought you'd gone to bed.' Charles appeared at her side. 'I'm just off myself.' With a wave, he was gone. But he knew she hadn't gone to bed, he'd been sitting right there when she'd said she was going outside for a smoke. *Had Charles been watching her through the window? If so, why?*

Shaking her head at her confused paranoia, Sasha took the stairs to her room, switching on the light and locking the door behind her, before pulling out her holdall and rummaging through the bits in the bottom. She'd been right – she still had the remains of the snacks she'd bought on the way to Parva Crossing. Sitting cross-legged on the bed, she ripped open the packet of cheese and onion crisps and pushed a handful into her mouth, leaning back as she savoured the taste, her eyes on the bar of milk chocolate. *Inspector Willow of the diet police could take a hike.*

~

Greg walked with Richard through the darkness of the gardens and reached for the gate.

'That's odd, it's not locked.'

Richard frowned. 'I definitely locked it when I came in.'

The sound of a car starting up was followed by the gentle crunch of footsteps on the gravel outside, and Greg pulled the gate open, feeling brave in Richard's company. Sticking his head out he caught a glimpse of a white car driving away and found himself face to face with Spencer.

'Spencer, what are you doing out here? I thought you'd gone home.'

Spencer smiled slyly at Greg, noticing the man hiding in the shadows behind him. 'Looks like we've all got our secrets, Greg. You don't tell mine and I won't tell yours.'

'Yes, well, you're not supposed to be here so you'll have some explaining to do if you're not careful.'

'Sure, Greg, whatever you say, but I reckon I've got more reason to be here than your... friend...' Spencer smirked at Richard and walked on into the gardens.

'He's too quiet, always tiptoeing around.'

Richard was aghast. 'He looked straight at me, he saw me, Greg. I can't have him tell anyone about this, not ever.'

After an agitated exchange, Richard departed, leaving Greg to lock the gate and head back inside.

SASHA INTERVIEWS HOWARD NORTON

Dr Taylor's reply arrived in D.I. Wendover's inbox on Thursday morning, suggesting that they meet at a coffee shop in Earl's Court on Friday afternoon, if convenient. Having replied in the affirmative, Steph Wendover stepped back inside the residence in Chiswick, the occupants of which had been found dead the day before, and threw her full concentration onto the matter in hand.

~

Sasha had finished her breakfast whilst keeping an eye on the door to the rooms, sure that at any moment Willow would arrive and make her feel guilty for eating eggs and bacon. No doubt she of the perfect bottom consumed a sliver of fruit for breakfast and not much else. About to leave her table, she was accosted by Jules.

'Message from Mrs Pringle, you're to meet her at Madam Couture's at nine-thirty.' Jules rolled her eyes. 'Sounds intriguing.'

Sasha groaned. 'Not the boutique on the high street, the one that looks like all the clothes are from the seventies?'

'Yep, that's the one.' Laughing, Jules took her plate. 'Looks like you've got a new best friend. Oh, you'll be able to return her cardigan all washed and dried – it's on your bed.'

Thanking Jules, Sasha hurried up the stairs, gathering her files and stuffing everything into her bag. She'd call in quickly as per Mrs Pringle's request – *demand?* – and see what it was all about. Perhaps the owner of Madam Couture needed her help with something, that would be it, theft of clothing perhaps. The thought made her smile as she drove along the high street, *the public is warned to be on the lookout – the perpetrator is likely to be wearing a floral pinafore over a big-collared blouse, and sporting clogs.* She was still grinning when she pushed open the door of Madam Couture.

'Sasha, dear, there you are. I want to introduce you to Mrs Winter, Beryl, the owner.' Mrs Pringle clucked around.

'Er, hello, nice to meet you, er, Beryl, and nice to see you again Mrs Pringle, um, Dolly. Oh, here's your cardigan back, thank you so much, you were very kind to me yesterday. And this is for you.'

'Oh, you shouldn't have, dear.' Mrs Pringle gasped as she took the box of chocolates. 'What a treat, oh my.' She beamed, her cheeks flushed.

'So, how can I help you?' Sasha smiled enquiringly at the two women.

'No, no, no, Beryl's going to help *you*, dear. There aren't too many cardigans in the shops at this time, Beryl knows all about it, it's to do with the season change, isn't that right, Beryl?'

Nodding, Beryl took over. 'Dolly told me about your predicament. We can't have you staying in Parva Crossing without a cardigan, you never know when the chills are going to come in, yesterday was a fine example. So, I've had a little sort out and I must say, I was surprised at how many woollies I had squirrelled away in the storeroom. There'll be a good discount, of course.'

With a sinking heart, Sasha became aware of the jumpers and cardigans laid out around her. She looked helplessly at the two women's expectant faces. She couldn't disappoint them, she just couldn't. Fixing a smile on her face, she reached for the closest item – a bottle green cardigan with brown toggles – and held it up, turning to look in the mirror. 'Too big for me, what a pity.' Feigning regret, she placed the ugly cardigan back on the chair, as the two women looked on anxiously.

Surely she could find something here that was wearable for someone under seventy? And she did need something warm... Her eyes roamed around the room, desperately trying to avoid the puce cable knit with toggles. *It had a collar – and a belt – and it was brown, for crying out loud.* She began to panic.

'How about this one, dear?' Mrs Winter and Mrs Pringle nodded knowingly at each other as the cardigan was held out for Sasha's approval.

It was a gorgeous soft, dusky pink, a thick chunky knit with a braided design in the knit of the full sleeves. Sasha slipped it on, twirling in front of the mirror as she admired the hood, the large pockets, and the length – falling to just below her knees.

'Boho, I think they call it these days.' Mrs Winter smiled at Sasha's surprised expression.

'It's beautiful, I love it!'

'Beryl always says there's nothing new under the sun.' Dolly Pringle grinned. 'It suits you, Sasha, and perhaps a nice scarf to go with it?'

'Or this?'

Turning, Sasha took the hanger from Mrs Winter, holding the cream-coloured dress against her body as she looked at her reflection. The swing, maxi dress was embroidered on the bodice, as well as the cuffs of the loose sleeves and the hem, with cream silk. *She wanted it.*

'A little Biba influence there. A good style will always stand the test of time, you know.' Mrs Winter sighed. 'It takes me back, that was a wonderful shop, so glamourous, I'm sure you remember us going there as young girls, Dolly – searching for something wonderful to wear to some club or other in Soho. I remember walking through the door in Kensington and thinking, one day I'll have my own fashion shop. I was just a young girl then, of course, and now here I am. It goes to show that dreams can come true...' With an effort, she pulled herself back to the present. 'You'll want a nice pair of boots to go with that.'

'I've got the perfect pair in my flat in London. But I'll take the dress and the cardigan, thank you.'

'Perhaps your young man...' Mrs Pringle murmured, with a gentle lift of her eyebrows, her eyes darting to the photo in the pendant hanging from the thong around Sasha's neck.

'My? Oh, you mean Eric. Yes, well, I'm not sure whether I want him to come and visit me now, that's the trouble.' Gasping, Sasha suddenly realised the time. 'I have to go, I'm so sorry, this has been amazing, thank you, both of you.' On an impulse, she leaned in and kissed each of the women on the cheek.

She paid for her new outfit and left the two women, both of whom had bright red spots of delight on their cheeks, to rush to Meadowvale, pondering, as she drove, the vagaries of life. She should learn to never be surprised, both at what life threw at her and at what she learned of people's old lives. It was almost impossible to imagine Mrs Pringle and Mrs Winter as young, fashionable, girls, in a Soho nightclub.

Which made her wonder, she continued her train of thought as she entered Meadowvale, just what the residents of Meadowvale's past lives may have consisted of, and whether any of them had something in their past that they wanted to remain hidden. If so, and Dorothy had found out about it, then her death had ensured that someone's old life remained buried in the past.

The jarring sounds of clashing cymbals and the rattling of maracas reached her ears, and she walked along the corridor, stepping inside the lounge just as the soft clonk of a hammer being dragged across the bars of a glockenspiel joined the discordant mix. Amused, but acknowledging that Willow certainly did fill the residents' time with varied activities, Sasha moved to the library and laid out her files and notepad in readiness for her first interview.

A movement caught her eye and she moved to the library door, looking out in time to see a swathe of boldly-patterned fabric disappear into one of the rooms. The musical mayhem must be over then, time to swoop before coffee, and no doubt some newly-baked biscuits or cakes became the next distraction.

'Has anyone seen Mary? Oh, hi, Sasha.' Tanya's expression was a little frazzled. 'I'm about to bring through coffee so feel free to help yourself, and there'll be some cheese straws coming through.' She looked up. 'Oh, Mary, there you are.'

'Sorry, I'll go and plate up those cheese straws.' Adjusting her tunic as she headed to the kitchen, her ample rear wobbled slightly as she moved, causing her brightly-patterned skirt to flap around her calves.

Chatter ensued as the residents ambled in and out of the lounge in preparation for their morning coffee. The Lovewell sisters entered the lounge and Sasha was struck again by the disparity in their appearances, the one so thin and the other so well-padded. And their style of dress... she gazed at Agatha's kaftan, decorated as it was with swirls of lime green, acid pink, and bright yellow – so different to her sister's restrained choice of blouse and skirt – the only similarity between the two women being their hair, styled as it was in a short, grey, bob.

'Here they are, the terrible twins.' Howard began playing to the room, encouraged by Davinia's and Agatha's giggling. 'Two's trouble and three's a crowd, but I hope you lovely ladies will join me for coffee?' He swooped his arm out, bowing, as the two women clucked and murmured, seating themselves either side of him.

Sasha headed towards them, smiling. 'Who wants to join me in the library for a chat?'

'Do I need a lawyer?' Howard winked, his eyes twinkling good-naturedly. 'I'll be happy to join you, Sasha, if you promise to go easy on me.' He pushed himself up from his chair, wincing slightly.

'D'you need a hand?' Not sure what to do, Sasha looked around as Tanya materialised with a walking stick.

'Here, Howie, unless you want the walker?'

'The stick will be fine, thank you, dearie, the old hip's just playing up a bit today, that's all.'

'No worries.' Tanya smiled at him and Sasha as she poured coffees.

By the time Howard was seated in the library, Tanya had taken his coffee through, together with a small plate of cheese straws.

Sasha placed her own coffee on the table, determined to resist the temptation of the freshly-baked pastries. This place would ruin what was left of her waistline if she wasn't careful.

'Thanks for coming to chat to me, Howard, are you sure you're alright?' The elderly man's face was strained, but he smiled brightly.

'Just the aches and pains of getting old, but you know old Howie, got to keep one's pecker up and all that. Right, shoot.' He held his hands up in front of his face, laughing, as he pretended to duck.

Sasha smiled indulgently. 'Now, if you can cast your mind back to the day of Dorothy's death, perhaps you can tell me what you remember. Start from first thing in the morning and just take me through it, even the smallest thing might help.' Sipping her coffee, Sasha picked up her pen.

Howard nodded. 'We were all up and about for breakfast, as I recall, and it must have been a bit on the chilly side because porridge had been laid on – they always bring out the porridge on the cold mornings. Agatha indulged, the girl's got a good appetite on her, might be why she wears those flowing dress things. For myself, I had toast and coffee.

'Total opposites those two, what with Davinia being on the thin side. She looked jolly cheery though in her bright blouse, I must say – might have teased her about it matching her red cheeks. I don't think she was quite herself though…

'We took a spin in the garden but not for long, the old pins not being so good these days, more's the pity. Casey's court, it was, all and sundry bombing around, and the love birds, of course, if you'll excuse the pun.'

Sasha looked up, momentarily lost, as Howard elaborated.

'Albert and Elspeth, him having the name Bird, one of my little jokes. Thought I saw Davinia walking with Elizabeth's daughter, Judith, but I must have got that wrong.'

Again, Sasha looked up. 'Weren't you walking with Davinia?'

'What's that? Oh no, I took my walk with Agatha, and then Richard visited, my nephew – he's a good lad, married a decent woman – armed with a batch of shortbread which we all had with morning coffee.

'Poor old Monty seemed to spend most of the day dozing in the conservatory, although I'll tell you one thing, he made sure not to miss out on the shortbread. He's another one who likes his food, is Monty. And I'm sure I saw Dorothy off on one of her walks around the garden at some point, she liked to go toddling off, always kept herself busy. Now, she was in the lounge for coffee, I remember that clearly, talking and whispering away at nothing, writing in her little book – had her eye on Richard – I said to him, good job you're married, she's got her eye on you.' Howard paused to take a long drink of his coffee, picking up a cheese straw and biting into it appreciatively.

'Jolly good, these are, can I tempt you?'

'I'm trying to resist, got to watch my figure.' Sasha grinned ruefully.

'You girls and your figures, you worry too much. It takes more than that to capture a man's heart, let me tell you. It's like that young Willow, our activities girl, skin and bone she is, and she's got the looks, I'll grant you, but all that bouncing around all bright and breezy with a pretty smile isn't much good when there's nothing going on between the ears.'

She was beginning to like Howard more and more.

'Agatha said she saw Richard in the garden in the afternoon but I said you've got that wrong, girl, he was here this morning, sure you're not losing your marbles?' Howard let out a cackle of laughter. 'She knows I'm only teasing of course, the two of them enjoy a bit of ribbing, keeps them young. Nice women, the pair of them, decent, respectable...' Howard nodded his approval of Agatha and Davinia Lovewell. 'Women were brought up properly in our day, and it shows, no scandalous behaviour, they've both lived their lives with decorum, yes, they're good, virtuous women, as my mother would have said.' He winked at Sasha. 'She'd have probably tried to marry me off to one or the other of them in our younger days.

'Now, let me see about the staff – Tanya and Greg were busy cleaning up on and off, although if you ask me, Greg did most of the work – the woman was off chit chatting with this one and that one, trying to set Elizabeth straight about something at one point, good luck with that, I thought to myself, and then in a huddle with Albert and Davinia, although what those two could ever have in common beats me, more like adversaries, well, these days anyway, and of course, he's courting Elspeth, sweet woman although somewhat fluffy, if you're with me.' Howard took a long drink of his coffee before continuing.

'And then we had the beading in the afternoon with Willow. Agatha roped me in so I couldn't say no, lucky old Albert ducked out of it completely, and Monty pretended to be asleep, but it wasn't all bad, I had the girls in stitches, they do like a giggle, and Agatha and I were the last two at the table in the end, oh, and poor Lillian. Maybe Agatha thought if she stayed there long enough, she'd be able to move straight onto dinner, I'm only teasing of course. Kirsty had informed us at lunchtime that it was chicken pie for dinner, she's a good cook, does us proud, and she'd been busy that day, she'd made us cake to have with our tea, as well.' Howard paused again to finish his coffee.

'Greg went prancing off into the garden and came back inside, red-faced, a bit later – wonder what he'd been up to? Nothing that I'd approve of, I'm sure, I've got no truck with his type, you wouldn't find me within a million miles of someone like that, ordinarily, no thank you, but he does his job well and with good humour, I can't take that away from him. I'm sure I saw Moira, that's my nephew's wife, collar Tanya out in the garden, I remember glancing out of the windows when I'd finished my poor excuse for a bracelet, although Agatha said she loved it – I gave it to her, it made the old girl happy, although I wouldn't have liked to see Davinia's face when she found out. Between you and me I sometimes wonder if there's trouble in paradise with those two, Moira's got her insecurities if you ask me, especially in the looks department, not really a pretty girl if you know what I mean – don't know why she doesn't grow her hair and wear a little make-up, too manly looking, especially in those trousers, and the poor girl looked quite white-faced. She was probably asking Tanya if she'd seen Richard, but the boy had been here in the morning so they'd got their wires crossed.

'But I'm getting the order all wrong, aren't I? Poor Lillian struggled to do the beading, which was just before tea.' He frowned. 'Elizabeth could have helped her, but, oh no, she's always in a rush to be off and she wasn't hanging around that day, not even for my jokes. Got a mean streak, that one. You should have heard her last night, Norwich and eating porridge, little digs about being bald – that'll be poor old Monty – she got them all going with her mimicking of Dorothy. The lot of them were coming out with all sorts of Dorothy's mumbo jumbo – Mum's the word, keys in the pot what have we got, something about a thief – Monty took off, all upset, poor chap – and lots of talk about dickie birds and eagles and magpies, oh, that was Albert who reminded us about that, something about them liking shiny things. She was three sheets to the wind by then, of course, likes her booze, does Elizabeth, harks back to her wild days in Africa, I reckon, which she never lets us forget, always on about when we this and when we that.' Howard's face had become quite red with indignation, and he sat back.

'You've been very helpful, Howard, lots of detail, thank you. So, one last thing, can you remember when you first noticed Dorothy missing? You mentioned that you saw her going off for a walk in the garden?'

Howard shook his head. 'I'm sure I saw her in the morning, yes, it was before coffee that she took her walk, of course it was, because after that Richard visited and we all had the shortbread with our coffee. I'm afraid I can't remember seeing her after that, but it's easy to confuse the days here, she must have been with us for lunch...' his voice trailed off and Sasha intervened.

'No problem, you've given me plenty of information, thank you.' It was clear that Howard couldn't recall anything else.

Sitting alone in the library, Sasha considered what Howard had told her. His references to the comments made by Dorothy were interesting, although could she really trust any of the phrases to be true to Dorothy's original words? She knew from experience how Dorothy had enjoyed her cryptic comments, when piecing together her poisonous missives for various residents of Parva Crossing the year before. But even if the phrases had been misquoted over time, surely the gist of them would remain the same?

It would be easy enough to check with each of the residents and find out their recollections of what was said, she'd do that as the opportunity arose. Standing up to stretch her back, she decided to go for a wander, and walked off along the passage, wondering which room had been Dorothy's. Presumably it was now unoccupied as it didn't appear that Meadowvale had taken in any new residents since her death. Deciding to go in search of Mrs Goodwin to find out, she turned round and found herself staring into the lens of a camera.

'Charles! What are you doing creeping up on me?' Feeling slightly unsettled, she studied his expression as it changed from intense to amused in an instant.

'Sorry, didn't meant to startle you.' He dropped his camera to his side. 'Willow called to say that I was welcome to come through and meet the manageress about taking photos of the residents. So here I am.'

'Yes, but I'm not a resident, Charles. No offence, but I'd honestly prefer not to have my picture taken unawares. Aren't the residents all in the lounge? I don't see any around here.'

'You're right, of course, I was just finding my feet, adjusting the camera and so on, and suddenly there you were deep in thought and I couldn't resist. But I'll leave you to it.' He turned and walked off in the direction of the lounge as Sasha watched him thoughtfully.

There was something off about his behaviour. He always seemed to be turning up unexpectedly. And she wasn't sure if she bought it about adjusting his camera. One thing she knew, he shouldn't be wandering around the corridors of Meadowvale unaccompanied. He was a stranger and no one really knew anything about him apart from his own proffered account of himself. She'd talk to Mrs Goodwin about it and make some enquiries of her own.

Tapping on the door of the office, she pushed the door open but found it empty.

'Looking for Mrs Goodwin?' Tanya stopped as she passed by. 'She's gone walkabout for a while, you'll have to try her after lunch, I'm afraid.'

'Thanks, Tanya, I'll do that.' Checking her watch, Sasha realised that she'd not be able to interview any other residents right now and, at a bit of a loss, wondered what to do with herself. Lunch. She could go and find somewhere for a bite to eat, there were plenty of little eateries in the village, she recalled from her previous visit.

~

Chantelle and her new friend, Lucy, walked nonchalantly across the school playing field, glancing back occasionally to make sure that no teachers were around. Lifting the broken section of mesh fencing, they squeezed through and wandered along the lane that ran parallel to the field, until they were out of sight.

'I haven't got much, Spencer said he was getting some more last night.' Lucy pulled out a small packet from her bag as Chantelle produced a cigarette, and the two girls pushed through the hedges, dropping their bags and sitting cross-legged on the grass. Opening a textbook, Lucy took the cigarette from Chantelle, expertly rolling it back and forth between her fingers so that the tobacco fell into the centre of the book. Shaking the last of her marijuana into the tobacco, she mixed the dried flakes before gently pushing the mixture into the cigarette. 'Got a light?' Lying on their backs, they passed the cigarette between them until it was finished, before picking up their bags and walking off in the direction of the high street.

~

Sasha stood at the counter of the Village Deli, perusing the goods temptingly displayed.

'What can I get you, love?' The woman behind the counter smiled encouragingly. 'Sausage roll? Quiche? We've got lasagnes and cottage pies as well, or I can make you a sandwich? Tuna, egg mayo, roast chicken? Or a wrap? Salad perhaps?'

Feeling positively saintly, Sasha settled for a chicken salad wrap and a bottle of water, taking a seat at a small table beside the window. The high street was busy and she contented herself with people watching while she ate her lunch, smiling at the sight of the two giggling schoolgirls on the other side of the road. Sitting up straighter, she looked again, sure that one of them was her niece, Chantelle. The jet-black hair of the girl accompanying her rang a bell, and as she turned to laugh at something her companion had said, Sasha noticed her heavily kohled eyes and dark lipstick. Surely that was Elspeth Parkhurst's grand-daughter? A white car tooted and pulled up alongside the girls and, after grinning delightedly, they clambered into the car before it drove off.

~

All was quiet when Sasha walked through the front entrance to Meadowvale, and she stepped quietly into the lounge, wondering if perhaps everyone was asleep after their lunch. The room was deserted apart from Lillian, her pen and book on the floor where they must have fallen when she nodded off. Sasha picked them up, placing them on the table beside the softly snoring woman, as a hum of voices reached her ears from the passage and she went to investigate.

Mrs Goodwin was coming out of one of the doors along the passage, a grim expression on her face. 'I'll look into it, Howard, of course I will, but I've told you before, you shouldn't leave cash lying around for all to see.' Looking up she spied Sasha and walked towards her, raising her eyebrows. 'Hard to tell when one of them's got themselves in a muddle and when it's the real deal. Still, we've had a few worrying incidents lately and I'm none the wiser as to who's behind it or if they're even connected.'

Falling into step beside Mrs Goodwin, Sasha asked, 'How much money has gone missing from Howard's room?'

'Two hundred pounds, if you please, said he was planning on giving it to Richard, his nephew, when he came to visit today. Howard's a kind man, adores his nephew – he's his only relative you know. He never married but he did alright for himself, I suppose it'll all go to Richard eventually – between you and me I think Richard's business is struggling and I think Howard knows, but he'd never embarrass him, just pops a folded bank note or two into his jacket pocket each time he visits. I expect he's done it ever since Richard was a young boy.'

'And has money ever gone missing before?' There was something in the back of her mind, a vague memory of something to do with money at Meadowvale, but it eluded her.

'Unfortunately, yes, we've had the odd instance. I had cash taken from the petty cash box in the office quite some time ago, and the following day Albert insisted that someone had stolen a hundred pounds from his room.' She turned to Sasha. 'But I've never known Albert to have cash lying around, maybe a few coins but never large sums, so that just muddies the water even further, and like I said, it's difficult with the elderly, they are inclined to forgetfulness and perhaps confusion so one can never be sure. And then we've had the other thefts, of course.' Mrs Goodwin sighed as they reached her office. 'Come in for a minute and take a seat while I tell you about them.'

Meadowvale was beginning to sound like a hotbed of criminal activity, Sasha decided, as Mrs Goodwin listed off the allegedly stolen items of jewellery belonging to Elspeth, together with a pen of Lillian's, a dress belonging to Agatha, a photograph of Davinia's, some kind of trinket belonging to Elizabeth, and Monty's cigarette lighter. In fact, it seemed that every resident had fallen prey to theft in some manner. The staff, however, had escaped unscathed.

'Mrs Goodwin, how much do you know about your staff's backgrounds? How long have they all worked here?'

'Well, there's often a connection somehow, and of course we do checks if necessary, that sort of thing, but Greg used to work in another care home that was managed by an old friend of mine, so of course he came highly recommended. Kirsty's been with us for years, she's from around here and an absolute star, never complains, runs her kitchen like clockwork and serves up top notch meals for the residents. She's helped by Mary, of course, who's also been here for quite some time, a year or two – her parents used to have the dairy farm – but Mary also works as a carer part of the time – mind you, Mary can cook very well too, and her cakes are popular, that's why we started doing the

Monday cake with afternoon tea – it's a nice event to start off the week on a bright note. We did one have one issue with Mary, about a year ago, the only blot on her record, when she helped herself to the contents of the petty cash box. She'd got herself into difficulty but was replacing the money when I caught her. We sorted it out, it'll never happen again.'

Mrs Goodwin's brow furrowed slightly. 'Then there's Spencer, young local lad, but I've got no complaints with him, he does what he's told, he's been with us about six months. The lad's dyslexic but it doesn't affect his work at all. Tanya's part-time, like Spencer, and she's a good woman if I ever I saw one, our oldest employee but keen to work and very sweet with the residents, helpful, nothing's ever too much trouble, she's especially patient with dear Lillian – she must have been with us for about five or six months, recommended by one of the relatives, if I recall correctly.'

Mrs Goodwin paused, drumming her fingers on the desk. 'Oh, and we have Willow now, such a lovely girl, so bright and bubbly. She's a breath of fresh air and really keeps the residents busy with all her ideas. I was a little sceptical when she first contacted me with the idea, I must admit, but it's going so well that I'm hoping to be able to make her position permanent.'

Such a lovely girl. A breath of fresh air. 'Wait a minute, Mrs Goodwin, you say that Willow contacted you? Didn't you advertise the position?'

'Yes, that's right, she e-mailed me suggesting the whole activities therapist idea and, between you and me, she offered her services for such a reasonable rate, I would have been foolish not to take her up on it.'

'Well, thanks for the information, Mrs Goodwin, and I just wanted to mention one concern to you, it's about the photographer, Charles. He was wandering along the corridor which runs past the library to the residents' rooms, when everyone was in the lounge, it must have been just about on lunch time. I wondered what arrangement you had with him?'

Pursing her lips, Mrs Goodwin shook her head. 'Well, I certainly didn't say he could walk around wherever he pleases – that's totally unacceptable. We don't know anything about him, it was Willow who vouched for him and what with all her bright ideas it seemed like a nice bit of fun for everyone. He offered a complimentary framed print for each resident, once he'd finished, which I thought was very kind. Now, I must find Davinia, I've got her replacement walking stick ferrule at last, had a bit of trouble finding one with the pimples for extra grip. And thanks for coming to me about the photographer, I'll have a word with him and make sure he sticks to the lounge and gardens.'

Sasha left the office deep in thought. Willow had told a little white lie about her appointment at Meadowvale, she was sure of it. Hadn't she said that she saw the position advertised? Maybe she was just embarrassed and didn't want to admit that she'd suggested the whole thing herself? And then there was Charles, aided by Willow in his insinuation into Meadowvale. Did one, or both, of them have an agenda at the home?

Walking back through the lounge, she headed through the conservatory and into the garden, where she could see heads bobbing above the shrubbery. Narrowly avoiding tripping over a gardening hoe, she smiled as the gardener appeared, muttering an apology as he picked it up. Talk of the devil. Willow's laugh rang out as Sasha rounded the, as yet, flowerless hydrangea bushes, and she stopped to observe the scene in front of her.

Elspeth and Albert stood together in front of a flowering cotoneaster shrub, smiling at Charles as he knelt down with his camera. A younger man, with similar facial characteristics to Albert, stood to the side, looking bored, as Elizabeth prodded at what looked like a large spiky-leaved weed, with her stick, where it grew profusely beneath the bird table.

'Ah, the Moonflower Vine, if I'm not mistaken. Such a beautiful night perfume when the flowers open. We used to have this in our garden when we lived in Rhodesia.' Elizabeth reached down to pick one of the leaves as the gardener suddenly appeared, putting out his hand and speaking to her urgently. Sasha's attention was distracted by Willow calling out instructions.

'Come and stand in front of these pretty foxgloves, it'll make a gorgeous photo, Elspeth. And how about the two of you, Davinia and Agatha? A nice photo of you both together, to send to a relative perhaps?'

'Howie and Richard, come and join us for a photo, we're all on our lonesome, we don't have anyone to send a photo to, do we, Davinia?'

'You don't want to be touching that, Mrs P, devil's weed is what that is, nasty bit of work, deadly it is, must have come from the birdseed. It'll have to come out.' The gardener began to attack the plant with his hoe as Elizabeth looked mutinously on.

'I think I know a moonflower when I see one.' She headed off along the garden path, muttering to herself.

'No, it's just the two us, Agatha, you know that, I don't know where you get your ridiculous fancies from, but perhaps a photo would be nice...' Davinia smiled vaguely as she reproached her sister, her mind seemingly elsewhere, before she looked around, enquiringly. 'Where is Richard, Howie? I thought he was right here.'

Monty turned away and raised his eyebrows at Sasha. 'Willow can't tell her foxgloves from her lupins, waste of time. Call this a garden walk?'

Richard and Greg appeared, deep in conversation, and Monty looked at Greg in surprise. 'I thought you were off today, young Gregory?'

'I'm on tonight, thought I'd come in early and see if I was missing out on any fun.' Greg minced off, blowing kisses at no one in particular, as Howard rolled his eyes. A rustle in the bushes further distracted Sasha, as she observed the man she'd seen the day before, hovering with his walking stick.

'Here to see your mother, Mervyn? I expect she's still napping in the lounge,' said Monty.

'You obviously know your flowers, Monty.' Sasha fell into step beside him, slowing her pace to match the elderly man's.

'I used to have a little florist shop in London, in my younger day.' Monty sighed. 'I can still smell it if I close my eyes, the sweet scent of the flowers, the buckets of freshly sprayed foliage, even the brown paper we wrapped the bouquets in. Ah, here's my bench, I think I'll have a little smoke break, care to join me?'

'Sure.' Sasha smiled. She liked Monty, he had a kindness about him. She sat down beside him and offered him one of her cigarettes. 'So, tell me more about your flower shop.'

'It was in Little Portland Street, a small street running between Regent Street and Great Portland Street, and our window display was a sight to behold. I ran it with my, well, my partner, Geoffrey.' He glanced at Sasha. 'Society was a little more permissive by then but we were still discreet, it was the way things were done. The girls from the little workshop above us used to sketch the flowers in the window – we prided ourselves on having the most exotic blooms and flamboyantly coloured flowers. They used the sketches to make artificial flowers, not the rubbish you see these days, I'm talking about a real skill, quite beautiful they were, they'd end up on hats in the milliners' and I'd say to Geoffrey, that's one of ours, made me quite proud.'

Old lives again. It was fascinating and illuminating, Sasha thought. 'It sounds wonderful, Monty, I expect you miss it?'

Monty sighed wistfully. 'Lots of memories, happy ones, but all good things must come to an end my dear. Geoffrey and I enjoyed many years together, but when he became ill and had to stop working it was never quite the same. And then he passed away...'

Sasha reached out and touched Monty's arm, her mind filled with images of him in his flower shop. 'I'm so sorry, Monty.'

He reached into his jacket pocket and pulled out his wallet, before gently removing a small photograph and holding it out to Sasha. The faded, colour photo, with its background of a florist's window filled with blooms, featured two, apron-clad, smiling men, in the foreground, their arms slung casually around each other's shoulders.

Sasha smiled as she handed the photo back to Monty. 'You look so happy together.'

Monty nodded. 'We were. We cared very much for each other.' He stared off into the past for a moment, before mentally shaking away the old memories. 'I expect you'd like to ask me about the day Dorothy died?'

The trundling of the wheelbarrow, loaded with the large weed which the gardener had just dug out, brought Sasha back to the present with a start. 'I would, Monty. How about we go to the library and you tell me everything that you can remember?'

SASHA INTERVIEWS MONTY MALLOWAN

Miles thanked the prison officer for his mail, knowing there was only one person it could be from. He wasn't feeling too happy with Charles, it had been a few days since his visit and he'd heard nothing up until now. Returning to his cell, he opened the envelope, resisting the urge to study the photo first, and read the short, printed e-mail.

Having a wonderful trip with my girl, it's brought us closer together. We're just having fun for now, but I feel the urge to take things to the next level. You know I'm ready, I proved it with Sally B, she was all my own work. Happy times. Hope you like the photo. Charles.

His hands shook with frustration as he turned his attention to the printed photo of Sasha. She was seated outdoors, possibly at a pub table, and gazing off towards a river, unaware of the photographer.

He was losing control of Charles. Impotence coursed through his body as he considered his situation. It would be years before he got out, if ever, and his protégé was taunting him. He forced himself to remain calm.

~

Monty rested his hands on his substantial stomach as he leaned back in his chair and began to speak.

'It was a rum start to the week, Mary was off sick – she usually makes a nice sponge cake for our afternoon tea on Mondays – so Mrs Goodwin sent Tanya out to buy cakes instead – they look after us here, can't complain. But it was Tuesday, wasn't it, when poor Dorothy was killed?

'Kirsty was on kitchen duty and we had porridge, the works, for breakfast, and at some point during the morning, Dorothy joined me in the conservatory for a while. Like the cat that got the cream, she was, but that's Dorothy, always with her little secrets – this time it was a secret assignation with her new friend in her favourite place – poor dear and all her imaginary friends. But I digress, there's no morning activity on Tuesdays so we're left to our own devices. Madam, of course, was full of her own self-importance as usual – you'd think it was the wedding of the year the way she goes on – she and her daughter were on about it and went off walking round the garden.

'Dorothy asked her something about her keys again, maybe she'd lost some? Although what she needs keys for, I don't know. Elizabeth just glared at her. There's been a lot of stuff going missing, of course, including my old lighter, reckon we've got someone helping themselves to things. I bought another one just like it, not gold, of course, it just looks like it. There's a name for it, klepto- something, they can't help themselves, of course, and I've got a soft spot for– well, let's just say I didn't feel the need to make a fuss. Wish I'd never mentioned it being missing, to tell you the truth, oh well, never mind.

'Then there was a fuss about a missing dress, I doubt that was pinched, wouldn't fit anyone else, well, apart from me, of course.' Monty grinned as he shuddered dramatically. 'And I can assure you that if I were to dress up in women's clothing it certainly wouldn't be one of Agatha's outlandish garments. Oh, that's who I meant, sorry, I do tend to ramble on,' Monty clarified, noticing Sasha's quizzical expression, smiling fondly. 'But come to think of it, that was the day after Dorothy's death, we were all still reeling from it, and no-one was too interested in Agatha's fuss.

'I think I saw Elspeth and her fiancé, as she loves to refer to him, taking a walk. His son Raymond was due to visit, but we had coffee before that, that's when Howard's nephew brought the shortbread. I think his wife made it, not sure if she came with him, saw her around the place once or twice, if I'm not mistaken – she seems to be quite friendly with some of the residents, takes time for a little chat with some of them – Davinia I can understand, but Albert? And Elizabeth? Steer well clear is my advice. Not that she was chatting the last time I saw her that day, marched right off round the side of the building, didn't even say goodbye to Howard. She was wearing trousers and I remember thinking how manly she was, how easy it would be to mistake her for Richard.

'Anyway, I was feeling very sleepy that day and kept skulking off to the conservatory for a nap to get away from all the hullabaloo. Elspeth was making a scene about a bracelet going missing and Albert spent hours searching for it. The woman should be more careful, telling all and sundry how valuable her jewellery is, then leaving it lying around for anyone to help themselves. Not quite sure how she came to have all the stuff in the first place, she doesn't strike me as the type, if I'm honest with you. Anyway, after lunch I took another nap, I didn't want to do the activity. Willow had everyone threading beads, I believe, some kind of crafting activity.

'I woke up and went to the bathroom, snuck off back into the conservatory, and that's when I nearly took a tumble over her wretched stick, sticks more like it, so many bits getting under your feet, when she came in from the garden, just as I turned to plump the cushion. Not even an apology, either, just disappeared off into the lounge. Red for danger, that makes sense. But we'd had tea and cake by then, I remember now, Kirsty surprised us with lemon cake. Gone in a flash, it was, not a crumb left, and plates cleared away before I even got back from the bathroom. That might have been Tanya, like a cat on hot bricks she was, in and out, face like thunder – might have been outside looking for Elspeth's bracelet, she certainly had grubby hands, something I just can't abide. Not sure if Agatha missed out on the cake, sure I saw her heading off somewhere in the garden when some of them were still busy with their beading.' Monty frowned. 'Not like her to miss out on cake, though, no, I must have got that wrong – although she's hard to miss, of course. Anyway, Gregory kindly fetched me another cup of tea and it was round about then that I wondered about Dorothy, couldn't remember when I'd last seen her.'

There were so many similarities between the accounts given by the residents, so far, thought Sasha, but small details were inconsistent, and hopefully therein would lie the key to what happened. She smiled at Monty. 'You've been marvellous, Monty, extremely helpful. What about lunch that day, do you recall what you had?'

Snapping his fingers, Monty exclaimed. 'Quiche and salad, that's what it was, and Dorothy was there, I remember now, because she was picking out the mushrooms, complaining about not liking them. So it must have been some time after that, that she...' his voice trailed off sadly before he looked across at Sasha. 'It's too sad, her last meal and she didn't even enjoy it. And she didn't get to have the lemon cake for tea. She'd have enjoyed that...'

Sasha reached across and placed her hand over Monty's. 'I can see that you cared about her, Monty. I'll do everything that I can to find out who took her life, but first I have to work out the why, then I can figure out the who.'

A message on her phone, suggesting that she drop in at the police station for an update, made Sasha's mind up, and she packed up her files before popping her head into the lounge to say goodbye. She had to admit it, she was becoming quite fond of the characters at Meadowvale.

A voice called her name and she looked round to find Charles hurrying out of the entrance.

'Finished for the day, Sasha? Where are you off to now, anywhere interesting?'

He was still holding his camera in one hand, his bag and camera case in the other. He was altogether too friendly, too charming, and too nosy, she decided.

'You look like you're in a rush, Charles, some kind of emergency?' She looked pointedly at his camera as he removed the lens and placed his camera in its case, still walking towards her.

'What? Charles slung the case over his shoulder. 'Oh, I couldn't find my phone, must have left it in the car.' He smiled at Sasha as the faint sound of a ringing phone reached their ears. Shrugging awkwardly, he reached into his bag. 'Looks like it was here all the time.'

'I'll leave you to it.' Sasha walked slowly to her car, one ear on Charles's side of the conversation.

'I told you, Megan, it's better that I call you, I can't have you disturbing everyone. Yes, it's going fine, you know what these conferences are like. How are the kids?'

Unable to hear him anymore, Sasha unlocked her car, threw her bags in, and settled herself in the driver's seat, taking out her phone and pretending to study it. She watched him surreptitiously as he got into his car, waiting for him to drive off, but he lingered, glancing in her direction before quickly turning away. Finally, when he saw that Sasha wasn't moving, he started his engine and pulled out of the parking area.

It must have been his wife calling, but why was he talking about a conference when he was taking a few days' holiday to indulge in a photography hobby?

Driving slowly into the village, Sasha wondered again about Howard's missing money. Charles had been sniffing around on his own in the corridor, hadn't he? But Mrs Goodwin had told her that money had gone missing before so it was more likely to be someone who was already at the home in some capacity. She tried to recall the patterned clothing that she'd glimpsed going into one of the rooms that morning, but all she could picture was a garish clash of colours. An image of Agatha Lovewell in her flamboyant kaftans came into her mind, as too, did Mary's ample behind, swathed in a patterned skirt, as she'd headed to the kitchen that morning.

Glancing in her rearview mirror she was annoyed to see a white car behind her. How could Charles be behind her when she'd left after him? But as the car drew closer, Sasha realised it wasn't him, but a man wearing a baseball cap. The car remained uncomfortably close behind her all the way until she pulled into a parking space outside the police station, when it continued on, the driver turning his head to grin at her, his eyes obscured by sunglasses.

Was she just letting herself get weirded out by everything, or were complete strangers following her around? And all of them in white cars, for crying out loud. Locking her car, she walked into the police station to be greeted by Pavani Datta.

'Afternoon, Sasha, Sergeant Weaver told me you'd be calling in, come through. Can I get you a cuppa?'

'Hi, Pav, actually a cuppa would be great, thanks.' Sasha smiled at the younger woman as she walked with her to Jane Weaver's office.

Sergeant Weaver looked up and smiled. 'Sasha, good to see you, how's it going so far?'

After a few minutes, Sasha had caught Jane up with the progress of her interviews. 'It's slow going, I'm afraid, there always seems to be something going on at Meadowvale, if it's not an activity it's morning coffee, afternoon tea, or lunch. Once I manage to interview the last four residents, I'll move onto the staff. I can't help but feel, though, that there's something more going on at Meadowvale besides Dorothy's death, I mean, obviously things have gone missing, or been stolen, but I'm not sure whether it's related to her murder...' Sasha shook her head. 'I doubt it, but it's interesting, all the same.'

Jane nodded. 'You never know what you might find out – it certainly didn't serve you too badly last time when you found us Dorothy's stash of poison pen letters in the old post box. Oh, that reminds me, Pav, where did you put the Burton box?'

'It's in the back office, shall I bring it through?' Pav jumped up but was stopped by Jane.

'No, I have to go, but if you've got a few minutes, Sasha, Pav will show you those clippings about the weed house that I was telling you about?'

Sasha picked up the clippings and scanned them, noticing the mentions of her name in relation to the discovery of information leading to the arrest of the people running the weed house: Jimmy Burton, his wife Nicola Burton, and their son Drew Burton. References were made to Sasha's involvement in the search for her niece, Chantelle; the deaths in the village; Dorothy Newton's letter stash of villagers' secrets; the cash heist leading to the arrest of the Spindleburys; and George Newton's victims in his killing spree spanning the decades, as well as his subsequent arrest.

She looked at the photo of her and Cal at the inquest into Barbara Fenton's death, as well as the one of her with her sister, smiling happily, together with Chantelle, after her release from hospital. She hadn't even known that these pictures had been taken, and felt vaguely uncomfortable about them. This, in turn, reminded her of Charles, and she turned to Pav.

'Pav, could I ask you to do something for me?' At the woman's nod, she continued, 'I don't have any solid reason for asking this, but there's just something about him that feels wrong, call it one of my paranoid crazy hunches. He's staying at The Spotted Dog, to all intents and purposes a tourist visiting the area to take photos, but now he's got himself inveigled into Meadowvale and it doesn't add up, at least not in my head. I mean, a bloke takes off for a few days while his wife and kids are supposedly with her sister, or something, and the next thing he's spending his time at an elderly care home, taking photos of the residents. Plus, he's a little too friendly, insinuating himself into everything, and always with his damn camera, which he seems to think he has the right to use to take my picture when I'm not looking, and that really creeps me out. Here's his car registration number.'

Sasha looked at Pav, ruefully. 'And now you're going to tell me that none of that is grounds to look into someone, aren't you?'

'Well...' Pav cocked her head to one side, considering. 'If he hasn't actually committed a crime...' She shook her head. 'I'm sorry, Sasha, we don't have grounds to investigate him.'

They were interrupted by the arrival of P.C. Canfield, his jovial face grinning as he saw the case name on the box. 'Ah, the famous weed house bust, wish I'd been here for that, bit of excitement in our quiet little village. And you can bet your life it's not over, someone's taken over the reins, set up somewhere else. It was never just the three of them, there must have been others involved, with distribution at least, and where are they now, that's what I'd like to know?'

Pav grinned. 'Our wannabe detective in the making. Ross, you're supposed to be dealing with new crimes, not harping on about old cases that were before our time.'

'Yeah, but there are drugs around, someone's dealing grass, we've had reports of schoolkids being seen smoking the stuff. It's coming from somewhere, that's all I'm saying.'

Sasha looked up sharply. 'Schoolkids? There's just the one secondary school isn't there?'

'Yep.' Ross nodded. 'The perfect supply of eager, young customers for a dealer, he or she just has to find their way in. I'm keeping my ear to the ground, but I can hardly spend all my time hanging around watching the school gates, and it could be being dealt somewhere else.' He shrugged. 'Gotta go.' Turning to hurry off at the sound of the ringing phone.

Sasha returned to the pub, her mind mulling over Ross's statement concerning drugs at the school, as she recalled Tessa's concern over Chantelle's new friends, her own observation of how tired Chantelle had looked, and the change she'd noticed in her, from friendly and open to slightly uncommunicative. But that was all just normal teenage stuff, wasn't it, behavioural changes? Especially so in Chantelle's case, she had a lot to recover from, all while growing up and making new friends.

Something hovered in the back of her mind, as she parked her car, noticing the white car, probably Willow's, at the end of the parking area. It was one of the names she'd read in the newspaper clippings, it had rung a bell, hadn't it? She was sure she'd recognised the name on some subliminal level. It was the son, Drew, that was it. But why had it come into her head now? Something had jogged her memory but she wasn't sure what. Feeling grimy from her day, she decided to take a shower and change into fresh clothes, and headed up to her room, taking her bag of files as well as her bag containing her new clothes with her.

Feeling refreshed from her shower, Sasha tried on her purchases and appraised her reflection, twirling this way and that, and wishing she'd brought her boots with her, they'd look so perfect with the dress. On an impulse, she took a selfie on her phone and posted it to her Graffic account. *Check out my gorgeous new outfit, from the local village boutique, Madam Couture, no less. Wish I had my fave boots here, they'd go perfectly with it!*

Changing out of her dress, she pulled on jeans and a tee shirt and reached for her bottle of perfume from the dressing table. That was odd, she frowned, opening the drawers to check, but it wasn't there either. That wasn't all, everything was just slightly out of place, as if someone had gone through her stuff...

With a glass of wine, Sasha perched on the bar stool, waiting until no one else was around. 'Jules, awkward question, my perfume's gone missing from my room. I was just wondering if your cleaning lady left my room open for a few minutes or something? Perhaps someone snuck in there and pinched it? I don't know, I'm just a little nonplussed, it's weird, isn't it?'

Jules's face fell. 'It is, I'm so sorry, I feel awful. We've never had a problem before. I'll call Sara, see if she can shed any light on it.'

Sasha sipped her wine while she waited for Jules to return, feeling bad for worrying her, but it couldn't just disappear on its own. Someone had filched it, which meant that someone had been into her room who shouldn't. She looked up as Jules re-appeared.

'Sara feels really bad, she cleaned your room as soon as you left after breakfast, and replaced your towels, but she'd forgotten the hand towel. She left your door ajar and popped down to the laundry room at the back. While she was there, she decided to put a wash load on, so all in all she was probably gone for about five minutes or so. She's so apologetic, as am I, and neither of us can believe it, but it's possible that someone accessed your open room during those few minutes. Which means–'

'Which means,' continued Sasha, 'that there was someone here, possibly watching Sara's movements. But why go into my room and only pinch my perfume? And who was it? There's no one else staying here except Willow and Charles, is there, unless someone sneaked into the pub at the perfect moment – but it's a weird thing to steal. Listen, Sara mustn't worry, it's not the end of the world, I'm sure I'll get to the bottom of it. For now, I'll just have to go scent free, and I suppose I can pick up something at Pringles Chemist, am I right?'

Jules laughed along with Sasha, relieved that her friend and guest was being so decent about it. 'Yep, our one and only Mrs Pringle will no doubt be delighted to help you.' A worried look passed over her face. 'Sash, if you wouldn't mind, you know what Mrs Pringle's like...'

Nodding, Sasha quickly put Jules's mind at rest. 'Don't worry, I understand, the last thing you need is gossip doing the rounds about something missing from a guest's room. Now, how about you tell me what's on the menu for tonight? I missed out on the chicken and chips last night, it was my own fault, I guilt-tripped myself into having salad. I'm calling it the Willow effect.'

'Oh, that reminds me, are you eating here tomorrow night? I mean, no plans to go anywhere else?' Jules flushed as Sasha looked at her quizzically. 'It being Friday night, that's all, it might get busy so I want to make sure my guests are looked after.'

'Well, probably, although I haven't spoken to Tess, she might suggest that I go round there...'

'We'll be serving pizzas...' Jules encouraged. 'I know it's your favourite, and toppings of your choice, they're really good.'

Laughing, Sasha nodded. 'Go on then, you've twisted my arm, I'm a complete pushover where pizza's concerned, count me in.'

ALL QUIET ON THE HOME FRONT

Zoe checked her packed bag, making sure she hadn't forgotten anything, before pouring herself a glass of wine. Sitting at her kitchen counter, she scrolled through Graffic, pausing to smile at the photo of her friend in her new dress. The caption gave her an idea and, pleased with herself, she popped her meal into the microwave a few minutes later as she read Eric's reply. They'd stop at Sasha's flat before they left London so that Zoe could pick up her boots and surprise her with them, as well as themselves.

~

'Chantelle, where are you going? Dinner will be ready in about half an hour, and surely you've got homework?' Tessa hurried to the front door as she heard it open.

'I'll eat at Lucy's, her mum offered.' Chantelle stepped through the open door, not looking at Tessa.

'Hold on, look at me.' Tessa held her daughter's arm, forcing her to turn round. 'What's with all this dark make-up? Your eyes are as black as your clothes, what's going on, Chants? And who is this Lucy? When are you going to bring her round to meet us?'

Chantelle stood there stubbornly. 'You should be pleased that I've got a friend, my last one was murdered wasn't she? I'm not a kid, Mum, you can't keep fussing over me. And I've done my homework. I can't let Lucy's mum down *now*, she'll have made us dinner.'

'But what about me? I've made you dinner.' Tessa stood there, feeling a little lost. 'Well, alright, if her mum's expecting you, but let me know next time, okay? And don't be late back, Chants.' She had an idea. 'Where does Lucy live? I'll get Dad to come and get you a bit later.'

Chantelle huffed irritably. 'They'll drop me home later, I don't need Dad picking me up. Can I go now?'

'They? But who's they? D'you mean Lucy and her mum? Let Dad do it, save her mum turning out later.'

'No, Mum, not Lucy and her mum, I mean Lucy and her boyfriend, Spencer. Oh, there they are now, I've got to go.'

Reaching up to peck Tessa on the cheek, Chantelle rushed off, waving at the occupants of the red car that had pulled up.

Closing the door after they'd driven off, Tessa told herself not to worry for the umpteenth time.

~

Sharon Cutter dumped the bloody bag onto the kitchen table. 'Here you go, Glen, I can't believe I did this for you, it's disgusting. Luckily Mr Alison had to go out otherwise I'd have had some explaining to do. You gonna tell me what it's for?'

Glen Cutter grinned at his sister. 'I knew it'd come in useful one day, you working for the butcher. Good work, Shaz, I'm going to have some fun with this.'

'Well, whatever it is, make it fast, it stinks. Put it out the back, will you?' Sharon wrinkled her nose in disgust.

~

Chantelle checked her watch subtly, not wanting Lucy to see. She liked being out with her, she did, but sometimes she felt like a spare part when Spencer was with them, plus, if she was honest, it did get a bit boring just driving around with them and having to sit in the back of the car like a kid, and it would be getting dark soon. For a moment she thought longingly of her bedroom, of her mum and dad sitting in the lounge watching television after dinner. Her mum was probably putting the kettle on round about now, then she'd have been calling Chantelle to help her bring the tray through if she was there, and she'd wink, opening the cupboard to take out a bar of chocolate. 'What?' She started, as Lucy prodded her knee, laughing.

'Well, I know you're not stoned, we haven't smoked anything yet.' Lucy grinned. 'I said have you got the money? I told Spence we'd chip in ten pounds each, remember?'

'Sure.' Chantelle pulled the ten pound note from her back pocket and handed it over. 'Where are we going?'

'I left my stash at work, I've got a nice little hiding place where I keep it, won't take long, then we'll find somewhere to go and have a smoke.' Spencer turned the music up as he slipped his arm around Lucy's shoulders.

Chantelle leaned back, anxiety knotting her stomach, as the music pounded in her ears from the speakers. She couldn't say anything without coming across as a total bore, and Lucy could be pretty mean when she wanted to be, so instead she'd have to face her mum and dad's worried faces whenever she did get home, and then defend herself by making up stupid stories about where she'd been. It all felt a bit pointless, if she was honest, and she wondered why life had to be so complicated. Her phone vibrated in her pocket – it would be her mum, she knew it – and she wriggled on the seat, extricating her phone from her pocket to read the message.

~

'Quite a subdued bunch tonight,' Greg remarked, as he and Mary cleared the last bits from the dining table and took them through to the kitchen. 'You missed all the to do last night, our darling Elizabeth got them all riled up – had them all on the bottle, as well, things got quite out of hand.'

'So I heard.' Mary grinned. 'She can certainly put it away, and what with harping on about the good old days in Africa it's not hard to see why. Reckon she was a lot more fun back then, don't you?'

Greg giggled. 'Ooh, I can just picture her, slinging back her gin and tonic at some party or another, and drunkenly demanding another one. It reminds me of something Dorothy goaded her about one time, something about parties, you should have seen the look she gave her. She's such a frosty, uptight old thing, I bet she was different in her younger days, don't you, a bit of a wild one, even? Anyway, enough of the chit chat, I must go and see who's still up, see if I can encourage everyone to have an early night.'

Having bustled around in the lounge for a while, plumping cushions and helping Lillian off to bed, Greg glanced a little despairingly at the bottle of whisky on the table, beside the remaining few. It would have to be Elizabeth, he thought, surprised to see Davinia and Albert still up and deep in conversation with her. His shoulders sagged, with Elizabeth there the drinking could go on for a while. Inspiration struck. 'Anyone for hot milk? I'll even offer room service tonight, how's that?'

'That sounds good, Greg.' Albert yawned. 'Yes, I'll take you up on your offer, might even get Elizabeth to slip me in a shot of whisky.'

'Waste of a good whisky, doing that, if you ask me,' Elizabeth scoffed. 'Davinia, can I pour you another?' She picked up the bottle clumsily, pouring herself another drink.

Davinia declined, pushing herself out of the armchair. 'No, thank you, Elizabeth, haven't you had enough? No, I'm with Albert, a cup of hot milk sounds wonderful, thank you, Greg.'

'No problem, Greg at your service. Does anyone need assistance? Albert, can I give you a hand, you look like you're struggling a little?'

'Oh no, I'll be alright, it's just the old knee playing up.'

'Right, well I'll get Mary to heat some milk.' Greg left the lounge to the sounds of Elizabeth's scornful imitation of Davinia spoken to the empty room.

'I'm a step ahead of you.' Mary turned to Greg, from the stove. 'The milk's on, and there's enough for you too, if you want?'

With his charges in their rooms, and their hot milk served, Greg walked back through the lounge, surprised to see that Elizabeth had also taken herself off to bed. Well that was a result. He picked up the whisky bottle, switched off the main lights and returned to the kitchen, where Mary was picking up her bag.

'I'll be off then, have a good night.' Mary left and Greg picked up his mug of milk, before guiltily opening the whisky and pouring a generous measure into his milk. Kicking off his shoes, he settled himself on the sofa in the adjacent staff room and leaned back into the cushions, perhaps he'd have a few minutes nap, there was no need to do anything until his rounds in a couple of hours.

~

Monty opened his eyes, half asleep, and tried to turn over in bed, before realising that he was still in the armchair. He peered at his watch in the darkness, trying to make out the time, when a small, moving light flickered erratically through the lounge towards the conservatory. Leaning back, he remained hidden in the darkness, watching the light's progress.

The figure made its way into the conservatory, the torch shining on the bag clutched in the person's hand as they fumbled with the handle of the door to the garden, so that the contents were revealed for a moment, a seeming patchwork of bright colours, before both the bag and its holder disappeared into the garden.

~

Spencer pulled the car off the road, switched off the music, and turned off the lights and engine, before speaking softly. 'Don't make any noise, okay? I'll just be a few minutes.' He walked silently to the gate in the side wall of Meadowvale, turning the handle, hoping that no one had slipped the bolt back across in his absence. Sliding inside, he crept along the wall towards his hiding place, freezing as he noticed the torchlight moving in his direction. Crouching behind the shrubbery, he watched as the shadowy figure slowly headed around the side of the small storeroom. His ears picked up the creaking sound of the door opening, and he crept closer, intrigued.

Straining to make out the dark figure, he peered through the grimy window and, gently wiping it with his sleeve for a clearer view, watched as the beam of the torch played over the storage boxes on the shelves, stopping when its light landed on the one its holder sought. The torch was placed down while the lid was removed, and the contents of the bag pushed in amongst whatever was in the box. The lid was replaced and, as the torch was picked up, its beam shone on the person's face for a second, before the figure was cloaked in darkness again as they made their way out of the storeroom and back towards the conservatory.

Well, well, well. Spencer thought about what he'd just seen. What the hell was that all about then? He waited until the torchlight had disappeared, before quietly entering the storeroom, taking his lighter from his pocket and using it to see the boxes. He opened the lid of the box in question and looked at the contents, mystified, before rifling through the pieces of fabric. Nonplussed, he replaced the lid and left the storeroom. As he reached through the window of the adjoining greenhouse to retrieve his drugs, he pondered what he'd just seen, wondering if he could turn it to his advantage in any way.

~

Watching from the darkness in the corner of the conservatory, Monty waited for the door to close and the person to turn round, before speaking. 'I saw what you had in the bag, I know what it was now.'

The gasp of shock was followed by silence.

'Why didn't you just put it back? No one would ever have known.'

The voice was ruminative as it began to speak, slowly. 'It was muddied and torn, I couldn't take the risk. It had to be hidden somewhere temporary until I could figure out how to hide it properly – the bottom of the rag bag in the kitchen sufficed, initially, but the police were sniffing around, and then she arrived, Miss Blue, with all this talk of turning the place upside down, searching for clues like some detective from the television. I had to get rid of it properly, somewhere it could pass unnoticed for a long time, not the damn rag bag where it might get pulled out for a cleaning purge any day.'

Monty nodded. 'So, it was you I saw in the garden the day that Dorothy was killed, quite ingenious. But what did Dorothy ever do to you that was so bad?'

'Dorothy and her little taunts,' the voice rasped bitterly, 'poking around in people's lives. She had no business playing her games, she could have spoilt everything. Do you think I could ever have let that happen? The past is the past, we've all got our secrets, but she just wouldn't let it rest, she enjoyed it, seeing our faces when she blurted out something that threatened to expose our old lies that we thought were safely buried forever. And always writing everything down in her blessed little notebook for anyone to find – if she'd ever let her handbag out of her grip. I had to put an end to it all, you see that, don't you?' The sudden laughter sounded a little hysterical. 'But the notebook was blank – she'd torn the pages out – after all that, I still didn't find her crazed scribblings.'

About to open the gate in the side wall, Spencer heard the soft murmur of voices coming from the conservatory and walked quietly towards it.

'So, she was right about you?' Monty nodded. 'I always wondered what she meant, but it makes sense now. Was it really such a terrible secret that you had to protect it at all costs? Ah, unless it affected someone else and they didn't know… maybe more than one person… yes, I can see how that might have happened, I think I understand now… I'm right, aren't I? But you didn't have to kill her, no one ever took her seriously. That was cruel and wrong – an unnecessary evil. It's over now, though, you realise that, don't you? What are you doing with that?'

Monty groaned as the first blow fell, his head falling sideways. The second blow landed with a squelching sound as his skull caved in slightly. On the third blow, his last breath left his throat with a gentle sigh, and his body slumped in the chair. The fourth, and final, blow caused his body to crumple a little further, his head lolling over the side of the chair, as blood began to drip and pool on the floor beneath it.

Hearing a dull thud as he reached the conservatory, Spencer crept silently up to the side window, looking through in time to see the torch-lit face of the person he'd seen just a few minutes earlier, walking quietly into the lounge. He squinted his eyes to make out the inert shape in the armchair. All was in darkness, apart from the soft night lighting in the lounge, but he guessed the bulky figure slumped in the chair must be Monty and that he'd fallen asleep out there, as he often did. About to leave, something about the awkward angle of Monty's head made him pause, even as he heard a dripping sound, and he quietly tried the door handle, finding it unlocked.

~

Greg came to with a start, not sure what had woken him from his nap, and looked at his watch anxiously. Relieved that he'd only slept for an hour, he stretched, before picking up his phone. Maybe it had been a message from Richard to say that he was coming through, he thought hopefully, but there were no new notifications on his phone, and he shifted his position, realising that his bladder felt uncomfortably full. He'd go to the bathroom and then do his first check of the night.

~

This was turning into the weirdest night of his life, Spencer thought, after his initial shock. He bent down and peered at

Monty's face. He'd never seen a dead body before, let alone a murdered one. The blackmail idea came into his mind as he realised what he could do with the information he had, for without a doubt he knew who'd done this, he'd virtually witnessed the actual murder. The thought of money gave him another idea and he held his hand against Monty's head to steady it as his other hand reached inside the dead man's jacket pocket, pulling out his wallet. Opening it quickly, he leafed through the different sections, grinning as he saw the twenty-pound notes. They'd do nicely. About to remove them, a movement caught his eye and he saw Greg pass the lounge door as he walked along the corridor. Slipping the whole wallet into his pocket, Spencer thought quickly – what had he touched? He grabbed some tissues from the box on the server, folding them into a thick wedge, before wiping it over the bloody side of Monty's head where his fingers had touched it. The hairpiece, holding on precariously to the top of Monty's head after the vicious assault, finally dislodged, falling to the floor and resting forlornly in the pool of blood. For a moment Spencer thought the top of Monty's skull had detached, and he stepped back, unnerved, before registering the white, bald, crown, as it glowed in the dim light. So old Monty had worn a wig, he thought, with surprise. Crumpling up the tissues, he shoved them in his pocket, left the conservatory and hurried back to his car.

'Spence, you've been ages,' Lucy whispered angrily as he climbed back into the car after opening the boot and throwing the wallet and blood-stained tissues in. 'What have you been doing? We both need the loo and I need to get home or my mum'll be on the warpath.'

'Alright, alright, I'll drop you both home.' He reached out and pinched Lucy's cheek, started the engine and headed off, laughing. 'I'll tell you what though, clever old Spencer has just come up with a way to earn himself a nice lot of extra cash...' He turned up the music and drove with a grin on his face.

Chantelle leaned back in relief, quietly typing a short message to tell her mum that she'd be home in a few minutes, glancing out of the car window as they passed the front parking area of Meadowvale, to notice the lone, white car parked at the end.

Lucy squealed. 'What's on my face?' She rubbed her fingers against the gooey wetness, looking at her hand in horror. 'Gross, what the hell have you got all over your hands, Spence?' Without thinking, she wiped her hand on her jeans.

'Relax, it's probably just something from one of the rubbish bins, I had to move them to get my stash.' He reached over and squeezed her leg as she squealed again and shoved his hand away.

'What was it, a dead body?' Lucy grimaced. 'It smells bad, I think I'm gonna puke.'

Chantelle leaned forward and handed Lucy a tissue, hoping she wasn't going to come over all drama queeny otherwise Spencer would stop the car, then they'd argue, then he'd want to roll a joint, and she'd never get home. She thought longingly of her bed, her hands clenched in anxiety.

~

Yawning, Greg walked along the corridor, noting all the closed bedroom doors. There was no need to check up on everyone, they'd all be off in dreamland now. He worried too much. Richard had told him. *You're too conscientious, Greg, you'll worry yourself into an early grave. How much harm can the elderly residents of a care home do in one night?* He could hear Richard's teasing tone in his head, and he smiled to himself as he remembered their jokes about them running riot and smashing up the place. He walked back to the kitchen – a cup of tea and a biscuit were what he needed, then he'd settle down and watch some TV in the staff room.

'Richard, you didn't tell me you were coming, how did you get in?' Pleasantly surprised, Greg allowed himself to be pulled into the other man's arms.

'I thought I'd surprise you, the side gate was unlocked and you hadn't locked the kitchen door – you should really be more careful, anyone could come in. I managed to give Moira the slip, it's becoming quite easy, she can't argue at the opportunity for me to find rare books of value, although,' his expression was rueful, 'she'll cotton on eventually to the fact that I hardly ever sell anything. I feel like an utter failure sometimes, I really do.'

'That's the last thing you are,' Greg burbled happily, 'and your uncle is so proud of you.'

'Yes, well, as long as it stays that way, but if he ever found out about us that'll be the end of any inheritance.' Richard's expression darkened.

'He won't find out, there's no one to tell him, is there? How about a drink? Let's pinch a bottle of wine and relax – it's all quiet on the home front.'

~

She'd had an extremely pleasant evening, Sasha decided, as she thanked Cal for the glass of wine. Jules's chilli and rice had been beyond tasty, and the icing on the cake had been that Willow had gone off out to visit a friend, which meant that Cal had joined her after her meal and she'd been able to bounce a few thoughts and ideas off him, just like before.

She sipped her wine, realising that the strange, somewhat creepy, Charles, was also noticeably absent this evening. Which was odd, if she came to think about it, seeing as he presumably didn't know anyone in the village, but maybe he'd just gone off out for dinner somewhere else.

Cal's touch on her neck made her jump. 'Sorry.' His eyes crinkled as his fingers slipped along the leather thong, to hold her pendant. 'It's a great photo of you both.' He let it go, leaning back in his seat as Sasha opened her mouth to speak.

The sound of the pub door crashing open and a voice calling out, distracted them, together with the other patrons. 'Someone's car's been vandalised, not sure what colour it is? Might be black? Hard to tell.'

Cal's eyes narrowed. 'Your car's black, Sash.' He jumped up and headed for the door as Sasha rushed to follow him. Others joined them and they stood in shock, staring at the dark, sticky substance coating the roof and windows of her car, lumps of bloody animals' offal sliding slowly down the windscreen to come to rest on the bonnet. Something that might have been a sheep's bladder fell from the back of the car to land with a squelching sound on the ground, and someone retched as the foul smell of rotting offal began to reach them.

Aghast, Sasha turned helplessly to Cal, and Jules, who'd rushed out and was staring in shock at Sasha's car. 'I don't know what to do. What should I do?'

'Call the bloody police, that's what.' Cal's voice was grim as he stepped a little closer to the gory scene. 'Call the cops, Jules, and tell them someone's made a threat against Sasha's life.'

'What?' Sasha stepped closer to see what Cal was staring at. The message written in the blood sent a chill through her body, despite the misspelling. YOUR NEXT.

~

Constable Ross Canfield was on night duty, but in Parva Crossing that meant putting his feet up on the pouffe in his sitting room while he tucked into fish and chips, and watched television with his wife, secure in the knowledge that if, and it was an extremely big if, an emergency arose, the call would be diverted to his mobile phone, which was diligently placed on the arm of his chair.

The plates had long since been taken out to the kitchen and washed up, and Ross was on his second mug of tea when his phone rang. Laughing at something on the TV, he absentmindedly picked up his phone to see who was calling at this late hour and realised it was official. Putting his mug down on the table, he walked out of the sitting room and answered the call.

'Nobody's to touch anything, that's the first thing, and keep everyone back, in fact, everyone should go back inside the pub and wait for me to arrive, I'll need to chat to them. Have you got someone who can take charge of that for you, Jules? Good, good.' Ross nodded. 'I'll be five minutes.'

Sticking his head around the sitting room door, he raised his eyebrows at his wife. 'Spot of excitement up at The Spotted Dog, someone's vandalised a car, sounds nasty.' He rushed off to change his clothes, and was out of the door in two minutes, having kissed his wife goodbye and assured her he'd be back in about an hour at the most. 'I expect it's just kids causing trouble.'

As Ross drove to the pub, he wondered about the vandalism. Contrary to what he'd said to his wife, he wasn't sure that it was just kids, not if the message scrawled in the blood on Sasha's car said what Jules had told him it did. A little quiver of excitement made its way through his body – he'd been yearning for some action and he'd finally got it. He thanked his lucky stars that he'd been on duty tonight and not Pav.

As he turned into the parking area, his car headlights swept over the parked cars and he picked out the scene of the crime with ease. Reversing so that his car faced Sasha's a little distance away, Ross switched off the engine but left his lights on, adding their illumination to the two spot lights which shone down from poles at either end of the parking area. Exiting his car, he pulled out his mobile phone and took photos of the scene, careful not to tread in the blood and entrails that had fallen to the ground around the car. Zooming in on the message he took more pictures, before returning to his car for a torch, which he shone around the area, looking for whatever had been used to write the message in the blood, but to no avail.

The room fell silent at his entrance, all eyes turning in his direction, and he thanked everyone for waiting, before walking up to the bar, nodding at Jules as a man stepped forward, holding out his hand.

'Cal. Jules asked me to move everyone back inside to wait for you.'

Ross shook the man's hand. 'Good to meet you, Cal, thanks for helping out, I might need further help, is that okay?'

'Sure, whatever you need. Sasha's here.' Cal stepped aside.

'Sasha.' Ross nodded. 'Sorry you've had this happen to you, we'll get to the bottom of it, you can rest assured.' He turned to face the room, clearing his throat.

'Thanks for waiting, everyone. I'm P.C. Ross Canfield, as most of you will no doubt know, of Parva Crossing Police. I'll need your names and addresses, and I'll have a brief word with each of you, then you'll be able to get off home.' He turned to Jules. 'Do you have a pad of paper that you could pass round, by any chance?'

Jules nodded and disappeared to fetch paper and pens as the door opened and Willow walked in, rushing to Cal, her eyes round. 'What's happened? I saw the blood and the police car. Oh—' She stopped as she saw the police officer and realised that no one was speaking.

'There's been some vandalism, Miss, if you'd like to join the others? From Meadowvale, aren't you?' Ross nodded in recognition before asking Sasha and Cal to join him outside.

'Sasha, I noticed your car had slight damage to the front bumper, was that there already?'

Grimacing, Sasha nodded. 'Yes, it happened the other day in the rain, someone overtook me at speed and pulled in too close in front of me, I hit the brakes and...' She shrugged. 'It felt a little aggressive, but maybe they were just in a hurry.'

'Or maybe it was the same person who did this to Sasha's car.' Cal was furious, his eyes flashing. 'Look, Constable Canning, is Sasha in danger? Is it related to her investigation into Dorothy Newton's death?'

At Sasha's protest, Cal held up his hand, addressing her directly, 'You've got no one watching your back, Sash, I don't like it.'

Ross watched the interaction between Cal and Sasha. *These two had history without a doubt.* 'I can't comment on that at the moment, of course, but let's see what we find out, before we go jumping to conclusions, yeah?' His eyes swept the parking area and he pointed at the two closest cars. 'Cal, could you ask the owners of these two cars to come and move them?'

While the cars were moved, Sasha studied the ground around her car. There were no footprints in the blood that had oozed to the ground – the perpetrator had got lucky in the way it had fallen. They'd obviously dumped the offal onto the roof and had enough time to scrawl their message in the gore on the windscreen, before moving away. *But what had they used to write the message?*

'You're wondering what they used to write the message in the blood.'

Ross was a quick study, she thought, approvingly. 'Yes, probably a stick, so it should be around here somewhere, no doubt thrown into the bushes.' She walked slowly, keeping her distance from the scene, her eyes to the ground, scanning, as Ross called Cal.

'I'll fix up some tape, if you can give me a hand, we're going to need to have a better look at the area in the daylight.'

As the two men finished up, a white car pulled in and parked on the far side, and Charles emerged, looking across at the scene before entering the pub. From what little she'd picked up on of Charles's behaviour, wouldn't he usually have come over and pushed himself into the middle of things?

'Ross, the man who just entered the pub is currently staying here, you'll no doubt want to have a chat with him too.' Pav might not be able to investigate him without good reason, but Ross was totally within his rights thanks to her car's vandalism. There was something very coincidental about both Charles and Willow being absent from the bar on the very evening that someone chucked blood and guts all over her car...

While Ross briefly interviewed the group waiting in the bar, Sasha went up to her room, she needed a moment, and she suddenly had an overwhelming urge to speak to Eric. Maybe she'd given him the silent treatment for long enough, she thought, sitting on her bed and calling him.

After a few minutes of chat, during which Sasha made sure not to mention any of her problems, they said goodbye, both of them feeling lighter – Sasha because Eric had been his usual fun self, had made her laugh, and had made her feel loved – and Eric because he felt that he'd come close to Sasha giving up on him and now felt forgiven for his latest foolishness. He pulled his bag from the top of the wardrobe and threw it on the bed. Everything was right in the world, he had a beautiful fiancée who loved him, he was surprising her for the weekend, and bringing her best friend along to boot. He began to pack his bag as he pictured their reunion, feeling a surge of love for Sasha. Being engaged wasn't so bad, maybe it was time to set a date for the wedding.

MURDER AND MAYHEM

Ross checked his watch, glad that he'd texted his wife earlier to tell her not to wait up. It was now past two o'clock in the morning and his night duty would officially finish at eight o'clock. Maybe he could catch a few hours kip and come back to the scene in the morning. His gut instinct told him that there was more to this than just a spiteful act and he didn't want to lose momentum. Resisting the urge to yawn, he bade the small group goodbye, realising that he'd inadvertently been part of a lock-in for the last few hours, even though he'd partaken of nothing stronger than a coffee.

Jules wiggled her empty glass. 'Last whisky for the ditch, guys?'

Sasha nodded, yawning, aware that she was more than a little sloshed. 'I won't say no, Jules, thanks, but then I must hit the sack.' She looked suddenly stricken. 'You must be knackered, Jules, I'm so sorry,'

'I think we're all knackered, and you've got nothing to be sorry about, Sash, you didn't do anything. Here.' She passed the re-filled glass to Sasha, and picked up Cal's.

The three of them sat in silence for a moment, as they sipped their scotch, each lost in their thoughts.

Cal was the first to speak. 'I think I should drive you around, Sash, your car's out of commission until the cops are done with it and we can get it cleaned up, plus I'd feel better knowing you weren't on your own.'

Jules nodded. 'I agree, there've been too many strange incidents now, I don't like it any more than Cal does.'

'Strange incidents? We're talking about the car that caused Sash to run off the road? Have there been any others?'

Wearily, Sasha rolled her eyes. 'Not really, nothing bad, someone had a snoop around my room and took my perfume, that's all. It hardly features as a life-threatening incident, it's just odd, that's all.'

'Hmm, well, I don't like it.' Cal downed his drink. 'So, am I your official chauffeur starting tomorrow?'

'Thanks, Cal.' Sasha smiled. 'I appreciate it.' She drained her glass and stood up, feeling a little woozy. On an impulse she turned to him and planted a kiss on his cheek, before leaning over the bar and doing the same to Jules. 'You guys are the best, thank you. I'm off to bed now.' She headed for the door leading to the rooms, aware that she was staggering slightly.

Murmurings of goodnight reached her ears from behind her, and then a touch on her arm. 'I've got you.' Cal's voice was gentle in her ear, as he guided her up the stairs.

They stopped outside her door as she fumbled for her key.

'Let me.' Cal took her key and turned it in the lock, opening her door.

For a moment they looked at each other, before Sasha turned and walked into her room.

'I'll see you in the morning, night, Cal.' She closed her door, leaning against it for a moment, her heart racing, before switching the light on and heading to the bathroom, pulling her clothes off as she reached for her toothbrush.

~

Kirsty arrived for her day shift at six o'clock, giving Greg a nudge as he lay fast asleep on the sofa in the staff room. 'Wakey, wakey, Greg, time to go home.' She laughed as he opened his eyes and groaned. 'Bad night?'

Greg rubbed his eyes blearily. 'No, all quiet, I'm pleased to say. Right, I'll be off then.' He stood up, sliding the empty wine bottle into the bin before stretching his arms, as Kirsty bustled around, putting her bag and cardigan in the cupboard.

The door banged as Tanya walked in. 'Morning everyone, lovely day out there. I'll get the kettle on shall I, Kirsty?'

The two women sat down at the kitchen table with their tea as Kirsty frowned, looking at the open cleaning cupboard door. Pushing her chair back, she pulled the door fully open, tutting at the bag of cleaning rags on the floor. 'Now who's been making a mess in my nice tidy cupboard, and not for the first time either?' She picked up the rags, stuffing them back in the bag, and replaced the bag on its hook.

Taking a last swig of her tea, Tanya stood up. 'Well, I suppose I'd better start opening up the curtains and laying the breakfast table.'

Pulling the curtains back as she made her away along the corridor, Tanya paused as she passed the manager's office – something had looked amiss. She turned and opened the door, taking in the dented filing cabinet – someone had forced the drawers open. Hurrying back to the kitchen, she informed Kirsty, who returned with her, and the two women stood, surveying the scene.

'Reckon I should call the police,' said Kirsty, 'looks like we've had a break-in.'

~

Since losing her husband, Peter having been the first to fall victim to the poison pen letter crusade which had so ravaged the village the previous summer, Maureen Ford had found herself a companion. His name was Douglas and he'd given her a reason to get up in the mornings again.

She smiled as his little legs raced through the grass, sleek, tan body shining in the early morning sunlight, his large ears flapping as he barked at an imaginary foe. 'Dougie, this way, boy,' she called, her heart overflowing as he turned his sparkling, almond-shaped eyes to look at her, before running towards her.

Picking him up, she smothered him in kisses, holding his soft body close for a moment as she breathed in his smell, before putting him back down on the ground, laughing as he charged off, nose to the ground. He barked excitedly, running back towards Maureen, before turning and disappearing again, making little snuffling noises as he buried his nose in the undergrowth.

Maureen stiffened as she heard him emit a low growl, and she rushed along the path, calling him anxiously. 'What is it, Dougie, what have you got?'

He began to bark, his high-pitched yap sounding urgent, and Maureen rounded the bend in the path to find him standing off against a tree in a small clearing, partially obscured by bushes. She picked Douglas up and pushed through the bushes, freezing on the spot as she stared at the tableau in front of her.

Douglas wriggled frantically in her arms and she clipped his lead back onto his harness, holding onto him firmly as her eyes took in the scene. The strong scent of a woman's perfume pervaded her nose and she looked around warily. Reaching into her back pocket, she pulled out her phone, taking a couple of steps closer as she brought up her camera. Still holding Douglas firmly under her arm, she took some photos of the dismembered doll, its body tied to the tree, daubed with a red substance, its limbs strewn beside it. What was this? Some kind of satanic ritual? Backing away, she turned and hurried back the way she'd come, still holding Douglas.

Once safely in her car with the doors locked, Maureen drove along the lane a little way, before pulling over. 'I think we need to call the police, Dougie, I didn't like the look of that, did you?'

~

Ross Canfield's wife shook him by the shoulders again. 'Ross, wake up, you've had a couple of calls.'

Groaning, Ross opened his eyes. 'What time is it?'

'Seven o'clock, you were out for the count. I think you've got a couple of messages, maybe it's to do with last night?'

Ross listened to the messages in disbelief. A suspected break-in at Meadowvale and possible signs of some kind of satanic ritual in Blackwater woods. What the hell? Had every criminal and lunatic waited for him to be on night duty to get into action? Talk about be careful what you wish for, he thought wryly. He was still officially on call for the next hour but, under the circumstances, a couple of extra pairs of hands wouldn't go amiss, he decided regretfully, making his first call.

'Sarge? Sorry to bother you so early, but you're not going to believe this...'

Sergeant Jane Weaver listened to Ross's account of the three separate incidents, before instructing him to reply to the calls and advise the callers that the police would be in touch during the course of the morning. She then told him to call Constable Datta and advised that they should all convene at the station as soon as possible.

~

Howard Norton had spent a disturbed night, the pain in his hip having woken him on more than one occasion and, as the morning light infiltrated his curtains, he reached for his glasses, putting them on and squinting at his alarm clock. Sounds of activity could be heard from further along the corridor and he guessed that the staff were busy laying the table for breakfast. They'd begin knocking on doors and checking on the residents soon, seeing who wanted a cup of tea, but he decided to get up. Having attended to his toilet, and feeling much better for being washed and dressed, he decided to take a quiet stroll in the garden to help stretch his hip out, as it was still only half past seven. After that he'd be just about ready for his toast and coffee.

~

Pavani Datta arrived at the police station first, and opened up, filling the kettle and laying out mugs in readiness. Her mind drifted as she spooned coffee into the mugs, and she thought about the three seemingly isolated incidents: Sasha's car gets vandalised with animal offal; kids or someone set up some kind of devil worship site in the woods; Meadowvale has a break-in. How much of that was linked to Sasha's arrival and investigation into Dorothy Newton's murder, she wondered? But no, however hard she tried to make it fit, some tied up doll in the woods could not possibly relate to Sasha. She poured hot water into the mugs as Jane and Ross arrived, stirring the coffees and adding milk. Once everyone had gratefully taken a coffee, they moved to the small conference room, and Ross brought them up to speed.

~

Moving slowly, with the help of his stick, Howard pushed the lounge door to the conservatory open and, having glimpsed the occupant seated there, called out, 'Morning, Monty, you're up with the larks.' He closed the door and turned back in Monty's direction, about to make a joke about how much he slept, when his jaw dropped. 'Monty?' Tentatively, Howard took a step closer, his eyes falling on the bloody mass which was the side of Monty's head.

His heart raced painfully and he placed his hand to his chest, forcing himself to take measured breaths as he took in the congealed pool of blood on the floor beneath Monty's awkwardly lying head, as well as the blood-stained, heavy, white marble vase which lay on the floor close by. Trying not to stumble, Howard backed away, pulling the door open with difficulty, and staggered into the lounge, where Tanya was calmly finishing off laying the breakfast table.

She looked up, her smile replaced by concern, at the sight of Howard's pale, horrified expression. 'Howard? Whatever's the matter? What's wrong?' She placed her hands on his shoulders, guiding him towards the closest armchair, as he pointed to the conservatory. 'Alright, you sit down, I'll be right back, darling.'

Forcing herself not to scream, Tanya ran from the conservatory to the kitchen at top speed. 'Kirsty, come quick!'

The two women stood just inside the conservatory door and surveyed the macabre scene grimly, shaking their heads in disbelief. Kirsty finally broke the silence.

'Poor old Monty, he didn't deserve this. Evil has darkened our doors again, Tanya. Now, be careful not to touch anything, and pull the curtains across the interior windows so the residents can't see into the conservatory.'

Still shaking, Tanya asked, 'What are you going to do?'

'I'm going to make my second call to the police in as many hours, that's what.' Kirsty took out her phone and pressed redial, looking sadly at Monty's forlorn hairpiece splayed out in the congealed blood, the indignity of the man's death making her own blood boil.

~

Pavani Datta returned from answering the call, her expression urgent.

'What is it, Pav?' Jane Weaver looked at her constable enquiringly.

'We've had another murder at Meadowvale, Sarge.'

~

Sasha and Cal walked out of the pub, pausing to look at the mess on and around Sasha's car.

'I wonder where the cops are?' Cal pondered. 'The sooner they deal with this the sooner we can get your car cleaned up.'

Feeling awkward, Sasha realised that Cal had obviously just offered to drive her around out of politeness last night and was now regretting it. 'Cal, you don't have to drive me around, I don't want to be a nuisance. I'm sure I can make some kind of plan. I expect the cops are just busy and will be along a bit later.'

'Busy? In Parva Crossing? Come on, Sash, you know what a sleepy village this is. P.C. Canfield looked like the cat that got the cream last night, landing himself a nice little case of vandalism.'

They were interrupted by Willow's exit from the pub, refreshed from her somewhat longer sleep. 'Cal, you weren't going to sneak off without kissing me goodbye, were you?' She wrapped her arms around him possessively, before turning to Sasha. 'Can I give you a lift to Meadowvale?'

'Well, I–' Unsure whether she should accept and let Cal off the hook, Sasha was prevented from replying by Cal.

'I've already offered to drive Sasha around until the police give us the all clear to get her car cleaned up.' Cal smiled at Willow, who looked put out.

'Well, fine, I just hope they don't keep you waiting for too long, I mean, how can they ever find out who did that to your poor car, Sash?'

It's called police work, Willow. 'You're right, it's a tricky one.'

'Well, I'd better be off, it's physical activity this morning, a nice energetic start to the day for the residents, they love it.'

Sasha doubted that, but conceded privately that keeping the elderly group mobile was obviously immensely important. Feeling the need to be friendly, she asked, 'How was your evening, Cal said you were out with a friend?'

Willow fiddled with her car keys, shifting her bag from hand to hand as she laughed. 'Look at me, all fingers and thumbs today. The evening was nice, thanks, we were just catching up, we stayed in and ordered pizza. I hadn't seen her for ages.' She rolled her eyes. 'We drank too much wine, of course.'

That was a lot of information for a simple question.

'Morning, gang.' Charles's beaming face appeared as he walked out to join them. 'I heard you all talking from the breakfast room.' He stepped closer to Sasha's car, frowning and tutting as he walked around the police tape. 'Nasty job, this, who did you upset, Sasha? Been making enemies?'

Gang? Enemies? Who did this guy think he was? And where had he been last night?

'Eat anywhere nice last night, Charles?' Sasha's voice and smile were equally sweet as she studied his reaction.

Charles motioned vaguely with his hands, his eyes fixed on Sasha. 'Oh, some Italian place, wasn't it? Can't remember the name offhand.' His eyes flickered and he turned away with a laugh. 'Well, I'd better get back to my breakfast, Jules will tick me off if I let my eggs go cold. I'll see you ladies later with my camera.'

'He's too familiar, Cal,' said Sasha, as Cal drove them away from the pub. 'Everywhere I look, he's there, it's almost as if he thinks he knows me.' She stopped, noticing Cal's troubled expression. 'What is it?'

'Oh, nothing really, I was just wondering about last night, Willow and Charles seem pretty friendly, don't you think? And they were both out last night, d'you think they could have been together?'

He was jealous, of course. 'I'm sure it's nothing like that, they're both just very friendly people.'

'Hmm, maybe.' Cal turned towards the village. 'Let's make a stop at the police, see what they're going to do about your vandalism case. If you're not in a hurry to get to Meadowvale, that is?'

'That would be great, I won't be able to interview anyone while they're doing their activity with Willow, anyway.'

~

Lucy Smithers pulled her school uniform on in a hurry, she'd be so late for school, good job her mum had already left for work. She picked up her jeans from where she'd thrown them last night, and looked at the stains. Whatever it was, it smelt rank, she thought, wrinkling her nose in disgust as she stuffed them in the dirty washing basket.

~

As they drove along the village high street, Sasha looked out at the shops and coffee shops as they opened up for the day, turning her head as she saw a familiar face. 'That's Maureen, isn't it? Maureen Ford?'

Cal glanced in his mirror. 'Sure is, want to stop and say hi? She can introduce you to the new man in her life.' He indicated and pulled over, switching off the engine, grinning at Sasha's quizzical look.

She and Maureen hugged, delighted to see each other again, before Sasha bent down to gently stroke the miniature dachshund who was sitting beside Maureen's chair, his bottom wriggling as he desperately tried to restrain himself from joining in all the excitement, failing utterly and rolling over, making little whimpering sounds of happiness.

'Oh, Maureen, he's gorgeous!' Sasha exclaimed. 'Can I hold him?'

'Douglas, meet Sasha.' Maureen laughed, picking up the squirming bundle and handing him to Sasha, who dropped kisses on his silky head as he turned and licked her cheek, enjoying all the attention. 'His owner passed away suddenly just before Christmas and there was an appeal to find a home for him. He changed my life overnight, didn't you, baby?'

They were distracted by the flash of lights and the sudden wailing of police cars, and turned their heads to watch the two cars head off past them along the high street.

Sasha looked puzzled. 'That was Ross in the first car, wasn't it? And Pav driving Jane in the second? What d'you think's happened?'

'No idea, must be something serious. I suppose we won't be stopping in at the station to ask about your car, now. Shall we join Maureen and Douglas for a coffee?' At Sasha's nod of agreement, Cal waved at the approaching waiter and ordered them both coffees, turning to Maureen to offer her a second one.

'No, I'm fine, thanks, I just got this. Douglas and I had a bit of excitement of our own this morning, didn't we?' She smiled at Douglas as Sasha regretfully handed him back, settling him on her lap. 'It can't be related to the cops going off like that though, it certainly wasn't any kind of emergency, it was just a bit weird.'

'What was it, what happened?' Sasha noted the woman's troubled expression.

'I took some photos, here.' Maureen picked up her phone, bringing up the first photo and handing the phone to Sasha. 'Douglas and I were out for our early morning walk. We often go to Blackwater woods as they've got lots of nice pathways to walk along. Dougie suddenly ran off and started barking and growling at something and I...'

A ringing sound filled her ears. *It couldn't be. It wasn't possible.*

'Sash? What is it?' Cal's voice was sharp as he looked at her white face.

He was locked away in prison. It was just some freaky coincidence. Dolls dismembered; daubed with red lipstick; tied with twine. D.I. Steph Wendover's words came back to her in a jumble as she remembered the detective inspector giving her, Eric, and Zoe, the account of Miles Bleak's twisted childhood, beginning with dolls, before he moved onto real women, culminating with Zoe and herself.

The touch of paws on her knees roused her, and she reached out to stroke Douglas's head as his worried eyes looked at her. Leaning down, she kissed his forehead, before looking up at Cal and Maureen. 'Sorry, I just zoned out for a second. Those photos, they reminded me of something bad.' Giving a small laugh, Sasha shrugged. 'It's nothing, just a stupid similarity. But you did the right thing to tell the police, Maureen, always best for them to nip anything of concern in the bud, or at the very least to look into it.'

They stood up and carried out protracted goodbyes, Douglas being the main cause for the drawn-out farewells, with promises to meet up again soon.

'I'm so pleased for Maureen.' Sasha smiled as she and Cal walked back to his car. 'They're both so lucky to have each other, it's a match made in heaven.' She noticed Mrs Pringle and Sheila standing outside the chemist and remembered that she needed some perfume. 'D'you mind if I just pop into Pringle's for a sec?'

'Hello, Dolly,' Sasha greeted the older woman warmly, ignoring Cal's amused expression at her use of her Christian name. 'Hi, Sheila, how are you both?'

'Oh, we're very well, dear, very well indeed.' Mrs Pringle's eyes sparkled with interest as she looked from Sasha to Cal. 'Come on in, what can we do for you? No tea today, I expect, as you've just had coffee with dear Maureen. And darling Douglas of course, what an absolute bundle of joy that little sweetheart is, he's turned poor Maureen's life around and put a smile back on her face. And we turn a blind eye, don't we, Sheila, when Maureen visits us, never mind about the no dogs rule, we say, Douglas is different, such a tiny little thing, he can't do any harm. We even keep a little box of treats on the shelf next to the custard creams, and d'you know, he's so clever, he runs to the back of the shop and looks up at the shelf. He does make us laugh, doesn't he, Sheila? And where are the police all off to, I wonder? Sheila and I were just saying, it's not good when you see flashing lights, and the sound of the siren fair made my knees go weak.'

Trying to keep up, Sasha's mind changed tack from talk of Douglas to talk of the police cars. About to speak, she was beaten to it again.

'And how's your poor car, dear? You've really been through the wars since arriving, haven't you? Do the police have any leads? Mean and nasty, I call it, doing that to a person's car. If I were the police the first place I'd look is the butcher's, not that I'm accusing Mr Alison, of course.'

In amazement, Sasha realised that Mrs Pringle was referring to last night's vandalism of her car – she should have known that word on the village grapevine would have reached Pringle's by now.

'No, it's the waste bins that I'm talking about. They sit out the back, there's a collection service, of course, but it only comes once a week, in between anyone could help themselves to what's inside.' Mrs Pringle shuddered. 'It makes my stomach turn, I said so to Sheila, didn't I, dear? Of course, those youths on the new estate...'

She was stopped from continuing by a warning glance from Sheila, who intervened.

'It's just a few bad seeds, most of the residents are quite lovely, like your sister Tessa and her family.' She looked meaningfully at Mrs Pringle, who flushed, realising her faux pas.

Sasha smiled, wondering if she was actually expected to reply to any of Mrs Pringle's questions. 'Well, I don't really have anything to tell you, I've no idea who did that to my car, or where the police were off to, but we mustn't keep you from your day, if I could just...'

'Yes, of course.' Mrs Pringle was all business. 'What can we help you with, I expect you need to get off to Meadowvale for more interviews.'

'Perfume, please, nothing fancy, I forgot to bring any with me.' She was careful not to fuel the rumour mill with the mention of her stolen bottle. Following Sheila, Sasha perused the small selection.

'Of course, we stopped stocking Lavender Dreams after it all came out about Mr Newton – it still gives me the shivers to this day. To think he was spraying it on his dead mother as she sat in her armchair.' Sheila shuddered. 'Oh no, dear, you'll not be wanting that one, I wouldn't think.' Her nose wrinkled. 'It's our cheapest one, a very inferior brand, but popular with some of our older clientele, Mrs Parkhurst, for instance. Poor thing's had such a hard life, widowed at such a young age and taking cleaning jobs from dusk 'til dawn to raise her daughter, and a fine job she made of it. Course, there's some will say it's wonderful that she's found love again in her golden years, but–'

'Sheila, dear, no one likes a gossip.' Mrs Pringle intervened, taking Sasha's arm and spraying a tester on her wrist. 'How's this? Yes? I thought so.' She whisked up a sealed box of the perfume and Sasha dutifully followed her to the counter, impressed as always by the woman's uncanny abilities.

'Now don't you go spoiling that little Douglas too much next time he visits, will you, ladies?' Cal winked as he turned to leave with Sasha, and the two women flushed, giggling delightedly.

Sasha and Cal were still grinning as they got into his car, and Sasha turned to him. 'Mrs Pringle was right about one thing, I do need to get to Meadowvale.'

~

Chantelle and Lucy hovered in the corner of the school netball court at morning break, talking about the night before.

'Did you get into trouble?' Lucy rolled her eyes. 'I was lucky, Mum was asleep when I got in.'

'No, we weren't that late, no big deal.' Chantelle pictured her mum's face again when she'd walked in the door, and her dad demanding to know where she'd been. They'd told her they wanted to speak to her tonight and she was dreading it, plus she was grounded for the whole weekend, but she couldn't tell Lucy and risk being laughed at.

'What shall we do tonight? Spencer's working, but we could go round to Sharon's and hang out with her and Glen?' Lucy looked up as a small group of girls walked up to them.

'We heard about that woman's car at The Spotted Dog, someone said she's your aunt, is she alright? It's so gross, my brother said there was blood everywhere. Was it human? Was someone murdered?' The girls clustered around as Chantelle looked from one to another in confusion. 'D'you think we've got another serial killer in the village?'

One of the girls sharply nudged her and her eyes widened as she realised her mistake. 'Oh my God, I'm so sorry, Chantelle, I forgot about Britney.'

Chantelle felt tears welling in her eyes and turned away as Lucy put her arm around her shoulders, lashing out at the girls.

'Shut your stupid mouths, you all know what Chantelle went through, leave her alone. And stop acting like we're all mates just because you want to find stuff out.' She steered her friend away from the group. 'Ignore them, they're just looking for drama.'

Grateful for Lucy's support, Chantelle turned to her friend. 'But was it my aunt's car? I haven't heard anything, I need to text her.'

~

Sasha read Chantelle's text and replied, putting her niece's mind at rest and telling her that she'd see her over the weekend. It was unbelievable that the story had already reached her at her school. Her phone rang.

'Tess, hi, everything alright?'

'It's me who should be asking you that, sis, I've just had a worried message from Chantelle saying something about blood all over your car. What's happened?'

'Oh, just a spot of vandalism, honestly, Tess, I was just unlucky. I expect it was kids causing trouble. They'd got hold of some animal guts and stuff, pretty disgusting. Look, I'll come round tomorrow if you like?'

'You don't really think it was kids, do you? Not with that message written in the blood.' Cal turned to Sasha as they neared Meadowvale. 'That story about someone running you off the road, that was the first thing, which on its own could have just been a spot of bad luck, but then someone was poking around in your room and nicked your perfume, then there was last night's incident. You need to be careful, Sash, someone's got it in for you. Whoah!' He pulled the car to the side of the road as a police car sped past, lights flashing. 'He came out of nowhere. That was Nick Crossley, I'm sure of it.' He indicated to turn into Meadowvale's approaching driveway as a police officer held her hand up to stop him.

Sasha craned her neck to see what was happening. Police and other official vehicles were parked in the parking area and she watched D.S. Crossley step from his vehicle and rush inside.

'I'm sorry, we're not allowing anyone in, you'll have to turn round, sir.'

'I'm working with the police as a consultant.' Sasha leaned over to speak to the police woman. 'Sasha Blue. If you could speak to D.S. Crossley or Sergeant Weaver, they'll confirm it.'

They waited while the officer spoke into her radio. Returning to the car, she leaned down to speak through the window. 'Sergeant Weaver says she'll see you, you can proceed, but I'll have to ask you to wait here, sir, the lady only, she said.'

Raising his eyebrows at Sasha, Cal thanked the officer and pulled the car over to the side of the driveway.

'Can you give me a minute? I'll just find out what's going on and come and let you know.' Sasha rushed off, filled with foreboding, something bad had happened, she knew that much.

An officer directed Sasha to the residents' lounge and she walked quickly, the sound of weeping reaching her ears from one of the rooms. Tanya's face was tearstained as she spoke to P.C. Datta, and a grim-faced, red-eyed Kirsty appeared from the kitchen with a trolley laden with tea and coffee pots.

As Sasha walked in, she was greeted by P.C. Canfield and, about to speak, her eyes were drawn to the police tape stretched across the lounge midway, preventing access to the conservatory and the area directly in front of it.

Sergeant Jane Weaver excused herself from her Inspector, Andrew Kavanagh, and approached Sasha, her expression harried.

'Someone's been killed.' As the words left her mouth, Sasha wasn't sure whether she was asking a question or making a statement, but guessed Jane's response would be the same, either way.

Dr Singh walked carefully out of the conservatory, accompanied by Chief Inspector Stanley Carpenter, from Rentham police station, and the two men joined Inspector Kavanagh as scenes of crime officers moved in and out. Sasha had her answer, even as Jane Weaver confirmed her fears. 'I'm afraid so. Monty Mallowan, resident. Head bludgeoned in with what looks like a marble vase.'

Speechless, Sasha stared at Jane in dismay. It was too awful to comprehend. Monty. That sweet, kind, loveable old man. How could anyone have done that to him? 'But, how? Why? I was just speaking to him yesterday. He's such a– was–' she corrected herself, 'such a lovely man. I just– I can't believe it.' Shock and grief made her feel sick, as the horror of it all hit her, and she put out a hand to steady herself.

P.C. Canfield hurried over. 'Side gate's unlocked, someone could have got in that way. Is it connected to the break-in, Sarge?'

'Break-in? What break-in? Here?' She had too many questions and knew that no one would have time for her right now.

Jane Weaver reached out and touched Sasha's arm. 'It's a huge shock for everyone. I'm not excluding you, Sasha, but can I ask you to leave for today? We'll have to put your interviews on hold for today, this new death complicates things. Two murders in a care home in a matter of weeks.' She shook her head in disbelief.

'Of course. Will you call me?' With a last glance towards the conservatory, Sasha walked slowly out of the lounge and made her way back to Cal's car.

Opening the passenger door, Sasha climbed in, turning to speak to Cal, her eyes wet with tears. He pulled her close, his arms holding her gently, his mouth moving in her hair as he asked her what had happened.

'Someone's murdered Monty. Such a kind, gentle soul – who would do that? He wouldn't hurt a fly. Everything feels so evil at the moment, so many awful things are happening.' Sniffing, she sat back as she reached down to her bag for a tissue.

'I don't even know what to say, Sash, it's unbelievable. What the hell's going on around here? Have the police got any ideas? How was he killed, do you know?'

'The poor man was hit over the head with a marble vase. They found the side gate to the grounds unlocked, so maybe someone came in that way. Apparently there was a break-in here last night, too. But, Cal, we can't tell anyone these details, we have to wait for the police to release information.' A thought occurred to her. 'Where's Willow? She was coming here for the morning activity, they must have turned her away.'

Cal frowned. 'I haven't heard from her, maybe she doesn't know what actually happened and just got told she couldn't go in. She could've gone back to the pub, or into the village, I suppose.' He started the engine. 'What shall we do? Where d'you want to go?'

'Back to the pub, I suppose, what a mess it all is.'

~

Chantelle sat in the last lesson before lunch, not taking in a word the teacher said. Her mind kept playing back the moment when Spencer came out of the side gate at Meadowvale last night. He'd opened the boot to put something in, before he got back in the car. And then he'd touched Lucy's face with his fingers and put something on it, something disgusting. And why had Lucy said that about a dead body? Had she thought it was blood? Did he get something from the old people's home, maybe some raw meat or something, from the kitchen? And why had he made that comment about money? Could he have been the person who vandalised Sasha's car? He could have gone to the pub after he dropped her and Lucy home. But why? He didn't even know her aunt. But she was interviewing everyone at Meadowvale about Dorothy Newton's murder, wasn't she? And Spencer worked there, so...'

'Chantelle, are we boring you?' Her teacher advanced in her direction and she hurriedly opened her book to the page that Lucy's was opened at.

~

Zoe picked up her bags, hugged her boss, Flavia, again, thanking her for letting her have the time off, and left the art gallery, grinning as Eric hooted. She threw her weekend bag in the boot and pecked Eric on the cheek as she fastened her seatbelt. 'This was a great idea, Eric, Sasha's going to be so surprised, it'll be fabulous. We're still going to stop at her flat so that I can grab her boots for her, aren't we?'

'Sure, anything for my girl.' Eric smiled happily. 'Oh, and I think I'm already out of the dogbox, my beautiful fiancée called me last night, I think she's missing me. It's going to be great, country air, a good, traditional pub, excellent food, and plenty of ale.'

A short while later, Eric pulled the car in outside Sasha's flat, as Zoe's phone rang.

'It's James, I'll speak to him while I'm getting Sasha's boots.' She grabbed her keys to the flat and jumped out of the car. 'I won't be long.'

'I'm jealous, it sounds like great fun.' James laughed as he grabbed himself a coffee. 'Wish I was going with you instead of being stuck in meetings on this trip.'

'I wish you were, too, I miss you. I'm going to have a whole double bed all on my own in a gorgeous country pub.' She took the stairs two at a time, unlocking Sasha's front door, leaving the keys in the lock as she entered the silent flat.

'Where are you? You sound out of breath.'

'In Sasha's flat, can you believe? I'm rushing because Eric's parked on a double yellow line. I'm getting her favourite pair of boots to take to her. She doesn't know, it's a long story.'

Laughing, James said, 'The mysterious lives of girlfriends. Well, I'll leave you to it, babe, love you.'

'Love you too.' Zoe smiled into her phone as she walked into Sasha's bedroom and opened the wardrobe. She groaned as she looked at the shoeboxes lined up in the bottom of the cupboard, putting her phone down on one of the shelves, and crouching down to search for the boots. Five boxes later and she'd found them. Grabbing the box, she rushed out of the flat, closing the front door and double-locking it.

'Success.' She placed the box on the back seat and fastened her seatbelt, leaning back happily. 'Let's go to Parva Crossing.'

SURPRISE

D.I. Wendover finished her meeting, checked her watch and decided it was time to set off for the coffee shop to meet Dr Taylor to discuss the doctor's concerns. It was intriguing, she had to admit, but she couldn't for the life of her figure out why the doctor wished to speak to her.

The two women arrived at the same time and both agreed on a pot of tea. Steph Wendover stirred the teabags in the shared pot as Dr Taylor spoke.

'I realise that it seems a little unorthodox to want to discuss this with you, and I obviously can't strictly repeat anything that Zoe actually told me, but perhaps we can get around it by my sharing of some concerns that I have.'

Steph Wendover nodded. 'Certainly, although I'm not really sure where I fit in?' She poured their tea as she looked at the doctor, enquiringly.

'The case, the man you arrested and put away, it's all closed to your satisfaction? You didn't feel that there was anything left open? No loose ends, so to speak?'

'Yes, we were happy with the result, we were able to tie him to both Zoe's abduction and imprisonment, her friend Sasha Blue's abduction, as well as the murders of a woman who'd been held at the same property as Zoe, and of another young girl. The evidence against him was overwhelming.' Steph leaned back. 'Something's obviously on your mind, why don't you tell me what it is that's bothering you?'

Nodding, Dr Taylor put her tea cup down and began to speak. 'I don't think Zoe herself is completely aware. It's more subconscious. I've encouraged her to talk through what happened to her and, without repeating her exact words, the conclusion I've drawn is that she had a sensation of someone else having been present.

Steph Wendover looked up sharply. 'Someone else? D'you mean like another woman being held?'

Dr Taylor shook her head. 'No, someone else there with Miles Bleak, or Blake Selim, however you wish to refer to him, the man who was holding her. We often commonly use the term *they* when we really mean *he or she*, that's quite usual in and of itself. So, if Zoe said *they* it would be quite natural to assume that she was referring to her captor, Miles, especially if she was trying to create mental distance between herself and him and what happened to her. But Zoe has revealed certain sensations she had which imply that there could have been another person in the room on at least one occasion when she was forced to wear items of clothing and pose in a particular way on the bed.'

Steph Wendover's mind whirred. 'Do you mean that she heard voices? People speaking to each other? Can you give me any idea whether it could be a male or female? I mean, she could have imagined it, couldn't she? The poor woman's head was covered with a hood so she couldn't see anybody, and I can only imagine how disorientating that must have been for her.'

Again, Dr Taylor shook her head. 'I don't get the impression that she heard anybody speak, it's more a feeling that she had, possibly a subconscious intuition. For instance, she talks about the man, Miles, ordering her to get dressed, and she makes reference to her hood being removed for a moment. My assumption is that photos were being taken of her just prior to this, as we know from the information you gave me, but with him standing beside her, the swinging closed of the door to the room could not possibly be related to him.'

'Zoe didn't mention this to us, I'm certain of it, but it's a tiny detail, I'm not sure if it means anything. Did she definitely see the door closing while Miles was standing right beside her?'

'I've pieced it together from small things that she said – we must remember that she finds the whole experience terribly distressing and although I'm sure that talking through it is helping her, she's not found it easy to recount incidents step by step, rather she has murmured recollections in no particular chronological order. It was while I was going through my notes that I realised that the two incidents seemed to occur in tandem.'

Dr Taylor took a sip of tea before continuing. 'And there's another thing – sense of smell is possibly heightened when we can't see, as is hearing, and I picked up on references to a different smell, a kind of strong soap smell, which she has only ever brought up in conjunction with the movement of the door.'

'So, to clarify, we have Zoe's impression that someone left the room where she'd been forced to lie on the bed with her head covered, pulling the door closed behind them, as well as her recollection of a smell other than Miles?'

'Yes, it's not much when you put it so succinctly, I admit, but I felt that you should know, in case she hadn't mentioned it to you when you interviewed her, which I suspect she hadn't, as it only cropped up gradually during our sessions as she released her deeper memories.'

'Well, I'm glad we met, Dr Taylor, and thank you for letting me know about this. I'll certainly give it some thought. I may need to speak to Zoe, of course, but will be careful not to directly reference her sessions with you.'

The two women shook hands and left the coffee shop, each going their separate ways, but as Steph Wendover mulled over what she'd been told, she decided to call Zoe and ask her if they could meet at the earliest convenience. She scrolled through her contacts and called Zoe, leaving a message for her to contact her as soon as possible, when she didn't answer.

About to head back to the office, she was called regarding one of her current cases and changed direction, needing to meet with a witness at the hospital. She made one more call, this time to Constable Graham Barnes, asking him to retrieve the closed case files on Miles Bleak from storage and to put them in her office. It wouldn't harm to skim back over the case and make sure they hadn't missed anything.

~

Mrs Pringle peered out through the window display, her eyes following the fair-haired man as he left the hardware store across the road. Now what was the visiting photographer doing in Pink's, she wondered, it was a strange establishment to be visiting when you were a tourist. He'd definitely made some purchases, the heavy-duty brown paper bags from Pink's were quite distinctive. 'Be a dear and pop the kettle on, Sheila, I'm just popping over the road for a moment.'

She returned a few minutes later, her mind mulling over the items that the man had bought. It was most strange, most strange indeed. Why would he have need of such things? Not sure quite what to do with the information, Mrs Pringle decided to keep it to herself for now.

~

Eric pulled off the motorway and into the service station. 'I need to fill up with petrol, won't take us long.'

'Oh good, I need the loo.' Zoe picked up her bag. 'I'll get some magazines from the shop, no doubt I'll be spending time in my room on my own later, while you two are enjoying your little romantic reunion.' She winked at Eric. 'I'll see you back at the car in a few minutes.'

As she paid for the magazines, Zoe rummaged through her bag. Her phone – where was it? She returned to the car, opening the passenger door and bending down to look under the seat. Maybe she'd dropped it in the box that Sasha's boots were in. She checked the box, before climbing into the back of the car and checking the footwells.

'What's up, Zo?' Eric leaned round to see what she was doing.

'I've lost my phone, can you call it for me?'

They listened for sounds of Zoe's phone but heard nothing.

'Maybe it's in the boot?' Eric jumped out and opened the boot as Zoe joined him, but there was no sign of it.

Groaning, as she looked at Eric, she realised what must have happened. 'I was speaking to James when I went into Sash's flat. I must have put the phone down to search for her boots and left it in her bedroom. Well, we can't do anything about it now, I suppose I'll just have to live without it for one weekend, it's not like I'm going to be called about an emergency, even Flavia can cope in the gallery without me for one day.'

'Sorry, Zo.' Eric pulled a rueful face. 'Good job you bought those magazines.'

~

The atmosphere at The Spotted Dog was deeply subdued. Sasha had told Jules about Monty's murder, but sworn her to secrecy until the police made the news public, and yet somehow word had filtered its way through and, as customers gathered for Friday afternoon drinks, the talk was of the latest murder up at Meadowvale.

Willow walked in, swinging shopping bags, and walked over to a glum-faced Sasha and Cal who were seated at a table in the corner of the bar. 'Have the police said anything yet? It seems a lot of fuss over a supposed break-in. I missed out on all my activities today, and Friday afternoons are usually such fun, we do napkin folding for Friday night's dinner. So, I went shopping instead.' She smiled, lifting up her bags. 'All a fuss about nothing and I don't know if I'm supposed to plan for tomorrow's quiz morning or not.' She stopped speaking, finally registering the expressions on the other two's faces, as she sat down beside Cal.

'You didn't hear?' Cal took Willow's hand. 'Terrible news, I can tell you I suppose.' He glanced at Sasha, who nodded, realising that Willow would hear about it soon enough anyway. He spoke in a low voice, 'Monty Mallowan was found murdered this morning. It must have happened last night.'

Willow's reaction was extreme. Her face turned white and she looked from Cal to Sasha in horror. 'Last night? Monty's dead? But how? Who? Is that why the police were there?' As her eyes welled with tears, she allowed herself to be comforted by Cal. 'Will the police want to speak to me?'

'The police will want to speak to everyone connected to Meadowvale, they'll need to know where we all were, but we must wait for them to finish their initial investigation of the scene. It's so dreadful, so cruel, I can't begin to imagine why anyone would do that to Monty, I only knew him for a short while, but he was such a lovely man.' Sasha shook her head sadly.

'Well, at least we can tell the police that we were all here, that's simple.' Willow nodded her head. 'That was when your poor car was vandalised, Sasha.'

'Yes, but we don't know exactly when it happened, babe, and you were out at your friend's, you'll just have to give them the details as they'll be checking everything, we are talking about murder, don't forget.' Cal squeezed her hand, before getting up. 'I'll fetch us some drinks.'

'What's all this about murder?' Charles appeared suddenly, hovering by their table.

Sasha groaned inwardly, this man had a habit of popping up and getting involved and she was getting tired of it. 'We can't discuss it, Charles, it's not a matter for gossip, but the police will want to know where you were last night.' *There, take that.*

'Last night? Are you telling me that someone was killed last night?' He snapped his fingers. 'Of course, it must have been at Meadowvale, that's why they wouldn't allow me to drive in. But why on earth would the police want to know where I was?'

Sasha took a moment's pleasure in his perturbed expression.

'It's not a problem, is it, Charles? You were out for dinner – you told us – they'll just want to know which restaurant, what time you were there from and to, that kind of thing. Of course, that was also when my car was vandalised.' She took another moment's pleasure in his discomfiture, but as she glanced at Cal, returning with drinks for the three of them, she remembered his musing from earlier, about both Willow and Charles being out and whether they could have been together, and wondered whether he could be right. She also realised that Charles hadn't asked who had been killed.

'What did you do instead?' Willow looked at Charles, enquiringly.

'Instead? Oh, you mean today?' Charles gave a small laugh, shrugging his shoulders. 'I just mooched about with my camera, visiting a few scenic spots, that kind of thing.'

'I thought I saw you in Rentham coming out of the toy shop and I thought, oh that's sweet, Charles is buying gifts for his children. What did you get them?' Willow waited expectantly.

'In Rentham? The toy shop? Ah yes, that's right, I popped in to have a look but I didn't find anything. Well, I'll leave you three to it.' Charles turned and walked away, leaving Sasha wondering. *That was a first, Charles being in a hurry to get away instead of trying to muscle in, and Rentham high street hardly constituted a scenic spot, in her opinion.*

Willow looked puzzled. 'I could have sworn he was carrying a bag from the toy shop when he walked out.' She laughed. 'But I'm such an airhead, I probably got it wrong.'

~

Freshly showered, after a little gardening and playing with Douglas in the garden, Maureen dried herself and dressed, reaching for her perfume to spritz herself with scent. She laughed as Douglas, who was following her every movement, sneezed. 'Oh, you poor thing, Dougie, did Mummy's perfume go up your nose?' She reached down and stroked his plump little belly as he rolled over onto his back, gazing at her lovingly. She frowned. 'Do you know, Mummy completely forgot to tell Sasha about the strong smell of perfume where my clever little boy found that poor doll all torn apart and tied up. We'll tell her next time we see her, won't we? Now, how about something to eat? Is it Dougie's dinnertime? Yes, it is.' Swooping him up in her arms, she carried him down to the kitchen, where they pleasurably discussed his dinner choices.

~

Draining her wine, Sasha stood up. 'Thanks for the drink, I think I'll take myself off to my room for a while. If I can't conduct interviews at the moment, I can at least go through my notes so far, and I need to do something to take my mind off poor Monty.' She picked up her empty glass and returned it to the bar where Jules nodded her thanks.

'Oh, Sash,' Jules called to her as she turned to go, 'don't forget you're here for pizza tonight.'

'I won't, thanks, Jules, a good dose of my favourite comfort food will be just what I need later.'

~

Miriam Smithers arrived home, tired from a busy day at the surgery, having had to deal with annoyed patients the whole day complaining about their appointments being either delayed or postponed. Dr Singh had been non-committal about his urgent call out that morning and it wasn't her place to know the doctor's business, only to deal with the appointments.

Her daughter was out and she did her best to contain her irritation, but really, it would be nice, just occasionally, to come home and find Lucy there. She kicked off her shoes and dragged herself up the stairs, retrieving dirty clothes from the dirty washing basket in her room before going into Lucy's room to do the same. Throwing everything into a heap on the landing, she sorted darks and lights, and took the larger pile of dark clothes downstairs, checking pockets as she placed things in the machine.

Pausing, as she held up Lucy's jeans, Miriam peered at the dark stains on the black denim, wondering what could have caused them, recoiling as the rank stench hit her. It looked a bit like blood and smelt like something had died, which sounded ridiculous, until she recalled the mention at the surgery of a car having been vandalised with animal blood and offal, but Lucy couldn't have been involved in something like that. Reaching for the stain remover, she sprayed it liberally over the offensive stains, before cramming the jeans in with the rest of the wash load and putting the washing machine on. There was no point in saying anything about it to Lucy, she could hardly get two words out of her at the best of times, and maybe, she uncomfortably admitted to herself, it was better not to know, just in case...

~

As she headed up to her room, Sasha glanced out of the window, wondering what to do about her car. It couldn't continue to sit there covered in gore and surrounded by police tape, she decided, throwing her bags on her bed, and with the police busy investigating Monty's murder, she doubted that her car's vandalism would be a priority for them.

'Jules, can I pinch a pair of disposable gloves? Oh, and a new, unused paper bag? I need to have a look around my car in daylight, see if I can find anything. Then I'm going to call Sergeant Weaver and ask her if I can clean it up, you can't have that mess sitting there for any longer, it's not fair on you.' Thanking Jules, who told her to call her if she needed a hand, Sasha approached her car and began to scour the ground around it. Someone had written the message on her windscreen and then disposed of whatever they'd used, they certainly wouldn't have kept it, she figured.

Concentrating on twigs to begin with, she checked any lying around for signs of blood on their ends, finding nothing. She began to probe the bushes beside the parking area, where it was most likely that someone had discarded their implement, carefully picking up any loose twigs, as well as pieces of rubbish that had lain hidden from view.

Most of the rubbish was clearly old, cigarette butts, empty match boxes, the obligatory, mystical, dirty sock, a broken key fob, and partially-disintegrated tissues, but a hint of something brightly-coloured caught her eye and she reached in hopefully to pick it up. She examined the plastic comb, feeling disappointed that it showed no signs of having been used to write in the blood. Parting the bushes where she'd retrieved the comb, she looked further, stretching out her hand to reach what looked like a new cigarette packet.

Nodding to herself in satisfaction, Sasha carefully turned the packet in her fingers, observing the blood stains on the squashed corner. She'd found it. And more importantly, she'd found a clue that could help identify the culprit. She opened the packet, surprised to find a few cigarettes still inside. After taking a photo, Sasha placed the packet in the paper bag, folded the top over a couple of times, and called Jane Weaver.

Sergeant Weaver had just returned to the police station after a long day at Meadowvale but was thrilled with Sasha's find. 'I'm sorry we couldn't attend to it, Sasha, I know you'll understand our priorities at the moment. I'll get Ross to drop by and collect it from you, and to organise the cleaning up of your car and the parking area.' But at Sasha's insistence that she'd do the clean-up herself, Jane acquiesced, 'Well, if you're sure, we'd certainly appreciate it.'

The two women chatted for a couple of minutes about Monty's murder, with Jane confirming that Sasha could join her up at Meadowvale the following morning, and Sasha then went in search of Jules.

Armed with rubber gloves and a large rubbish bag, she set to and began to pick up the remains of the offal as it lay rotting on the ground. Satisfied that she'd got it all, she then rolled up the police tape and added it to the rubbish bag, looking up as the sound of something scraping along the ground headed in her direction.

'Cal, you don't have to, I can manage.'

'Let me help, it's no problem, I'd have come out earlier if I'd known what you were doing. Shall I open the nozzle?'

They stood beside each other, watching the pressure of the water as it hit the roof of her car, forcing the dried blood and stuck-fast remnants to dislodge and wash away on the ground. Closing the nozzle, once the car looked clean, Cal dropped the hose. 'And now for my next trick.' He quickly strode off round the side of the pub, returning with a bucket. 'Soap and sponges, we'll have your car looking spotless in a few minutes.'

They worked in companionable silence, sponging soapy lather over the car, the sounds of cars coming and going in the car park, slamming doors, and voices, heralding the start of Friday evening drinking.

'We thought we'd surprise you with our company, but it looks like you don't need it.' Eric's petulant tone caused Sasha to drop her sponge in surprise.

'Eric! What are you doing here?' Sasha smiled in disbelief, her eyes widening as she realised that Zoe was standing beside him. 'Zo? I don't believe it, this is wonderful.' About to step forward and embrace them, she looked down at her soap-drenched clothes.

'Is it?' Eric's eyes were cold. 'Sure we're not interrupting a little wet tee shirt competition here?'

'Look, mate, go easy, Sasha's had some crap going on and she needed someone to–'

'I'm not your mate.' Eric looked from Cal to Sasha, nodding his head. 'Why am I not surprised?'

'Eric, will you shut up for a minute?' Rolling her eyes in frustration, Sasha turned to Cal. 'Thanks for your help, Cal, but I'll finish up here, okay?'

'Sure?' Cal's eyes were concerned as he picked up the sponges and dropped them in the bucket. 'You'll just need to hose off the soap.' At her nod, he walked off with the bucket.

Taking a deep breath, Sasha smiled at Eric and Zoe. 'It really is wonderful to see you both, you have no idea. Look, let me just hose off the soap, then I can take a shower and get some clean clothes on. And then we can have a drink in the bar while I tell you everything that's been happening. And perhaps,' she looked meaningfully at Eric, 'you can buy Cal and his *girlfriend*, Willow, a drink to apologise.'

Eric had the grace to look sheepish. 'Fine, I'll get our bags.'

'Does Jules know you're coming?' Realisation shone in her eyes. 'Of course she does, that's why she wanted to make sure I was going to be here this evening.' She laughed happily as she sprayed the soap away, closing the nozzle as a police car pulled in beside them.

Ross Canfield stepped out of the car and greeted Sasha. 'The Sarge said you had a piece of evidence for me?'

'I do, here it is, Ross, whoever vandalised my car was dumb enough to use their own cigarette packet to write their stupid threat with.'

'What makes you think it was theirs? Couldn't they have just picked up an empty packet from the ground?'

'They could.' Sasha nodded. 'If it had been empty. But this pack still has a few smokes in it, which tells me that they pulled it out of their pocket on a whim, when they decided to write in the blood. My guess? Whoever did this is pretty stupid overall.'

Ross grinned. 'So, we're to be on the lookout for someone stupid, who smokes this cheap brand, can't spell, and might be covered in animals' blood and guts. I don't suppose it could be connected to the possible satanism worship, could it? Oh, you won't have heard about that, of course.'

Zoe watched the exchange, her eyes widening as she listened to what was being said, hushing Eric as he came to stand beside her with their bags.

'Actually, I did, and I saw the photos. Maureen's a friend of mine. Listen, Ross, it might be worth checking out the scene if you get the chance, otherwise I could take a drive out myself, if you don't mind?'

'I don't mind at all, I don't feel like a particularly good investigator at this moment, anyway. I'm sorry I didn't find this, Sasha.' Ross was feeling a little stupid himself, if he was honest.

'It was dark, Ross, and the middle of the night, you couldn't have found it, I promise you. It's only because it's daylight that I managed to find it at all, and you had far more important things to attend to, in light of poor Monty's murder.' Sasha smiled at him sadly.

Waving Ross off, Sasha turned back to the open mouths of Eric and Zoe. 'What's wrong?'

'Animal blood and guts? Vandalism? Satanism worship? Threats? Monty's murder?' Zoe looked incredulously at Sasha.

'Bloody hell, Sash, you came here less than a week ago, to investigate an old lady's murder and it sounds like it's turned into a horror film,' said Eric, his eyes wide.

Zoe touched his arm, gently. 'Maybe that's why Cal tried to tell us about what's been going on, but you didn't really give him much of a chance.'

Sasha grinned at them. 'Come on, let's go in and get Zoe's room key. And the minute I get out of the shower, I'm going to give you both the biggest hugs, then we're going to hit the bar and get hammered.'

'Well, you might want to put some clothes on before that, not that I mind, but the other customers might.' Eric winked at them both as Sasha and Zoe burst out laughing, and the three of them walked into the pub.

THE PERFECT PLOT

Mrs Goodwin surveyed the forlorn group of residents and staff gathered in the lounge. It had been a terrible day, but she'd felt it essential that she speak to everyone together. She cleared her throat.

'Thank you, everyone, and those staff who would usually have gone home or only come in later, for coming together. We've had one of the worst days of our lives and suffered unimaginable shock and sadness. We've lost a dear friend, a special person who only ever had kind words to say of, and to, others. We've not been able to see our loved ones today while the police have been working here, but we've contacted all your relatives now and asked them to come to see you tomorrow morning if possible.' She paused, looking around at the faces, both young and old.

'The police will return and ask questions. This is the second time that we've experienced this now, but I would like to assure you all that you are perfectly safe here at Meadowvale. We have police officers on round the clock duty – one at the entrance and one at the side gate, where there is a high likelihood that the cruel person who did this gained entry.' All was silent as their minds considered this.

'But why?' Howard's voice was upset. 'Why would someone come through the side gate, come into the conservatory, and do that to Monty? Was he the reason that they came in? Or was he in the wrong place at the wrong time? And how did they get in when the gate's always kept locked? Did someone leave it open? But how would they know that? I just don't understand it at all.' He removed his glasses, wiping his eyes with his handkerchief, as both Davinia and Agatha reached out to pat his arms.

'We don't have those answers yet, Howard, but we must let the police do their job, they will get to the bottom of this, there's no doubt about it.'

'They didn't with Dorothy.'

All eyes turned towards Lillian as her eyes stared around the room, through her large glasses.

'We're all slowly being murdered, one by one, and nobody can stop it. Who's next? It could be any one of us.'

'Now, Lillian, that kind of talk isn't helping. Thank you, Tanya.' Mrs Goodwin nodded at Tanya, who'd moved to sit beside Lillian and taken her hand, whispering to her in hushed tones.

'Well, it's not good enough, that gate being left unlocked. Lillian's quite right, we're all at risk as we sleep in our beds at night. Although I'd like someone to try it with me, I shall be sleeping with a weapon handy from now on, I don't mind telling you.' Elizabeth made a harumphing sound as the other residents nodded in agreement, and she looked around, her wide eyes betraying concern hidden beneath her bravado.

'I'm sure it was just a mistake and nothing to do with the murderer.' Spencer appeared, directing the comment at Greg although his eyes moved around the room.

'Yes, I'm sure it was, Spencer.' Greg shifted on his feet, not looking at Spencer. 'And if you don't mind, we shouldn't use that word, it's so distressing.'

'Well what else would you call him?' Albert chimed in. 'Murder's murder, my boy, simple as that, and the person who did it is a murderer. It's gone too far now.' He glared at the group. 'One murder was bad enough, but another one...'

'How do you know it was a him?' Davinia glanced around. 'Maybe it was a her? It's alright, Tanya, no need to fuss.' She shrugged off Tanya's attempts to shush her.

Elspeth shuddered. 'Oh, Davinia, stop it. Stop it, all of you, I can't bear it.'

Mrs Goodwin regained control, having been temporarily caught off guard. 'We all have opinions, of course we do, but now's not the time to be sharing them, or to be making guesses about what might or might not have happened. Now, Kirsty and Tanya have worked very hard today, making breakfast and lunch for you all, as well as providing refreshments for the police throughout day, but I am aware that most of you have hardly touched any food all day. They've stayed on and helped Mary with tonight's meal, which won't be our usual Friday night restaurant experience but which, nonetheless, has still taken considerable effort.'

Murmured acknowledgements and approving nods followed.

'So, I'd like you all to join us for this evening's meal, residents and staff alike. We'll all sleep better with some food in our stomachs, and perhaps we can use the time at the dinner table to honour and remember dear Monty. How does that sound? Can I count on you all?'

Pleased with the response, Mrs Goodwin smiled around at everyone and left them to their chatting.

~

Once they'd ensconced Zoe in her room and left her to shower, Sasha and Eric climbed the second set of stairs to Sasha's room, where the sound of slightly raised voices could be heard from behind the door opposite hers. Trying not to eavesdrop, Sasha turned the key quickly and ushered Eric inside.

'Let's get you out of those dirty clothes and into the shower.' Eric dropped his bag in the middle of the floor and began to pull his clothes off. 'If I remember rightly, we had some unfinished business here on my last visit...'

A while later, showered, and with their unfinished business pleasurably and enthusiastically attended to, Sasha waited impatiently for Eric to dress. 'Come on, we told Zo we'd meet her in the bar, and I for one am looking forward to a drink tonight.'

The two friends chatted at their corner table while Eric stood at the busy bar ordering drinks. Realising that he was struggling with his pint of lager and the two glasses of wine, Sasha jumped up and went to help him, her eyes catching sight of Charles as he handed some small items over to Jules.

Jules glanced at her, rolling her eyes, after he'd walked away. 'He could just leave them in his room.' At Sasha's blank look, she held up the wrapped soaps. 'Allergic apparently, brings his own, only ever uses one particular brand, some kind of tar soap. Sounds old-fashioned to me, but hey, whatever floats your boat.'

'I shouldn't keep saying it, but there's something odd about him, Jules, I just can't quite put my finger on it.'

Jules laughed. 'You need to switch off your super sleuth brain, at least for tonight, and enjoy yourself, especially after such an awful day.'

'You're right.' Smiling, Sasha turned to go. 'Oh, and Jules? This surprise was just what I needed, although it's taught me what a dark horse you are, keeping secrets from me so successfully.' She winked and waltzed off back to the table, settling herself in beside Eric and nuzzling up against him as she took a welcome gulp of wine.

'I feel so happy right now, it's hard to believe.' She put her glass down. 'There's so much to tell you, some terrible things have happened since I arrived, but right now I'm just basking in the pleasure of having my two most favourite people in the world right here. I still feel like I need to pinch myself.'

Figures loomed beside the table and, looking up, Sasha locked eyes with Cal, his arm around Willow who was beaming delightedly at the three of them. A moment's guilt hovered in Sasha's mind as she acknowledged her moments of attraction to him during the days since she'd arrived but, with relief, she realised it had just been confusion, the re-opening of old wounds perhaps, and felt a sudden fondness rush through her. Cal was a good friend now, nothing more, and she stood up to introduce everyone.

Eric was charm itself, all signs of his earlier jealousy gone, now that Willow was so clearly partnered with Cal, and he shook Cal's hand before swooping Willow into an ostentatious hug. As Willow shrieked girlishly, Zoe exchanged an amused look with Sasha, before hugging Cal and then Willow.

'More drinks!' Eric bellowed, as they all clustered around the table, laughing and chatting. 'Why don't you join us? I'll get them in. What are you drinking?'

'Let me get them.' Charles insinuated himself into the group. 'This looks like a fun party, what's the occasion?' He smiled enquiringly, as Sasha felt her familiar irritation with the man.

Never one to refuse someone's offer to buy the drinks, Eric grinned happily, throwing his arm around Charles's shoulders. 'The occasion is me surprising my gorgeous fiancée with my irresistible presence.'

Laughing, Zoe joined in the banter. 'Don't forget me, my presence is irresistible too.'

Willow began to make introductions, which further irritated Sasha, and she wondered if she was just becoming a crotchety old cow.

'And let me guess, 'You must be the beautiful Zoe, Sasha's best friend?' Charles opened his arms wide, enveloping Zoe in a friendly hug.

A small alarm sounded in the back of Sasha's brain. She'd never spoken about Zoe to Charles, had she? One look at Zoe's face and she moved to her side, easing her from Charles's grasp. Her friend had turned as white as a sheet, and Sasha moved her away in concern. 'Are you alright, babe? What is it? Come with me.' She steered Zoe to the ladies, her arm around her shoulders protectively.

'Sorry.' Zoe leaned back against the hand basins. 'I don't know what came over me, I just, I don't know, suddenly I felt really weird, kind of pukey. I was fine, and then...' Her eyes were puzzled as she tried to figure out what had just happened.

'Maybe you need to eat something? We can order food now? Or I can get some crisps? Maybe that'll help.'

'Yeah, maybe some crisps.' Zoe's tone was doubtful, her mind clearly distracted, but she shook her head, as if to banish her thoughts, and smiled at Sasha. 'Some crisps and another glass of wine, that'll sort me out, come on.'

They re-joined Cal and Willow as Eric and Charles made their way back through the bar with the drinks, and Sasha hurriedly whispered to Cal. 'Could you do me a favour? No questions?'

A few minutes later, Cal said casually, 'I think we should leave these lovely people to themselves, don't you, Wills? I'm sure they want to enjoy their catch-up without us all being in the way. Charles, why don't you join us?'

Smiling her thanks at him, Sasha felt herself relax. She'd get to the bottom of whatever had upset Zoe, but right now she just wanted them to have a great evening, and to put from her head the cruel events of the past few days, and to not think about Monty's death, at least for tonight. And tonight included pizza, she thought happily, glancing up at the chalkboard listing the choices of pizza toppings.

~

It was late and she was hungry, but a niggling feeling of doubt from her meeting with Dr Taylor prompted D.I. Steph Wendover to return to her office. Picking up a burger and chips on the way, she settled herself at her desk, took a bite of her burger, and pulled the box containing the Miles Bleak case files towards her. Popping some chips into her mouth, she opened the top drawer of her desk and pulled out her scissors, cutting the strings holding the box tightly closed.

She removed the lid, dropping it on the floor and, with another mouthful of chips, stared at the envelope sitting on top of the files. She stopped mid-chew. That had not been there when she'd placed everything into the box, she was sure of it. Consternation trickled into her subconscious as she picked up the envelope and read the address written in spidery hand-writing.

How the hell had an envelope addressed to Police Officer Stephanie Wentworth, London Office, found its way to her sealed case files box? How had it even found its way anywhere at all, more to the point? When had it been placed there? And when had it been posted? She tried to decipher the smudged postmark unsuccessfully. She couldn't be sure that the contents were even intended for her, maybe it had landed up here by mistake, but no, she reasoned, as she felt the open edge of the envelope, someone had read it and felt sure that it was for her, and that it belonged with the Miles Bleak/Blake Selim case files.

With a feeling of trepidation, Steph Wendover slid the contents of the envelope out onto her desk and picked up the slightly faded, colour photograph of two boys. The larger of the two was dark-featured, his eyes staring unsmiling into the camera as his arm lay around the younger boy's shoulders. The smaller, fair-haired boy, gazed up at his companion adoringly, his beaming smile for him alone. She peered closer at the larger of the boys, she'd know those dead eyes anywhere, it was Miles, or Blake, as he'd been called then.

Holding the hand-written letter, Steph first looked for a date and, not finding one, turned the paper over to see who had written the letter, struggling to make sense of the spidery writing.

Irene Weatherall. The name felt familiar. She racked her brains, staring at the photo as if it would magically produce a memory for her. Boys. Children. Of course, Irene and Frank Weatherall had run a foster home and Blake had been one of their charges. She'd visited them during the course of her investigation, as she'd delved into his past. So, the letter *had* been intended for her, Irene must have just got a little confused.

A small, icy chill, settled along Steph's spine as she read Irene's letter, certain phrases seeming to jump from the page: two boys; joined at the hip; hero-worship; dismembered dolls; your recent visit; Charles Priestley.

And there it was. She had a name. Appalled, she leaned back, still holding the letter. How could they have missed this? How could *she* have missed this? At the very least she should have tracked him down at the time and interviewed him, shouldn't she? But they'd had no reason to suspect that anyone else had been involved, everything had pointed to Miles Bleak working alone. Everything, that is, until Dr Taylor had voiced her concerns over Zoe's sessions and her sensations of someone else having been there. Had that someone else been Charles Priestley?

Steph sat up straight in her chair. She'd speak to Irene Weatherall. How long had it been since her visit? Irene's reference to it being recent was incorrect, surely it had been the previous year? Yes, some time in December, she was sure of it. So, almost six months ago, six months during which time they'd been completely unaware that Miles might possibly have had an accomplice.

She screwed up the wrappers containing the remains of her now-cold food, throwing them in the bin. This was all supposition, it might mean nothing, the woman had been, after all, purely voicing a concern over a young boy who'd been in her care many years earlier. Rummaging through the box, Steph retrieved the contacts book for everyone related to the case, and flipped through to find the phone number for the Weatheralls.

Checking her watch first, and deciding that it was just within the socially acceptable timeframe for making evening calls, Steph dialled the number.

'Er, good evening, sorry for the late call, this is Detective Inspector Steph Wendover, I wonder if I could speak to Irene, please?'

There was a slight hesitation at the end of the line. 'Would that be Irene Weatherall? As in Frank and Irene?' At Steph's confirmation, the woman spoke again. 'We bought the house from them a little under half a year ago, when they moved into a care home.' She hesitated again. 'In fact, it was all very sad, we received a letter from their son, Scott, it must have been around February, or perhaps March, advising us that they'd both passed away within a few weeks of each other. We only met them a few times, a lovely couple, such a pity.'

Thanking the woman, Steph put the phone down. Well, that was that, she thought sadly, allowing herself a moment to remember the kindly, elderly couple.

Bringing up a list of Charles Priestleys on her computer, she stared at the total: one thousand two hundred and forty-four. One thousand two hundred and forty-four men called Charles Priestley, spread out around the United Kingdom, and one of them might be him, or he may have moved abroad, or have died, or be in prison, the possibilities were many, and even if she tracked him down, there was no physical evidence to say that he had been involved in any of Blake Selim's sick games.

She hit print, as the last thought made her pause, there might have been physical evidence, but they hadn't known to look for it amidst the long list of trace evidence found in the house where Zoe Pullman had been held. There had been no need to attempt to identify anyone else from fingerprints, hairs, or anything else found in the house, as he'd been working alone.

Steph pulled up Zoe's name on her phone and called her, leaving a message again when the call went unanswered, repeating her earlier request that Zoe call her as soon as possible. She then scrawled an instruction for her officer, Graham Barnes, requesting that he prioritise contacting everyone on the list which she'd printed out, with a brief explanation of what she wished him to ask. Hopefully by the time she returned to work in the morning he'd have found the correct Charles Priestley. Picking up her bag, she switched off lights as she went, and left the offices, heading home.

~

Doing their best to cheer everyone, including themselves, the Meadowvale staff tried to make light conversation, as music played softly in the background.

'Kirsty, these carrots are so sweet, I really don't know how you do it.' Mrs Goodwin nodded across the table. 'And Mary, your roast chicken is so tender and succulent. Don't you agree, Agatha?'

Agatha looked up from her plate, nodding enthusiastically. 'I do, roast chicken is our absolute favourite, isn't it, Davinia?'

Her sister placed her knife and fork down on her plate. 'It is, and this is very nice, but I just can't eat much, I'm sorry, poor Monty... I just don't understand why he was killed, it can't be, that is, I hope, oh dear...' She picked up her wineglass, her distressed eyes looking at Greg. 'Perhaps a little more wine?'

Greg jumped up and walked around the table, topping up glasses as everyone fell silent again.

'How about a toast to dear Monty? We should remember him as our friend and fellow resident, in happier times.' Tanya held up her glass.

'I was very fond of old Monty, you know,' Howard said, after they'd all sipped from their glasses, 'I still can't understand how anyone could have done that to him.'

'Howard, we really don't want to get into that, dear,' Mrs Goodwin said gently.

'But we can't just ignore it, it's all we can think about.' Elspeth's eyes were wide as she nodded across the table at Howard. 'And poor Howie saw it all, didn't he?'

'Saw it all? What on earth do you mean, my love?' Albert stared at Elspeth. 'You can't mean he saw Monty being murdered? You didn't, did you, Howard?'

'Of course he didn't, it was the middle of the night, we were all in bed asleep,' Elizabeth quavered.

Greg patted her arm in sympathy as he sat back down beside her, surprised to witness the elderly woman's rarely seen vulnerable side.

'Well, not everyone, Monty hadn't gone to bed, had he?' Spencer spoke for the first time.

'Quiet, Spencer, not helping,' Kirsty hissed under her breath.

'Yes, but everyone else had gone to bed, I should know.' Greg glanced uncomfortably in Mrs Goodwin's direction.

'All I'm saying is, maybe someone else was out and about and saw who did it, maybe someone was out doing all sorts in the middle of the night. They could have looked through the window and seen the whole thing. If they did, I wonder why they didn't tell the cops. Course, they could be planning a spot of blackmail. Ow.' He winced as Kirsty's shoe made sharp contact with his shin.

'Spencer, come and give me a hand in the kitchen, will you?' Mary pushed her chair back.

Lillian nodded sagely. 'It's the perfect plot, the murderer doesn't know they were seen, and then they receive a blackmail note. Of course, the blackmailer would usually be the next to be murdered. But first we have to consider why Monty was murdered and whether it was connected to Dorothy's murder. He probably knew who her murderer was and was threatening to expose them, that'll be it.' She smiled around the table at the shocked faces. 'I always wanted to write a murder mystery, you know.'

There was a moment of stunned silence at Lillian's unexpectedly coherent pronouncement, followed by the sound of something falling to the floor.

'I'm sure I'm going to have nightmares, what did Spencer mean? Who was out there?'

'No one was out there, Elspeth, he's just young and silly, watches too much television, I expect.' Mrs Goodwin spoke calmly, inwardly annoyed with Spencer. 'Has everyone had enough? I'll help you clear the plates, Tanya.'

'Is there pudding?' Agatha looked hopefully towards Kirsty, as Davinia nudged her.

'There is.' Kirsty smiled. 'Syrup sponge pudding and ice cream, in honour of Monty, as it was his favourite.'

'I still don't see why he had say that about blackmail.' Elspeth's puzzled face stared down at her plate.

'I can't get over it, seeing his head all bashed in like that.' Howard shook his head sadly. 'You're not the only one worried about nightmares, Elspeth.'

'Excuse me.' Elizabeth stood up awkwardly, dabbing at her face as she walked unsteadily from the table.

'Funny, didn't realise she was so fond of the old chap.' Albert watched Elizabeth head out of the room.

'He did love his pudding, poor, dear, Monty. How nice of you to make sponge pudding, Kirsty, I must say, I'm looking forward to it, what a treat.'

Davinia tutted to herself, really, sometimes her sister was a little too food obsessed.

'Should I go after Elizabeth?' Greg glanced at Mrs Goodwin.

'Give her a moment, otherwise I'll go.'

Dumping her pile of dirty plates on the counter, Mrs Goodwin glared at Spencer. 'What was all that about, young man? The whole purpose of this evening was to try and take everyone's mind off what happened, not make things worse with stories about people lurking around. Can't you see how upset everyone is? I honestly don't know what got into you.'

'Yeah, well, I was only saying.' Spencer was sullen as he scraped the plates over the bin.

'Well don't.' Mrs Goodwin was firm. 'Now, let's get pudding served, and no more mention of it all.' She went in search of Elizabeth.

'I couldn't eat pudding, perhaps a brandy.'

'Yes, of course, dear, you settle yourself in a chair and I'll bring you one.'

With pudding dispensed with, Howard and the Lovewell sisters joined Elizabeth, accepting their glasses of brandy from Tanya.

Greg cleared the table with Mary, bending down to retrieve the fork beneath his chair. 'I could do with a brandy myself after this dreadful day,' he murmured, bundling up the table cloth, his thoughts on Richard and his unexpected visit the night before.

'Brandy for you, Lillian? Albert and Elspeth?' Pouring three brandies, Greg carried them over, pleased to see everyone sitting together peaceably. Monty would have liked that, he thought sadly.

COPYCAT

Sasha leaned back, groaning, her hands over her belly. 'I shouldn't have eaten that whole pizza earlier.'

Zoe burst out laughing. 'You say that every time, Sash, no one takes you seriously anymore.' Exaggeratedly, she put her hand over her mouth. 'You didn't take a photo.'

'Oh no.' Sasha slapped her forehead, theatrically. 'How could I have forgotten? But you didn't take one either.' They collapsed against each other in fits of laughter as Eric looked on nonplussed.

'I don't get it.' He looked at his mad fiancée and her best friend. 'What is it with all this taking pictures of food and posting it online?'

'No idea,' spluttered Sasha, prompting fresh peals of laughter from Zoe, as the remaining customers looked across in amusement.

'It's what we do. We take pictures of our food, before we eat it, and then we post them on Graffic.' Zoe's voice was slurred as she picked up her wine glass. 'Except I couldn't take a picture because I don't have my phone.' She stared forlornly down into her wine. 'I left it in Sash's flat.'

'My flat? You couldn't have left your phone there, Zo, you've had too much wine, babe.'

'Nope.' Zoe shook her head. 'I went to get your boots and I left my phone in your bedroom. Poor James, he won't know why I don't reply to his messages.'

'Wait a minute.' Sasha's brain was struggling to follow Zoe's seemingly haphazard remarks. 'What are you on about my boots for?'

'You explain, Eric, I need the loo.' Zoe stumbled up and wove her way unsteadily to the ladies.

'Well, not sure if I get it all, but Zoe saw some photo of you with a dress or something and then she wanted to stop at your flat on the way, to get your boots, as if somehow she knew you wanted her to bring them. But if you'd wanted your boots, you'd have asked her to get them, wouldn't you?' Eric's eyes screwed up in puzzlement at the vagaries of women's behaviour.

'Eric, darling, I couldn't ask her because I didn't know you were coming, did I?' Sasha smiled hazily across the table at Eric, draining her wine glass. 'I shouldn't drink anymore tonight, I'm finished.'

'Oh rubbish, I'll get us some whiskies in before last orders. I'll meet you girls outside for a smoke, yeah?'

'Okay.' Nodding, Sasha decided to go to the ladies.

Zoe stood frozen, straining her ears to listen for sounds. Someone had come in after her, she was sure of it. But they hadn't used the other loo, they'd just walked up and down outside the cubicles. And now they were standing outside her door, she could hear their breathing. Sounds of talking and laughter swelled in for a moment as the door to the bar opened and swung closed, then all was quiet.

The outer door opened again and Sasha called out, 'Zo? Are you still in here? I'm desperate for a pee.'

Zoe's shoulders relaxed, and she opened the cubicle door. 'Right here, babe, I'll wait for you.' She washed her hands, realising they were trembling slightly. What was the matter with her?

As Sasha washed her own hands, she glanced in the mirror at her friend. 'You look freaked out again, what's going on, Zo?'

'Nothing, I– Did you see anyone come out of the ladies before you came in?'

'No, I don't think there are any women left in the pub, except for Willow. Why, hun?'

'I'm gonna sound like a drama queen, it's just, I thought someone followed me in and stood outside the cubicle.' Zoe shook her head. 'I'm either going mad or I'm just completely hammered.'

'Come here.' Sasha pulled Zoe into a hug. 'You're not mad, so you must be hammered.' They left the ladies, laughing, and headed outside to join Eric at the table by the river.

Cal and Willow were about to go back inside, and Cal stopped to speak to Sasha, telling Willow to go on ahead. 'I was about to come and look for you, I had a message from Maureen earlier, I've just remembered, saying if we want to meet her and Douglas tomorrow morning, she'll show us where she took those pictures. She said there was something else weird about it that she'd forgotten to mention, didn't say what though. They go out early though, about six o'clock.' Cal grinned at her. 'So what d'you think?'

'What do I think?' Sasha groaned. 'I think six o'clock sounds like hell right now, but I also think that a walk with the adorable Douglas sounds irresistible. What d'you say, guys? Early morning walk, with the cutest little sausage dog, in Blackwater woods?'

'Count me out.' Eric shook his head. 'I'm having a lie-in, it's not normal, going out at that time in the morning, especially on a Saturday.'

'Zo? Join us?' Sasha raised her eyebrows at Zoe, who shook her head.

'I'm with Eric, a lie-in is called for, but you go.' She yawned. 'I have to go to bed.'

'Come on, down your drinks, Jules will be wanting to close up soon, we should all go to bed.' Picking up the empty glasses, Sasha followed Eric and Zoe back into the pub, agreeing to meet Cal early the next morning.

'I really, really, love you.' Sasha pulled Zoe into a hug as she took her boots from her. 'And I'm sorry about your phone, d'you want to use mine to call James?'

'No way, thanks, hun, if he hears how drunk I am he'll ban me from weekends away in the countryside with my best friend. I'll call him tomorrow. Love you, sleep well. I'm going to pass out now.' Closing her door, Zoe pulled her clothes off, brushed her teeth as her head nodded, and fell into bed.

Sasha and Eric were asleep within minutes, Sasha's last conscious thought being whether she'd actually wake up in time for her early morning walk.

Not sure how long she'd lain there, Zoe suddenly stiffened, feeling wide awake, as her eyes followed the shadow moving back and forth in the dim light shining beneath her door. In the silence of the night, the gentle creak of the floorboard sounded deafening. Had she locked her door? She must have; doubt suffused her; silently stepping from her bed, she tip-toed to the door, pausing to listen, her hand poised to check if the key was turned properly.

Someone was standing the other side of her door, she just knew it. Her hand reached for the key as the door knob slowly turned, and she twisted the key savagely, relieved to find that it had been locked. Holding her breath, she watched as the shadow paused, before moving away.

She got back into bed, forcing herself to lie down and be calm. She was being ridiculous, here she was, away on a country weekend break in a village pub, and all she could do was freak herself out. Maybe it was because of her sessions with Dr Taylor, she pondered, as her eyes began to feel heavy, all that recalling of buried memories from her ordeal. Soap. Suddenly she was smelling the strong smell of soap, a particular kind, the type her grandparents had used, coal tar, that was it. A flashback of herself lying on a bed, unable to see anything, was gone as quickly as it had come, and she jumped up, running into the bathroom and lifting the seat of the toilet as she gagged.

Damp with sweat, Zoe poured herself a glass of water, drinking it down in one go, as she stared at her crazed, moon-lit reflection in the mirror. She picked up the small soap from the soap dish on the basin, sniffing its delicate scent of jasmine, before replacing it. Why in hell had the smell of coal tar pervaded her senses just now? And why had she twice felt like throwing up tonight? Miserably she crawled back into bad, curling up under the covers. She was falling apart, maybe she'd contact Dr Taylor when she got home and ask if she could have some extra sessions. She wanted to move on with her life but couldn't, not until she'd banished the demons of Miles Bleak once and for all.

~

Yawning, what seemed like only five minutes after going to bed, Sasha forced herself to step into the shower and, feeling refreshed, if not fully awake, pulled on some clothes, dropped a kiss on Eric's forehead, and turned the key in the door. Except it didn't turn. Well that had been clever of them, leaving their room unlocked all night, she thought, before reminding herself that they were in Parva Crossing, in The Spotted Dog, not in some dodgy inner city hostel. She laid the key on the bedside table, for Eric to find.

'How's the hangover?' Cal's eyes twinkled as she appeared. 'I wasn't actually sure you'd wake up, come on, we'll pick up coffees on the way.

As they drove to Blackwater woods, sipping their coffee, Cal glanced at Sasha. 'I'm pleased you're happy, Sash, it was good to see you enjoying yourself last night.'

Leaning her head back against the headrest, she smiled. 'Thanks, Cal, I'm pleased for you and Willow, too.' Surprised, she realised that she actually meant it.

'How did you sleep after your crazy evening?' Grinning, Cal pulled into the lane that led to the parking area for the footpaths through the woods.

'I think passed out might better describe it, although I had some totally weird dreams, one time I was wide awake and looking at a figure standing at the side of the bed as if it was staring at us.' She laughed. 'Except I was asleep, of course. Tonight will definitely be a more sober affair and I doubt I'll get any objections from Eric or Zoe. Oh, there's Maureen and Douglas!' Her face broke into a grin at the sight of the little dog wiggling his bottom ecstatically as his tail whizzed back and forth in a frenzy of excitement.

Once Douglas had licked Sasha's face to his satisfaction, he leaned into her body as she held him, whimpered happily, and looked up at her with eyes that melted her heart. She dropped soft kisses on his velvety forehead, before placing him back on the ground, and turned to Maureen to hug her. 'I've never been so jealous of another woman in my life.' Sasha laughed. 'And I'm so glad I hauled myself out of bed to join you, it's such a beautiful day.' Her face darkened momentarily, as she thought of Monty. About to speak, she hesitated, not wanting to spoil their walk, perhaps she'd tell Maureen afterwards.

They set off, laughing at Douglas's antics as he ran on ahead, snuffling in bushes and letting out the odd, excited, yap, running back to Maureen every minute or so to reassure himself of her presence, before charging off again, panting in happiness.

'Cal said there'd been something odd that you'd forgotten to mention, Maureen, about the doll you found?' They'd been walking for about fifteen minutes and Sasha was beginning to feel uncomfortably warm. She pulled off her long-sleeved tee-shirt, tying it around her waist, thankful that she had a vest top on underneath.

'Yes, it may be nothing, but the smell was so strong, I–' she stopped, anxiously calling Douglas as he slowly reversed from behind some shrubbery, emitting low growls and baring his teeth. Swooping down, Maureen picked the little dachshund up, holding him firmly in her arms. 'It's through there.' She nodded across the bushes.

The smell hit Sasha as they pushed through the bushes, stopping in the small clearing in front of the tree to which Maureen and Douglas had found the dismembered doll tied. 'That's my perfume.' She looked at Cal, a horrified expression on her face. Crouching down, she sniffed the air, nodding.

'Maureen?' She remained in her crouched position. 'How many dolls did you find here yesterday morning?'

'How many?' Maureen was confused. 'Only one, at least, I think it was one, I didn't count its arms and legs, they were torn off and thrown on the ground.' She stepped forward to stare at the scene she'd taken a picture of the morning before, only to gasp in surprise. 'That wasn't here yesterday,' she whispered, backing away slightly.

'He's been back,' Sasha murmured her thoughts as she stood back up, taking out her phone to take photographs.

'He?' Cal's voice was sharp. 'Why he, why not they, as in kids? You don't seem surprised by this, Sash?'

'It's got to be a copycat,' Sasha was still murmuring to herself, 'it's the only explanation, someone who knew what he'd done as a child. But why take my perfume and pour it on the dolls? And who? Who got into my room and took it?'

The three of them stood in silence for a moment, staring at the two dolls tied to the tree, the first, familiar from Maureen's photos, the second, a torso only, the smiling face painted on the detached, blond-haired head, seeming to mock them from its position, spiked onto a nearby branch. The four limbs were lined up neatly together, nearby, and, as with the first doll, a red substance had been painted onto the doll to portray blood.

'Is it some kind of satanism?' Maureen peered in disgust at the horrific sight, as Cal called out.

'Here's an empty perfume bottle. Yours, Sash?'

'Almost certainly.' Sasha leaned down, removing her top tied around her waist and using it to carefully pick up the bottle, which she wrapped securely inside the top. 'We should get the police to work this scene, but I don't know if they can spare the manpower right now.'

'Maureen, I should tell you some sad news from Meadowvale, you'll hear about it soon enough anyway. I'm afraid there's been a murder of another resident, it happened the night before last, his name was Monty Mallowan.'

'Oh no, that's terrible. Is it related to Dorothy Newton's death?' Maureen was upset, the grief from her husband's unfortunate death, as well as that of her friend, and a young girl – all related to Dorothy's meddling and the woman's husband's cruel manipulation – painfully resurfacing.

'I can't say, not yet.' Sasha shook her head. 'I hope to find out more today. This,' she said, waving her arms at the gruesome sight in the clearing, 'can't be related, it seems to be a re-creation of the acts carried out by a disturbed young boy many years ago, the same boy who grew up to abduct my best friend, and eventually me, late last year.' At Maureen's shocked face, she hurriedly offered reassurance. 'He's safely behind bars, it's got to be a sick copycat, but it does beg the question: why now, why here, and, of course, who?'

'But how did anyone know the details? Add to this the incident with your car when someone trying to run you off the road, not to mention the vandalism with the bloody offal, and we've got a whole lot of nasty stuff going on, Sash, and you seem to be right at the middle of it all. Someone's out to get you.' Cal's face was unhappy.

'Could it be to try and scare you off from investigating Dorothy's death?' Maureen held onto a now-struggling Douglas.

'I don't know, I can't connect the dots, maybe they're just not connectable.' She reached out and stroked Douglas. 'Come on, let's walk back and let Douglas back down, he's going crazy, poor little fellow.'

~

Constable Graham Barnes pulled his chair up to his desk, yawning loudly, as he took a gulp of coffee. Being new parents was wonderful, but the sleepless nights were a killer, he thought ruefully. Scanning the boss's instructions, he picked up the phone and began calling the list of people with the name Charles Priestley, wondering why the name rang a vague bell.

~

Night terrors, decided Zoe, as she stretched out luxuriously in her bed, that's all it had been. The sunlight shining in the window worked its magic, and she emerged from the shower a little while later feeling happy and looking forward to the day. Wondering if Sasha was back from her early morning walk, Zoe took the stairs to the top floor and knocked on her door.

A pallid-faced Eric opened the door, his hair flattened to one side from the pillow. 'I thought you were Sasha, where is she?' he asked grouchily.

'She went for a walk with her friend and her dog, don't you remember?' Zoe wrinkled her nose at the stale smell emanating from the room.

'Nope.' Eric shook his head. 'Which friend?'

Great, thought Zoe, now she was going to have to deal with his insecurities. 'A woman called Maureen, Cal invited us all last night, but we both declined.'

'So, she's with him?' Eric ran his hands through his hair, making it stick up ridiculously.

'No, she's not with him, she's with them.' Zoe sighed, 'Eric, open the window and take a shower. Come on, I could do with some breakfast, how does a full English sound?'

'It sounds perfect.' His grin transformed his sulky face. 'Give me ten minutes and I'll meet you down there.' As Zoe smiled and turned to go, he called out, 'Zo? Sorry, I can be a grumpy old bastard sometimes.'

'Don't I know it,' Zoe replied, laughing. She descended the stairs a few minutes later, the aroma of eggs and bacon reaching her nose as she opened the door to the breakfast room.

Sasha and Cal arrived back at the same time as Eric appeared and, Cal having declined to join them, Sasha sat down and added her breakfast order to the other two. While they waited, they nursed cups of tea, and Sasha grinned at their hungover faces.

'You should have come walking with us, although it was more an investigation than a walk, as it turned out. Zo, how did you sleep?'

Not wanting to burden her friend with her paranoia and spoil the mood, Zoe informed her that she'd slept like a log, enquiring what they were going to do for the day.

Groaning inwardly, Sasha thought quickly. Eric and Zoe had been so pleased with themselves for surprising her, how could she disappoint them by telling them she had to go to Meadowvale to continue her initial investigation, as well as to find out more about Monty's death? But time was running and she'd arranged to meet Jane Weaver – maybe she could buy herself a couple of hours. 'I just have to pop through to Meadowvale for an hour or two, no longer, I promise, so I thought I'd send you two off into the village this morning, you can be tourists for a couple of hours, it's so pretty with the river running through the middle of it, and then I've got an idea about this afternoon, but I need to check with Tess. All good so far?'

Eric shrugged. 'As long as there'll be a few pints involved somewhere, I'm a happy man.'

'Ugh.' Zoe shuddered. 'I can't believe you're thinking about drinking this early in the day, especially after last night. It's fine, Sash, I'll keep an eye on him for you while you go and do what you have to do.'

'Nothing a good breakfast can't fix.' Eric's eyes lit up as his plate was placed in front of him, and he liberally applied salt and pepper, before tucking in, groaning in appreciation. The two women rolled their eyes at each other before applying themselves to their own plates.

'Why are you shutting me out?' Willow's voice was upset as she appeared beside Sasha. 'I don't see why I couldn't come with you this morning. And why do the police want to interview me? Am I a suspect? In a murder?' Her voice became increasingly shrill. 'I already told you that I was with my friend. Why can't you just tell them that?'

'Excuse me.' Sasha left the table, steering Willow out of the breakfast room. 'Listen, no one's shutting you out, and as to the police wanting to interview you, I already told you, they'll be speaking to everyone.' She stopped as Cal appeared, looking apologetic. 'You just need to tell them the truth, the sooner they can find out who killed Monty, the sooner everything can return to normal.'

She watched Willow walk away with Cal, wondering why the woman was so concerned about being interviewed. Although it was strange that Willow had been on the scene just after she'd been run off the road, and Willow did drive a white car, and she'd been out with her friend, allegedly, while Sasha's car was vandalised which, she realised another thing, was when Meadowvale had had the break-in, as well as possibly when Monty had been killed...

Slipping her phone from her pocket, she called her sister. 'Tess? Hi, babe, listen, what are you guys up to this afternoon? I've got a favour to ask, and I did tell Chants that I'd see her over the weekend.'

Pleased, Sasha returned to Eric and Zoe. 'We're going to Tessa's this afternoon for a barbeque. I thought you could pick up some goodies from the village, Dave will sort the meat and the booze. How does that sound?'

With plans made to the best of her ability, Sasha finally left for Meadowvale, not a little anxious about her slow progress with her interviews.

SASHA INTERVIEWS DAVINIA AND AGATHA LOVEWELL

Success. He'd found him, there was no way that two boys called Charles Priestley had both been fostered at Golden Oaks. Pleased, he looked up as D.I. Wendover walked through the office. 'Morning, Ma'am, I've just found your man.'

'Steph Wendover smiled tightly. 'That's great, constable, my office, please.'

She took the envelope from the case file box and waved it at him. 'Is this familiar to you at all, Graham?'

Taking the envelope, Graham turned it over, recognising the incorrect name and address. He slipped the letter out, bending to pick up the photo which fell to the floor. 'Yes, Ma'am, it came after you'd gone on leave, when the offices were being redecorated.' Sensing that he may have made a major error, he attempted to justify his actions. 'I took a chance and opened it, in case it wasn't for you, but it related to the Blake Selim case, which I knew was closed, and I popped it into the box before I took it down to storage. It didn't contain any pertinent information, as far as I could judge, seeing as the man himself had already been tried and imprisoned. Did I do wrong, Ma'am?'

Steph Wendover nodded, her expression grim. He was right in one way, the case had been closed, the perpetrator locked away and if it hadn't been for her meeting with Dr Taylor, she probably would have done the same thing. Or would she? Mightn't she have wanted to at least check out Charles Priestley, after Irene Weatherall's disclosures of his involvement with some of the disturbing childhood acts carried out by Blake?

She shook her head. 'Yes, no, I'm not sure, something's come to light.' She motioned to him to sit. 'What did you find out about Charles Priestley?'

'Well, I spoke to his wife, Megan, they've got two young children, all sounds perfectly normal. He's off at a conference somewhere, so I couldn't actually speak to him, although she did give me his mobile number but it's switched off. Oh, and he was definitely fostered at Golden Oaks. She was adamant that he didn't know anyone by the name of Miles Bleak, or Blake Selim, although she said she did recall the case last year, of a woman being abducted.'

'Hmm, okay, I want you to make one more call for me, thanks, Graham.'

Relieved not to have been hauled over the coals, Graham Barnes hurried back to his desk and placed the call to Wakefield Prison.

~

'Well, your funny game with the blood and guts didn't exactly make front page news, did it, little bruv?'

Glen Cutter crossed his arms as he leaned against the kitchen counter. 'Nah, that was just another little taster for the cow, felt good though.' He cackled. 'I've got something else up my sleeve, what's that word, you know, when it happens like it's supposed to, or something?'

'You what?' Sharon's eyes were confused.

'When someone gets what they deserve, that's it. What's that word?'

'Oh, you mean karma. Yeah, I heard that somewhere. How you gonna do that then? How you gonna give her karma?'

'I'm not gonna give her karma, sis, karma's gonna get her, that's how it works.'

'Yeah, whatever.' Sharon was getting bored. 'What's your great plan then? You gonna tell me or not?'

~

She didn't need to hear anything further. The fact that Charles Priestley had visited Blake Selim in prison was all she needed for her worst fears to be confirmed. Blake, known to them at the time as Miles Bleak, had had a protégé from an early age, and not only that, the adoring fair-haired boy, who had so clearly hero-worshipped Miles, had grown up to become an accomplice, almost definitely, in Zoe Pullman's abduction. They needed to find him and speak to him, but it was the weekend so there was no chance of speaking to his employer, and his wife didn't seem to know where his conference was. Pondering her predicament, Steph Wendover decided to let the situation simmer on the back burner while she attended to some other matters.

~

'Any progress?' Sasha looked from D.I. Nick Crossley to Sergeant Jane Weaver, who both shook their heads.

'All very odd.' Nick frowned. 'There were remnants of tissue found in the wound to Monty's head, as if someone had wiped over it. 'I can't think of any reason other than that they wished to remove their fingerprints, but why touch him there? After killing him? Doesn't make any sense.'

The scene had been cleaned up, and the three of them stood in the conservatory, looking around them.

'Taken from that tissue box?' Sasha inclined her head towards the box of tissues sitting on a server. 'Seems like a bit of an afterthought. And the weapon was a marble vase, you say? Obviously no fingerprints on it? Was that also wiped with tissues?'

'No, we think someone was wearing gloves,' Jane chimed in.

'So they wore gloves to kill him, then touched him with bare hands afterwards? There's a contradiction there.' Sasha pondered for a moment. 'Was anything taken from Monty? He had a wallet in his jacket pocket, he took it out to show me a photograph earlier in the day.'

Jane frowned. 'No wallet was found on him, nor in his room, that's odd.'

'A lot of things seem odd about just about everything lately. What about the break-in? No signs of forced entry to Meadowvale anywhere at all? If not, then unless they had a key, someone came in through the conservatory, is that right? Could they have entered the grounds through the side gate? So, did Monty let them in? Did he know his killer? What was taken?' She forced herself to stop with all the questions. 'Sorry, I'm babbling like a mad woman.'

'No forced entry, and we did find the side gate unlocked, so we're thinking along the same lines at the moment, and that's another odd thing, it doesn't seem like anything was taken. But someone wanted to get into the filing cabinet in Mrs Goodwin's office, they forced it open and the files had clearly been rifled through. I dunno, murders, break-ins, and your car was vandalised, I understand? Takes me back to the good old days of last year when we had old George Newton, the most unlikely serial killer, terrorising our village. Phew, that was a real nightmare, what did we call it? Death Cottage? Thought I'd seen it all when we found both his parents murdered and kept in the cottage.' Nick shook his head in disbelief.

'And it all went back to Dorothy Newton...' Sasha stared into space as her mind tried to fathom everything. 'And this all started with Dorothy Newton's murder. Look, if someone broke in undetected somehow, or was let in, and killed Monty, what did they want? His wallet? Makes no sense. Isn't it more likely that it's connected to Dorothy? That Monty maybe saw something, or worked something out, and her killer had to silence him? If so, I'd like to continue with my interviews with the residents if they're up to it, is that okay?'

'Yes, of course, as long as they're fine with it, and Mrs Goodwin.'

Sasha, having received the go ahead from Mrs Goodwin, took a seat in the lounge, where the residents were gathered. The worried faces of relatives looked up at her, and she introduced herself, recognizing the man with Lillian as the man she'd seen walking with a stick and getting into his ancient car.

'You must be Lillian's son – Mervyn, isn't it?' He nodded without smiling, as Lillian stared at Sasha, her eyes clear.

'Someone dropped their fork at dinner after Monty died.' She nodded her head, knowingly. 'Because of what he said. It's a clue. Did I tell you I'm going to write a murder mystery?' Her eyes clouded over again as a snort sounded from somewhere in the lounge.

Elspeth and Albert were seated with a man who put his hand out, shaking Sasha's. 'I'm Raymond, Albert's son, nothing's more important than being here to support Dad and Elspeth today.'

'Poor Miriam's at work this morning, she's terribly worried about me, but she can't let Dr Singh down.' Elspeth fiddled with her rings as Albert patted her knee, whilst at the same time giving his son a slight nod.

'I'm Elizabeth's daughter, Judith.' The smartly dressed woman sitting with Elizabeth inclined her head towards Sasha with a tight smile that didn't reach her brown eyes, her distinctive hook-like nose reinforcing her imperious manner. 'I'm not happy about all this, my husband is David Bertram the member of parliament, you know, it really won't do, this type of scandal, not at all. Mother's so upset, aren't you, Mummy? And poor Gemma, that's my daughter, she's getting married soon. The last thing we need is the newspapers getting hold of this and making a big fuss, it could ruin everything.'

Trying unsuccessfully to control her immediate dislike for the woman's attitude, Sasha forced herself to smile. 'Yes, well, I'm sure that Monty would have preferred for it not to happen at all.'

'Oh, really, it's too much, I must go to my room.' Elizabeth reached out, clutching her daughter's hand, in a surprising display of emotion.

Davinia and Agatha Lovewell sat together, and Sasha felt a pang of sadness for them, as she recalled that they had no family other than each other.

'This is my nephew, Richard, and his wife, Moira,' Howard piped up, introducing Sasha as their lady detective. 'She's investigating Dorothy's murder, but I suppose we must add Monty's to the list now.'

Sasha shook their hands, surprised at the strength of the rather manly-looking Moira's handshake compared to the limpness of her husband's.

She made her decision, moving to the chair beside the Lovewell sisters. 'I know it's been a terrible time, but I wondered if either of you felt up to having a chat with me? Or you could do it together, if you'd prefer?' It wasn't ideal, but she realised that she had to work with what she had, and what she had right now was a group of traumatised elderly people, and the two sisters clearly depended on each other heavily. 'It's to talk about Dorothy and what happened the day of her death, we won't be talking about Monty,' she said gently.

Looking at each other and nodding, the sisters agreed.

'I'll tell you what, you make your way to the library and I'll go and see if I can rustle us up a pot of tea from the kitchen. How does that sound?'

'And perhaps some biscuits?' Agatha looked at Sasha hopefully.

'Yes, of course, I quite fancy one myself.' Sasha smiled, standing and heading to the kitchen as she heard Agatha complain to her sister.

'There's no need to nudge me like that, Davinia, Sasha wanted a biscuit too.'

'Kirsty, you must be exhausted, weren't you in all day yesterday?'

Kirsty turned to Sasha, mid-yawn, and nodded. 'I was, I am, but it's all hands on deck to be honest, so many comings and goings what with the police in and out and the relatives all visiting. Now, how can I help you, dear?'

'I don't want to be a bother, but would you mind if I made a pot of tea to take to the library? I'm meeting with Davinia and Agatha, for a chat, oh, and if there are any biscuits...'

Kirsty chuckled. 'No problem, I know how Agatha enjoys her biscuits, here, let me pop the kettle on while you tell me what you've found out about our break-in.' She filled the kettle, switching it on, as she continued speaking. 'I should have known the day was going to turn out bad the minute Tanya rushed back to tell me about Mrs Goodwin's office, and that wasn't the first thing we found amiss, and then to find poor Monty sitting there in the conservatory like that, well, I don't think any of us will ever be the same again. Terrible shock for poor Howard, and him such a joker usually. But why did they have to kill Monty? Lord knows why anyone was poking around in my kitchen or the office, but the old chap was clearly just minding his business out in the conservatory. Why didn't they leave him well alone? Makes no sense.' She shook her head sadly, warming the pot and making the tea.

Pressing rewind on Kirsty's chatter, Sasha paused it at the part about her kitchen. 'Kirsty, what's all this about someone in your kitchen? I'm not sure that I heard about that?'

'Yes, and not for the first time, I take a pride in everything being in its place, that's how I work, everything runs like clockwork, you ask anyone. I can lay my hands on anything with my eyes closed, so to find my rag bag hanging off its hook with half its contents on the floor, well, it put me in a bad frame of mind I don't mind telling you. It was the door ajar that alerted me, that's not right, I thought.'

'Someone rifled through your rag bag, you say? A bag of old cloths for cleaning?'

'That's it, old cloths, torn pillowcases, stained napkins, anything not fit for purpose anymore goes in my rag bag, even sheets, course I cut the larger things up into usable squares. A little thriftiness goes a long way, you know.'

'And you think this happened the night of the break-in and Monty's murder?'

'I know it, there's not a staff member would dare touch my cleaning cupboard or leave anything out of place, and Mary was on that night – she knows what a stickler I am.'

'And you found the door ajar? Was that the kitchen door? To the outside?'

'No, dear, I'm talking about my kitchen cupboard.'

'Oh, right, and you say this has happened before? Can you remember when?' Was she actually hoping to go anywhere with this? Still, sometimes it was the small, unexplained incidents that shed light on the bigger things. Every little anomaly was worth paying attention to, experience had taught her that.

Kirsty frowned as she cast her mind back. 'Now, it was quite a while ago, a good few weeks back, round about the time of Dorothy's death.' She grinned at Sasha. 'I know what you're thinking, woman's got a crazy obsession with her cleaning cloths. But it's odd, isn't it, that someone's been at my rag bag twice?'

'I don't think you've got a crazy obsession at all, Kirsty, I think it's strange too. I've got no idea what it means, but still...' An idea occurred to her. 'D'you think you could do something for me? When you get the chance, of course, I know you're busy.'

'Sorry for the delay, ladies.' Sasha placed the tea tray on the library table a couple of minutes later as Agatha exclaimed.

'Oh goody, malted milks, my favourite.'

'Shall I start?' Davinia glanced reprovingly at her sister as Agatha brushed biscuit crumbs from her ample bosom. At Sasha's nod, she began.

'It was a miserable day, I remember it clearly as I wasn't feeling quite myself. I didn't even put my nose outside all day.'

Agatha interjected, 'It was very dull, but the sun did come out eventually and a few of us took walks in the garden.'

Davinia continued, 'I read my book which I'd got from the library after breakfast, which was tea and toast – The Body in the Library – Agatha Christie of course – the book, that is, I'd read it as a young girl and found it very enjoyable – although it was an unfortunate choice under the circumstances, not that Dorothy was found in the library.'

'Murder on the Orient Express was my favourite growing up,' Agatha enthused, 'do you remember how clever we thought it was the way they each–'

'Quiet, Agatha, we're not here to reminisce, we should keep to the day in question and not waste Sasha's time. And do wipe your mouth.'

'Sorry.' Hurt at her sister's rebuke, Agatha picked up another biscuit, taking a large bite and spraying crumbs as she spoke again.

'Howie's nephew was visiting, he told me how much he was looking forward to it when we breakfasted together.' She glanced triumphantly at her sister. 'I had a banana, porridge – such a treat – and some toast. Howie teased me about my appetite, but it's the weather, those dull days always make me hungry. Anyway, Howie and I took a walk around the garden together, so did Dorothy, Elizabeth and her daughter, and I saw Elspeth and Albert out in the garden but I think they were looking for something, she's always losing things. And then Richard brought delicious shortbread which we all had with coffee.' Agatha sat back, taking a sip of her tea.

'Not to speak ill of the dead, but Dorothy was being her usual wretched self at coffee, writing her little secrets in her notebook as well.' Davinia sipped her tea as her sister gasped.

'What a thing to say, Davinia. Well, talking of coffee, I definitely saw Mervyn with his mother – poor Lillian – he's always got papers for her to sign, she doesn't know what she's doing half the time. Was that the day Tanya was huddled with them? I'm sure Lillian's her favourite, she often sits and has little chats with her – very kind. She was a writer, you know. And yes, Dorothy was there at coffee for a while, fiddling in her little book, but then she went off to her room and came back without it a few minutes later, and I suppose Davinia's right, she was making lots of her little comments. She had imaginary friends, all very sad. I think she upset you, didn't she, Davinia?

When she came back from her room? Something about the bathwater? Whatever did she mean? You don't even use the bath, do you dear.' Agatha looked proprietorially at her sister. 'Poor dear can't manage the bath these days, what with her poorly hip and knees, but we have such marvellous walk-in showers here, don't we?' She looked back at Davinia. 'Do you remember when you had to go away? Mother and Father had a bath fitted and I was so excited for you to see it. No more tin baths in the kitchen. We felt like royalty, didn't we?'

'Really, Agatha, you do go on.' Davinia gave a dry laugh. 'Sasha's busy and we should really hurry up and finish, not talk about bathrooms and nonsense.'

'I was only remembering.' Agatha looked upset. 'You know how my mind runs away. Oh, you went off to your room not long after that, d'you remember? Of course, Dorothy was always upsetting someone. I think we were all pleased that she nodded off then, slept like a baby right until lunchtime.'

'Goodness, your memory, Agatha, I don't know where you come up with these things, I really don't. I went to have a rest in my room after coffee, that's all, and I must have dozed off because I missed lunch completely.'

'Lunch was quite a nice quiche, it's a shame you missed out.' Agatha patted her sister's hand. 'Dorothy definitely had lunch, I can remember her picking bits out of the quiche and putting them on the side of her plate. And then we did beading with Willow, such a sweet girl, she'd only been here a few days, or perhaps a week. She helped me and Lillian thread some of the difficult beads, she's so attentive, so interested in us old crocks, full of questions about when I was born, where I lived, that kind of thing. She wanted to know all about you as well, Davinia. It's so nice when the younger generations take an interest in us oldies and she said it was so sad that neither of us married or had children, but I said we have each other.' Agatha beamed.

Davinia gave a tight smile. 'It doesn't do to gossip though, I've told you that before, sister dear. I came through to the lounge to have a cup of tea, I was feeling a little better.'

'Yes, but that was after the beading. Elizabeth had cleared off, I remember because she was quite rude, finished her beads in about five minutes flat and off she went. Then the delicious lemon drizzle cake came through, gone in a flash, it was a good job I left a piece in Davinia's room for her – you did find it, didn't you, darling? And after that we all drank our tea.' Nodding happily, Agatha sat back.

'Yes, thank you, dear, I'm sure I was feeling quite hungry from missing lunch, having been in my room the whole day. I came through, and we were all there drinking tea, every one of us, no visitors though, not sure that I saw any all day, not that I was around much, oh well, of course, Elspeth's daughter must have visited because she was sporting a new cardigan, spinning around like a little girl, showing it off, so I suppose they'd been shopping.'

'Oh, and I saw Richard's wife in the garden.' Agatha wiped the crumbs from her mouth as her sister tutted. 'At least I think I did, it was in the afternoon, maybe she'd come to fetch Richard. That's odd, no, perhaps it was in the morning, yes, it must have been, unless she came back after she changed out of her pretty dress, I really don't know why women must wear those awful trousers... yes, she must have because we were busy with our beading and I saw her and Tanya out of the window–' Her eyes widened. 'But you're wrong, Davinia, and so am I, we weren't all there drinking tea, not the whole time, I remember now, Elspeth had saved a chair for Albert, she was a little flushed, and Tanya rushed in from outside to collect plates, and you'd only just come through when Monty moaned at–'

Sasha's head had been swivelling back and forth between the two sisters as they'd taken turns at recounting the day's events.

'That's when Monty came in asking about Dorothy.' Davinia's voice was firm. 'And you're just going to confuse Sasha with all your ramblings, dear, you're not remembering things clearly.'

Agatha clarified, 'He came in from the conservatory, he must have been napping out there, and he was complaining because–'

Davinia interjected, placing a hand on Agatha's arm, 'He asked if any of us had seen Dorothy, and the dreadful thing was that none of us seemed able to recall when we'd last seen her, I remember clearly because I asked Elizabeth – she'd been beside you the whole time, don't you remember? And Albert and Elspeth were first in for tea, so we were all there. Agatha, do wipe those crumbs off, you look untidy, my dear.'

'Yes, but she didn't– but what about the cake?'

'You and food, Agatha, it's all you think about, we're here about Dorothy, not to discuss cake. I really think you've remembered everything that you can.'

About to thank them both for their time and for the many important details they'd remembered, Sasha closed her mouth as Davinia spoke again.

'I do remember hearing noises from her room while I was resting, it must have been before lunch. Her room is next to mine. It was definitely a good while after morning coffee, and then, of course, they found her in the pond, so maybe it happened at lunchtime – I think it was actually the young boy, Spencer, who found her. We were all terribly shocked and upset. Poor Kirsty had made dinner, but no one had much of an appetite, obviously. I can't even remember what it was.'

Instinctively, Sasha's eyes turned to Agatha, as did Davinia's.

'Dinner was homemade chicken pie, Kirsty made it, and it was delicious, but the mashed potato was cold – not that any of us complained – it was hardly surprising. Don't you remember? You said it was the first thing you'd eaten since breakfast and you were quite starving.' Agatha smiled and nodded, pleased to have recalled the final event of the day.

Remembering something she'd been meaning to ask, Sasha directed her enquiry to Agatha. 'I heard that you had a dress go missing? Can you remember when that was?'

Screwing her eyes up in an attempt to pinpoint the day, Agatha slowly shook her head. 'Not the actual day, sorry, I just suddenly realised that it was missing, it wasn't in my wardrobe, and I'd known it was there because I'd almost worn it on the Sunday, it was such a nice, bright, colourful design, very cheery, you know? And I thought I'd dress up for Sunday lunch, but then I changed my mind and wore something else. I think it was the day after Dorothy's death that I noticed it missing, I wasn't going to wear it, of course, it was much too bright. I suppose it was stolen early in the week. Can you believe it? Someone stole my dress. Why would they do that?'

'Any ideas about all the other items that have gone missing?' Sasha noticed Davinia's slightly impatient glance and shake of her head towards her sister. She should probably wrap things up, she decided.

'Someone took Monty's lighter, I believe, then Elspeth claims to have had what sounds like the crown jewels taken, and money has gone missing, of course, but those are two entirely different things, then there was my photograph.' Davinia looked at Sasha, shaking her head. 'Why take an old photo of me as a young girl?'

'It's in such a pretty little frame.' Agatha beamed. 'I can't wait to get our pictures from that charming photographer, do we know when he's coming back? Such a lovely surprise to have a professional arrive on our doorstep and start taking photographs of us. Although why a young man would ever want to spend time with an old bunch of geriatrics, I'll never know.'

And that, thought Sasha, after she'd thanked the sisters and seen them off back to the lounge, pretty much summed up the mystery about Charles Priestley. Why did a young bloke want to hang out at an old people's home? Unless there was something else there that was the attraction, or someone else...

COAL TAR SOAP

About to make her escape from Meadowvale, she was accosted by Jane, with a pleased-looking Constable Canfield.

'Sasha, my officer here has found something interesting. Come out to the garden, he was just about to show me.'

Intrigued, Sasha accompanied the two police officers to the furthermost part of the gardens, where the two women were prevented from proceeding, as Ross held out his hands.

'Careful, now.' Ross pointed to the ground beneath a dirty window in a small outbuilding. 'Looks like someone's been loitering here and having a look through the window. See the glass? It's been wiped by someone so they can see through it to the inside, and those boxes don't half look untidy in there on the shelf, can you see which ones I mean? All the others are all lined up neatly, it's just those three, like someone was rooting around in a bit of a hurry or something. Might have nothing to do with the murder, can't say, but it's odd, don't you think, Sarge?'

'It's certainly odd, and anything odd where a murder has been committed is worth investigating. Good work, Constable.' Jane looked around her as Ross beamed with pleasure. 'Fetch some tape and cordon off the area and we'll have a look inside. Oh, and find the gardener, I'm sure I saw him earlier.'

Jane turned to Sasha. 'It might be nothing, but we don't have a lot to go on at all at the moment. A second murder at Meadowvale and no idea who did it.' She handed Sasha a latex glove. 'Pop this on.'

Taking care where they stepped, the two women entered the small storeroom. 'Ross was right about the orderliness of everything.' Sasha glanced around. 'All the boxes are labelled as well.'

'Crafting supplies, fabric, paper,' Jane read out the labels from the disturbed storage boxes.

'Fabric.' Sasha mulled over the word for a moment, looking at the coloured and patterned pieces of material, as Jane carefully opened the lid.

'What are you thinking?'

'I'm thinking,' Sasha said slowly, 'that it's a strange coincidence that this box of fabric has been disturbed, and that Kirsty had someone rifle through her rag bag in her kitchen cleaning cupboard.'

Jane nodded as she deftly searched through the piles of fabric. 'It's just fabric, oh well, we'll see whether forensics can get a decent footprint.' Lifting the lids of a few of the other boxes, she shook her head. 'Nothing of interest, old bits and pieces, party decorations, old books in this one – I don't know, maybe it was just a coincidence.'

They left the storeroom at the sound of voices, and Ross presented Colin Hartley, the gardener.

Colin proved to be a quiet type, which, thought Sasha, no doubt served him well, working as the lone gardener at Meadowvale with nobody to talk to all day. Having expressed his disbelief and sadness at Monty's violent exit from the world, he answered Sergeant Weaver's questions quietly and with few words.

Wrapping up her few questions, Jane confirmed, 'So the storeroom's never been locked?'

He shook his head. 'No need, nothing valuable in there. Like I said, just the stuff that the young lady fetches for her activities, most of the other stuff's not been touched for years. There'll be the Christmas decorations, of course, one of the staff takes them in each year then brings them all back out again after the festivities.' His eyes darkened for a moment. 'And I don't take kindly to anyone poking around my greenhouse, neither.'

'Er, could you show us, Colin?'

Not sure how he could tell that anything had been touched, the two women stood inside the ramshackle greenhouse, next to the storeroom, as Colin folded his arms. Sasha voiced what both women were thinking. 'So, what exactly made you think someone had been poking around in here?'

'Window was left open, my seed packets mucked about with, and potting soil dropped on the floor. Seen it before, too.'

'Well, thank you, Colin, you've been most helpful.'

'Jane, I'm just going to try something.' Sasha stepped outside and reached her arm through the window. 'There, that pot of soil.'

Jane transferred the soil into another pot, smiling as a small bag fell out. 'Here it is and I'd say we've found ourselves someone's stash of grass, any ideas?'

'Could be the young lad, Spencer?'

'I'll hold onto it, maybe he's responsible for the disturbance in the storeroom as well, but we'll get the whole area checked to be sure.'

They left the greenhouse, stepping round a large pile of cuttings and garden waste, topped with an enormous, wilted and shrivelled, weedlike plant, with spiky pods, wrinkling their noses at the unpleasant stench of rotting vegetation.

Ross finished taping off the area around the storeroom, including the greenhouse as a last-minute instruction from his sergeant, and joined the women to walk back to the house. 'Kirsty was looking for you, Sasha, I almost forgot. Forensics will come on Monday, Sarge, they've got a bit of a backlog in Rentham.'

'We'll come back on Monday as well, I think, Ross, give everyone here a chance for a little peace and quiet for what's left of the weekend. See you Monday, Sasha?'

'Sure.' Sasha popped quickly to the kitchen, anxious to get back to Eric and Zoe before Eric began to get twitchy with her about leaving them for too long.

'You wanted to see me, Kirsty?'

'What d'you make of this?' Kirsty stepped aside to reveal a roughly cut square of garishly patterned fabric lying on the table.

'Er, bright?' She wondered where Kirsty was going with this.

'You can say that again, and who likes their brightly coloured patterns all over their clothes?'

'Agatha.' Realisation dawned on her and she repeated the name. 'Agatha.' Although she'd seen someone else in a brightly patterned outfit, but who it had been eluded her for now.

Nodding, Kirsty continued, 'I found this near the bottom of the rag bag and I know I never cut up material like this. Just the one piece, mind, but it made me wonder.'

Peering closer, Sasha noticed the dried mud along one edge of the fabric. She turned it over, observing that it was part of the hem. 'Do you have a paper bag by any chance, Kirsty?' Having taken photographs of the piece of material, Sasha carefully placed it inside the paper bag. She'd drop it in at the police station on her way back to the pub. She had one last thing to do. Thanking Kirsty, she went in search of Agatha, finding her in the lounge where the residents now sat alone, their relatives having gone.

'Agatha, I'd appreciate it if we could keep this between us for now, is that okay?' At Agatha's nod, she showed her one of the photos on her phone, watching as the woman's eyes widened in surprised distress.

'That's a piece of my kaftan,' Agatha hissed, 'someone cut it up into pieces.' Her face was upset as she looked at Sasha. 'Who would do that? Where did you find it?'

'You're sure? It's definitely yours? This is the one that you couldn't find?'

Nodding her head agitatedly, Agatha confirmed, 'It's mine. What a horrid thing to do.'

Sasha left her, having elicited a promise from her that she wouldn't say anything to anyone.

She drove back to the pub, her mind going over everything that had come to light in her short visit to Meadowvale that morning. Did everything connect, or were some incidents unrelated? She yearned to finish her interviews with the remaining residents, Elizabeth and Albert, but that would have to wait for Monday. And those interviews were only concerning the day that Dorothy Newton had been murdered. She hadn't even begun to interview the staff or the relatives, then there was Monty's murder, the break-in at Meadowvale, the damaged filing cabinet in the office, the mystery of Agatha's missing kaftan and the discovery of a muddied piece of it in Kirsty's rag bag, the fact that someone had been disturbing the boxes in the storeroom, that someone had been keeping drugs in the gardener's greenhouse, and, she shook her head in frustration, there was her own unpleasant experience of being run off the road, as well as her car's vandalism, and last but not least, there was Charles Priestley.

Pulling into the car park at The Spotted Dog, Sasha pushed it all from her mind. Right now, she wanted to relax and forget all about it.

~

Glen Cutter watched from his car as Sasha stepped out of her vehicle, the car key jammer poised in his hand. Once she'd entered the pub, he walked quickly to her car, pleased to find that it had successfully remained unlocked and, looking around, opened the door, pushing the little packet of white powder deep inside the tissue box in the glovebox. Next, he popped the boot open, lifting the carpet so that he could slip another, larger packet, underneath it. The whole exercise had taken him less than thirty seconds. Now he could bide his time until he chose to make the call.

~

'Uh oh, they've come in a cab, you know what that means don't you?' Dave laughed as he shook Eric's hand, before hugging Sasha and Zoe.

Tessa rushed to kiss her sister, before hugging Zoe and Eric. 'It's so good to see you both again, it's been too long. Come in, Dave will pour us some drinks. Oh my goodness, look at all the food you've brought with you.'

As the group moved to the garden, Tessa pulled Sasha aside, rolling her eyes. 'Chants is upstairs, grounded for the weekend.'

'More problems, sis? What happened? Want me to go and speak to her?'

'You could do, she might be more forthcoming with you. I just can't figure out the change in her, these new friends, staying out late, we never know where she is, and Thursday night she had us worried, not a peep from her, then I get a text and she rolls in late, refusing to tell us anything. She doesn't even seem all that happy. Anyway, long story short, she's grounded this weekend, so we've got a sulky daughter lurking in her room. Maybe you can convince her to join us, might do her good?'

Chantelle hovered on the landing as she listened to her mum talking to Sasha. Great, now Sasha would try to find out where she'd been, and she couldn't tell her. She rushed back into her room and flung herself on the bed as she heard Sasha climbing the stairs.

Knocking on her bedroom door, Sasha called out, 'Chants? Can I come in?' She pushed the door open, peering around it. 'How's my gorgeous niece? Are you coming down, your dad's lighting the barbeque. Eric and Zoe are with me.' She sat down on the bed beside Chantelle, drawing her into a hug.

'Hi, Sash, it's good to see you. Oh, wow, I love your outfit.' Chantelle hugged her aunt back.

'Thanks, would you believe me if I told you it was from Madam Couture?' She grinned at Chantelle's expression. 'Listen, you don't have to tell me anything, but your mum and dad are worried about you. Why don't you come down? And you should invite your friend round, there's so much food, Eric and Zoe went crazy and bought every type of salad imaginable at the deli, and there's bangers, chicken kebabs, burgers, we'll never eat it all. Your friend's name's Lucy isn't it? I met her and her mum up at Meadowvale. She seems nice.'

Chantelle smiled. 'You met Lucy? She is nice, she's a good laugh. She won't want to come round for a family barbeque though, she's way too cool for that. She's going out with Spencer, he works at the home.'

'Hey, what's not cool about a family barbeque?' Sasha nudged Chantelle's arm, laughing. 'You know Spencer? Small world, isn't it? I haven't interviewed him yet, but I know who he is.' She didn't like the fact that there was a connection between her niece and Spencer, if the drugs turned out to be his.

'Why d'you need to interview him? Was your car alright, Sash? D'you know who did it yet?'

'I'm interviewing everyone, I'm sure Spencer doesn't have anything to be concerned about. And my car's fine, don't you worry about things like that. I'm sure it was just stupid kids playing a prank. I probably just got unlucky. Come on, come down and say hi to Eric and Zoe.'

Tessa gave Sasha's arm a squeeze as she watched her daughter laugh at one of Eric's lame jokes. 'How's your investigation at Meadowvale going? I don't suppose you can tell us much.'

Sasha sighed. 'It's all got rather complicated, terribly sad news, I'm afraid. There was a break-in on Thursday night, we're not quite sure what they were after, and we have no way of knowing whether it's related or not, but an elderly resident called Monty was violently killed that night. I only knew him for a short while but he was a kind and gentle man, really lovely.'

'Thursday night?' Chantelle blurted out the words and immediately wished she hadn't, as all eyes turned to her.

Nodding, Sasha eyed her niece. 'Yes, didn't your friend say anything? I would have thought her boyfriend would have told her, seeing as he works there?'

Chantelle shook her head. 'No, Lucy didn't say a word.' She threw a dark look towards her dad. 'I'm grounded so I only saw her at school yesterday, then I've been stuck at home.'

'Thursday night?' Tessa looked surprised. 'The same night your car was vandalised?'

'Yep, not a good night all round.' Sasha watched her niece's face as it whitened. Something was clearly bothering her, but now wasn't the time to ask, not in front of everyone.

'I have to go to the loo.' Chantelle stood up abruptly, rushing inside. Her head was spinning. She pictured Spencer getting back into the car outside Meadowvale, his hand wiping something gooey on Lucy's jeans and face. And there'd been that white car in the parking area outside, as they'd driven off. It could have belonged to whoever broke in, or worse, whoever killed the old man, but if she told Sasha, she'd be dropping Spencer in it. And then it might come out about the grass. And what if Spencer had been the one breaking-in? Had he nicked something? He'd said something about money, hadn't he? And what had he put in the boot? She was already worried that he might have done something to Sasha's car, but now she didn't know what it was all about. There was no way he'd killed someone though. Despairingly, she stood in the bathroom. She couldn't say anything, it was as simple as that, Lucy was her friend, her only friend, she couldn't lose her.

'I remember what it was like at that age,' Zoe said into the silence after Chantelle rushed off, 'full of angst.'

'You've got that right.' Dave groaned, reaching across to squeeze Tessa's knee. 'We try not to go too hard on her after everything that happened last year, but it all feels pretty complicated at times. Right, time for me to start cooking, I reckon.'

Basking in the praise for his skills at barbequed food, a good while later, Dave topped up glasses as Tessa and Sasha collected plates. Zoe brought through the remains of the salads to the kitchen and the three women chatted, laughing at the raucous sounds from Eric as he regaled Dave with one of his stories. Tessa's eyes narrowed as her daughter wandered through, eyes glued to her phone screen, fingers tapping furiously.

'Chantelle, enough with the phone now, there's such a thing as real conversation, you know.' She reached over and grabbed the phone out of Chantelle's hands, putting it down on the counter. 'You can have it back when our guests have gone, okay?'

'Sure, whatever.' Chantelle stomped off to the lounge, where they heard the sound of the television being switched on.

Sasha took her own phone from her pocket to check the time, laying it down on the counter as she cling-wrapped salads. 'We should go soon, let you have a bit of family time.'

'You are family, idiot, and so are you, Zoe, and Eric. Dave's just poured more drinks, come on, let's join the men outside for a last drink, I'll sort the rest of this lot out later.' Turning back, she picked up the phones. 'I'll bring these out otherwise madam will be back on it the minute my back's turned.'

The last drink turned into two or three and, as the chill of the evening made itself felt, Zoe shivered. 'I'm glad I bought a jumper with me.'

'And I'm glad I wore my new cardigan, but I'll call us a cab now, I just need to nip to the loo.'

'I'll call one for you, don't worry.' Tessa reached for her phone.

'Five minutes,' Tessa informed her sister when she returned, and Sasha picked up her phone, slipping it into her pocket, as they all hugged each other goodbye, stopping in the hall to hug Chantelle who'd appeared from the lounge.

They piled back into the pub as Eric announced he would get them a bottle of wine, and Sasha and Zoe looked around for a table as Willow waved at them.

'Come and join us, the pub's full.' She wriggled closer to Cal and they thanked her, taking a seat with the couple.

~

'Fancy watching a film, Chants?' Tessa walked into the lounge. 'I could murder a cup of tea, what about you, darling?' She put Chantelle's phone down on the coffee table, smiling at her. 'And there's a bar of chocolate up in the kitchen cupboard with our name on.'

'Yeah, that sounds good, I'll make the tea, you sit down.' Chantelle stood up. 'Oh, and Mum? You can leave my phone off, I don't mind.' She really didn't, she realised – hadn't sitting in the lounge watching telly with her mum been all she'd wanted to do the other night when she'd been stuck out with Lucy and Spencer, driving around dead bored? And if she didn't read Lucy's messages moaning about her not coming out then she wouldn't have to reply to them, would she? 'Dad, d'you want tea? Are you going to watch a film with us?' she called out, happily.

'Be right down.' Dave frowned as he looked out of their bedroom window at the white car waiting just along the road, its engine idling. He stared at it until it drove off. He hadn't liked the look of the bloke driving, he was too old for his daughter, he knew that much. The girl in the back had looked younger, but maybe he was worrying over nothing, best not to say anything to Tess for now.

Tessa smiled at Dave as he walked into the lounge, inclining her head towards their daughter's phone. 'The phone's off, wonders will never cease, eh? Tell you what, let's switch ours off too, it'll be nice to be disconnected for a couple of hours.' She raised her voice as she called out, 'Hope you're not eating all that chocolate in there!'

~

'You lot look like you've had a good evening.' Cal grinned at their flushed faces, as Eric appeared swinging two bottles of wine and five glasses, all precariously threaded between his fingers.

'It's not over yet.' Eric stumbled as he sat down and Sasha grabbed the bottles as Zoe rescued the glasses. 'Two bottles to start with, plenty more where this came from. Ha ha, get it? Plenty more where–'

'We get it, babe, we know we're in a pub.' Sasha groaned, Eric was painful, but he was good fun. She snuggled up to him as he snaked his arm around her shoulders, glancing across the room to find Charles Priestley's eyes fixed on them in concentration.

She zoned out from the conversation around her as she looked away from him, noticing Zoe's momentary expression of consternation. 'What is it, Zo?' she murmured quietly. 'Fancy a quick smoke?'

'I don't know what's wrong with me, Sash.' Zoe took a drag of her cigarette, once they were outside by the river. 'I don't know if it's from my sessions with Dr Taylor, or what.'

Sasha touched her friend's arm. 'It's bound to bring stuff back to you, love, I suppose that's partly the point, to get rid of the demons once and for all?'

'Yes, I suppose so, it's just, I don't know, I've had so many flashbacks, or something, it's got worse since I've been here and that doesn't make sense, does it?'

Charles Priestley. The name boomed in her head. Appearing out of nowhere, pushing himself in, taking photographs of her when she was unaware, his inexplicable familiarity with Zoe, the dismembered dolls in the woods, her stolen perfume poured over them – and hadn't Willow thought she'd seen him coming out of a toyshop with a purchase, which he'd denied? Had it been a doll? And last night – Zoe had reacted badly to his hug, had felt physically sick, and then later... in the bathroom, had been convinced that someone had followed her. Zoe wasn't a drama queen, quite the opposite – something had triggered those responses, something deep inside her subconsciousness. And everything that had just raced through her head brought back unpleasant memories of Miles Bleak. Was Charles a copycat?

'Zo, tell me honestly, does that bloke, Charles, freak you out?'

Zoe let out a deep sigh. 'Yes, he does, I don't know why, and Sash, I think someone tried to come into my room last night.'

'Oh, Zo, why didn't you say anything?'

'I didn't want to spoil our weekend, babe, and it's just flashbacks, like I said, isn't it? Like the bloody coal tar soap smell. I mean, what the hell could have triggered that? It makes me feel like throwing up just thinking of it.'

'Coal tar soap?' Sasha's voice was sharp. Someone else had mentioned coal tar soap, hadn't they? Jules, it had been Jules, and it had been about Charles, surely?

'Zo, tell me the first thing that comes into your head about that smell.' She didn't even know why she was asking her, but a sixth sense was pushing her.

Zoe's eyes were wide as she turned to her. 'Someone else was there. Oh, God, Sash, someone else was there when I was tied up, and he smelt of coal tar soap. I didn't know that I knew it until this moment.' She sank down onto the bench behind them. 'That bastard Miles was taking photos of me and he pulled the hood off of me for a moment, I saw the door closing and I knew it couldn't be him, he was standing right beside me, it had to have been someone else leaving the room. It was the smell, that's what made me feel sick last night. It must have brought it back to me. The other person smelt like coal tar soap.'

Sitting down beside her friend, Sasha held her close. 'I'm so sorry, Zo, that's awful, I had no idea. I wish I could make it all go away for you.' She needed to think, needed to try to make sense of everything, it was inconceivable, surely, that Charles Priestley had been involved with Miles? But if he had, and he was right here, staying in the pub, then that meant... what, though? Was he here to finish something that Miles had started? But how could he possibly be involved? Surely the police would have had knowledge of him? Anger coursed through her veins at her friend's distress, as well as frustration at the lateness of the hour, the amount of alcohol she'd consumed, and her inability to make sense of all the facts. And, she realised, her dream of the night before – that someone was standing in her room watching her and Eric in bed – might not have been a dream at all...

MRS PRINGLE MAKES A PHONE CALL

D.I. Wendover cursed loudly as the thought burst into her head. She should have considered the implications of their newly found knowledge immediately, not pondered it, not left it on the back burner like it wasn't important. There were two women out there who were unfinished business as far as Miles Bleak and his accomplice, Charles Priestley, were concerned. Here she was focusing on trying, unsuccessfully, to make contact with Charles Priestley, when it was Sasha Blue and Zoe Pullman who should be her priorities. They were potentially in danger and neither of them had a clue.

Niggling in the back of her mind was the fact that she'd left two messages for Zoe and received no reply. Please don't let it mean anything sinister, she muttered under her breath, as she scrolled through her phone for Sasha's number. All she had to do was to let Sasha know about Charles Priestley so that she was aware of the situation. Sasha would know where her friend was and would be able to warn her too. At the end of the day, the chances of Charles Priestley being remotely close to either woman were extremely slim.

She stared at her phone angrily as the disembodied voice informed her that the number was not available right now. What did that mean? That Sasha had switched her phone off? That she was out of the signal area? It couldn't mean that anything had happened to her. She looked around for something wooden to touch, having to resort to a pencil as the recipient of her superstitious tap.

~

'You've been out here for ages, we'll have to get another bottle of wine.' Eric's slurred words were loud in the quiet of the evening. He lurched towards them, belching, and kept going towards the river bank, his eyes bloodshot and glazed. Jumping up, Sasha grabbed his arm to steer him away.

'S'alright, I'm alright, I'll just sit here for a minute, just for a–' Eric slumped to the ground, falling over onto his back.

'Zo, can you watch him for a second? I'll get some help, we need to get this clown up to bed. Why does he always have to overdo it?' Sasha turned and went into the bar in search of Cal and the three of them manoeuvred Eric up the stairs to bed.

'You're sure you don't mind me sleeping in your room, Zo?'

She switched Eric's phone off and left it on the table beside the bed, grabbed her toothbrush and a tee shirt and, with a last look at Eric's sleeping face, turned off the light and went back to the bar.

~

Mrs Pringle hovered uncertainly over her telephone, trying to decide what to do. It wasn't strictly acceptable to make a phone call at this time of night, but it wasn't to someone's home, so there was that... and she didn't want to be a nuisance, but Sasha was a dear girl and very bright, she would understand her concern. She picked up the receiver, decision made, if she didn't get it off her chest, she'd be awake half the night worrying about it like she had been last night.

'Sash, phone call, darling.' Jules motioned for Sasha to come round behind the bar, handing her the phone as she mouthed, 'It's your friend.'

'Hello?' Who could possibly be calling her at the pub?

'Oh, hello, dear, it's Dolly here, Dolly Pringle. Oh dear, I don't want to be a bother, but when you know something's wrong somehow then you just feel that you have to tell someone, don't you? It just didn't make sense you see, I watched him go in there and I thought, now why on earth would a visitor to our parts be going into Pink's of all places? And so, I decided I'd just pop over and ask Mr Pink about it and, well, it was what he bought you see, it feels, well, ominous, I think.'

'Dolly, hold on, I'm a few steps behind you here, what is Pink's exactly? And who are you talking about?'

'Oh goodness, I'm not being clear, am I? It's because I've been agitating over what to do, you see. Pink's is our hardware shop in the village, so you'll see why it would seem strange to me to see a tourist going in there. I mean, I know that he's a photographer, but still, I can't see what he needs with a hardware shop, can you?'

The sounds from the bar seemed to crowd in on her for a moment, before receding, Mrs Pringle's words capturing her full attention.

'Dolly, what did he buy?' Sasha held her breath as she awaited the woman's reply.

'Well, here's the thing, it was duct tape, rope, and some kind of retractable cutting tool, you know, those ones with the terribly sharp blades.'

Mrs Pringle waited. 'Sasha? Are you there, my dear?'

'I'm here. Thanks for telling me, Dolly, you were quite right to be concerned. Leave this with me, alright? And not a word to anyone, I know I can count on your discretion until I can find out what it's all about. You're not to worry now, you get yourself off to bed.'

'I will, I feel much better now that I've told you. Be careful, Sasha.' Mrs Pringle replaced the receiver. She'd make a small pot of tea and have a read of her book, then she'd be ready for her bed.

'Everything alright, Sash?' Jules looked at her quizzically.

'I'm not sure.' Sasha's tone was perplexed as she spoke softly. 'I don't think that everything is quite alright, but I don't know if I've just allowed old fears to resurface. Jules, where's Charles Priestley at the moment? Is he here? Don't let him see you looking.'

Jules glanced around the pub as she handed two glasses of whisky to Zoe, who hovered at the other end of the bar. She turned back to Sasha. 'He's just walked out of the pub. What's going on, Sash?'

'I'll tell you in a minute, I just need to speak to Cal.' Sasha rushed over to where he was sitting.

'Cal, can we have a quick word?' She hurriedly explained what she wanted him to do, then joined Zoe back at the bar.

'You're acting weird, what's going on?' Zoe handed Sasha her whisky.

'Something or nothing, Zo, I'm not sure yet, but just stay here by the bar, okay? Don't go off on your own, promise me, Zo.'

'Now you're scaring me.' Zoe gave a small confused laugh.

Sasha placed her hand over her friend's. 'Everything's fine, just stay here with Jules.'

~

Steph Wendover growled in frustration, her sudden brainwave of calling Sasha's boyfriend, Eric Latimer, having fizzled out like a damp squib. How the hell could all three of them have their phones switched off? Now what was she going to do?

~

She threw back her whisky as Cal re-entered the pub. 'Jules, don't let Zoe out of your sight, okay? I know I sound crazy, I probably am.' She stood up as Cal walked over.

'Yeah, he took a brown paper bag from his boot and stuffed it into his daypack. He's coming back in now.' Cal glanced casually around. 'Are you going to explain what's going on yet?'

'Not yet, I just have to make a call to someone. Sorry.' She looked apologetically at Cal. 'And thanks for doing that, I just don't want him getting suspicious.'

Sasha took her phone from her pocket and swiped her fingers across the screen. But it wasn't her phone, she realised, as the snippets of visible messages registered with her brain. Not wanting to invade her niece's privacy, she hurriedly closed the screen. Damn. She must have picked up Chantelle's phone by mistake when she left Tess and Dave's house earlier.

But... the misspelt word had caught her attention, reminding her, as it did, of the ominous message written on her windscreen. Her hand hovered over Chantelle's phone, maybe she could just check who had sent it...

Your missing out, Chants, come on, theres plenty to go round. Pick you up at eight.

It was painful to read, and plenty of what to go round? The sender's name was Glen, and who the hell was Glen, she wondered?

There was no time to give it any further thought right now. She needed to get hold of D.I. Wendover but needed the number from her phone. Using Chantelle's phone, she scrolled through the contacts for her own name and called it, only to be told that the number was currently unavailable. Calling Tessa, listed as Mum, and Dave, listed as Dad, she received the same messages.

Oh, for crying out loud, they must have switched all their phones off.

Her mind frantically sought another option. Sergeant Jane Weaver had D.S. Tony Palmer's contact details, and he, in turn, could get hold of the detective inspector. She turned to Jules and explained what she needed to do.

~

Steph Wendover lunged for her phone, hoping inexplicably that it would be one of the three people she'd been trying to contact. 'Tony Palmer, this is a surprise, how are you?'

'All good, Steph, all good. Sorry to disturb you late on a Saturday night, but I've got a strange question for you. Does the name Charles Priestley mean anything to you?'

Steph's mouth gaped in surprise as she tried to formulate a coherent response.

~

Charles nursed the last of his pint, his daypack down by his feet under the table, as he looked around the bar, surreptitiously noting the behaviour of certain of the customers. They were definitely acting a little strangely, Zoe looked worried, Sasha looked tense, Cal looked wary, and the owner, Jules, looked watchful. He didn't like it, not one bit, but to do anything out of the ordinary might attract their attention although, he pondered, they couldn't know anything about him, it was impossible. No, it must be all the other stuff that had been going on up at the retirement home.

He leaned back, trying to suppress his smile as he thought about what he was going to do later. The dolls had been a pleasant little trip down memory lane and a fun little appetiser but now it was time for the real thing. Two for the price of one. It was perfect, they were actually going to be in the same room, thanks to her useless, drunk, imbecile of a fiancé. He had to stop himself from giggling. Miles would be proud of him in the end, once it was all over, and Charles would have shown himself to be worthy to carry on where Miles had been forced to leave off.

~

Sergeant Jane Weaver listened in disbelief to what D.I. Wendover had to tell her, before thanking her and assuring her that her team could capably deal with the situation. She called D.S. Crossley first, followed by Constables Datta and Canfield. Finally, she called The Spotted Dog and was put on to Sasha, who kept her expression carefully neutral as Jane spoke rapidly.

Calmly, Sasha thanked Jane and, holding the handset to her mouth as if she was still speaking, stretched her foot out to nudge Jules. 'I'm pretending to still be on the phone. We need to keep Charles here until the police arrive. Can you get Cal to buy a round and sit with him? He mustn't suspect anything.'

Jules grinned over at Cal and Willow, grabbing a bottle of Sambuca and shot glasses, as she walked around the bar and over to them. 'Shots are on me.' She expertly filled the small glasses as she murmured Sasha's instructions to Cal.

'Cheers, Jules, nice one.' Cal downed his shot, before standing up and walking over to the bar where Tristan, the barman, poured him drinks.

Jules continued to pour shots for her few remaining customers, including Charles, who was trying to work out if her behaviour was odd or not.

He was distracted from his thoughts by Cal's large presence as he dropped onto the banquette seat beside him, effectively trapping him at the table. He began to feel a little edgy, but forced a smile as Cal handed him the pint of lager.

'How's it going, Charles? I thought I'd get us a quick pint in before last orders.'

'Er, thanks, you didn't have to, I was about to go to bed actually.'

'Rubbish, it's too early to hit the sack.' Cal stretched out, placing one arm along the back of the banquette, casually.

Sasha repeated her earlier instruction that Zoe stay at the bar with Jules, before getting two glasses of wine and taking them over to a rather non-plussed looking Willow. 'Let's join the guys.'

Feeling a little sulky, Willow acquiesced. Why did Sasha think that everyone would just jump to attention and do her bidding? She was so bossy. And always huddling with Cal, getting him to help her with things. And Cal always had to rush to please her, when she had her own boyfriend to run around for her. Ha, except he was a useless drunk, anyone could see that a mile off.

~

Miles stood outside his cell as the prison officers searched through his meagre possessions, his expression betraying him as they removed his precious photos of Sasha. He watched them glance through his correspondence from Charles, the one officer's finger pointing at something on the most recent message as they both nodded.

'I'd like to speak with Detective Inspector Wendover.' He spoke instinctively, realising that it must be all over for Charles – his sweet Charles, his loyal follower, but also, ultimately, his unfaithful servant – because what else could have happened but that Charles had betrayed him and killed Sasha, *his* Sasha, after he'd expressly forbidden it, and got himself caught? At least the bitch was dead, but Charles had taken all the pleasure for himself, and he could never forgive him for that. He would take the only course of revenge that he could for such treachery. 'I want to tell her about Charles Priestley.'

~

'Where's Eric?' Willow enquired sweetly, once she and Sasha were seated at the table.

Cal shook his head at her, gently.

'Oh, I forgot, he passed out, didn't he? Has he always had a problem with alcohol? That must be so hard for you.' Willow cocked her head to one side, avoiding Cal's eyes, as she held her wineglass.

Controlling her irritation with Willow, Sasha forced herself to shrug her comments off, laughing as she took a swig of wine from her glass. 'Eric just overdoes it sometimes, that's all, but he's a good bloke underneath.' She looked down at the table, hurt by Willow's subtly cruel perception. She needed to concentrate on what they were doing here, until the police arrived. Her mind was still reeling from what Jane had told her about Charles, and it took all her self-restraint not to reach across the table and punch him in the face for his involvement in her best friend's ordeal.

How long had it been since she'd spoken to Jane? She watched as a couple of customers dropped their empty glasses at the bar, before heading out. Soon they'd be the only ones left and Charles might get suspicious.

'So, when do you head home, Charles? Where is home, I don't think you ever mentioned it to us?'

'Maybe tomorrow.' Charles forced himself to sound casual. Something was definitely up, he could read the signs. He shifted in his seat, uncomfortably aware of Cal's arm stretching behind him along the seat.

'And home is...?' Cal pushed him.

'Just a boring semi-detached in London.' Charles shrugged. 'But my family's there, so that makes it special.'

Oh please, Sasha felt like gagging, to think that he had a family and yet all the while he'd been as warped and twisted as Miles Bleak. She glanced at her watch. What was taking the police so long? There were now only three other customers left in the bar, but they were standing up, gathering their things and making moves to leave.

~

D.I. Wendover leaned back in satisfaction. Miles Bleak had just given her everything she needed to arrest and charge Charles Priestley for the abduction, torture, and murder of Sally Birchmont, the woman whose body they'd found in the basement of the property in Nun's Lane, where Zoe Pullman had been held captive. She thought back to Miles's question, at the end of his supervised video call, when he'd asked how Charles had killed Sasha. Nothing had given her greater pleasure than the look on his face when she'd informed him that Sasha was alive and well.

~

Headlights played fleetingly across the windows of the pub as the faint sound of car tyres on gravel could be heard. The last customers exited the bar, and Charles suddenly tried to stand up from his confined position on the banquette.

'I think I'll head off to bed now.' He held his daypack in his hands as his knees tried to push against Cal. 'Excuse me.'

'I don't think so, Charles.' Cal's grip was vicelike on Charles's shoulder as he pushed him back down onto the seat.

The door to the pub opened and D.S. Crossley, Sergeant Weaver, and Constables Datta and Canfield entered, making a beeline for the group. Relief flooded through Sasha as the officers surrounded their table, while additional officers from Rentham stood inside the door.

'What's going on?' Charles's voice was high-pitched in alarm.

'Charles Priestley?' Jane Weaver's voice was firm and confident. 'You are under arrest on suspicion of murder, intention to abduct, and intention to murder. You do not have to say anything...'

She completed the caution, raising her voice to be heard over Charles' laughter.

'This is ridiculous.' His voice was shrill as Cal moved out of the seat to allow the officers to take him into custody. 'I don't know what you're talking about.'

'Oh, I think you do.' Nick Crossley's tone was triumphant. 'It was extremely helpful of you to put it all in writing to your friend, Miles Bleak. Oh yes.' At Charles's crestfallen face, Nick nodded. 'And he's been most helpful at filling in the gaps.'

Jules locked the door behind the officers once they'd taken their prisoner away, and Sasha rushed to Zoe, giving her a hug. 'You helped that to happen, babes, now you'll be able to heal. It's over, it's really over.'

'Why didn't you tell me what was happening?' Willow was angry with Cal, her face white. 'I thought they'd come for *me*.'

'For you? Why on earth would you think that?' Cal laughed. 'Unless you're a secret serial killer.'

'Not funny, Cal.' She fumed. 'I just got freaked out after everything at Meadowvale. Is anyone going to actually tell me what just happened here? I feel like I'm the only one in the dark.'

Appeased, after a condensed explanation from Sasha, *which surely had been hugely over-dramatized, it couldn't possibly all be true, could it?* Willow sulkily announced that she was going to bed.

Jules poured drinks for the remaining small group, and they sat at the bar, slightly stunned from the revelations regarding Charles.

'You'll still sleep in my room tonight, won't you, Sash?' Zoe shrugged her shoulders. 'I know there's nothing to worry about, but I'd just feel better.'

'I'm definitely sleeping in your room, Zo, don't worry, Eric's probably snoring at top volume and sprawled across the whole bed. I'll let him sleep it off and we can tell him everything in the morning.'

'Thanks, Sash.' Zoe yawned. 'I'll head up then and see you in a minute, yeah?'

'Jules, thanks for everything, you're always so cool, calm, and collected, nothing seems to faze you.' Sasha squeezed Jules's arm.

Jules laughed. 'I dunno about that, I thought I'd seen it all over the years, but this was a new one for me. Listen guys, I'm going to get off to bed, someone's got to open up in the morning.'

~

Sasha and Cal sat at the bar, the silence heavy around them. 'I haven't thanked you, Cal, you really came through for us tonight, without you, things could have gone badly wrong.'

'No need, Sash, honestly, pleased to help, you know that, although if you've got a spare fag, I could do with a last smoke, I'm all out.'

'Sure.' Smiling, Sasha picked up her packet of cigarettes, and Cal unlocked the door to the car park, holding it open for her.

~

Not sure what had woken him, Eric grimaced at the foul taste in his mouth. He climbed out of bed, his head thumping, room spinning. Where the hell was Sash? He couldn't even remember going to bed. Still drunk, he blundered to the window, hearing a noise, and looked out, seeing the two figures standing close together, their cigarettes glowing in the dark of the night. He needed to pee badly, and he stumbled to the bathroom.

~

'Well, I should go up.' Sasha yawned. 'It's been another traumatic time, I'm starting to wonder if I attract all this stuff. I suppose it was Charles who vandalised my car, although it doesn't feel like it fits, somehow... and there are still two murders to solve.' She groaned.

'Come here.' Cal pulled her into a hug, holding her close for a moment. 'Don't stress, and whatever you need, you just ask me. Now go and get some sleep, okay?'

~

Eric stopped at the window again, on his way back to bed, and looked out at the two figures embracing, before falling onto the bed. So it was alright for Sasha to mess around with other people, but not him, was it? He fell asleep trying to figure out what to say to her when she came up to bed.

SINGLEDOM

'Sasha, I know you're in there.' Eric shouted as he hammered on the door. 'Get out here now.' He kicked the door for good measure, before standing back, folding his arms as he waited for her to open the door.

'Eric? What the hell are you doing?' Sasha appeared from the floor below, staring up at him in horror. 'You'll wake the whole damn village.'

His head swivelled as Cal's door opened and Cal stepped out, half asleep.

'What's the problem, Eric?' Cal yawned, rubbing his eyes.

'I saw you both last night, I know what happened.'

Sasha stormed up the stairs in her tee shirt. 'Get in our room, now, Eric,' she hissed, pushing him ahead of her and shutting the door behind her. She stood against the door, glaring, 'You don't know anything about last night, in case you've forgotten, you were completely bloody pissed. You almost fell in the river and it took three of us to get you up to bed, did you know that?'

'Yeah? Well I know you didn't sleep in the bed with me, Sasha, so what've you got to say about that? I saw you, I saw the two of you outside all cosied up. You think you're so high and mighty, don't you?' His voice took on a girlish inflection. 'Eric cheated on me again, Eric kissed a girl in the bar, Eric doesn't know the meaning of faithful.' He gave a vindictive laugh. 'Well, you know what, Sash? Eric did cheat on you again, and why the bloody hell shouldn't he, when first chance you get, you're back in bed with *him*? And just for the record, yeah, it was the night I was out at The Woolly Sheep.' His voice was cruel. 'There were two of them, I had my pick, I could have had both of them if I'd wanted.'

Energy drained from Sasha as she slumped against the door, wrapping her arms around herself as if for protection from his sadistic words. She raised her eyes to look him squarely in the face. 'Pack your things, Eric, and get the hell back to London.' She pulled off her engagement ring, throwing it at him. 'And take this with you.' Turning, she pulled the door open, walking straight into Zoe, who'd come up to find out what the fuss was all about.

'Eric will be leaving soon, Zo.' Her voice was toneless. 'I'm sorry it's been such a rotten weekend for you.'

Zoe looked angrily through the doorway, at Eric. 'You stupid idiot, I heard everything you just said to Sasha. You can't help yourself, can you? And just for the record? Sasha slept in my room last night because you were in a drunken sprawl across the bed, which we put you in, with the help of Cal, who's nothing more than a friend to Sash. You've monumentally ruined everything that was good in your life, Eric. And if you weren't so utterly selfish, you might have enquired about what happened last night.' She paused for breath, before looking at Sasha. 'Get some clothes on, babe.'

'What? Oh.' Sasha looked down, realising she was only wearing a tee shirt, and pushed past Eric, back into her room, to grab a pair of jeans.

Eric had one last parting shot for her. 'I was going to suggest we set the date while I was here.' He laughed cruelly. 'Instead, I had a lucky escape from marrying an uptight bitch with a serious persecution complex and a personality disorder called I don't have one.'

'I could kill him, I really could, Sash.' Zoe held Sasha tight, half an hour later, as they said goodbye outside the pub. 'You're sure you're going to be alright?'

'I'll be fine, thanks, Zo, I'm just sorry you're stuck with him all the way back home. Thanks for sticking up for me, not that I care what he thinks anymore. I've got more important things to think about at the moment, there's a killer on the loose and I'm going to focus all my attention on that.'

She stood in the car park after waving Zoe off, having pointedly ignored Eric, feeling humiliated and lonely. Slowly she turned and walked back into the pub, where Jules stood, looking sympathetic.

'Cup of tea, babe?'

Feeling better after tea and a chat with Jules, Sasha returned to her room and, once showered, settled herself cross-legged on the bed with her notes. What she needed right now was to keep her mind busy. She began to jot down the points from each interview that seemed to have some kind of relevance.

A couple of hours later she rubbed her eyes, and was about make herself a cup of tea and read back through her list, when there was a gentle tapping on her door.

Tessa's smiling face greeted her, and she pulled the door open wide. 'Oh crap, Tess, I forgot all about having Chantelle's phone by mistake.'

'No worries, she survived without her phone and, if you can believe this, actually told me to leave it switched off last night while we watched a film. She forgot all about it and it was only when she turned it on this morning that she realised it was yours. We're not stopping, Dave's taking us out for Sunday lunch, fancy joining us? Have Eric and Zo gone back to London?' Tessa finally registered Sasha's pale face, realising that something was amiss. 'Something's happened, hasn't it?'

'Yeah, loads, it was a crazy night after we left yours. I'll give you the bullet points. Eric got hammered, made a fool of himself, and had to be put to bed by me, Zo, and Cal. This morning he accused me of spending the night with Cal, when I'd kipped down in Zo's room, then informed me that he'd cheated on me after I came up to Parva Crossing, so I sent him packing. It's over for good this time, no more chances.'

'That bastard, and just as I was beginning to think it was all going to work out for you guys. I'm so sorry, sis.'

Sasha contorted her face into a twisted smile. 'That's not the half of it, Tess, we figured out that Charles Priestley, the photographer who'd been staying here, was an accomplice of Miles, the sick freak who took Zo and then me. It was a kind of collaboration between local police, D.I. Wendover in London, and Zo, Cal, Jules, and me, oh, and not forgetting Maureen Ford, Douglas her adorable sausage dog, and Mrs Pringle. Turns out he'd killed the woman whose body was found at the house where Zo had been kept and, get this, they've got his confession in writing in an e-mail he sent his mentor, Miles, in prison – who, in turn, has chosen to spill the beans on Charles to D.I. Wendover. Turns out he'd been playing with dolls in the woods here, just like when they were kids, he'd even pinched my perfume – all to get himself psyched up – and had purchased duct tape, rope, and a knife, ready to finish what he and Miles started.'

Tess was aghast, her mouth gaping in disbelief.

'I know, we all felt pretty much the same, sis, and the worst thing is that he'd got himself in with everyone, hanging out with us, taking our photos. Creepy bastard.' She shuddered. 'He's off to join Miles behind bars, so maybe we can all finally forget about that chapter in our lives.'

Tessa was shaking her head. 'How are you so calm?'

'I'm relieved, if you want the truth, I know it sounds weird, but things had been niggling in the back of my mind since I met him, and they were getting in the way of the reason that I was here. Now I can get back to trying to figure out who murdered Dorothy, as well as poor Monty, too.' She hesitated for a moment, wondering whether to mention the strange message she'd read on Chantelle's phone, but then thought better of it. She'd invaded Chantelle's privacy, albeit partially accidentally, and should try to find out more before throwing out her concerns and causing upset. 'Listen, go and enjoy a nice lunch out, yeah? And thanks again for yesterday, it was fun, even if it was the last time we'll all ever see Eric.'

The two sisters hugged and exchanged the phones, promising to catch up soon, and Sasha resumed her position on the bed with her notes and a fresh cup of tea. She studied the points which she'd considered salient, wondering if she should discard most of them, scribbling and crossing out until she yawned, rubbing her neck, wondering if anything she'd jotted down would actually help her. There were discrepancies, things that didn't quite add up, and comments made which required further investigation. Overriding everything was the sad fact that Monty appeared to have been the only person who'd noticed that meddling Dorothy was missing.

She added a final note – *everyone at Meadowvale obsessed with food, especially cake* – smiling to herself. Checking the time, she was surprised to find that it was lunchtime already and, as her stomach rumbled, realised that she hadn't eaten anything all day.

~

Sunday lunch was going to be poorly attended, Kirsty observed, wishing that the relatives would inform her in advance when they were taking residents out for lunch. It would have to be bubble and squeak for Monday dinner, that would take care of the excess vegetables, all Mary would need to do would be to make some mashed potato. She could serve it with the cold roast beef. Satisfied with her plan, she checked on her roast potatoes, turning the oven up a little to help them crisp.

The first to be collected had been Howard, by a rather determined looking Moira. 'Richard and I think you should be with family at a time like this, Uncle Howie, and you know how much we enjoy your company. I've got a nice roast chicken in the oven and I left Richard to finish off the roast potatoes. A proper home-cooked meal is just what you need to take your mind off things.'

Kirsty had done her best not to feel affronted, after all, what were the meals she served at Meadowvale if not home-cooked? She'd rolled her eyes at Greg, who'd asked Howard if he wanted him to fetch his slippers and a cardigan from his room.

'I'll get them, thank you, Greg, I think I'm best placed to know what my uncle needs.' Moira had swooped off, leaving Howard to wink at Greg.

'I feel like I'm being kidnapped,' he'd joked, 'but she's a good egg, old Moira.'

A rotten egg, Greg had thought privately, wondering why Richard hadn't come and collected his uncle himself. Maybe Moira was putting her foot down, the old bag.

David Bertram had marched into Meadowvale a few minutes after Howard's departure, wife and daughter in tow. 'You fetch Elizabeth, Judith, I want a few words with Mrs Goodwin.' He'd headed straight to her office, not looking in a particularly good mood.

'A word please, Mrs Goodwin. We're taking Elizabeth out for lunch, the more time she spends away from here at the moment, the better, quite frankly. How on earth can there have been another murder in a home for the elderly, for God's sake? The whole thing is quite unacceptable, the last thing we need is scandal associated with our family. Poor Gemma has her wedding coming up and I'm sure I don't need to remind you that it's the society wedding of the year. Alec Crouse's father is most unhappy about it all, most unhappy, I don't mind telling you, and in my position in parliament I can certainly do without questions about killers on the loose at the very place my mother-in-law is supposed to be living in safety.' David Bertram stopped to draw breath and Mrs Goodwin took the opportunity to get a word in.

'Firstly, Mr Bertram, I can assure you that we didn't orchestrate a murder at Meadowvale, neither did we invite killers on the loose to pay us a visit. As for scandal, I really don't see how it has any bearing on your family, or Gemma's wedding, or, indeed, Alec Crouse's father. If anyone is feeling unhappy right now, it's those who cared about the victims of these heinous crimes, which includes the residents, the staff, myself, and their friends and relatives. Your mother-in-law, Elizabeth, has been terribly upset by everything that has happened, as have all of us, and what she needs right now is love and support, not speeches about scandal by association.' There, that told the pompous so and so, she thought, feeling quite proud of herself.

David Bertram was an imposing man, and a member of parliament, but he was no match for Mrs Goodwin, manager of Meadowvale, when she was being accused of condoning murder.

'Yes, well, I've said my piece.' Chastened, he turned to find his wife and daughter behind him, with Elizabeth. Turning back to Mrs Goodwin, he attempted to re-assert his authority with a final jibe. 'Just make sure it doesn't happen again.'

'I'll certainly do my best.' Mrs Goodwin smiled tightly, holding in her anger with difficulty.

'Come on, Mummy.' Judith steered Elizabeth towards the front door, as Miriam Smithers appeared, looking flustered.

'Oh, Elizabeth, have you seen my mother anywhere? I thought I'd take her to mine for lunch to take her mind off things.

Elizabeth was prevented from replying by the arrival of the Lovewell sisters. 'You've missed her, Miriam dear, Raymond collected Elspeth and Albert a while ago, I believe he's taken them both to lunch.' Davinia had the grace to look sympathetic.

Miriam's face fell. 'Oh no, I should have called, but I've had so much to do, I just suddenly thought of it and drove straight up here.'

'I think he's taken them for burgers and chips,' Agatha chimed in, 'those Birds do love their fast food.'

Elizabeth snorted derisively, burgers and chips for Sunday lunch, and dolled up Elspeth probably thought she was being taken out to a nice restaurant. This would make for some entertainment later, she thought, cruelly. 'What time is our table booked for at The Crown, David?'

'Gosh, The Crown, how lovely, I've never been there, that's the hotel in Rentham, isn't it? A little beyond my budget, unfortunately.' Miriam smiled kindly at Elizabeth. 'Have a lovely meal, it'll do you good to be out and have your mind taken off things.'

'Yes, well, it's certainly very upmarket, they have an excellent à la carte menu.' Elizabeth wasn't sure why she felt very slightly uncomfortable as she turned to go.

'Well, come on, Davinia, it looks like it's just us and Lillian for lunch, let's go and see if we can squeeze in a sherry first, shall we?' The Lovewell sisters moved off to the lounge and joined Lillian.

'Kirsty, I've printed out cards with the details on for Monty's small memorial, there's to be no fuss, he didn't want any. I thought you might organise getting them to our residents, and their relatives as many of them knew Monty and might like to attend. It will just be held in the garden on Tuesday afternoon. He'll be cremated in Rentham. Give the staff cards as well, so that they can make arrangements, it being rather short notice, thank you.' Mrs Goodwin took herself off to her office, having had enough of dealing with fractious relatives for one day.

~

The impact of her break-up with Eric hit Sasha when she walked into the bar, where a number of couples sat enjoying The Spotted Dog's Sunday roast buffet. Welcome back to singledom, Sash, she muttered under her breath, as she made for the bar.

A woman's brightly-coloured skirt caught her eye and she recognised Mary from Meadowvale. *Mary from the dairy*, she intoned silently, trying to recall where she'd heard the phrase. About to order a drink, she stopped – she'd forgotten to drop the piece of muddied kaftan, found in Kirsty's rag bag, off at the police station.

'Rain check, Jules, I'll come back later, there's something I need to do.' She went back up to her room, fetched her car keys, and headed out to the car park. Someone would be on duty at the police station, she was sure. Clicking her car remote, she tried to open her driver's door, but found it locked. That was odd, she must have left it unlocked the day before, which was unlike her. Shrugging, she clicked it again, and opened the door.

~

Ross Canfield looked up, grinning, as Sasha walked into the police station. 'Afternoon, Sasha, please tell me you're not here to report any more criminal activity or murders, my wife's just been on the hooter, there's a Sunday roast at home with my name on it.'

Sasha smiled. 'Nothing today, Ross, at least I hope not. No, I forgot to drop something off for your attention. It may be nothing, but it bears inspection, I think.' She placed the paper bag on the counter. 'This was found in Kirsty, the cook's, rag bag in her cupboard in the kitchen at Meadowvale. It appears to be a roughly cut piece of Agatha Lovewell's missing kaftan, and what's more, it's got dried mud on it. Kirsty's rag bag has been disturbed twice, the first time may have been around the time of Dorothy Newton's murder, which makes me wonder...' She smiled, raising her eyebrows. 'Actually, I'm not sure what it makes me wonder, but it's just strange. The second time the rag bag was disturbed was the night of Monty Mallowan's murder, which makes no sense, but that's what makes it so interesting.'

Ross picked up the bag, nodding. 'I get you, we'll have it attended to and see if we can link the mud to the pond. Anything else while you're here?'

Pausing, Sasha wondered whether to be a nuisance or not, the poor guy obviously wanted to get home. On the other hand, it would only take a minute or two... 'There is just one thing...'

~

Back in her car, Sasha pondered what to do with herself. She could go back to the pub in time to catch lunch, but wasn't sure if she fancied a roast dinner, or if she wanted to sit there eating on her own. She glanced at the box containing Dorothy Newton's letters, retrieved by herself originally, from the old post box at the end of the woman's garden, as well as from the coal bunker at Meadowvale where Dorothy had spent her final months, and now this time, all from their final resting place in the box file which Ross had fetched from the back office for her, having extracted her assurances that she wouldn't lose them and would return them within a day or two. Her stomach rumbled and she had an idea.

She found a petrol station on the outskirts of Rentham and went inside to see what she could find for a makeshift lunch. The selection was pretty decent, no doubt holiday visitors called in regularly, and having eaten nothing all day, she lost the plot, picking up a pack of egg mayonnaise sandwiches, a couple of packets of crisps and, about to hit the chocolate display, turned as the aroma of freshly-baked pastries reached her nose – hot sausage rolls and pies were being placed into the warming cabinet.

She drove off, munching on crisps, and headed back towards Parva Crossing, finding a quiet spot to park beside the Black River. Gulping down some coke, and with a mouthful of sausage roll, she picked up the first of Dorothy's letters. The words drifted through her mind as she glanced through page after page of Dorothy Newton's crazed missives; messily glued individual letters cut from newspapers and magazines formed words and odd disjointed sentences, all finished with childish stickers of seemingly arbitrary items, and adorned with glitter in some instances.

You're a cheap whore; I know why you sleep all day; Devil's work at night; Mary, Mary, from the dairy, took the money, thief; I saw you, Richard, kissing.

Painfully, Sasha was reminded of reading these very words out loud to Cal, when they'd worked the case together. It all seemed a long time ago now. She sat up straighter in her seat, putting down the sandwich she'd begun to eat, and picked up the last piece of paper again, studying the flowery paper. The letter was addressed to Greg. At the time it had seemed of no importance, just another spiteful disclosure which, in the normal scheme of things, would never have seen the light of day.

But Dorothy had continued to observe and record the actions of those around her, had delighted in finding out people's hidden secrets, either from their current lives or from their old ones. Not content with recording her findings in her notebook – which had presumably been taken by her murderer – she'd taken to making little snipes within earshot of her prey – her comments causing much disquiet, their meaning only apparent to her target. Had one of those little snipes sealed her death warrant?

Two words, she'd said to Lillian, he wants you to write two words – who? Mervyn, her son? She'd asked Elizabeth about keys, Davinia about bathwater, and how many other comments had she made that Sasha was so far unaware of? One thing she knew for sure, Dorothy never said anything without it having a hidden meaning.

Discarding her sandwich, Sasha opened a bar of chocolate, breaking off a piece and popping it into her mouth, her thoughts returning to Greg. She really liked him, he had a wonderful way with the residents, was fun, as well as kind, and seemed popular with everyone. But Dorothy had seen him kissing Richard... could it be Richard Carding, Howard Norton's nephew? Richard who was married to Moira? Richard who owned a struggling bookshop and was constantly being given cash by his uncle? His uncle who had made it quite clear to Sasha that he had no tolerance for homosexual behaviour, or any behaviour which, by his own, immeasurably strict moral code, constituted scandalous, indecent, or immoral behaviour.

What if Richard was banking on inheriting from his uncle, and his alleged affair with Greg could throw a spanner in the works? Was it a possibility? It seemed hard to believe, but yes, she conceded, Howard was clearly rigid in his beliefs. She needed to find out for sure, because if so, then Dorothy's silence would ensure his inheritance... an inheritance which would benefit Richard, but also his wife, Moira, if he stayed with her, or Greg, if the two were planning on being together with Moira out of the picture... Could any of them have been Dorothy's murderer? Greg was certainly there that day, and had been seen in the garden, as had Richard, and, she remembered, Moira had been seen arguing with Richard, but had that been in the morning or the afternoon? She shook her head frustratedly, it all hung on the recollections of a few elderly people, all of which were contradictory and muddled.

Turning her thoughts to Mary *from the dairy*, she recalled having seen Mary, possibly, entering a resident's room on the day that Howard had reported cash being stolen from his room. Had Dorothy known that she was a thief? Probably. But had Sasha seen Mary or had the flash of patterned fabric been

Agatha in one of her kaftans? But would Agatha steal money? And there was nothing suspicious about Mary entering residents' rooms, it was her job after all, plus Mrs Goodwin had mentioned that Mary had one blot on her record which she would never repeat. Maybe the thefts witnessed by Dorothy had been someone else altogether...

About to break off another piece of chocolate, she stopped herself, closing the wrapper to avoid further temptation. Agatha... Sasha pondered the woman. No, she couldn't see Agatha as that kind of thief, she surely had no need, but Monty had inferred that the other items had been taken by someone with kleptomania, hadn't he? And hadn't he made reference to having been fond of whoever it was? What was it he'd said, *got a soft spot for*? And then he'd begun to talk about Agatha's kaftan going missing, or being taken... he'd definitely spoken of Agatha in very fond terms...

It was a bit of a leap but if Agatha did suffer from kleptomaniacal tendencies, and Dorothy had known about it, which Dorothy being Dorothy she probably would have, then she had likely taunted Agatha with her knowledge. But to kill her to prevent her secret from coming out? No, Sasha leaned her head back against the headrest, it just wasn't the kind of secret someone would commit murder for, at least, it wasn't unless the revelation was likely to affect her life in such a way as to make it intolerable... but what on earth could that reason be? Plus, she remembered, Agatha herself had been a victim of theft, having had her kaftan taken, which rather muddied the waters.

There was nothing else of interest in Dorothy's letters, so Sasha turned her thoughts back to the comments made by Dorothy, according to Monty and Agatha.

Monty had mentioned something about keys in relation to Elizabeth, that Dorothy had implied that she'd lost some? *Again*, he'd said, so it hadn't been the first time, and Elizabeth had clearly been unhappy with Dorothy's taunting, she'd glared at her, he'd said, if she was recalling his words correctly. But what the hell could be so upsetting in relation to some missing keys? If only she knew what the exact words had been, but sadly, Monty would never have the opportunity to summon up those words from his memory, ever again.

As for Agatha's mention of Dorothy's comment to Davinia which had apparently upset her so much, it just wasn't enough to go on. Bathwater. What about bathwater? It must have meant something to Dorothy, and likewise, Davinia, but Agatha seemed unaware of any hidden implications to whatever the remark had been.

If only she had Dorothy's notebook, Sasha thought, then all would be revealed, but that was presumably long gone by now, for surely the killer's purpose in drowning Dorothy had been to prevent something from their past from being exposed, which meant they'd wanted to get their hands on the notebook too, hence the fishing out of Dorothy's handbag from the pond. Of course, it was all supposition, this idea that Dorothy had been murdered because of something she might reveal, but if it was true then it had to relate to either someone's old life and something they'd lied about then perhaps, or something which they were lying about now.

The only other references that she had to any of Dorothy's snipes were those recounted by Howard when she interviewed him, and those, of course, were thirdhand, so their reliability was heavily called into question. Nonetheless, she considered them.

They'd come from Elizabeth, initially, and then others had joined in, according to Howard. *Norwich and eating porridge* – that was interesting... possibly... if you took the porridge reference to mean, yes, thought Sasha, excitedly, prison perhaps? She made a note to check whether there was a prison in Norwich. Maybe someone had done time in their old life, and if that was the case, they could have every reason to want that fact to remain hidden. But one of the residents of Meadowvale an ex-con? It was so unlikely as to be laughable, but you never knew...

Digs about being bald, well, Howard had said that was about Monty, poor chap, and he was correct – she had, after all, seen the crime scene photos and could picture the sad spectacle of Monty's bald head hanging over the chair, his hairpiece resting in the pool of congealed blood. Monty's hairpiece had been rather dark in colour for his age, which could have given it away to an eagle-eyed person such as Dorothy.

But it hardly constituted a reason for murder. No, Sasha smiled to herself, Monty had been fond of Dorothy, and the residents obviously knew that he wore a wig, so that was just dear old Dorothy being mean. And Monty was dead now, so that kind of excused him from the whole thing.

Mum's the word – what possible hidden meaning could that have? There was no knowing in what context Dorothy might have said those words, but if she did, then the obvious reason was *keeping quiet*. Someone had kept quiet? Dorothy was saying that she'd keep quiet about something? Well, that would have been a first, so, no, unlikely. Was it a reference to a mother? Dorothy knew something about someone's mother? Or child? If that was it then it excluded Howard Norton and the Lovewell sisters, *as far as she knew*, but she didn't know which staff had children, although, at a guess, Greg and Spencer were unlikely to be parents – and she wasn't sure about the relatives.

Keys in the pot what have we got. Keys again. So that had to have been the Elizabeth connection. What pot, though? Sasha considered what she knew about Elizabeth, so far – but this was from Howard – she likes to drink. If Howard was aware then it was probably public knowledge and hardly a reason to commit murder. She'd lived in Africa – her wild days in Africa, Howard had said, but again, he'd also said that she was always talking about it, so no secret to guard there. And what the hell did a pot have to do with anything?

Dickie birds and eagles, not forgetting magpies. Dickie – Richard? Or birds – as in Albert Bird, perhaps? It was no good, none of this was getting her anywhere.

SUNDAY LUNCH SHENANIGANS

Tessa studied the menu and looked at her husband, a worried expression on her face. 'It's a bit pricey, Dave, d'you think we should have gone somewhere else?'

'It's fine, why shouldn't I treat my family once in a while? Besides,' Dave grinned as he leaned back in his chair, 'I've got some good news that I've been keeping quiet, waiting for the right moment. I've been promoted. There was a bit of a gap left after old George Newton was put away.' He looked across at his daughter, sympathetically, reaching out to stroke her pale face. 'I know he took your friend's life, Chants, among others, and we don't really talk about it, but maybe it's something good that's happened for us at last. I'll be taking over his role, and getting a nice pay rise to go with it.'

'Something good?' Chantelle looked at her dad in horror. 'He killed my best friend and you're celebrating getting his job? What's wrong with everyone? What's wrong with this place? Everyone just does bad shit and laughs about it.'

'Chantelle, language.' Tessa put her hand on Chantelle's arm. 'It *is* good news, love, I'm proud of you.' She smiled at her husband. 'What other stuff are you talking about, Chants? What did you mean?'

'Oh, nothing, it's just that things keep happening, don't they? I mean, someone vandalised Sasha's car, didn't they? Then there's always murders.' Her voice rose by an octave. 'Murder, murder, murder, someone's always being killed, and we all just carry on like it's normal.'

'Shh.' Tessa soothed her daughter, noticing the glances from surrounding tables.

'Are you alright, Mother?' Judith Bertram looked at Elizabeth's face, in concern. 'You're upset about the murders, of course you are, I wish people would keep their voices down.' She glared at the Watsons' table, pointedly, before turning to her husband. 'David, do something.'

'Oh, Daddy, it's all too dreadful.' Gemma Bertram blew her nose. 'I'm getting married and all everyone talks about is murder.'

'No!' Elizabeth's voice was forceful as she thumped the table. 'I won't have it. No more talk of that, it's all so unsavoury. We've got a wedding to plan and nothing is going to spoil it for us, nothing, do you hear me? I won't allow it.'

'That's all very well, Elizabeth, but just because you won't allow it doesn't mean that this wretched killer is going to stop, does it? How many more of you are going to be killed? For God's sake, it could be you next. And how would that be for a scandal? Hmm? Member of parliament's mother-in-law murdered at Meadowvale – the home of murder. It's an absolute disgrace, and more than that, it's bringing scandal on our family, Lord knows what questions will be thrown at me by these dratted reporters if word gets out in London. And as for the fellows in the house, they're going to have a field day with this.' David Bertram scowled at no one in particular, before taking a mouthful of roast beef and Yorkshire pudding.

'Daddy, stop it!' Gemma Barton pushed her chair out from the table, rushing off to the ladies, her mother in hot pursuit, having first cast a reproachful glance at her husband.

'Well done, David.' Elizabeth smirked at her son-in-law. 'You handled that superbly.' Sarcasm dripped from her every word, but she shifted in her chair, leaning in closer to him. 'But I agree with you, we'll have no scandal brought on our family, it simply must not be allowed. Whatever it takes. I'm quite sure that all will be well from now on, and all forgotten about before darling Gemma's wedding. And I can assure you of one thing, without any shadow of a doubt, I will certainly not be getting myself killed.' She sat back, smiling, as Judith and Gemma returned to the table. 'Now, is someone going to refill my wineglass? The bottle's empty, would you believe it? Really, the service levels here are abysmal.'

Chantelle looked across at the elderly woman who seemed to rule the roost at the next table, having heard everything that had been said. So, she was a Meadowvale resident. A bit full of herself, wasn't she? Maybe someone should polish her off, she thought harshly, feeling fed up. She was missing Lucy, her only friend, and so much for being grounded for the weekend, that was all fine until Mum and Dad wanted to go out, then it was all, come on, Chants, we're going out for lunch. Last night at home had been okay, she supposed, watching the film with tea and chocolate, but now she just felt like a stupid little girl out with her mummy and daddy.

'I have to go to the loo.' Chantelle stood up just as their food arrived.

'Oh, Chants, your food will go cold.'

'I won't be long, what d'you want me to do, wet myself?'

Tessa and Dave watched their daughter walk out of the dining room.

'Devil daughter's back,' said Tess with a sigh, 'our little armistice didn't last long, did it?'

Chantelle pulled her phone out as she entered the ladies, scrolling through her missed messages. There was a message from Glen. Hold on though, it had been opened. She couldn't believe it, talk about a total invasion of privacy, by her own aunt who she trusted. At least he hadn't given anything away, Sasha would have had no idea what he was talking about. They must have come to pick her up last night, then given up when she didn't reply. Her loyalty to her family swung over to a renewed allegiance to her friends and she tapped out a belated reply.

Sorry, had a boring family do last night, missed your message. What about tonight?

She texted Lucy, suggesting getting together later. She'd work out how to get out of the house later.

'Haven't you had enough, Mother?' Judith Bertram looked disapprovingly down her hooked nose at Elizabeth as she waved the empty bottle in the air.

'Nonsense, dear, the day your mother can't handle her drink will be the day you bury me six feet under. Now, let's go over the seating plan again, where did we decide to seat the prime minister? Oh and, Gemma dear, no dahlias or gypsophila anywhere in the church or the reception.'

'But, Gram, we've already decided on the flowers, and gypsophila's one of my favourites.'

'Hay fever, we can't have people sneezing and carrying on, all focus must be on the family, and on you, of course.' Elizabeth quickly corrected herself. 'No, roses and astrantia will be far more suitable, I think.'

'Mother's quite right, oh, look sharp, everyone, someone's taking our photo.' Judith pulled in her stomach, fixing a smile on her face, as Elizabeth patted her hair, and David reached over to affectionately tweak his daughter's cheek. That would make a good picture, he thought, happily, *MP and loving father, out for family lunch.*

~

Spencer yawned in boredom, Sundays were the worst, and only three of them there for lunch. Still, at least he hadn't had to do much. Plus, he'd got a nice Sunday roast out of it, Kirsty was a good cook, even if she was a bit sniffy with him. He sidled out of the kitchen door, making his way to the old greenhouse. He'd grab the last of his stash and smoke a quick joint before his shift ended.

He stopped in his tracks as he found his path cordoned off with police tape. Now what? And why had they included the greenhouse? Maybe he could just sneak through and grab his grass, there was no one around. Unless they'd found it...

'Spencer, you can get yourself back inside and finish off those saucepans, if you don't mind. No good will come from sniffing around here, like I don't know what you're up to. The police have cordoned it off for a reason, you know.' Kirsty stood behind him, her hands on her hips. 'And did you pinch that last slice of cake in the kitchen? I was going to have that with my tea, you and your sweet tooth. 'She rolled her eyes in mock despair.

What the hell, the woman *was* the bloody police, the way she behaved.

'Alright, alright, I was just taking a breather, that's all.' He walked back, wondering what to do. Had the cops found his stash? They wouldn't know it was his, at least. He didn't have anything at home, and no money to buy any more from Glen. Money, that's what he needed, and he knew exactly where to get it. He just needed to work out how to get the message to the person and also where to tell them to leave the money.

Kirsty smirked to herself, that had shown him. No doubt he'd been wanting to smoke one of his joints. Well, not with her in charge, he wouldn't be. Remembering Mrs Goodwin's instruction from earlier, she called out to his retreating back, 'Oh, and Spencer, when you've done the saucepans, I've got a little job for, but you'll have to be quick about it.' That would keep him busy.

~

Glen Cutter grinned as he read the messages. Everyone wanted to meet up tonight, including little Chantelle. He replied, arranging the time, nodding to himself. They were a hungry little lot, keen to get stoned, but he had a nice surprise for them. It was time to get them onto the harder stuff. His new contacts in Rentham would be pleased with him if he could hook them some new customers. And it would all tie in so nicely with his plan to destroy little miss perfect, Sasha Blue.

~

'Thank you, Moira, my dear, an excellent roast, as usual. Richard, you're a lucky fellow.' Howard kissed his nephew's wife on the cheek, before heading out to the car to be returned to Meadowvale by Richard. 'Oh well, back to barracks, let's hope all is calm, I'm looking forward to a nice nap.'

'Straight back, Richard, it shouldn't take you more than twenty minutes.' Moira's expression was guarded. 'Make sure he doesn't dilly dally, Uncle Howie.'

They arrived just as Elizabeth was being escorted in through the front door by her daughter. 'Look out, she's had a few too many by the looks of it.' Howard watched the woman's unsteady steps in amusement. 'Oh, and here are the lovebirds back from their lunch.'

'Cooee.' Greg appeared, smiling and bustling around everyone. 'Welcome back, did everyone have a nice time? Richard, are you coming in for a cup of tea?'

Hesitating, Richard Carding looked at his watch, as Howard piped up. 'Not a chance, old boy, your wife looked like she meant business. You'd best get yourself straight home, there's a good chap.'

Richard and Greg exchanged glances as Richard shrugged his shoulders helplessly, and got back in his car. About to drive off, he looked up as Greg tapped on his window.

'What's going on? Is Moira being a bitch again? You shouldn't let her treat you like this, Richard.'

'What can I do? She's all over me, if Uncle Howie gets wind of us, it's all over, you know what he's like. I'll be out in the cold. Moira wants the money as much as I do, she's as keen to keep him sweet as we are.'

'Yes, but Moira's not going to be in the picture in the future, is she?' Greg was mutinous.

'No...' Richard groaned, 'but I need her to think she is, we both do. Look, we've just got to be careful, we've been lucky so far but we just need to lie low for a while, alright?'

'Okay, but I miss you, that's all.' Greg pulled a sad face, before turning round and resignedly walking back into Meadowvale as Spencer rushed past him to hand something to Richard.

Elizabeth pushed Judith's hand away, 'I can manage, thank you, dear. I think I know the way to the lounge, I do live here, after all.' She turned her attention to her son-in-law and grand-daughter, who were hovering behind her. 'David, thank you again, for lunch, and, Gemma dear, remember, we'd like that wedding dress to fit, I'm not sure that dessert was necessary today, are you? You did, after all, have three roast potatoes. Ah, Elspeth.' Her eyes gleamed cruelly. 'Come and join me in the lounge and tell me all about your lunch. You look so pretty all dressed up, Raymond must have taken you both somewhere special.'

Spencer rushed to catch up with them, as Judith and David Bertram hurried their daughter, Gemma, away from Elizabeth, each with one arm around her shoulders, the sounds of their rising voices reaching those gathered in the reception, as they remonstrated with each other.

'Well, really, yes, it was such fun, Raymond is a joker, you know.' Elspeth fluttered her hands as her face flushed. 'He takes after his father, doesn't he, Albie?' She clasped Albert's arm as they entered the lounge. 'So clever, really, the way he described lunch – a nice piece of beef, crispy potatoes, vegetables, and all finished off with a nice pudding.'

Albert Bird guffawed loudly. 'You're a good sport, old girl, I have to say, Raymond got you good and proper, didn't he? One of your best yet, son, I reckon.' Albert clapped a grinning Raymond on the shoulder, as they all walked into the lounge. 'Beefburgers, chips, and onion rings, then a nice whippy ice cream. Just the ticket, if you ask me, and as Raymond said, better that than sitting here all forgotten about. Family's who you choose, that's what we always say. We're your family now, that's what it's all about.'

'Well, Elspeth's still got a daughter, hasn't she? Perhaps she was too busy today.' Elizabeth harrumphed. 'I must say I had the most wonderful lunch with my daughter, and the rest of my family, at The Crown, really very civilised, and an excellent roast.'

'Yes, but I'm sure Miriam...' Elspeth's voice faded off as Davinia Lovewell appeared.

'Ah, Elspeth, did Elizabeth tell you that Miriam came by just after you and Albert left with Raymond?' Davinia's eyes glinted triumphantly at Elizabeth, who had the grace to look slightly abashed. 'She wanted to take you back to hers for lunch, she was most disappointed to have missed you. She's a good daughter, she might not be able to take you to fancy restaurants, but how lovely to have someone to think of you, and to want to take you home for a nice cooked meal.'

'Oh, thank you, Davinia.' Elspeth flushed happily. 'Yes, Miriam's a good girl, and she works so hard, you know, what with raising Lucy and working for Dr Singh.'

Spencer drifted over, taking Raymond Bird aside to hand him an envelope, before speaking to the small group. 'I've put your envelopes in your rooms, so you can read them later, Mrs Goodwin's sorted out the memorial for Monty, that's what it's about.'

'Elspeth, what a gorgeous ring!' Agatha swooped into the lounge, her eyes fixed on the large, glinting, adornment to Elspeth's right hand. 'How were your lunches, everyone? Kirsty made us an entirely adequate roast lunch, didn't she, Davinia? You enjoyed it, didn't you, Lillian?'

All eyes turned to Lillian as she sat, almost lost in the large armchair, her hands moving ceaselessly back and forth above an open magazine.

'Poor old girl.' Howard joined the group. 'Always writing her next book. Oh, where did you spring from, Mervyn? Been here long? Were you looking for your mother in her room? She's over there, being swallowed up by the armchair by the looks of her.

Did Spencer give you one of his envelopes? He did? Oh, good lad, good lad. Ah, the lovely Lovewells, did you miss me, ladies?'

Much flustering and flushing later, and things calmed down enough for Greg to bring in some tea, which was gratefully received by all.

~

She may as well go back to the pub, Sasha decided. Lunch would be over and she couldn't spend the day sitting in her car. Suddenly she felt at a complete loss, not sure quite what to do with herself. It was the Sunday afternoon affliction, common among those who found themselves alone and away from their home comfort zone. There was nothing to do, no one to do it with, and the hours seemed to stretch ahead endlessly. She could have a drink, she supposed, but that might end messily, no, she really needed to keep herself occupied, at least for a few more hours. How unacceptable would it be to pitch up at Meadowvale? She could try to chat to Elizabeth or Albert, the last two residents she had yet to interview. Shrugging her shoulders, she started her car, might as well pop by and test the water, at least. They'd either be fast asleep after their Sunday roasts, or as bored as she was, and happy to have someone to chat to.

Elizabeth was holding court, when Sasha entered the residents' lounge, a glass of sherry tilting precariously in her hand. 'So, I told David, I certainly won't be going and getting myself murdered, I simply won't allow it. Oh look, it's our very own private detective, here to sniff out the killer hiding in our midst. How are you, Sasha? Join us for a sherry?'

'Good afternoon, Elizabeth, you're looking well. No sherry for me, thanks.' Sasha smiled, glancing around at Elizabeth's companions, all of whom were either asleep or, in the case of Davinia and Elspeth, flicking through magazines and clearly not interested in her chatter.

'No sherry? Teetotal are you? When we lived in Rhodesia, we always had sherry on a Sunday.' Elizabeth giggled. 'Sherry on Sundays, gin and tonics every afternoon for sundowners, and wine every evening with dinner. Whisky, of course, after dinner, yes...' For a moment Elizabeth's gaze was distant as she was transported to a past life, but she pulled herself back to the present. 'Now, where was I?'

'You were talking about your time in Rhodesia. Did you live there long?'

'My whole life, until we moved to England when my husband retired, beautiful country, and, oh, the parties we used to have.' She winked at Sasha. 'Wouldn't you like to know?' Her sherry spilt on her blouse as she adjusted her position. 'Whoops, look at me, that's the trouble with not finishing one's drink in a timely manner.' Throwing the rest of the glass down her throat in one go, Elizabeth looked around her, wincing theatrically as Howard emitted a loud snore. 'No stamina, this lot.'

'Well, look.' Sasha stood up, deciding it had been a bad idea to come. 'I think I'll leave you to rest.'

'Nonsense, I could do with the company. You haven't interviewed me yet, don't you want to know who killed Dorothy? And what about Monty? You'd better hurry up before any more bodies turn up.'

A loud tut came from Davinia's chair and Elizabeth leaned towards her, exaggeratedly. 'What's the matter, Davinia? Did I say something to upset you?'

'I just think you could be a little more respectful, Elizabeth, it's not a joke and it's gone quite far enough. Besides, you don't seem to be in any fit state to be interviewed.' Davinia shot daggers at Elizabeth before returning to her magazine, lifting it up in front of her face, pointedly refusing to engage further.

'She's right, Elizabeth, maybe you should have a lie-down,' Albert said firmly, 'you don't want to be boring Sasha with a load of old mumbo jumbo. Better to speak to her when you're sober so you can get your facts straight.'

'Oh, shut up, Albert, what's the matter? Worried I'll spill the beans? Tell Sasha all your secrets?' Elizabeth's laugh was harsh as everyone looked uncomfortable.

'Maybe Albie's right.' Elspeth fluttered, not enjoying the unpleasant atmosphere. 'And of course he's not worried about secrets, my Albie doesn't have any, do you?'

'Course I don't, old girl, don't I always say I'm an open book?' Albert's laugh was drowned out by Elizabeth's guffaw.

'Oh, you're all so priceless, so worried about secrets. Well, here's one for you–'

'Elizabeth!' Kirsty hurried in, called by Spencer to deal with the disruption. 'That's quite enough, you're upsetting everyone. Now, are you going to behave yourself or do you need to have a rest in your room?' She made an imposing figure, hands on her hips, her eyes fixed on Elizabeth, who shuffled in her chair, smiling up at Kirsty, innocently.

'I'll behave myself, in fact, I'm going to have my interview with Sasha.' She stood up, swaying slightly, bumping Howard's chair so that he came to with a start, and headed for the library.

'Are you trying to bump me off, Elizabeth?' Howard grinned, before nodding off again, his head falling forward to his chest.

Sasha looked uncertainly at Kirsty, who nodded. 'Might be a good idea to have her out of the way for a while.'

Shrugging, Sasha followed Elizabeth's slightly haphazard progress along the passage to the library. She might as well see what Elizabeth had to say, even if she was more than a little under the influence, maybe it would be interesting.

'Uncle Howie? Oh, you're awake, Richard forgot to bring your slippers back with you, so I thought I'd pop them through. Shall I put them in your room for you? Anything else you need? Well, if you're sure, I'll be off then. We should have you home for lunch more, it's so nice, just the three of us, isn't it?' Moira Carding leaned down and pecked Howard on the cheek, before leaving the lounge.

'Mrs Carding.' Spencer walked quickly towards Moira, waving the envelope, before stopping in surprise as it was snatched from his hand.

'I've got it, thank you, Spencer.' Greg walked up to Moira, smiling as he handed her the envelope. 'Details of Monty's memorial service in case Richard doesn't tell you about it, although I'm sure he tells you *everything*.' He waltzed off, winking at Spencer.

'Kirsty asked me to give out the envelopes, not you.'

Greg sighed, over dramatically. 'Does it really matter, Spencer? And since when were you so conscientious? Are you sure you're feeling alright? Not ill, are you?' Sniggering to himself, Greg waltzed off.

SASHA INTERVIEWS ELIZABETH PAYTON AND ALBERT BIRD

'So how do we do this?' Elizabeth leaned back in the armchair in the corner of the library, leaning her walking stick against the wall. It fell with a clatter, and Sasha picked it up, standing it beside the armchair.

'Damned thing with all those feet, I'm told I need the extra stability.' Elizabeth's voice was bitter. 'I can thank my daughter for that, no one else uses such a monstrosity.'

Sasha smiled. 'Better to be safe than sorry. Right, it's probably best if you just tell me everything that you remember about the day Dorothy died. I'll stop you if I have a question. How's that?'

Nodding, Elizabeth began to speak. 'I awoke early, as I always do, and I seem to recall it being rather chilly. I had my cereal and went through my notes for the wedding in preparation for my daughter's visit.

'We were spared any morning activity with the wretched Willow, as Tuesday mornings are our own time, but when the sun came out, Judith and I took a stroll in the garden. Judith took a phone call and so I returned first, that's when Monty almost had me over, he will stretch his legs out when he's napping in the conservatory. Oh–' Elizabeth corrected herself. 'I should have said he used to, shouldn't I? I forgot for a moment. Poor old Monty, I don't suppose he remembered about that, did he? Perhaps he told you? Are you writing this down? It was in the morning – he probably blamed me, the man did like to complain.' Pausing to sip her sherry, she looked across at Sasha, who smiled non-committally, giving an encouraging nod.

'Right, well, we didn't see Dorothy at all, not even at morning coffee, which was when we enjoyed Moira's shortbread. Richard brought it through, of course, he spends a lot of time here, you may have noticed him always hanging around, and not just with his uncle?'

Again, Sasha ignored Elizabeth's attempts to get a reaction from her. 'Go on,' she said.

'Well, anyway, I was feeling a little tired, it had been a long morning, so I had a rest in my room before lunch.' Elizabeth paused, her blue eyes looking a little watery. 'I remember glancing out of my window and seeing Lillian's son getting into his car, oh–' She fidgeted, clearing her throat. 'Do you know, I think that perhaps that was in the afternoon, just before the crafting session. Do you know what time Dorothy was murdered?'

Surprised at Elizabeth's sudden change in tack, Sasha replied, 'Well, not exactly, no, but why do you ask?'

'Oh, I was just thinking that Mervyn Springer was clearly in the right place at the right time, and perhaps he was unhappy with Dorothy, she did have a habit of upsetting people, you know.'

'Did she upset you, Elizabeth?' asked Sasha softly.

'Me? Goodness, it would take more than a few snipes from a batty old fool like Dorothy to upset me. I would say that she amused me, yes, that's how I'd put it. But I'm getting distracted, aren't I? Now, let me see, lunch was salad, and possibly quiche, and I do recall lots of fuss from Elspeth about a piece of jewellery. The woman's quite irresponsible – when we lived in Rhodesia we kept our jewels under lock and key, to be taken out for dinner parties.' She cupped her mouth with her hand and leaned forward. 'And other types of parties... lots of fun in those days, happy times, we were young and beautiful, had our whole lives ahead of us...' Elizabeth appeared to pull herself from her reverie with difficulty.

Yawning loudly, she continued. 'Our activity girl was hanging around like a spare part, not sure why she was there when there was no activity, she seems to like asking questions, always wanting to know things. And then, of course, she had us stringing beads together for our afternoon craft session. Do I look like I belong in a nursery school? Anyway, we all suffered it like good little children and then we had our afternoon tea, no homemade cake, that's a Monday treat only, and this was Tuesday.

'Elspeth was preening in her new cardigan, just like a small child. I told you that I saw Richard, didn't I? And Moira too, I believe, out in the garden.' Elizabeth frowned. 'Although, he brought the shortbread in the morning, so...' She shook her head, stifling another yawn.

'We're almost done, Elizabeth, I expect you'd like a lie-down.'

'Yes, I am a little sleepy, and there's not much else to tell you, Albert was all over the place, Elspeth's gallant knight in shining armour, searching for her bracelet, inside, outside, round and round the garden, but he wasn't the only one, Agatha was out there in one of her ridiculous kaftans hiding her huge body, well really, just about everyone spent some time in the garden. The cook informed us at lunchtime that dinner was to be chicken pie, which we all liked the sound of, nothing like a homemade pie, is there? Now, I did see her going out through the conservatory, that must have been in the afternoon, you can't miss her in those awful kaftans. And, of course, then someone asked if anyone had seen Dorothy.'

'Thanks, Elizabeth, you've been very helpful.' Sasha looked across at Elizabeth, realising that she'd fallen asleep.

Had she learned anything new? Not really, she decided, glancing at the points which she'd jotted down.

The residents were beginning to stir, the sounds of slow footsteps making their way along the passage, doors opening and closing, toilets flushing, the murmur of voices, all reaching Sasha's ears. She gently nudged Elizabeth, concerned that she'd fallen asleep with her head at an awkward angle.

'Can I help you to your room?'

At Elizabeth's sleepy nod, she helped her out of the chair, holding her elbow as they made their way to her room.

Sasha looked around with interest, it being the first of the residents' rooms that she'd been into. Framed photos adorned the chest of drawers, a silver hairbrush and mirror nestled among them, and an old-fashioned writing case lay open on the small table, accompanied by a bottle of sherry and a small crystal glass on a tray. Sasha picked up the photo of a young Elizabeth on her wedding day, gazing adoringly at her new husband. Replacing it, she smiled at the other photo, Elizabeth's husband again, but this time as a joyful father holding his young daughter, his blue eyes staring proudly directly at the camera.

Walking to the large window, she looked out at the garden, thinking what a nice view it was for Elizabeth, nothing but trees and the immaculate lawn dotted with beds of flowers in a riot of colour as they bordered the pathways winding through the garden.

'You've got a lovely room, and such a nice view. Are you alright? You look a little pale.'

'I'm fine.' Elizabeth tucked the card back into the torn envelope, placing it into the pocket of her skirt, before smoothing her hair and turning towards her bathroom door.

'Well, I'll leave you to it then. Thanks again for the chat.' Sasha left Elizabeth's room a little uncertainly, but the reason for Elizabeth's pale face soon became clear.

'Oh, it's too awful, I can't bear to think about it.' Agatha held a card in her hand as she stood outside a doorway at the end of the passage, from within which Davinia's voice could be heard.

'We have to be strong, sister dear, it's what Monty would have wanted. It will be a lovely way to remember him, you know how much he enjoyed the garden.'

Albert Bird appeared from around the corner and joined Agatha. 'Got your invitation to Monty's memorial then? Let's hope it's a nice day.'

'Will we have to wear black? I don't think I own anything black.' Elspeth's worried face emerged from the door next to Davinia's.

'No, you wear one of your pretty outfits, my girl, that's how it should be, plenty of colour, not all dreary. Agatha will be in one of her colourful dresses, won't you?'

'Yes, I'm afraid I don't have anything black either.' Agatha shivered. 'I'm not looking forward to it, not at all.'

Howard walked towards the group, having come from the same direction as Albert. 'Is this about Monty's memorial? I shall wear my red bow tie, we should make it a jolly occasion, Monty was a fine chap and we must remember him in style. I expect Kirsty will lay on some good food, perhaps a nice cake.' He winked at Elspeth as Agatha's face brightened.

'Oh, do you think so? Yes, what a lovely idea, a nice memorial tea. I must speak to Kirsty about what cake would be best, I know Monty enjoyed her lemon cake. Oh–' she paused, looking stricken. 'I think the last time we had that was the day that Dorothy was killed.'

Elizabeth's voice carried from her room, 'We didn't have cake the day that Dorothy died, and quite frankly,' she walked out, passing the small gathering, 'I think it's in very bad taste to be discussing food when it's the memorial we should be focused on.'

Howard rolled his eyes at Sasha, who'd been hovering nearby. 'She's made a quick recovery, trust her to put the dampener on everything.'

'For what it's worth, I think you've all got the right idea. From the little that I knew of Monty, he loved his flowers and the garden. He was a lovely man. Er, when is the memorial?'

'Tuesday afternoon, and I'm sure he'd like you to be there too, dear.' Howard smiled as he nodded his head, to murmured agreements from the others.

'I'd be honoured to attend, thank you.' Sasha glanced towards Albert, wondering if she could try and catch a few minutes with him. 'Er, Albert, are you free, by any chance?'

'Free as a bird, that's me.' Albert laughed at his own joke. 'I'm the last man standing, I believe, the only one who hasn't been interviewed. Wouldn't want you to think I'd got anything to hide. My life's an open book, don't I always say that, my girl?' He pulled Elspeth close and hugged her.

'Oh yes, Albert's a very open man, we have complete trust with each other don't we, Albie?'

'Complete and utter trust.' Albert kissed the top of Elspeth's head before releasing her. 'Which is why, after Monty's untimely demise, I've been thinking, and I shall be making a new will leaving everything to you, my beloved.'

'You mustn't do that, what about poor Raymond?'

'Raymond can take care of himself, and I'm sure you'd see him right if need be. No, it's what a married couple does, we take care of each other first. Of course, you'll make your own decision, Elspeth, but you know I'd always look out for Miriam, don't you, even if she does seem too busy to visit you very often.'

Clocking Elspeth's expression, a mixture of hurt and confusion, Sasha regarded Albert thoughtfully. Had the man seriously got an agenda somehow? Marrying for money at the age of, what, eighty-five odd? And just how much money had

Elspeth got? She certainly appeared to have some impressive jewellery...

'In fact, I think I'll get Raymond to take me to the solicitor's tomorrow, get that all finalised, there are some other things I need to attend to in the village, as well.'

'I need to go into the village too,' Agatha piped up, 'I could ask Mrs Goodwin if she can organise the minibus for us, we can have a day out.'

'Well, I'd been thinking of going in as well.' Elspeth's expression took on a look of resolve, as Howard spoke.

'I need to go to the bank, as a matter of fact, not to rob it, my bank robber days are over.' He chuckled at no one in particular. 'We might as well ask about that minibus.'

The group dispersed and Sasha gave Albert a smile. 'Let's go into the library, shall we?'

Elizabeth's back was disappearing along the garden path leading from the library door, as they entered, the door left open. 'She'll be in trouble with Mrs G for leaving it swinging, never closes it, she doesn't. I reckon it's on account of her la-di-da life in Africa she likes to remind us about, servants swarming around doing everything all the time. And all those parties, there was a chap I met when I was– well, it doesn't matter where I was, a long time ago now, but he used to live out there, Kenya, then Zimbabwe, which he called Rhodesia, said the stories he could tell, made some joke about it being the happiest place on earth. I never did quite get what he meant by that. I mean, what, did they all take happy pills or something? He said *it still goes on, Albie, all over Africa, not just in the valley, in little mining towns in the middle of nowhere, the big cities, all those places full of the settlers, all on account of the boredom, it's never changed.* I can still see him giving me a knowing wink.'

Sasha moved things along. 'Right, well, perhaps we should get to the day that Dorothy was killed? If you can just tell me everything that you can remember about the day, from when you woke up.'

'Righto, don't suppose I can tell you anything that Elizabeth didn't? Helpful was she?'

With a non-committal bob of her head, Sasha indicated that he should continue.

'Not much to tell, I took Elspeth for a walk in the garden, poor thing was all upset about a missing bracelet, you know, we've got a thief here and nothing gets done about it. Worth a bob or two, her jewellery is.' Albert whistled to add weight to his statement, before continuing.

'Dorothy was doing her mad walking around and muttering, none of us paid much attention to her, always coming out with nonsense, she was. We all ended up in the lounge for morning coffee, the lot of us, I'm sure, including Judith and Richard – he'd brought shortbread. There was a lot of coming and going that day, plenty of visitors, what with Judith and Richard, oh, and his wife, sure I saw her with him in the garden, might have been in the morning when I was looking for Elspeth's bracelet. Oh, and my son visited, he's a good lad, is Ray.

'But I've shot ahead, first Davinia disappeared off to her room and that must have been before lunch as I'm pretty sure she missed out on the meagre offerings. I don't think the old dear was feeling too well. Anyway, that's what reminded me about Ray, he popped in just before lunch and said how about if he sneaked in burgers and chips for us for a late lunch.'

Albert arched his eyebrows at Sasha, a wry grin on his face. 'I'm making it sound like we're in prison here, not at all, of course, but they do frown on fast food, and it was an opportunity, what with Elspeth being out shopping with Judith. So while they were all dozing off in the lounge, we scoffed our grub in the library, out of sight of our beloved leader, Mrs Goodwin. That's between you and me, of course, no food in the library, that's the rule.'

Sasha shifted uncomfortably, aware that she'd also broken the rule albeit unknowingly.

'Like naughty schoolboys we were, creeping out of the library with the wrappers, needing to dispose of the evidence, we had a good laugh about that. We squashed them in the bins round behind the greenhouse, had a panic when Ray thought Agatha had spotted us, but she was a way off and had her back to us so I think we got away with it.' Albert guffawed at the memory, making Sasha smile even as she made her notes.

'Not sure what young Spencer was doing round there, I saw him walk off just before we got there, might have been around the time that old Dorothy copped it, not that I'm suggesting he had anything to do with, I doubt the old girl had anything on him, ha ha, not that I'm saying she had anything on any of us, it's just, she liked to talk, say too much, upset people. I expect the others have mentioned it to you?'

A number of the residents seemed quite concerned to know whether she was aware of Dorothy's comments, but what was it they were worried about? Surely they didn't all have things they were hiding? Old lives – the phrase popped into her head, not for the first time – was someone keeping an old lie hidden from their past? Were they all keepers of old lies which they wanted to keep buried at all costs? It seemed absurd.

Receiving no response from Sasha, Albert continued, 'I didn't do the crafting activity, I ask you, beading, for a bloke! We saw Greg and Richard having a bit of a ding dong outside but I can't remember if that was before or after I saw his wife.' Albert shook his head ruefully. 'The old memory's not what it was, although I reckon I've had a better recollection of it all today than I did at the time, when we had to speak to the old bill.

'And I've remembered another thing, Lillian's son, Mervyn, was around, funny, I'd clean forgotten about him being there until now. It was before lunch that we saw him, that's right, it was when Ray called in to say did I fancy him going and getting us burgers – he saw Mervyn getting into his car, face like thunder on him, he said. I didn't have my specs on, can't stand the things, so I couldn't really make him out. Not a happy chappy, that one, don't know why he visits his old mum so much, never looks very cheerful about it.' Albert appeared to have finished speaking and Sasha opened her mouth to thank him when he began again.

'It was quite a day all round, really, and then a nice bit of cake with our tea in the afternoon, which was a surprise, but I'm not complaining. And it was round about then that someone asked where Dorothy was. Shame really, none of us knew how long she'd been missing.' Albert lapsed into silence.

'Well, thanks, Albert, you've been a huge help, I think your memory could give mine a run for its money.'

Elspeth appeared in the doorway, hovering uncertainly. 'Are you done? Am I interrupting? It's just that they're laying the table for dinner.'

'I'm all yours, beautiful.' Albert pushed himself up and out of the armchair as Elspeth flushed happily.

Sasha smiled, before looking at her watch in surprise. Well, she'd successfully kept herself busy, and finally completed her interviews with the residents. She left the library and headed further along the passage to use the visitors' cloakroom. Bedroom doors stood open, revealing empty rooms, everyone, presumably, gathered in the lounge for dinner.

A grunting sound from one room was followed by a heavy thud and the clattering sound of things falling on the floor and, glancing in through the doorway, she was presented with Agatha's vast kaftan-clad rear as she bent down between the bed and the wardrobe.

'Can I help you, Agatha?' Stepping into the room, Sasha walked round the bed as Agatha looked up red-faced, a gold metallic object in her hand, which she hurriedly dropped into the box on the floor, where it landed on top of a jumble of items, the topmost being a small framed photo of a young woman.

'No! Sorry.' Agatha pushed the lid back onto the box. 'I didn't mean to sound rude, I just got flustered. I was having a bit of a tidy up, do excuse me. I'm a little out of sorts what with all the talk about dear Monty's memorial on Tuesday.' She nudged the box under the bed with her foot as Sasha retreated.

'Sorry, Agatha, I didn't mean to disturb you, I know it's an upsetting time for you all. I'll leave you to it.'

With her bag and notebooks collected from the library, Sasha decided to spend a few minutes in the garden before leaving. Wandering in no particular direction, she found herself at the bench on which she'd come across Monty having a smoke, when she'd been arguing on the phone with Eric. She sat down, enjoying the peace and quiet, and took out her cigarettes and lighter. About to light her cigarette, she stopped, had the gold-coloured object in Agatha's hand been a lighter? More specifically, could it have been Monty's lighter? And the photo of the young woman? Someone had had a photo stolen, but who had it been? She flicked through her notebook, finding the page where she'd listed the items that Mrs Goodwin had reeled off to her.

She glanced through the list again – cash belonging to Howard and Albert, various pieces of Elspeth's jewellery,

Lillian's pen, Agatha's dress, Davinia's photo, a trinket of Elizabeth's, and Monty's cigarette lighter.

Sasha leaned back, wondering again if Agatha could be a kleptomaniac. But Monty had been her friend, would she really have taken his lighter? He'd made a cryptic reference to someone though, and she'd wondered if he'd meant Agatha, but had decided against it due to the fact that Agatha had also had something stolen. And Davinia was her own sister, had she helped herself to Davinia's photo? Aware that someone was walking towards her, Sasha looked up, greeting Kirsty and shunting along the bench to make room for her.

'I'm feeling my age.' Kirsty yawned. 'All that cooking today and only three for lunch. Still, it won't be wasted, most of it'll do for tomorrow night. Cold roast beef sandwiches tonight is what they've got, I don't expect they've got much of an appetite. I came to look for Spencer, I don't suppose you've seen him?'

'No, I haven't sorry.' Sasha shook her head.

Kirsty's expression darkened. 'He'd better not be off smoking one of his joints. Oh yes.' She nodded. 'I've held my own counsel so far, but if he carries on leading Elspeth's granddaughter astray I'll have to have a word with Mrs Goodwin.

'Er, remind me, Elspeth's granddaughter is...?'

'Lucy, always in black, you know what these young girls are like. I expect you've seen her visiting her grandma at some time or another.'

'Lucy, yes, I know who you mean, I think my niece is friends with her. Her and Spencer are an item, aren't they?'

'That's right, well, if your niece is friends with her, you'd better keep an eye on things, they slip into drugs easily at that age. Well, I'd better go and find him, he's got work to do and I'm wanting to get off home, my feet are killing me and my husband will be wanting his dinner.' She rolled her eyes. 'Sometimes it feels like the cooking never stops.'

Watching Kirsty walk away, Sasha called out to her. 'Kirsty, what colour car does Spencer drive?'

'Him? Oh, I think it's red, it's a bit burnt out, but gets him from A to B. Bye, love.' Kirsty's wave of her hand as she walked off was a clear message, this was a woman who wanted to get home.

Sasha drove back to the pub, her head buzzing. She needed to have a look at the box in Agatha's room, hell, she needed to check all the rooms, although what she hoped to find after all this time she couldn't say, she needed to find out a little more about Chantelle's extracurricular activities which, she considered, included finding out who the owner of the white car was that she'd seen Chantelle and Lucy getting into in the high street, and she absolutely needed to find out exactly what knowledge Dorothy had taunted each resident with, as well as any visitors or staff, for surely it had been the desire to keep an old lie a secret that had resulted in Dorothy's murder. Could it have been Agatha, wanting her kleptomaniac tendencies to remain hidden? Had Dorothy taunted her about it? Agatha had been seen in the garden, by more than one person, possibly around the time of Dorothy's death, hadn't she? Or was she just barking up the wrong tree completely? She pulled into the car park, looking forward to an ice-cold glass of wine.

'Hi, Sash, how are you feeling, have you had a good day, my darling?' Jules smiled as she reached for a wine glass.

'I did in the end, thanks, it didn't start off great, understatement of the year, but it's been productive.' In amazement, Sasha realised that she'd kept herself so busy that thoughts of everything that had happened between her and Eric had not crowded her head or upset her. The ice cubes clinked enticingly as she took the glass of wine from Jules and she lifted it to her lips, swallowing thirstily.

THE OLD MOTEL

Spencer brought through the plates of sandwiches, together with cream cheese bridge rolls for those might struggle to chew the cold meat, placing them on the table. Returning to the kitchen, he collected Kirsty's freshly-baked cheese scones and picked up the bowl of crisps. That just left the angel cake, which still needed slicing, as per Kirsty's instructions, but he'd call them all to the table first, he decided, and then help himself to a slice, he was partial to a bit of sponge cake with those creamy bits in between. And where was Greg? He wanted to head off, have a shower and meet up with Glen and Lucy for a bit of fun.

'Sorry.' Greg hurried into the dining room, smiling. 'I was just on the phone.'

'Oh yeah?' Spencer smirked knowingly. 'Talking to your boyfriend?'

'Shh.' Greg frowned at him. 'You respect my privacy and I'll respect yours, alright, Spencer? You can go now, I'll be fine, thank you.'

Dismissed, Spencer removed his tunic, waving over his shoulder as he went to the kitchen, where he sliced up the cake and stuffed a slice in his mouth, wiping the crumbs away as he left. He wondered what the reaction had been to his little blackmail note, not having had the opportunity to watch it being opened. If they did as he'd told them, he'd find a nice little wad of cash placed where he'd instructed, tomorrow. He grinned as he walked out to his car, this was going to be easy money, he could milk it forever, it was fantastic.

~

'Oh, goody, cheese scones, my favourite.' Agatha plonked herself down at the table and reached for a scone as Albert laughed.

'Everything's your favourite, Agatha, is there anything you don't like?'

'Nothing wrong with a girl having a good appetite.' Howard winked at Agatha as she blushed a deep shade of crimson. 'What about you, Davinia? Nice cheese scone?'

'Yes, perhaps a small one, I ate quite a large meal at lunchtime.' Davinia patted her stomach.

'The day you eat a large meal I'll eat my hat, but I must say, you do keep a nice trim figure, Davinia.'

It was Davinia's turn to blush deeply, as Elspeth piped up.

'You don't even have a hat, do you, Howie?'

'Did Mervyn visit me today?' Lillian looked around. 'I think he did, but I can't quite remember...'

'He popped in after lunch, but he seemed in a rush to be off, perhaps he was busy.'

'Yes, he's always busy.' Lillian lapsed into silence again.

'So, who's off to the village tomorrow? Our trusty leader said she'll organise the minibus for us. We could have some lunch out, how about it?' Albert squeezed Elspeth's arm.

'Perhaps I'll get my hair done.' Elspeth patted her curls. 'I could do with a trim.'

'Me too, Elspeth, I'll make appointments for us in the morning, shall I? I've got quite a lot to do, so we should leave early.'

'You all heard Elizabeth.' Howard mock saluted. 'An early departure is called for. I myself need to get to the bank, but afterwards perhaps a nice spot of lunch somewhere...'

Agatha nodded enthusiastically. 'Lunch out would be lovely, and Davinia, you said you needed to go to the bank as well, so perhaps I'll go too, it's always handy having a little spare cash around. Oh, we could go to the patisserie for lunch, they have such lovely little cakes there. They put them in little boxes for gifts, we should buy one for Mrs Goodwin.'

Various murmurings ensued, the need to call in at Pringle's chemist, perhaps a peek at the clothes in Madam Couture, peppermints to be purchased at the supermarket, appreciative comments made over Kirsty's scones...

'Make way for the teapot and the angel cake.' Greg placed the pot in the centre of the table, followed by the cake. 'Everyone okay? Yes?' He left the dining room, wishing that he had something to look forward to. With Richard telling him they needed to lie low for a while, he was feeling quite miserable. Honestly, their jaunt to the village in the morning sounded more exciting than anything in his life lately.

'Who'd like some of this cake?' Agatha asked, reaching for the largest slice.

~

Arms embraced Sasha from behind, the scent of perfume enveloping her. 'Oh, poor old you, single again. Are you alright? Cal told me all about it.' Willow's face was the perfect picture of sympathy, as Sasha turned to her.

'I'm fine, thanks, Willow.' Why was it that the woman irritated her so much? She smiled a greeting as Cal joined them. 'Can I buy you both a drink, I was just about to order another?'

'I'll get them.' Willow leaned over the bar to attract Jules's attention, her pert bottom, encased in a tight-fitting denim skirt, attracting the attention of the male customers nearby.

'Are you good?' Cal spoke softly, concern showing in his eyes as he looked down at her.

'I am, honestly, it's the best thing that could have happened, now my head's clear and I'm focused on what I came here for.'

'Any more news about Monty's death?'

She shook her head. 'Not that I know of, but I'm still working on Dorothy's murder, and if they were killed by the same person then something will reveal itself in due course.'

Willow handed round the drinks and, at a wave of a cigarette packet from Cal, they made their way out to the river, sitting down at a bench table where they lit their cigarettes under the disapproving gaze of Willow.

'Will I be able to go back to work tomorrow? I usually do a literature activity on Monday afternoons.'

'I would think so, yes, I was there this afternoon and everything's pretty much back to normal. Oh, there's going to be a memorial for Monty in the garden on Tuesday, I don't expect you'd heard.'

'Someone left an envelope for you at the bar earlier, with the details, didn't they?' Cal pulled Willow close. 'You got quite upset about it, didn't you?'

As Willow snuggled into Cal, nodding, Sasha looked across at her. She studied Willow's face, wondering why she'd insinuated herself into Meadowvale, snippets of Agatha's conversation springing into her mind, *so interested in us oldies, wanted to know where I was born, interested in Davinia as well... do you remember when you went away?* What had Agatha been talking about? Something about baths, a comment Dorothy had made about bathwater... Willow had been out the night of the break-in at Meadowvale when someone had rifled through the filing cabinet, which surely contained personal information about the residents. It had also been the night that Monty had been murdered. What was the connection? Was there even one?

'Sash?'

Realising that Cal had been speaking, Sasha looked at him distractedly. 'Sorry? I think I zoned out for a second.'

'I said do you fancy joining us?' At Sasha's blank face, he repeated himself. 'We're going out for tapas in a while, there's a great spot on the river on the way to Rentham.'

'It sounds great, but I've got work to do.' Pasting on a rueful expression, Sasha excused herself. 'In fact, I really ought to get on with it, I need to go through my notes before tomorrow. Thanks though. You two have a good time, yeah? And thanks for the drink, Willow.'

Finding a corner table inside, Sasha ensconced herself with her notes and tried to assimilate the haphazard thoughts that crashed around in her head.

What was it Dorothy had taunted Davinia about? Bathwater. The old saying sprung into her mind, *don't throw out the baby with the bathwater*. But a baby? Davinia's? But there was no child. Unless... She shook her head, the whole idea seemed ludicrous.

And Willow? Why had she been so keen to work at Meadowvale? Dorothy had been killed shortly after her arrival... maybe Willow wasn't even her real name... Willow the murderer...

It was an appealing idea, she thought, looking up as Willow's tinkling laughter rang out from the bar, where she and Cal had dropped off their empty glasses. It was also more than a touch insane, but maybe she was going a little mad...

~

Tessa removed her hand from her wine glass. 'Oh, go on then, one more, then I need an early night.'

Dave topped up both their glasses, grinning. 'An early night sounds good, we could watch a film in bed, maybe open another bottle...' He turned as his daughter came back into the lounge. 'Have you done all your homework, Chants?'

'Good time to ask me, Dad, on Sunday night.' Sighing, Chantelle nodded. 'Yeah, all done, school uniform ready, all set for another exciting week of my life. I think I'll go to bed.'

'Bit early, isn't it? Don't you want to watch a film with us, love?' Tessa smiled gently at her daughter as Dave nudged her.

'She doesn't want to get stuck with us, and besides, we're going to watch a film in bed, I need to rest my poor old back.'

'There's nothing wrong with your back.' Tessa slapped his arm, giggling.

Embarrassed, Chantelle called out goodnight and went upstairs, it was so gross when they behaved like that and she knew exactly what they were going to do. She also knew that they wouldn't come into her room later to check on her, not once they'd got all romantic in their bedroom with wine. She texted Lucy and arranged a time to meet her and Spencer at the bottom of the road.

~

'Oh, Lucy, you're not going out on a Sunday night, surely?' Miriam looked at her daughter helplessly, feeling her control as a mother slipping further and further away. It was so late and she had school tomorrow. 'Where are you going at this time of night?'

'I'm just hanging out with Spence, Mum, he is my boyfriend, and besides, it's not even nine o'clock yet, what am I, a five-year old?' With a last approving check in the hall mirror, she opened the front door, slamming it behind her, and looked for Spencer's car.

~

Satisfied that her parents were ensconced in their bedroom, Chantelle tiptoed down the stairs, opened the front door quietly, and slipped out, before making her way to the end of the road just as Spencer and Lucy pulled up.

'We're meeting Glen at the old motel out on the Rentham old road,' Spencer announced to his passengers as they drove off.

'Uurgh, that place gives me the creeps.' Lucy shuddered exaggeratedly as she turned round to grin at her friend.

'Me too.' Chantelle laughed. 'I've driven past with Mum and Dad. What happened to it? Why did it close down?'

'Dunno exactly, something to do with when they built the new road, which was years ago anyway, so no one went that way anymore, and then they didn't get many people staying there so it closed. There was a story that someone was murdered there, she was the only guest and the bloke working there went mad and topped her.' Spencer sniggered as the girls squealed in a mixture of fear and delight.

'Maybe it was like in that film, you know, when he dressed up like his mother and killed that woman?'

'Psycho, oh my God that was so scary, that sound when he stabbed her through the shower curtain.' Lucy put her hands over her face as Chantelle made the sounds from the film.

'Nah, he pulled the curtain back first then he stabbed her.' Grinning, Spencer turned onto the old road. 'I've seen that film loads of times, but it might have been like that in this murder, yeah, come to think of it, my mate showed me which room it was, I'll show you, if you're brave enough, it's still got all the bloodstains.'

More squeals followed as both girls pretended a bravado they weren't quite sure they actually felt.

'There's Glen's car.' They pulled into the pot-holed parking lot, overgrown with weeds, parking down the side of the building, next to Glen, and Spencer got out of the car. 'Come on, what, scared now are we?'

'No, course we're not, are we, Chants?'

The girls huddled together, giggling, as they followed Spencer in the gloom of approaching twilight.

Spencer and Glen had a huddled conversation, the odd word reaching the girls as they stood a little distance away, *money, grass, tomorrow, white, my treat.*

'Come on then, my treat.' The last words were repeated as Glen turned to the girls. 'I've got something a bit different for you ladies tonight. That includes you, Spencer.' He cackled at his own sense of humour, then turned to the derelict motel building, stepping through the open doorway into what used to be the reception. 'Watch your step, it's a bit of a mess in here.'

Chantelle looked around in interest. Fast food wrappers littered the floor, rotting upholstery, on what had once been two armchairs, had disintegrated to reveal crumbling foam padding, and the yellowed, curled, pages of a phone book indicated just how long the motel had been abandoned. The light was fading fast now and she hurried to catch up with the others as they headed along a corridor.

'We'll go in here.' Glen walked into what had once been a guest room, as Spencer turned to the girls.

'This is it, this is the one she was killed in.' He winked at Glen, who nodded, going along with the wind-up.

'Yeah, that's right.'

'I don't see any bloodstains.' Lucy was peering around as she stepped into the small bathroom.

'That's 'cause it's too dark, but it's all over the floor, you're standing right in it.' Spencer grinned at Glen. 'I told them about the bloke who worked here, how he killed the woman who stayed here one night.'

'They're winding us up, Luce.' Chantelle pulled her squealing friend back out of the room, nevertheless.

'Bit like that old bloke up where you work, Spence, eh? What happened, someone stab him or what?'

'Bashed him over the head.' Spencer nodded knowingly. 'Blood everywhere.'

'Did you see it?' Lucy looked at Spencer in horror as Chantelle, again, pictured his hand leaving something bloody on Lucy's face that night when he got back in the car.

Glen had pulled a small table into the middle of the room and, having squatted down on the floor, was busy tipping a small amount of white powder onto the surface. 'You're going to enjoy this.' He grinned, as he began to chop at it with a razorblade which he produced from his back pocket.

'What is it, is it cocaine?' Chantelle looked nervously at Lucy. She'd thought they were just going to smoke a joint.

'Yeah, white, blow, whatever you want to call it.' He expertly divided the powder into smaller piles, before scraping them into thin lines. 'Careful now, don't blow it away.' He laughed at his own joke.

They watched him as he took a ten-pound note from his wallet and rolled it into a tube. Lucy cast a glance at Chantelle, raising her eyebrows slightly and shrugging. 'I'll try it.'

'You just snort it up, a little up each nostril, like this.' Glen leaned over the table and demonstrated, tapping the rolled banknote on the hard surface afterwards and dabbing at the residue with his finger, which he then proceeded to rub onto his gums, before opening a new packet of cigarettes and lighting up.

Chantelle picked up his discarded packet. 'You've still got two in here.'

'Keep 'em, I'm feeling generous.'

'Thanks.' She slipped the packet into her back pocket, she and Lucy could have one each at school tomorrow.

She felt so great, it was so cool, Lucy was the best friend ever and Spencer and Glen were so funny. There was so much to talk about, everyone was just so interesting, she'd thought life was boring in Parva Crossing but it was amazing. Her mouth felt a little numb, or was it her tongue? Giggling, she and Lucy clutched at each other in the gloom, a circle of light from Glen's mobile phone torch illuminating his hands and face as he prepared them another line of cocaine. 'What?' she looked at the guys as they burst out laughing.

'You've been talking non-stop for about ten minutes, Chants, feeling good?'

'I feel fantastic!' She grinned at Spencer, before telling them about her fabulous aunt. 'What was I saying? Oh, yeah, she solves murders and stuff, and she's really cool, she drinks and smokes and has these gorgeous boyfriends, although the one did abduct her and try to kill her. He'd killed other women before and been to prison and stuff.'

'I can't believe your aunt went out with a murderer, I want to meet her, can I meet her? Has she caught the killer at the old people's home yet? Spencer, what's she like? You better not fancy her.' Lucy jabbed him in the ribs as she pulled her hair back in preparation to snort another line of coke.

'Yeah, she's alright.' Spencer was on a major high, Glen was being so cool about everything, giving them free coke and letting him pay him tomorrow, after he got his money, for the bag of grass he'd given him earlier. 'I might be able to help her out about the murder, might have seen something, might have seen who did it. But it pays me to keep my mouth shut for now as long as they pay up. I gave them a nice little blackmail letter today.' He laughed, pleased with himself. 'Spencer's not just a pretty face you know, he knows how to make money out of a bit of good luck. Talk about being in the right place at the right time, I couldn't believe it, the way his head fell over and his wig fell off.'

'You never saw it, Spence, don't lie.' Lucy's eyes were wide.

Unable to resist showing off, or to stop his tongue running away with him, Spencer carried on bragging.

'Prove it,' Glen said, his eyes narrowed, 'tell us something no one else knows or how do we know you're not just making it up?'

Jumping up, Spencer announced, 'I'll do better than that, I'll show you something I took from him.' He ran off into the darkness, whooping as he tripped over a discarded table, returning a minute or two later with something in his hand, which he held out triumphantly.

'Took it from his pocket just after the murderer bashed his head in, wasn't much cash in it though, which was a bit of a let-down.'

'Give us it here, let's have a look then.' Glen held out his hand, taking the wallet and folding it open to look inside. 'Monty Mallowan... Ooh, what's all this then, a picture of him with his boyfriend, is it? Old poofter was he?' Glen went to remove the photo but Chantelle spoke out.

'Leave it, don't touch it.' She grabbed the wallet from Glen's hand, folding it closed, remembering how sadly and fondly Sasha had spoken of the old man. 'It's just,' she explained awkwardly to their surprised faces, 'a bit of respect, that's all, you know?'

'Nah.' Spencer lunged, grabbing the wallet from her, laughing as Glen tackled him and they rolled on the floor, the wallet finally being ejected from their wrangling to disappear beneath the rusting bed frame topped with an old rotted mattress.

'Where'd it go?' Spencer tried to look beneath the bed as car headlights illuminated the room, but Glen pulled him back.

'Leave it, don't matter, we need to go, looks like someone's pulled in out there. I've got a bit of business to sort out anyway. Let's go, might be the old bill.' At this, they hurried from the room and made their way quietly through to the old reception, where Spencer peered out at the newly parked car.

He shook his head. 'It's not cops, it's a bloke and a woman, I think they're fighting.'

'Watch and learn, children, watch and learn, I'll give them a fright.' Glen walked out to his car, followed by the other three. 'And, Spence, don't forget my money tomorrow.'

Glen revved his car's engine before switching on his headlights to full beam, he then drove straight at the parked car, veering around it at the last second, his hooter blaring. He twice circled the car containing the astonished man and woman, before driving out with a final blast of his hooter, waving his arm out of the window at his admiring groupies.

Spencer laughed as the man hurriedly started his car and pulled out. 'That's stopped their little fight, anyway.'

'Spence.' Lucy's voice was tense. 'That wallet you had in there, is it really from the dead man, from Monty? But you didn't– you didn't kill him, did you?'

Leaning across to smooch Lucy on the lips, Spencer seemed to remember something. He jumped out, opening the boot to retrieve something which he screwed up and threw on the ground. Back in the car, he started the engine and drove out. 'Getting rid of the evidence, nah, I'm only kidding. I didn't kill him, Luce, course not, but the person who did is going to give me a nice lot of money, whenever I ask for it, to keep my mouth shut, starting tomorrow.' Whooping loudly, Spencer drummed his hands on the steering wheel. 'Who fancies a joint? No one? Roll me one then, will you, Luce?'

She'd had a great time, Chantelle thought sleepily, as she got out of the car and waved goodbye. Now she just had to get indoors without waking Mum and Dad up. At the top of the stairs, she quickly used the bathroom before scooting into her bedroom as she heard her parents' bedroom door began to open. She yanked her duvet back, jumped into bed and covered herself up to her neck with it, closing her eyes tightly.

Tessa yawned, rubbing her eyes as she glanced at Chantelle's open bedroom door. Moving to stand in the doorway, she smiled at her daughter's hair as it fanned out on the pillow. Closing the door quietly, she tiptoed into the bathroom, where someone had left the light on, probably Dave, she decided sleepily.

Chantelle's heart was racing, it had been a close one. Cautiously turning back her duvet, she slipped out of bed and undressed, careful not to make a sound. She slid the cigarette packet from Glen into her schoolbag before getting back into bed gratefully, she felt so tired.

An hour later she was still tossing and turning, unable to sleep, her mind wide awake and working overtime. Thoughts careered through her head of what they'd done, the things they'd said, the things Spencer had said, she pictured the derelict motel room, could smell its abandonment – the story about the murdered woman, it couldn't be true – but the story about the poor old man at the home, did Spencer really know who did it? She should tell Sasha, shouldn't she? But then she'd be betraying Spencer, well, Lucy, she supposed, as panic suddenly hit her, she'd forgotten to do her maths homework. She sat up in bed, about to reach for her light switch, when she remembered that she'd done it on Friday night. Relieved, she laid back down, where she tossed and turned throughout the night.

A LITTLE JAUNT TO PARVA CROSSING

Monday morning dawned bright and sunny and Sasha leapt out of bed, jumping into the shower before breakfasting alone on poached eggs on toast. First on her list was to be a quick courtesy call at Pringle's, to update Mrs Pringle on Charles Priestley – the woman had, after all, been a great help with her eagle-eyed observation of his visit to Pink's Hardware – but as she drove into the village she was pleasurably distracted by the sight of Maureen Ford and Douglas, and she pulled into a parking space, jumping out of the car with her arms outstretched.

After hugs and exclamations of delight between the two women, tail-wagging and a series of excited barks from Douglas, which showed no sign of stopping, it was agreed that a cup of tea was in order. Maureen swooped up Douglas's trembling body and they crossed the road to take a seat at The Village Deli. By the time they'd caught each other up on their news and Maureen had expressed her absolute shock over the Charles Priestley affair, followed by suitable commiseration over Sasha's break-up with Eric, their tea had arrived and they sat back in companionable silence for a moment, Sasha's hand resting on Douglas's velvety body as he nestled on her lap.

A minibus parked just along the road and disgorged its occupants onto the pavement, the strident tones of Elizabeth Payton being the first voice to be heard as she announced that they had only five minutes until their hair appointments, joined swiftly by the flutterings of Elspeth Parkhurst as she worriedly arranged a time to meet up with Albert, who, in turn appeared to make a general plan amongst the group with regard to lunch. Davinia and Agatha Lovewell headed in the direction of Pringle's chemist and Howard, after waving them off, turned to Lavinia, offering to accompany her to the supermarket as he too needed peppermints.

Sasha and Maureen observed the activity with smiles on their faces, as Sasha commented that it was a good thing she'd completed her resident interviews yesterday. They watched

Elizabeth and Elspeth walk past Pringle's and turn into Hair by Patricia, at which point Sasha gulped down the rest of her tea and said she'd better be moving.

Sasha entered Pringle's to the sound of Dolly Pringle holding forth about the murders at Meadowvale.

'Of course, my dears, it could have been any one of you, couldn't it? After Dorothy's death it's a wonder you didn't all refuse to come out of your rooms. And you say he was just sitting there in the conservatory? Well, it's like I said to Sheila, what's the world coming to when you can't sit safely in your armchair in your own home? And who knows where the killer will strike next?' Mrs Pringle shook her head. 'I don't know what the world's coming to, I really don't.' she paused, turning her head to check on Sheila's progress with the tea. 'Let it brew for five minutes, dear, and don't forget the custard creams. Ah, here's Sasha, how are you, dear?' She slipped a notebook into her pocket as she spoke.

Not waiting for a reply or to draw a breath it seemed, Mrs Pringle continued, not wanting to lose her momentum. 'It never would have happened in the old days, and as for the vandalism, well, that was unheard of in our day.' Finally, she had to draw a breath and Agatha took the opportunity to get a word in.

'We've both been very upset, haven't we, Davinia? I'll just take the one biscuit, thank you, Sheila, oh, well, they are quite small, perhaps two, it'll be a while until lunch, I expect. Oh, those hairclips are so pretty, I'll just have a look...'

'Good morning, everyone.' Sasha took the gap, not wanting to get caught for hours. 'Dolly, I thought I'd just pop in to thank you for your call on Saturday, your observations were most helpful and you were quite right to be concerned.'

Mrs Pringle beamed, turning the same shade as the name of the hardware store. 'Yes, well, as soon as I saw him going into Pink's I knew that something was wrong. You must tell me all about it, not that I'd expect you to divulge sensitive information, but perhaps just the basics, I shan't breathe a word to anyone, of course. Oh there, that's right, Sheila, thank you, no, I insist, Davinia, you sit down and rest your legs, I expect you've got lots of walking to do this morning. I saw the minibus arrive, it looks like you've all come out for a little trip? And Elizabeth and Elspeth have gone into Patricia's, she'll send them out looking ten years younger. I had a little trim just last week.' She patted her hair. 'And I must say, I clean felt like a young girl when I walked out. She just has a way with hair, I said so to Sheila, didn't I, dear?' Her brow furrowed. 'Although that young girl she's taken on isn't really experienced enough, if you know what I mean? Just put the tea there for Agatha, that's right, thank you, Sheila. Now, can we pour you a cup, Sasha, the tea at the Deli isn't always the best...'

Sasha shook her head in amusement, declining the offer. 'I'll give it a miss, if you don't mind, I've quite a lot to do today.'

Nodding, Mrs Pringle whipped around the counter and led Sasha to the bubble bath section, lowering her voice as she spoke. 'So the police arrested him? But you don't think he was connected to the Meadowvale murders?'

'Yes, he's under arrest, but nothing to do with Meadowvale. It'll all come out in due course, it was related to the abductions–'

'I knew it, was he a copycat, is that what they call it? No? Then he was working with him, goodness, no, I quite understand that you can't discuss it.' Her eyes glanced at Sasha's neck. 'You're not wearing your necklace, I do hope everything is alright with you and your young man, or perhaps...'

'Let's just say he's not my young man anymore, but for no reason other than that Eric's always been the same and I should never have believed that he'd change.' *She had to get out of here if she didn't want to cave in under Mrs Pringle's adroit interrogation.*

'Well, we should be off, thank you for the tea, Sheila, it was just the fortification that we needed for a morning at the shops, wasn't it, Agatha? Yes, just the hairspray for me, thank you, dear. What's that, Agatha?'

'Could you pay for these hairclips for me? They're so pretty, and I don't have any cash until we go to the bank.'

'They'll be running out of money at the bank, I see Mr Bird's already been in, and it looks like Mr Norton's headed in there now.' Sheila returned to her post at the till as Mrs Pringle gave her a reproving look.

'Now, Sheila, we shouldn't go spying on the bank's customers, I'm sure we've got quite enough to do in here today.'

After much clucking and goodbyes, the Lovewell sisters departed and Sasha opened her mouth to say goodbye, too, when she remembered something. 'Oh, where do I find the butcher's, Dolly? I thought I'd take your advice and pop in to ask about their waste disposal. Not that my car's vandalism is exactly top of the list of priorities, but I'd like to know who did it just the same.'

She walked to the door to the sound of Sheila muttering, 'Really, Agatha Lovewell is quite untidy, look at this hairclip display. Didn't we have two of the pearl clips left? There's only one here now, that's odd.'

Leaving the chemist, and the two women's mystified discussion, Sasha smiled to herself, it looked like Agatha might not be restricting her kleptomania to just Meadowvale. It was still only a suspicion at this point but once she'd been to the butcher's she'd head to Meadowvale and see if she could take a look at the residents' rooms. With everyone out on a jaunt it was the ideal opportunity, if Mrs Goodwin would allow it.

She walked past Hair by Patricia, glancing in to see both Elizabeth and Elspeth swathed in floral capes and seated at mirrors, a rather elderly lady attending to Elizabeth, while a woman in her late fifties wielded her scissors on Elspeth's curls – presumably the young girl that Patricia, the owner, had taken on, as described by Mrs Pringle, she thought with amusement.

~

'Not too short, please, Patricia, do be careful,' Elizabeth commanded imperiously, 'I need to be able to fix it up in a bun, and of course, with the wedding coming up I'll need to look my best.'

Patricia nodded, her mouth full of hairpins, as she grappled with Elizabeth's rather wiry hair.

'Elspeth reached up a hand to touch her fringe. 'It won't curl up too short will it, Hilary? Once it dries, I mean? I must look nice for Albie for the wedding.'

'All these weddings.' Hilary chattered away. 'To think we've got a bride-to-be here, as well as a grandmother of another bride-to-be, you must be so excited, both of you. How long is it until the wedding?' She combed through Elspeth's hair, snipping off a few errant wisps before standing back and appraising her work.

'Six more weeks,' Elspeth said, beaming, 'until I'm Mrs Bird. I never thought I'd find love a second time, I feel like a young girl all over again.'

Elizabeth snorted. 'A young girl indeed, you must be realistic, Elspeth, you're not in the first flush of youth anymore, far from it.' She turned her head to gauge Elspeth's reaction to her harsh remark.

'Keep your head still please, Elizabeth.' Patricia, who didn't take kindly to being given orders by her clients, or to any discord between her ladies, regained control of her charge, turning her head back to face the mirror.

Elizabeth retaliated. 'How much longer will you be, Patricia, can't you hurry it up? I still have to get to the bank and do some shopping before we all meet for lunch.'

'Now you don't want me to rush and make a mistake, leaving you all lopsided, imagine that.' Patricia, the clear winner of the round, glanced at Hilary. 'I should get Elspeth under the drier in a minute, if I were you, we've got Mrs Grover in shortly for a wash and blow dry, don't forget.'

'I'll wait for you, Elizabeth, we can go to the bank together.' Elspeth smiled cheerfully as she settled down under the drier with a magazine, oblivious to Elizabeth's rolled eyes.

~

'Mr Alison's out this morning, so it's just the pre-cuts 'til he gets back.' The woman behind the counter spoke without looking up, her head bent over a magazine.

'That's okay, I just wondered if I could ask a couple of questions.' As she spoke, Sasha realised that there was something familiar about the woman's bleached hair. She'd seen her somewhere before, had noticed her dark roots.

The woman looked up sharply, a glint of recognition in her eyes as she looked at Sasha. 'Well, I can't really speak for Mr Alison, I mean, he's the boss.' Contradicting herself immediately as her curiosity got the better of her, she asked, 'What was it you wanted to know?'

She'd been in the pub with a younger guy, it came back to her now, as she saw the tattoo on the woman's arm, and they'd both had an unfriendly air about them. 'I just wanted to enquire about where the waste is stored, I understand it's collected once a week, is that right?'

'Not from the health, are you?' Something about the tone of the woman's voice told Sasha that she didn't believe that for one minute.

The door to the shop banged open and a large man entered, holding a box in his arms. 'There's one more box in the car, Sharon, if you could just grab it for me.' Realising that they had a customer, he placed the box down on the counter and smiled at Sasha. 'New in town, are you? And what can I help you with?' He reached for his white coat, hanging on a hook behind the counter, shrugging it on as he looked at Sasha enquiringly.

'Mr Alison?' At his nod, Sasha introduced herself and repeated her enquiry, conscious that the woman was hovering by the door, clearly wanting to eavesdrop. She waited until she'd left before explaining a little more.

'I'm working with the police.' No need to specify exactly in what capacity she was working with them, she decided. 'There was an incident up at The Spotted Dog on Thursday night, a car was vandalised with what appears to be animals' offal, and we're trying to establish where it might have been acquired. I understand that you have a waste collection once a week?'

'Dear me, yes, but I can tell you right away it couldn't have come from here. Very careful, we are, with our waste, all kept in the big bins out the back and the gate's kept locked. The only people who can unlock that gate are me or Sharon, the key's kept in the office, and there's no other way in. Here, come with me, I'll show you.'

'Now, you tell me how anyone could get over that.' Mr Alison stood back, his arms folded.

'Yes, I see.' Sasha looked at the high walls surrounding the small back yard as Mr Alison unlocked the gate and beckoned her through to the lane running behind the shop. There was nothing outside that anyone could stand on, so the only access would be via the gate. Mrs Pringle's hunch must have been wrong, perhaps she should check out the supermarket although, to the best of her knowledge they didn't have a butchery department.

Thanking Mr Alison for his time, Sasha walked out of the butcher's, smiling politely at the woman who flicked her hair from her face and turned back to her magazine. *Not very friendly, that one.*

She drove on to Meadowvale, her mind still on the unfriendly woman at the butcher's, unaware that Sharon Cutter was calling her brother. That tattoo on her arm, of the name, Drew, had niggled at her before, she was sure of it. White cars, the pub, the unfriendly couple... Drew – that had been the name of the son involved in the weed house! It came back to her in a rush, the newspaper clippings she'd been shown at the police station – Jimmy Burton, his wife, Nicola Burton, and their son, Drew Burton. And all three were now serving time for their crime. But what if there'd been others, as Ross Canfield had suggested, what if Drew had a girlfriend whose name was Sharon, who had a tattoo of his name on her arm? It would explain her animosity towards Sasha and could potentially link her in some way to the vandalism of Sasha's car, for she definitely had access to the waste bins of offal. But who was the other bloke? The young one? The one who drove a white car... Could it be the same white car that had tried to run her off the road? Was this all possible? Did they blame her for the weed house bust and incarceration of the Burtons?

A further worrying thought occurred to her – if he was involved in drugs then what if he'd been the driver of the white car who'd picked up Chantelle and Lucy, the day Sasha had seen them in the village? Hadn't Kirsty, the cook at Meadowvale, told her that Lucy was involved in drugtaking? Was she taking too many leaps of the imagination, something she was occasionally inclined to do, or was she onto something? The first and best thing to do would be to speak to Chantelle, she decided – her niece was her overriding concern and far more important to her than who might have vandalised her car or tried to run her off the road. If Chantelle had got involved in drugs, she needed to know as soon as possible so that she could put a stop to it. She'd go to Chantelle's school at lunchtime and text her to come out and meet her. Relieved to have a plan, Sasha pulled into Meadowvale, ready for her next mission of the day.

'Well, I'm not sure that it feels quite... right, Sasha, to be poking around in the residents' rooms while they're out...' Mrs Goodwin's tone was dubious as she considered Sasha's request.

'I understand, but I did inform them when I first spoke to them all when they were gathered together, that I'd need to look in their rooms and no one raised any objections. Look, Mrs Goodwin, I know it feels slightly uncomfortable, it does for me too, but let's face it, it'll be much quicker with them all out of the way, and we mustn't forget that not only have we had two murders but we've also got a thief in our midst...' Having played her trump card she waited for a response.

'It sounds so awful when you put it like that, but yes, someone has been taking things, that's true... and you'd leave everything just as you found it?'

'Oh, absolutely, they'll never know I was there. So, is that a yes then?'

At Mrs Goodwin's nod, Sasha remembered one more thing. 'Oh, and I wonder if you could show me which room was Dorothy's, I did go to it when I visited her last year but I can't recall where it was, and I can't remember what happened to her belongings?'

'I'll show you now if you want to walk with me, then I'll leave you to conduct your searches, but I can't imagine what you hope to find after so long. As for Dorothy's belongings, they were boxed up and placed in storage. There's a storage room at the end of the garden, next to the greenhouse, it was cordoned off while the police had something or other checked, but I see that they've removed the tape this morning, so that's alright. It's unlocked, and the boxes are labelled, you'll find them easily enough. Right, here we are, this was Dorothy's room, not the best room I'm afraid.' Mrs Goodwin stopped at the end of the passage before it turned to the right, waving her arm at the door standing open to an unoccupied corner room on the left.

'When she came to us, we didn't know for how long it would be, whether it was just for a visit. We popped her in here to see how she got on, and she settled down well so we opted not to disrupt things for her when her stay became permanent. Although it has a partial view of the garden, it mainly overlooks the car park, unfortunately, being on the corner as it is. But she was very happy in here though, always talking about her nice view of the garden, so that was something. All the other rooms look fully onto the gardens which is much nicer for everyone. Then next door is Davinia's room, you'll see nameplates to the side of each door.'

'That's perfect, thank you, I'll get busy then.' Sasha walked into the room, looking around at the unadorned furniture, the bare mattress, and the empty shelf running along the wall above the chair. She stood in the centre of the room, picturing Dorothy the last time she'd seen her when Dorothy had invited her into her room and shown her the stationery box containing such life-changing information for some. She gazed up at the shelf, remembering Dorothy's dolls lined up, an exotic collection from around the world, and how possessive Dorothy had been of them, not allowing Sasha to touch them.

Smiling, she walked to the window and looked out at the car park, before moving to stand at the other window with its partial view of the garden. What was it Dorothy had said about her dolls? *You can't talk to them*? Was that it? Poor Dorothy, she'd obviously sat here in her room and talked to her dolls, just like a little girl. Sasha moved on to Davinia's room.

Davinia's room was pristine and lacking any personal touches other than two framed photographs, side by side on the chest of drawers. One pictured an elderly couple, possibly Davinia's and Agatha's parents, the man austere and unsmiling, the woman looking down at her lap where her hands twisted together. The other photo was of Davinia and a much slimmer Agatha and looked like it had been taken on holiday, perhaps in the West Country. The two sisters were laughing at the camera as they stood, arms entwined, on the sandy beach with the blue sea sparkling in the sunlight behind them. They must have been in their forties or early fifties, Sasha estimated sadly and appeared to have shared their lives with no one else, still to this day. With nothing of interest to be found after a check of the room, Sasha moved on.

She knew just where to look in Agatha's room and, reaching under the bed, she found the box, together with a smaller one and a zipped bag, all of which revealed a cornucopia of delights, confirming to Sasha that Agatha had given in to her kleptomaniacal urges at a good few places other than Meadowvale and for a considerable length of time.

Sifting through the contents, Sasha shook her head in wonder at the odd assortment of items; a small bag of children's marbles, a cellophane-wrapped pack of cards celebrating the Queen's silver jubilee in 1977, a hair comb, a pack of elastic bands, hairclips galore, a pair of slightly grubby leather gloves, a plastic torch, a keyring with a plastic photo of Parva Crossing, a coaster from a restaurant called The Grill, a bride and groom cake topper, a teaspoon from the Cornish Cat, a pen from The Seaview Hotel, a pair of men's socks, a vinyl pencil case patterned with unicorns, an open packet of cigarettes, handkerchiefs, and an old diary from 1984 belonging to Frances Ridgeway aged sixteen.

Her eyebrows raised in wonder, Sasha opened the box that she'd seen the day before, lifting out the photograph from the top and studying the woman's face. Yes, this was a younger Davinia and she had been quite pretty.

She thought back to Davinia's expression when she'd listed the items that had gone missing – hadn't she seemed rather perplexed about her missing photo, but not so mystified by the disappearance of the other items? Was that because she was aware of her sister's predilection to take things that didn't belong to her? Had she protected Agatha over the years?

The lighter had to have been poor Monty's – he'd probably guessed that Agatha had taken it and kept quiet, owing to his fondness for his friend.

The blue bow tie reminded her of Howard – didn't he usually wear a bowtie? Plus she was sure he'd mentioned something about wearing his red one to Monty's memorial, so this one probably belonged to him too.

A couple of rings, which appeared to be costume jewellery, lay on a small bundle of fabric and Sasha examined them carefully – she wasn't an expert by any means, but they didn't look valuable up close, she couldn't see any hallmarks and the stones in the rings looked quite dull and scratched. Could these be Elspeth's, and if so, why had she made such a fuss about her jewellery being valuable?

The fabric bundle turned out to be a doll and she guessed immediately that it must be one of Dorothy's, from her collection. The large, flat-topped hat and full, brightly-patterned costume indicated that the doll was possibly from

Peru. She held it in her hand, straightening its skirt and adjusting its hat, which had slipped sideways, frowning as she noticed a piece of white paper sticking out from beneath it. Easing the hat from the doll's head, she carefully extricated the slip of folded paper and opened it up, reading the words written in Dorothy's spidery handwriting.

There once was a crook who cooked the books, he did his bird, but haven't you heard? They're plotting to take all the money.

Well, that was in true Dorothy style, she observed as she felt a rush of excitement. It all came back to her now, being in Dorothy's room last summer when Dorothy had stopped her from touching her dolls. *You can't talk to them, they... keep my secrets or, look after my secrets? They'll never tell.* Had Dorothy hidden notes in all her dolls? If so, then whatever Dorothy's murderer had hoped to keep a secret by killing her and taking her notebook, could still be revealed.

She tapped a few words into her phone, remembering that Dorothy had made a comment about Norwich and porridge. Yes, there certainly was a prison in Norwich – a men's prison. But who were *they* and what money were they plotting to take?

She picked up the last two items in the box, a pink pen, which had to be Lillian's, and a small carving of an elephant in some kind of heavy stone, which might be Elizabeth's, a memento from her years in Africa, perhaps?

Well, Agatha was truly a little magpie, ah, Howard had said something about that, someone had recalled a comment made by Dorothy about magpies liking shiny things – she could well have been referring to Agatha, even if the old myth wasn't technically correct.

Would Agatha have done whatever it took to keep her kleptomania a secret? Or would Davina, for that matter? She looked at her watch, surprised at how much time had passed already. She barely had time to check the other rooms and she badly wanted to have a look at the boxes of Dorothy's belongings from her room, especially now that she was sure that her doll collection would offer up the secrets that the elderly woman had unearthed about her fellow residents and possibly the staff and relatives. Deciding to prioritise examining Dorothy's belongings, Sasha made her way to the storeroom to find the boxes labelled Dorothy Newton.

There were just the two, neither of them heavy, and there appeared to be a fair number of dolls contained within them. Carrying them back to the house, Sasha popped them on the floor by the front door and walked along to tap on Mrs Goodwin's office door.

'I have something quite urgent to attend to, would you mind if I took the boxes of Dorothy's belongings with me so that I can look through them this afternoon, in my accommodation?' With Mrs Goodwin's blessing, Sasha collected the boxes and put them in the boot of her car before driving to Chantelle's school. She'd make it for the lunch hour with a few minutes to spare.

~

Glen Cutter looked up as Sasha's car pulled out of Meadowvale, pleased that Sharon had called him earlier. If she was sniffing round the butcher's then she might be getting warm, and he couldn't have that. It was time to put his plan into action, but he needed it to be convincing. Where are you off to now, little miss bitchy blue, he wondered? His face broadened into a wide grin when he saw her pull up outside the school, this was perfect. Taking out his prepaid burner phone, he called Rentham Police.

~

Sasha texted Chantelle to tell her that she was outside her school, asking her to pop out and meet her. She leaned her head back and closed her eyes for a few moments.

~

Sergeant Snow thanked the caller, before flicking his fingers to get the attention of his colleague.

'Concerned member of the public – reckons there's some woman pushing drugs to the schoolkids at the comprehensive school in Parva Crossing. Says it's been going on for some time and he's worried about his own kid, sounded like he was in quite a state. He says she's getting drugs out of the boot of her car. Wouldn't give his name though, said he was scared of retaliation. We've got a description of the car and the numberplate, but we'll need to get a couple of officers out there right now if we want to catch her in the act. Who have we got available?'

'Constables Baxter and Shore are in the vicinity, I'll get the information through to them.' Sergeant Lang picked up his radio and passed on all the details before turning back to his colleague. 'They'll be there in under five minutes.' He paused, consulting his screen. 'The car belongs to a Miss Sasha Blue, who lives in Shepherd's Bush, she's quite far from home.'

~

A tap on her driver's window jarred Sasha awake and she opened her eyes in surprise, feeling disorientated. Expecting to see Chantelle's face, she was confused by the police officer standing there and opened her window, smiling.

'How can I help you, Officer?'

'Sasha Blue? Would you mind opening your boot and stepping out of the car, please, Sasha? Is it alright to call you Sasha?' At her bewildered nod, he continued. 'We've had a complaint from a concerned member of the public and we've reason to believe that you're in possession of drugs of some kind, which you're supplying to members of the public. Would you consent to a search of your car to clear things up?'

'What? But that's crazy.' Stunned, Sasha reached down and popped her boot open, before opening her door and stepping out. 'There's been a mistake, I don't know what's going on but I'm here to see my niece, she's in school. Go ahead, search my car, you won't find any drugs, I don't have drugs in the car because I don't use drugs, full stop.'

The officer nodded politely whilst keeping an eye on his colleague who was searching through Sasha's boot. Constable Shore held up a bag filled with white powder.

'Perhaps you'd wait in our car, Sasha, while Officer Shore looks through the rest of your car?' Officer Baxter guided Sasha towards the patrol car as Sasha craned her neck to see what the other officer had held up.

'What's he got? What did he find? Is it drugs? Someone's setting me up, you must see that. What's that he's holding, where did he find it? This is ridiculous. Please be careful, I've got important stuff in those boxes.' The car door was gently closed on her and she sat, dazed, as the sound of voices reached her ears back and forth over the radio as one of the police officers reported their findings.

Officer Baxter got into the police car and turned to face Sasha. 'Sasha, Officer Shore has found what we believe to be a substantial quantity of what may be cocaine in your car, do you admit to having these drugs in your possession?' He held up the two bags of powder as Sasha shook in shock and disbelief.

'What? No, I don't. No way. Someone's planted them, they must have.'

'Sasha Blue, I'm arresting you for the possession of...' The words came and went in her head... 'You do not have to say anything but it may harm your defence...' The loud ringing sound in her ears drowned the rest of the words out as she laughed at the craziness of the situation. Sitting in the back of the car, she watched Officer Shore start her car and drive it away as Officer Baxter followed, barely registering her surroundings as they left the village.

Feeling numb, Sasha allowed herself to be escorted into a building and, after being received by the custody sergeant, found herself in a room described as a custody cell, minus her belongings. She'd handled just about everything wrong, she knew that, but shock had taken over. At least she'd asked them to call her sister and, more forcefully, had insisted that they speak to Nick Crossley. As soon as he heard, they'd be opening the door and offering her a huge apology.

~

Elizabeth and Elspeth left the bank and went their separate ways to make their visits to other establishments, before heading along to The Parva Patisserie to join the others.

There was a slightly festive air to the group's lunch as they exclaimed over the menu, made their selections, and indulged in the tasty offerings served up at their table.

'I don't think I've ever tasted such a delicious sausage roll.' Agatha sprayed pastry crumbs as she spoke. 'Oh, Lillian, did you see Mervyn? I bumped into him coming out of the bank earlier.' She forked up another piece of her sausage roll with one hand as her other brushed crumbs from her substantial bosom.

'I must say that looks good, Agatha, although this tomato tart is quite exceptional.' Howard nodded approvingly, dabbing his mouth with a paper serviette. 'I was surprised to see Richard and Moira at the bank, perhaps the lad's finally sold a rare collector's item and made his fortune.'

'I've never quite understood the attraction for military history,' Albert chimed in before taking a large bite of his sandwich.

'Oh look, there's Miriam.' Elspeth waved through the glass at her daughter as Miriam hurried along the pavement. 'I expect she's in a rush, it'll be her lunch hour.'

As everyone looked up, Greg's face appeared at the window and he smiled and waved, before pushing the door open and entering. 'Well, look at you all out on a jaunt. I was just running some errands before going to work. Raymond's around somewhere, Albert, did you know? He said he'll visit you later this afternoon. I'll see you all back at the ranch.' He twirled, waved, and left the patisserie as Elizabeth snorted.

'Since when did the staff have to behave like they're our friends? Oh, good Lord, there's our activity girl swanning along the road, don't any of them have work to do?'

They watched Willow for a moment as she headed through the entrance to the bank, before returning their attention to their respective lunches.

'Did you see those gorgeous little heart-shaped cupcakes in the display?' Agatha looked longingly at the cakes. 'So romantic, a gift for your love...'

'Oh, imagine that.' Elspeth clutched her hand to her breast. 'Sending your love a cake in the shape of a heart. Dear Lucy brought me a cupcake from here the other day for a treat, so pretty, in its own little box.' She beamed happily. 'She told me she left one for her boyfriend, Spencer, as a surprise, she's always doing things like that, he's got a sweet tooth you know, young love is truly romantic...'

'Utter nonsense,' Elizabeth scoffed.

'Everyone wants money today.' Lillian's voice was loud in the lull in conversation.

'What's that?' Albert asked, his tone sharp.

'She just means that we all had to go to the bank today, don't you, Lillian.' Elspeth flustered as she nodded around the table. 'Is Judith visiting you today, Elizabeth, I thought I saw her earlier?'

Talk turned to weddings as Elizabeth held forth on the many items still to be finalised for her granddaughter's approaching marriage and the others took the opportunity to finish their meals.

Everyone regretfully agreed that they couldn't possibly indulge in the delicious-looking carrot cake, since Mary would be serving them cake with their tea later and, once Agatha had chosen a cupcake for Mrs Goodwin, they made their way along to the minibus for their return to Meadowvale, waiting impatiently as a forgotten shopping bag was retrieved from beneath the table in the patisserie by one of their group.

~

Spencer arrived at Meadowvale for his shift, just after lunch, in high spirits. He stuck his head around the kitchen door, greeted Mary, and went to check his designated spot for the cash he'd demanded be placed there. Reaching his hand behind the row of children's books by Lillian Springer, he nodded to himself, nothing yet, give it time. He slipped quietly from the library.

~

Chantelle returned to her afternoon lessons wondering why Sasha hadn't been there when she'd told her she was waiting outside her school. She'd hovered around for a few minutes but Lucy had appeared and they'd gone and got lunch in the canteen where they'd both admitted they felt so rough that they hadn't even wanted to smoke the cigarettes Chantelle had in her bag. They'd had rubbish nights and would never do that stuff again, they agreed, although it had been kind of fun at the time...

~

Glen Cutter was proudly regaling his sister with the tale of Sasha's arrest and the two of them were falling about laughing. 'I told you I'd deal with her, Shaz, you should have seen her face. I wish I could see what was going on now.'

'Stuck up bitch, she deserves it after what she did to Drew and his mum and dad. You should have seen her at the butcher's making her investigations. Tea?' At Glen's nod, she filled the kettle and switched it on. 'You sure she won't know it was you?'

'How could she? She hasn't got a clue. We'll tell Drew all about it when we next visit, maybe we'll visit her as well.' Glen cackled in amusement. 'Got any biscuits to go with that tea?'

~

Meadowvale was abuzz with activity as the residents settled themselves back in, placed their purchases in their rooms, and finally gathered in the lounge for their afternoon activity with Willow. Agatha was last in, informing them all that she'd popped the cupcake on Mrs Goodwin's desk as she'd gone out for a bit.

'Did I see you with two of those little cake boxes, Agatha?' Albert nudged Elspeth as Agatha flushed, her denial fooling no one.

'Not sure I'll stay awake for this,' Howard whispered sotto voce to Davinia and Agatha, who giggled conspiratorially.

'I heard that, Howard.' Willow smiled brightly. 'I've got some wonderful books from the library for us to discuss. We all remember Jane Eyre...' Willow's voice droned on as residents dropped off, and she finally gave up, returning the books to the library before going into the kitchen to make herself a cup of tea.

~

Judith Bertram was the first visitor to arrive, just as the group began to wake up, followed shortly by Raymond and Mervyn, minutes apart from each other, a harried-looking Miriam – who rushed in shortly afterwards, telling Elspeth that she couldn't stop for long – and Richard and Moira, who walked in and nodded to Greg, who was hovering in the lounge as he announced that cups of tea would be served shortly, together with Mary's homemade Madeira cake.

Short walks in the garden were taken by some, whilst Mervyn sat with his mother in the corner. Miriam left after twenty minutes, having been assured by Elspeth that she was fine and that she would go and find Albie and Raymond in the garden and stretch her legs a little before tea.

Judith marched into the lounge from the direction of the library, looking around for Greg. 'Mummy needs her walking stick, please, Greg she overdid it today with all that walking around in the village. I don't know why you don't keep a closer eye on things, it's too much for them at that age, it really is.'

Reigning in his irritation, Greg smiled sweetly. 'I'll take it to her, don't you worry, where is she?'

'I left her sitting on the bench by the greenhouse, she was quite exhausted. Now, I must go, see to it that she gets it right away, won't you?'

Moira returned from the bathroom, looking around. 'Where's Richard gone?' Her eyes darted around the lounge, fixing on Spencer as he walked past. 'Have you seen Greg? He was here just now.'

'Why, do you need him for something?' Spencer's tone was cocky and Moira flushed.

'I just saw Greg up in the garden.' Raymond Bird walked through and left, as Davinia and Agatha walked in from the conservatory making a beeline for armchairs, into which they both sank.

'My poor legs,' Agatha exclaimed, 'still, we've worked up a good appetite for tea and Mary's cake. Save a chair for Howie, Davinia, he was looking a little tired.'

'Where are you rushing off to, Moira? Come and sit down and have some tea with us.' Howard eased himself into a chair, wincing.

'I was looking for Richard, is he outside?'

'We took a little walk but I had to turn back, he's coming though, said he'd dropped something and went back to get it.'

'I'm fine, Greg, thank you, Judith was making a big fuss about nothing, and I absolutely did *not* fall into the garden waste heap, not a word to anyone about something you *thought* you saw, do you hear me? I'm going to my room now, yes, a cup of tea would be welcome, thank you.' Elizabeth walked off to her room, leaning on her stick, as Mary wheeled the tea trolley into the lounge.

'I thought you'd gone.' Davinia looked up as Willow walked into the lounge from the conservatory carrying a box.

Laughing, Willow explained. 'I thought I'd take my work home with me and get the bits I need from the storeroom to prepare for our next crafting session. I've got lots of fun lined up.' She bounced off, disappearing with the box.

'She's keen, oh, Mary's cake looks delicious.' Agatha eyed the tea trolley greedily.

The day finally caught up with everyone and, once tea and cake were dispensed with, pleasant naps were enjoyed while Mary, Spencer, and Greg cleaned up and began preparations for Monday's dinner of cold roast beef and bubble and squeak.

~

Sasha banged on the door of her cell, for what else could she call it? With no idea of how long she'd been kept locked up, she was losing the plot. Surely someone had cleared this up by now? One call to Tessa and she would have explained everything. And where was bloody Nick Crossley when she needed him? She knew exactly who'd done this, it had all slotted into place. She just needed to *tell* someone. 'Hey!' she shouted at the door, banging on it again before throwing herself on the bed.

CHANTELLE COMES CLEAN

Tessa was waiting at the door for Chantelle, car keys in her hand. 'Where the hell have you been, Chants? I've been texting you.'

'Alright, relax, Mum, we just walked down to get a bag of chips.' she rolled her eyes. 'I didn't hear my phone.'

'Dad's working late and there's a massive problem, I don't know what's going on. I've had a phone call from a police officer, Sasha's been arrested and is in Rentham in some kind of custody suite. He wouldn't tell me anything so I'm going through and you're coming with me, no arguments.' She closed the front door behind her.

'Sasha's been arrested?' Chantelle's mouth gaped as she hurried to keep up. 'Why? What's she done? She told me she wanted to meet me at lunchtime but she never showed up. What's happened, Mum?'

'That's what I'm going to find out. 'Tessa's expression was grim. 'Let's go.'

~

Nick Crossley looked across the table at a frustrated Sasha. 'I'm sorry about this, Sasha, I had no idea about any of this and got here as soon as I could, but it's a different department, that's the trouble. Let's start at the beginning, shall we?'

Taking a deep breath, Sasha forced herself to remain calm, at least Nick was here now and they could sort this mess out.

'I was waiting for my niece, Chantelle Watson, outside her school at lunchtime when suddenly two police officers ordered me out of my car. Baxter and Shore, I think their names were, and then they searched my car and produced two bags of white powder. Which, by the way, I'd never seen in my life. Was it cocaine? They said it was. I've been set up, Nick, I've worked it all out, it goes back to the drugs house bust, when—'

'Hold on, one thing at a time.' Nick held his hand up. 'Yes, it is cocaine, in quite a sizeable quantity, more than we would expect to be found on someone for personal use. If you think you've been set up then someone must have had access to your car at some point. Did you leave it open at all?'

Frowning, she tried to recall. 'There was one morning when I clicked my remote and my car locked instead of unlocking. That was at The Spotted Dog, and I thought maybe I'd forgotten to lock it the night before, but if I did, then it's a first. But it's a bit of a stretch to think that someone was waiting for me to forget to lock my car so that they could plant drugs in it. Could it have been one of those jammer things?'

'Key jammers, it's possible, yes, they are in use in the Rentham area. Now, tell me why you're linking this to the drugs house bust.'

Sasha began to explain, her words tripping over themselves as she told Nick about the newspaper clippings that Jane Weaver had kept, which mentioned her name, about how she'd registered the name of one of the family members arrested – Drew Burton – about how she'd been to Alison's the butchers, to find out about their offal waste storage, and seen that the woman called Sharon, with the tattoo of the name Drew on her arm, worked there. She told him about the white car chasing her off the road, a white car at the pub in which the same woman and a young man had driven off after they'd eyed her with attitude in the pub. 'Nick, I'm pretty certain this Sharon was the one who got the offal which was thrown all over my car, maybe the bloke carried out the actual deed, but I don't know who he is. If she's the girlfriend of Drew Burton then it would all make sense – she could have a huge grudge against me and blame me for her boyfriend being in prison.'

A worried expression shot over her face. 'Oh God, I've just remembered something else, my niece and her friend got into a white car in the village one lunchtime, I saw them, and I think it was the same car. That means that Chantelle knows him, and knows him well, I even think she was dropped home by him one day when I was there.'

'I'm going to pop out and make some calls, okay? I'm afraid I'll have to ask you to stay here while I do that, but what you're saying all makes sense. Look, Sasha, I don't believe for one minute that the drugs are yours, but the officers were responding to a call from a concerned member of the public, they were only doing their job and acting on information received. From what you're saying, I think it's highly likely that the so-called concerned member of the public was probably the person who was setting you up. Bear with me, okay?'

'Alright, but can you check whether they called my sister, Tessa? And, Nick, I've got important evidence in my car, or it *was* in my car, I don't know what they did with it, but they mustn't mess around with the contents of those boxes, it concerns Dorothy Newton's murder. I need to get out of here urgently and get back to doing what I came here to do, which is to find Dorothy's killer, and the evidence in my car is crucial to that. If it tells me what I think it's going to then I hope to be able to figure out who it was and it will more than likely turn out to be the same person who murdered Monty Mallowan.'

'Nick? D.S. Crossley?' Tessa looked up as Nick walked into the waiting area. 'It's Tessa, Sasha's sister. Is she alright? What's going on? They won't tell me anything.'

'Tessa, how are you? Hi Chantelle. Sasha's fine, this is all a big misunderstanding, I'm sure, I've made a couple of calls and everything she's said to me pans out.'

'But why was she arrested?' Tessa's face was grey with worry.

Sitting down beside them Nick spoke softly. 'It sounds like someone's set her up and planted drugs in her car.' About to continue, he was interrupted by a small cry from Chantelle.

'Drugs? What sort of drugs?'

Why do you ask?' Nick looked intently at her. 'Do you know something about some drugs? Know someone who deals them, perhaps? Do you know anyone who drives a white car?'

'Chants?' Tessa studied her daughter's troubled face. 'What is it, love? Something's bothering you.' She suddenly realised that the concerns she'd had for her daughter may have been justified.

'Oh, Mum.' Chantelle's eyes filled with tears and she leaned into her mother as Tessa held her, stroking her hair. 'I need to tell you something, you promise you won't be angry? I think I know who he is.'

'Look, let's all go and have a chat together, alright? I'll get us some tea.' Nick showed them through to the interview room where Sasha was pacing anxiously.

'Tess! Chantelle! I'm so glad you're here. It's alright, Chants, don't be upset, it's all a big mistake.' Sasha hugged her sister and her niece in relief.

With mugs of tea on the table, Nick turned to Chantelle. 'Tell us everything you know.'

~

Greg walked along the passages, closing windows and collecting discarded items, a cardigan left on a chair, a book on a windowsill, and the odd pen or cough sweet wrapper. Turning to enter the library to return the book, he bumped into Spencer walking out. 'Looking for something to read, Spencer? I didn't have you down as a bookworm.'

Spencer laughed. 'I happen to be very interested in books as a matter of fact.'

'What did you choose then?' Greg looked pointedly at his empty hands.

'What? Oh, couldn't find anything I fancied in the end.'

Spencer walked off jauntily. He was in the money now and it would just keep coming, whenever he demanded.

The cardigan was Davinia's, and Greg placed it on her bed, before walking back through reception. A small box on the counter caught his eye and he picked it up, noticing the name written on it. That was odd, he frowned, why had it been left there, and how long had it been sitting there? He took it through to the kitchen. 'Look what the fairies have left you.'

'Cheers, Miriam must have brought it from Lucy. Where was it?'

'She must have put it down in reception and forgotten, she was in a bit of a rush. It's a good job I found it. How sweet, a little cupcake from your girlfriend.' Greg winked, taking a last look around the kitchen. 'I'm off then, I'll leave you to it, sure you'll be alright?'

'I think I can manage, we've only got to serve up the dinner.' Spencer grinned, opening up the cake box and taking a large bite of the cupcake before putting the kettle on. Glen would be wanting his money but he'd have to give it to him tomorrow, those cops were still hanging around at the gates. He made his tea, putting his feet up on the table and stuffing the rest of the cupcake into his mouth, grinning as he sent a message to his girlfriend, before texting Glen.

~

'So, let me get this straight, Glen Cutter's been supplying marijuana to Spencer, who works up at Meadowvale and who is also Lucy's boyfriend? And he's also been supplying it to Lucy? And you? He's the brother of Sharon Cutter, whose boyfriend Drew is in prison for being involved in the weed house in Parva Crossing?'

Chantelle nodded miserably, she might as well come clean about everything. 'He got coke, too. It was last night, but it was the first time, I promise, Mum.'

'Cocaine?' Nick looked up sharply from his notes.

'Last night?' Tessa was dumbfounded. 'But you didn't go out last night, what are you talking about?'

'I sneaked out, I'm sorry, Mum.' Fresh tears fell down Chantelle's face and Nick handed her a tissue.

Tessa picked up Chantelle's schoolbag, emptying the contents onto the table. 'I'd better not find any drugs in here, Chantelle. And what's this, you're a smoker now?'

'Glen gave them to me, I'm sorry, Mum.'

Sasha stared at the cigarette packet, she'd seen that cheap, unfamiliar brand before...

'And do you know anything about the vandalism of your aunt's car? Was it Sharon? Did she get the offal from the butcher's where she works?'

'Sorry,' Sasha interrupted. 'Nick, this cigarette brand, it's the same as the packet I found near my car. It had been used to write the message in the blood. Ross was taking it to be checked for prints – it must have been this Glen Cutter.'

'Looks like we'll be able to place him at the scene with any luck, I'll check with Ross, well spotted. Carry on, Chantelle.'

'I thought it was Spence, he came out of Meadowvale that night with stuff on his hands and then wiped it on Lucy's jeans – we thought it was blood. He said he'd moved the bins to get to his stash or something. After I heard about Sasha's car, I thought he must have got some old bits of meat or something from the bins, to throw on it, because he talked about money, so

I thought someone must have paid him to do it. But it wasn't that, it was that old man.'

'Monty?' Sasha's voice was sharp. 'Spencer came out of Meadowvale with blood on his hands the night Monty was murdered?'

'He was bragging about it last night, he said he might have seen who did it. Then he said something like it was better to keep his mouth shut, as long as someone paid. He said he'd just given them a blackmail note, that was on Sunday, yesterday, and they'd be giving him lots of money starting the next day – Monday. Glen didn't believe him but he said his head fell over and his wig fell off.' Chantelle's voice was little more than a whisper and they leaned in to hear her words.

'Glen still didn't believe him and said prove it, so he went to his car and got the man's wallet. He showed it to us – it was his, it had his name in it on something.'

'And where were you all last night while this was going on?'

'We went to the old motel, Spencer picked us up after work, that derelict place out on the old road. We met Glen there and he'd brought the cocaine and we tried it. Oh, Mum, I'm sorry, I know I've been stupid, you won't tell Dad, will you?'

Tessa blew her nose. 'I'll have to tell him, love, he's going to find out anyway, but it's all going to be alright.' Her voice was soft.

'Where's the wallet now, Chants?'

'It's still there. They were messing about, kind of fighting but not really, and it went under the bed in the room the woman was murdered in. Well, that's what Spencer reckoned, but I think he was just making stuff up. D'you think he made the stuff up about the old man?' She looked up hopefully.

'No.' Nick's voice was grim. 'I don't think he was making that up. But he was making it up about a murder at the old motel, no one was killed there. We need to speak to Spencer. I need to make some calls and get Glen and Sharon Cutter brought in for questioning. Chantelle, can you show us which room you were in if we go to the old motel? We need to find that wallet.'

Nodding, Chantelle spoke again, her face the picture of misery. 'There's one last thing, that night, the night the old man was killed, I saw a white car parked in the car park outside Meadowvale when we drove off. It was the only car there, and then I heard about the murder and the break-in, and I know I should have said something but then it would all have come out and I didn't want to get anyone into trouble.'

'A white car?' Did you recognise it, Chants? No? Anything noticeable about it at all?'

'It had something pink on the back shelf, I remember now.'

Sasha directed her next words to Nick. 'Willow drives a white car, and I know from personal experience that she keeps a pink blanket on the parcel shelf. Nick, Willow could have been up at Meadowvale the night of Monty's murder, she's been a little vague about where or who she was with that evening. It's possible that she accessed the filing cabinets in Mrs Goodwin's office in an attempt to find out something unrelated to this.'

'Go on.' Nick waved his hand in a circular movement. 'Why do you think she was snooping around in the files?'

'It's just a theory, but Mrs Goodwin told me that she suggested the position of activity therapist herself, and yet Willow implied that she'd replied to an advert. I have a suspicion that she was trying to find out information about the residents, I'm not sure why, yet, but something doesn't add up.'

'She suggested the job herself? So she insinuated herself into Meadowvale? How did we not know this?'

'Look, it's just a theory, I haven't even checked it out yet and I'm certainly not saying that she had anything to do with murder, but she might have seen something without realising its significance...'

'We'll have a word with her – unless she had a legitimate reason to be on the premises at that time then she shouldn't have been anywhere near the place. She's staying at The Spotted Dog, isn't she? Right, let me make some calls and get the ball rolling and then Chantelle can show us where this wallet is.'

'And what about me? Am I free to go?'

'You are, I'll clear it with Officers Baxter and Shore and make sure that everything is replaced in your car. I'm sorry that this happened to you, Sasha, but as long as everything matches up once we've interviewed Glen and Sharon Cutter, then this whole unfortunate incident will be erased from the system, you have my word.'

~

'No, no, get away, get off me.' He tried to fend off the giant spiders as they crawled towards him and up his leg. 'Aargh.' He dodged the clown as it lunged for him with a maniacal laugh. 'Help! Somebody help me!' Tearing at his clothes as he overheated, he ran from the kitchen, discarding his tunic and his tee shirt, and trying to pull his jeans off over his trainers. 'My eyes, turn off the lights, it's biting me, get it off, I'm on fire, help me, put it out, put it out, who are you, no please, not my arm...'

The residents seated around the dinner table looked in confusion at a half-naked Spencer as he writhed on the floor, his limbs twitching spasmodically, incoherent mumblings coming from his mouth, his face a deep shade of red.

'Whatever's the matter with the boy?' Albert pushed his chair back and went to Spencer, peering down at him.

'Somebody call Mary.' Davinia looked around worriedly as Howard joined Albert.

'He looks like he's having some kind of seizure. Spencer! Spencer, can you hear me?'

'He's very red, perhaps he's got a fever, I'll get a wet cloth.' Elspeth went to the kitchen as Mary appeared.

'Oh, Mary, thank goodness, there's something wrong with Spencer.'

Mary stood beside the two men, looking down at Spencer. 'His eyes are like saucers.' She bent down to listen to the small noises coming from his mouth, shaking her head. 'He's not making any sense and why has he taken his clothes off?'

'Here's a cloth.' Elspeth reappeared, the cloth dripping as she handed it to Albert, who knelt awkwardly to mop Spencer's face.

'I'll call the doctor.' Mary was unsure. 'Or perhaps an ambulance...'

'Call Dr Singh.' Elizabeth spoke authoritatively, sensing Mary's indecision. 'Let him come and have a look first, we shouldn't panic. He can take charge and decide about an ambulance, we're not experts after all.'

'What about our dinner?' Agatha whispered to Davinia, who turned on her in irritation.

'For once, can you not think about your stomach, Agatha?'

They all waited silently as Mary called Dr Singh.

'He'll be here in a few minutes.' Mary fetched a cushion from an armchair, lifting Spencer's head to place it underneath it.

'He's stopped moving.' Albert grimaced from his kneeling position. 'Help me up, will you, Howard?'

'He's very quiet.'

'His eyes are still open.'

'Spencer, can you hear us?'

'He's been murdered. I told you this would happen.'

'Oh, Lillian, please, now is not the time for your fanciful ideas.'

'Elizabeth's quite right. Howard, here's a chair.' Mary pulled a dining chair over. 'You sit beside him and watch him. Albert, could you go and wait for the doctor and bring him straight through when he gets here? I'm calling Mrs Goodwin.'

~

Sasha looked around her as they entered the derelict motel. What an awful place, what on earth made youngsters want to come and hang out in a place like this at night, she wondered? 'Can you remember which room it was?'

'I think so.' Chantelle led them down the corridor as Tessa looked at her sister in horror.

Nick Crossley grimly took in the small table in the centre of the room, white residue adhering to its surface in minute quantities. He inclined his head towards the bed. 'You think the wallet ended up under there?' Kneeling on the floor, his mouth twisted in distaste at the filth, he peered under the bed, reaching for the wallet. 'Here it is.' He stood up, dusting down his trousers, and held up the wallet in his gloved hand. Opening it carefully, he studied its contents, nodding slowly. 'It's Monty Mallowan's alright, looks like young Spencer has a lot of explaining to do.'

About to get into their cars, Chantelle stopped and looked around the parking area.

'I've just remembered something.' She walked slowly, her head down. 'Lucy was in a panic about whether Spencer had killed the old man, and he got back out of the car and threw something away from his boot. It looked like crumpled paper or something. We were parked here, and he made some comment about destroying evidence or something, but I just thought he was doing more showing off, oh, this might be it.'

'Don't touch it!' Nick's tone was sharp. He hurried over to where she stood, slipping a fresh glove on and opening an evidence bag, into which he placed the bloodied tissues.

They departed ways outside the motel, Nick to Parva Crossing police station where he would meet up with Jane Weaver and await Spencer's arrival, as well as Willow's – Glen and Sharon Cutter were to be taken to Rentham. Tessa took Chantelle and headed for home, while Sasha drove back to the pub.

~

'Cal's face was angry when she walked in. 'What the hell, Sash? Is this your doing? What did you say to the cops? They've taken Willow in for questioning, something about the night Monty was killed and her car being seen outside.'

'Listen, Cal, I'm sorry, okay? It just came up – a white car was seen at Meadowvale and I had to tell them about Willow's car and that she hadn't really accounted for her whereabouts that evening. But it doesn't mean that she's under suspicion, she may have seen something that can help us. There was a lot going on that night, my car vandalism, the break-in, the murder. If she did break in and access files in the office then maybe she can help us, even if she doesn't know it yet. I certainly never accused her of murder.'

'Are you serious? Break-ins? Murder? You're making it sound like she's got something to hide. And what are you on about files? Why would she want to go through files at Meadowvale? Are you trying to cause trouble for Willow because of what happened with us? Is that it? I mean, I know you and Eric have split up, but this is really scraping the barrel, especially after she's been so nice to you. You need to have a good hard look at yourself in the mirror, Sash, I'm serious, you might not like what you see, you're turning into, a bitter, jealous woman, lashing out at a harmless, gentle girl who's got nothing to hide and who wouldn't hurt a fly.'

Miserably, Sasha watched Cal storm outside to the garden, wanting to follow him and explain, but unsure – she'd never seen him so angry. She'd said too much as usual. Feeling hurt, she realised that she should leave him alone for now and bring the boxes in from her car. She needed to go through Dorothy's belongings and examine the dolls. She had to keep her priorities on track and that meant concentrating on trying to figure out who had murdered Dorothy, not worrying about how much Cal disliked her at this moment.

~

Dr Singh stood up, shaking his head. 'I'm calling for an ambulance but this doesn't look good. Did he have any health issues? Any allergies? Had he eaten anything out of the ordinary?'

Mary shook her head. 'Not that I know of, he was fine earlier.' She turned around as Constable Pavani Datta entered the room. 'Officer Datta, are you here about Spencer, how did you–?'

Pavani Datta glanced at the residents seated around the dining table. 'Sorry to disturb your dinner, but I'm afraid we've been dispatched to bring Spencer Brent down to the station to answer some questions. Is he here?' As she spoke, she became aware of Dr Singh's presence and her eyes fell to the figure lying prone on the floor. 'What's happened?' She turned to Dr Singh as he finished his call.

'I've called for an ambulance. Could I have a word, Officer?' Leading Pavani out of earshot, Dr Singh shook his head. 'I don't like the look of it, something's wrong here, could be an overdose perhaps, or, I'm not sure...' his voice trailed off as Constable Canfield joined them.

'What aren't you sure about, Doc?' Ross's voice was sharp.

'The residents tell me that he came into the room shouting nonsense and pulling his clothes off before collapsing, red-faced and twitching. His pupils are severely dilated, consistent with the intake of stimulants, but the behaviour is odd, it's almost as if he'd ingested poison of some kind. We'll know more when he gets to the hospital.'

Ross Canfield bent down beside Spencer and checked the pockets of the jeans crumpled around his ankles, pulling out a small bag of what he was sure was marijuana, a packet of cigarettes and a lighter. Reaching into the back pockets of his jeans, he frowned as he felt the folded notes, and pulled them out. 'Five hundred pounds.' He whistled, looking up at Pavani. 'That's a lot of cash. You'd better let the sarge know what's happened, Pav.' Standing up, he addressed Mary. 'Has Spencer eaten or drunk anything since he came on shift?'

'Just a cup of tea, as far as I know, his mug's on the table in the kitchen.' Mary indicated that she wished to speak privately and they moved away. 'The residents need their dinner, that's if any of them still have an appetite after all this, what should I do?'

'Just give me a minute to have a look in the kitchen, then you can go ahead.'

He'd craved excitement such as this, thought Ross ruefully, as he carefully bagged the empty mug sitting on the table in the kitchen, but it was all becoming a bit much, he conceded. Noticing the crumbs on the table beside the mug, he peered closer – they looked like cake crumbs.

He turned to Mary as she hovered in the doorway. 'Did Spencer eat any cake by any chance?'

Mary sniffed. 'He was always eating cakes, Kirsty was always complaining about him pinching slices of leftover cake. I made a Madeira cake for them today, he might have eaten the last slice of that? The empty plate's over there, he must have washed it up.'

Ross nodded, it made sense, and the bag of marijuana just served to confirm what he'd suspected for some time – drugs were definitely making a re-appearance in the village. Was this why he and Pavani had been tasked with bringing Spencer in for questioning? Had something drug-related happened and if so, why hadn't anyone told them? He bagged the cake crumbs, all that remained of Mary's cake, satisfied that he'd done all that he could for now.

KEEPERS OF SECRETS

'Fancy some company?' Jules raised her eyebrows at Sasha, taking in her miserable expression and the boxes by her feet. 'Can I help with anything?'

'I'd love some company.' Smiling, Sasha shrugged. 'But I won't be much fun, I need to go through these boxes and then get drunk.'

'I'm your person, and I'm off duty, Tristan's managing the bar, it's a quiet Monday evening. Come on, we can use my flat, I'll get some wine brought through, let me take one of those boxes.'

The two women settled themselves at Jules's dining table, having placed the boxes on the floor, and Jules poured them both glasses of wine.

'These boxes contain Dorothy Newton's belongings and, I'm hoping, clues to her killer. This is going to sound weird, but she had a doll collection that she was extremely territorial about. She wouldn't let me touch them – referred to them as her keepers of secrets or something.' Sasha gulped a mouthful of wine. 'I found one in another resident's room, hidden in a box, where she'd been stashing items stolen from the others.' She rolled her eyes. 'I know, right? Meadowvale's got a kleptomaniac hiding in plain sight. It seems that some, or possibly all, of the residents had secrets they didn't want to be discovered, but Dorothy delighted in exposing people's lies and secrets, whether current or from their old lives, and I'm wondering if the fear of one of these secrets being revealed by Dorothy led to her murder.'

'Wow, that's pretty kind of – surreal, I guess.' Jules's eyes were wide. 'Tell me you've got the doll collection in these boxes?'

'Uh-huh.' Bending down, Sasha opened the first box and retrieved a doll, placing it carefully on the table between them, as their eyes studied it. The doll's shiny, brown, plastic head was adorned with a basket of fruit, her painted face staring blindly up at the ceiling. A lace bodice was attached to a voluminous silken skirt in what had once been a rich array of brightly-coloured bands of purple, yellow, and red, each trimmed with lace. Her arms had become detached, clinging by remnants of withered elastic bands to her body. A crumpled, pink, sash, lay across her breast. 'Rio, Brazil,' Sasha read the words aloud.

Picking up the doll, she explained. 'The stolen doll which I found had a folded slip of paper hidden underneath her hat. I put the doll back so as not to arouse suspicion at this point, but I took the piece of paper.' Sasha took the piece of paper from her bag and laid it flat on the table. 'It looks like it's been torn from a notebook.'

There once was a crook who cooked the books, he did his bird, but haven't you heard? They're plotting to take all the money.

One of the doll's arms fell onto the table with a small clatter as Sasha lifted its skirt to examine it. 'Oh wow, look at this, Jules.'

Gently, she eased the skirt up and over the doll's head, to reveal – another head – complete with a fruit basket atop it. The same painted face stared up at them, albeit with a darker complexion, but this time the clothing was less extravagant – dull cotton with a simple design, although the doll was adorned with a necklace and beaded waistband. Both arms were missing, leaving small holes where they had become detached. Shaking her head, Sasha placed the doll on the table. 'No note.'

Jules picked up the doll, holding it up as she peered into the small holes where its arms should have been. 'Sash,' she breathed, holding it out to her.

Sasha's eyes glinted. 'Have you got a pair of tweezers?'

Easing out the small piece of paper, she unrolled it and pressed it out flat on the table as they both read the spidery words.

All that glitters is not gold. The giggling little princess is a tin pot fake telling her lies to get what she wants.

'Now just what exactly does this cryptic little note mean? Not gold...' Sasha screwed up her eyes. 'Someone is faking something to get something...' She picked up another doll as she spoke, turning it around in her hands as she examined it.

'She looks like she's from South America somewhere... funny little hat, hmm, nothing hidden under there, it's stuck on firmly. Just what secrets are you hiding?' Her fingers deftly moved over the doll's clothing, checking beneath the brightly-coloured waistcoat over the balloon-sleeved shirt, before lifting the stiff, red, skirt fabric and checking beneath it as Jules held her phone out.

'Looks like she's from Bolivia.'

Sasha's eyes scanned the images on Jules's phone, clicking on one and reading the description out loud. '*Most important to the traditional outfit is the multi-layered skirt, or pollera, with five petticoats*. That's why the skirt is so stiff. Jules, I swear, you are my hero right now. Look–' she gently eased the layers of petticoats apart, removing a photograph with writing on the reverse. 'I missed this, I thought it was just stiffened fabric.'

They both leaned forward to read Dorothy's spidery writing.

He got your keys and more while you were happy in your little valley.

Turning the photo over, they again leaned forward, this time studying the faces of the group of people smiling at the camera.

'The Salisbury Club,' Jules read out the words printed on the sign behind the trio.

'It's in Africa.' Sasha noted the men's short-sleeved jackets and suntanned faces, the frond of a palm tree drooping in the corner of the photograph. 'This is a young Elizabeth Payton, look how beautiful she was. She's from Zimbabwe, which was–'

'Previously known as Rhodesia until nineteen-eighty,' Jules read from her phone.

'What else does it say?'

'The Salisbury Club was renamed The Harare Club after Zimbabwean independence. Women weren't allowed to become members although they later opened a ladies' restaurant which, listen to this, had a separate entrance as they weren't permitted to use the front entrance.'

'That's incredible. This photo must have been taken before nineteen-eighty, quite a bit before, I'd guess, as Elizabeth looks like she's only in her twenties.'

'Her daughter's Judith Bertram, isn't she?' Jules brought up a photo on her phone, of Judith at a fundraiser with her member of parliament husband. 'That one must be Elizabeth's husband, talk about the spitting image.' She pointed to the brown-eyed man in the old photo whose arm hung lazily around Elizabeth's shoulders. 'And look at their hooked noses, talk about like father like daughter.'

Sasha was gazing out of the window, her mind racing as she tried to make sense of Dorothy's word games. Subconsciously registering Jules's words, she picked up the photo, glancing over the writing on the back again. 'So, what's she getting at? Why hide this photo? Something about one of the group, perhaps? 'Maybe it's about her husband... perhaps he had an affair... or she did... perhaps that's what the little comments about being happy in the valley are referring to... but Elizabeth's so proper, so...' She searched for the right word. 'Upright. She, the whole family, is so concerned with their social status, I can't imagine any of them ever putting a foot wrong, especially not Elizabeth. The very notion that she would commit murder to keep something in her old life a secret is absurd.' She shook her head. 'I just can't see it – it seems too fantastical.'

'The whole thing sounds mad though, doesn't it, if you think about it? You're uncovering old lies from the pasts of a bunch of elderly residents in a care home, one of who you think might have committed murder.'

'Well, when you put it like that... although there will no doubt be a few secrets about relatives or staff hidden in this lot as well...' Sasha grinned, shrugging, before slugging her glass of wine back. 'Let's have some more wine, this is, if nothing else, quite fascinating, and is just what I needed to take my mind off my own miserable life.' She reached in, picking up another of the dolls. 'Here.' She pushed the box towards Jules. 'Pick a doll.'

Jules smiled as she picked up the little doll. 'He looks like he's from Greece, some kind of traditional outfit, he's so cute. Here we go.' She tweezed out a small roll of paper from the doll's sleeve and folded it flat, squinting at the tiny writing.

The unhappily married liar just wants her money.

'What d'you think that means?'

'Okay, so it's aimed at a married woman and she's not happy... She's a liar because she's pretending to be happy? And she has money because of her marriage, or maybe she wants money, there could be some kind of expectation of money to come? I'm trying to think who the married women are. Let's see, there's Judith Bertram, of course, who's certainly wealthy because of her husband, and it's hard to tell if she's happy or not, I'm not sure I've ever seen her crack a smile, and Moira Carding, Richard's wife, come to think of it I've never seen her smile either, but no money there, I'm fairly certain. We've got Mrs Goodwin, the manager, but I think she's widowed, so not her, oh, and Kirsty the cook, I'm sure she mentioned a husband at some point, but again, I doubt there's any money there.'

'So, who d'you think it is?'

'Could be Judith Bertram, if it's something to do with the daughter's hugely expensive wedding they spend their time planning. Or Moira Carding, she's an option – there might be something going on with her husband and Greg, who works there – it was hinted at in an old letter of Dorothy's. If it's true, and Howard were to find out, who knows how he could react? I think Richard's struggling financially – Howard's always giving him cash apparently. If Moira knows about her husband's affair, she could be putting up with it until she can get her hands on her share of any inheritance. They're an unlikely couple, I swear she's more man than he is, in appearance and behaviour.'

'Makes sense.' Jules nodded. 'He's got the bookshop at the end of the high street, some kind of antiquated establishment specialising in old war books and stuff. I don't think I've ever seen anyone go in there, poor chap.'

'Moira Carding...' Sasha murmured thoughtfully, 'would she kill to safeguard an inheritance? It's possible... but whoever killed Dorothy had to also have been able to kill Monty, if my hunch is correct that he was killed because he discovered who her murderer was. Of course, if she had an accomplice... her husband perhaps... I don't know, first, we work out all the people who felt threatened with exposure, then my next job is to see whether I can place them in both scenarios.' She held up the doll she'd taken from the box.

'Look at this little cutie, isn't she adorable?' They both smiled at the fur-jacketed baby-faced doll, its large eyes looking out from beneath the fur hood. 'She's even got a little bag, and she's standing on a block of fake snow.' She held up the maple-leaf-shaped tag, with the words *Crafted in Canada*. 'A little Eskimo doll, although I think Inuit is the correct term these days. Have you got a secret for us?' she asked the doll.

'It has to be in this sweet little bag.' She gently eased it open, smiling in delight. 'Here we go.'

You threw it away with the bathwater, your brave heart will never love you now.

'That reminds me of the saying about throwing the baby out with the bathwater – imagine if one of our elderly ladies had become pregnant when she was a young girl – having a baby out of wedlock about sixty-odd years ago would have been a scandal for many families. So did she get sent away to have the baby? And then what – give it up for adoption? If so, I wonder where he or she is now. And who is brave heart?'

She'd picked up a Spanish flamenco doll and her fingers unconsciously played with its gaudy pink satin and lace-frilled skirt as she pondered her last question. 'Nothing hidden in this doll, it seems.' She looked down at it.

'Look at the little fan she's holding, can I see?' Jules held her hand out eagerly. 'The detail in these things is quite amazing, oh look, there's a bull on it, poor thing, oh, wait... hold on...'

'What is it?'

'The fan's not right, it's like it's been folded in half, the picture is all wrong, look, oh–'

Their eyes followed the slip of paper as it fell from the folded fan onto the table.

Once upon a time there was a little boy and a little girl, but they didn't live happily ever after.

'It sounds like the beginning of a children's bedtime story.'

Sasha looked at her friend in delight. 'There's a children's author living at Meadowvale called Lillian Springer. Her books are experiencing something of a revival and she earns quite extensive royalties from them. Her son, Mervyn, is always hovering around with papers for her to sign, but there's something...'

'What is it, Sash? You don't like him? Don't trust him?'

Sasha frowned. 'Trust, I think, Lillian always seems to be under the impression that she has to sign new contracts with her publisher, but there are no new contracts, she hasn't written anything for years. She's easily confused poor thing. Greg said she talks about an imaginary daughter in Australia or something, but it's all rather vague, and then, again according to Greg, she's left her fortune to a children's home somewhere. Thanks, love.' She took her re-filled wine glass from Jules, sipping it thoughtfully. 'There's definitely something worth looking into there.'

~

Ross Canfield returned to the kitchen, something niggling in the back of his mind... what had he missed? His phone beeped with a text from his wife and he turned round, replying quickly as he walked back through to the front door, adding a row of kisses in the hope that she wouldn't feel too upset with him for missing dinner.

Ross re-joined Pavani and they followed the paramedics as they carried Spencer out to the ambulance.

'I'll go with them,' Pavani volunteered, stepping forward and climbing into the back of the ambulance. 'The sarge wants me to keep her updated on the situation and for you to head back to the station once you've finished up here.'

~

'I wish I knew what was going on down at the police station.' Sasha threw her head back, groaning. 'For all I know Spencer has told them everything and they've already arrested Monty's murderer and here we are going through Dorothy's things and reading all her little secrets and it could all just be a massive waste of time – it has to be the same person who killed both of them. I tell you what, you check the other dolls and I'll just give Pavani Datta a quick call, see if she can tell me anything.'

She listened, aghast, to Pavani as she explained what they'd found when they arrived at Meadowvale to take Spencer in for questioning.

'Well, how is he now? Has he said anything yet?'

'He's unconscious, Sasha, and it's not looking good. Between you and me, we're not quite sure why we had to fetch him.'

'Sergeant Weaver didn't tell you? He might have seen Monty Mallowan's murderer, he was bragging about it last night to his girlfriend and my niece.'

'Oh, wow, I left Ross there, you could give him a call and see if he knows anything more?'

'Thanks, Pav, I'll do that.'

Ending the call, Sasha looked at Jules. 'I think someone's poisoned Spencer to keep him from exposing them – if he dies this will be the third murder, and all by the same person. I'm calling Ross.'

'I'm just getting back to the station, I take it you've heard the news?'

'I have, Pav told me, what can you tell me, Ross?'

'Not much at this point, we were dispatched to bring him in but no one told us why, it all sounded a bit chaotic to tell you the truth. All I know is that he was drinking a cup of tea in the kitchen, and eating a piece of the cook's leftover cake, and the next thing is he's tearing his clothes off as he runs around in the dining room making strange noises before collapsing in front of everybody. Here's an interesting thing, I checked his pockets and he had a bag of grass and five hundred quid on him.'

'That is more interesting than you know, Ross. Anything else on him at all? Was that it?'

'That's the lot. I've got to go, the sarge is calling me in.'

She thanked Ross, thoughts and ideas buzzing through her mind. The five hundred pounds had to be his first payment from whoever he was blackmailing, but how had he blackmailed the person? And how had the person known it was him or had he been stupid enough to tell them? Not only that, she realised, someone would have had to be able to lay their hands on five hundred pounds in cash, which meant they would have had to go to the bank.

'There's nothing hidden in these other dolls.'

Jules's voice stopped her jumbled thoughts and she sighed. 'Okay, thanks, Jules, maybe we should call it a night, oh, and thanks for helping me, I'll take the stuff up to my room and get an early night, I think I'll go into Meadowvale early tomorrow to see if I can talk to the residents about what happened to Spencer. It's Monty's memorial service in the garden in the afternoon so I'll probably be there all day.'

Jules hugged her. 'It's been fascinating, thanks for letting me help.'

'Thanks for the wine and for taking my mind off my miseries for a while, darling.' She picked up the boxes and headed for the door.

'Shall I bring you up a toasted sandwich?'

'That would be so good, thanks, I'd forgotten about food completely, which isn't like me.'

She was still smiling as she made her way across the bar, reaching awkwardly for the handle as the door to the rooms flew open, catching her shoulder, so that the boxes fell to the floor, spilling their contents.

Cal rushed through, pausing to glance unapologetically at her. 'I'm on my way to collect Willow from the police station, they must have finished wasting her time by now, and don't worry, I'll be sure to let her know that she's got you to thank for being dragged off like a common criminal.' He marched off without a backward glance.

'No, Cal, it wasn't like that, I wasn't–' But Cal had gone. Sudden unwelcome tears blurred her eyes as she miserably gathered Dorothy's sad assortment of belongings, replacing the dolls in the box and picking up the small photo album which had fallen apart as it hit the floor. A photo of Dorothy and George Newton on their wedding day smiled up at her and she picked it up forlornly, frowning as she felt the unusual thickness of the paper.

Her tears forgotten, Sasha carefully removed the tape holding the small pieces of paper to the back of the photo and looked at them in delight. Here were the rest of Dorothy's notes, torn from her notebook and hidden for safekeeping. She bundled everything back into the box and hurried up the stairs with renewed energy.

~

'What do you mean she's still helping you with enquiries?' Cal's voice was raised in frustration. 'You can't seriously think that Willow knows anything about all this? Look, Nick.' He forced himself to remain calm. 'Sasha's got a hand in this, things have got a little personal, there's a history and, well...'

Nick looked sympathetically at Cal, nodding as he spoke carefully. 'Cal, I can understand your frustration, but it's possible Willow may have seen something which can help us if, as we believe, she was at Meadowvale at the time of Monty Mallowan's death.'

Cal looked at him incredulously. 'But you can't have any reason to think she was there? She was with her friend, they spent the evening having pizza at her house, she must have told you?'

Nick sighed. 'A white car, which we've now identified as belonging to her, was seen in the parking area and she has admitted to us that she was there. There was no friend and there was no pizza. You're going to have to trust us on this one when I tell you that we have good reason to be speaking to your friend, there are other matters of concern that we're addressing, unrelated to Meadowvale and, incidentally, unrelated to Sasha in any way, in fact, Sasha's completely unaware of our enquiries. Willow might not be– well, she isn't who you think she is, Cal, and that's absolutely all I can say, for now, I'm, sorry.'

Leaving the police station, Cal walked slowly back to his car and returned to the pub, his anger still directed towards Sasha, no matter what Nick Crossley had said.

~

Sasha read through Dorothy's notes again as she sat cross-legged on the floor, the papers spread out haphazardly in front of her.

Kissing in the cupboard, kissing in the garden, but it's all over if you kiss and tell.

He just wants her to write two words, but she won't sign the contract.

Hair today gone tomorrow.

Can you nose out the truth Mrs La de dah? The camera doesn't lie.

They're all lying dirty birdies. They've been naughty girls and the little dicky bird likes to sing to a different song. Poor brave heart.

It's time to come home children but she's already here. Why did you choose him?

A brave heart could never love a little magpie stealing all the shiny things.

The kissing note was obvious, and the two words? Well, that was easy to guess, for wasn't Lillian always saying things about him wanting her to sign a contract? She paused in her musings to open the door, thanking Jules for the sandwich, suddenly feeling ravenous. Sitting back on the floor she ate as she continued to analyse the notes. The hair must be poor old Monty Mallowan, nothing cruel so maybe Dorothy had a soft spot for him; she paused over the next note – It couldn't mean–

? Was it referring to–? She hadn't paid proper attention earlier – had almost missed this, she realised, rummaging through the box and her notes simultaneously. Yes, she nodded to herself, Dorothy had definitely been on the right path. This was very interesting... Her mind flashed back to Albert's interview and his recollections of what someone had told him, and she tapped a few words into her phone, reading the results with great interest.

Pushing her plate aside, she leaned back against the bed as she moved on to the next phrase - lying dirty birdies – it made her grin – well clearly she was accusing more than one female of something, but also referring to who else? Richard again? And there it was for the second time, brave heart – just who was this for? And come home children, what did this mean? Sasha rubbed her eyes, frustrated at Dorothy's cryptic offerings – just who exactly was already here? It was specific, clearly referring to someone in particular... home children – on impulse she again tapped some words into her phone, feeling sure that she'd heard the phrase somewhere in the past, possibly in a documentary.

Having read enough, she placed her phone back on the floor. It was hard to believe that this kind of thing had happened in England's past. It was achingly sad, but had Dorothy been correct? Was someone connected to Meadowvale a home child? And if they were, then who exactly had given them up? Someone had said something about making a choice, something about choosing him? Who had that been? She'd spoken to so many different people. But, most important of all, who was the home child?

Brave heart again, aha, slowly it began to make sense, for she knew exactly who the little magpie was, which meant that she knew who brave heart probably was. A quick internet search on her phone confirmed it and she expressed silent admiration for Dorothy's clever games.

There were three individuals, targeted by Dorothy, who were hoping for something from brave heart, but they were all covering up lies in their lives, and brave heart had no time for liars, no time for scandal even in its smallest form. The question was – would one of them kill to protect their secret?

Things were beginning to take shape in her head, they were murky, but she felt that she had almost all the information that she needed to figure out Dorothy's killer. It should be simple – who had the most to lose? But that was relative as even the smallest thing could take on huge importance if it was the focal point in someone's life – if they felt their very happiness depended on it. Her phone rang, it was Pavani Datta.

'Sasha, bad news I'm afraid, the sarge asked me to call and let you know. The lad didn't make it, Spencer Brent died about half an hour ago. Wilson Mwabila will conduct an autopsy tomorrow.'

'I'm so sorry, thanks, Pav.' She placed her phone back on the floor, stunned and saddened at the news. This killer was bold and able to act fast when the need arose, eliminating any threats to their exposure at the first opportunity. The stupid boy, he'd thought he was being so clever and instead he'd signed his own death warrant the minute he'd delivered his blackmail note, which had been delivered on... Sunday, yesterday. Chantelle had said that he picked them up after work which meant he'd delivered his demand to someone at Meadowvale.

She looked down at Dorothy's pages torn from her notebook. In total, she'd recovered fourteen notes from Dorothy's hiding places – thirteen of them her comments about others. Concealed within her words was the vital clue which would lead her to not only Dorothy's killer but Monty's too, and now Spencer's. Someone who'd been at Meadowvale yesterday had received his blackmail note, made a plan to get hold of the cash today, delivered it to Spencer, and poisoned him. Why pay him though? To keep him quiet in case their plan to kill him didn't work? And what the hell had they poisoned him with? It's not like the average person kept a stash of poison just in case they needed to polish someone off. It would take weeks for results from anything found during the autopsy so she needed to try to figure it out on her own.

She studied the fourteenth note of Dorothy's again. This was different – it wasn't about anyone else – it was about Dorothy.

I've got a new friend from the Wizard of Oz. Shh. She's going to tell me a secret this afternoon.

A chill crept along Sasha's spine – this must have been Dorothy's last entry in her notebook – she was referring to her appointment with her own death. But a new friend? Why new? Because they hadn't been friends before? Or had it been a stranger? No, a stranger would have been noticed, without a doubt, although... fragments from her interviews popped into her head... both Elspeth and Lillian had mentioned possibly seeing an unknown man in the garden the day that Dorothy had been drowned... but Dorothy's new friend had been female...

She phoned Pavani Datta back. 'Sorry to bother you, Pav, but are you going to attend the autopsy tomorrow? Could I ask you a favour? Could you let me know what Wilson finds in Spencer's stomach contents?'

Thanking Pavani, she stood up and stretched, suddenly feeling like a glass of wine. She was supposed to be having an early night though... Oh, to hell with it, maybe a quick glass and a ciggie...

Taking her wine out to the beer garden, she stopped, recognising Cal's figure hunched at one of the tables as he faced the river, and she quietly slipped into the furthest bench seat, lighting her cigarette and sipping her wine. The small group at the only other occupied table suddenly stood up and left, disturbing Cal, and causing him to look round. She kept her eyes down, not wanting another unpleasant confrontation.

'You were wrong.'

Cal's voice was soft and she wondered if she'd heard him correctly. Maybe he was on the phone.

'You were wrong.'

This time he spoke a little louder and she looked up to find him facing her.

'I'm sorry?'

'You were wrong about Willow. Whatever you thought you knew, you'd got it all wrong. Nick Crossley told me. They're holding her, something about other enquiries and her not being who I thought she was.' He smiled wryly. 'So it seems I owe you an apology.'

'I don't know what you're on about.' She was confused. 'They can't be holding her for other enquiries, there aren't any, this is about the murders and there was no suggestion that Willow had anything to do with them. You must have misunderstood.'

'Nope, he was quite clear, although he couldn't give me any details. I'm sure Willow will be alright, it must be a misunderstanding, you couldn't find a more sweet, open person if you tried.'

She wasn't totally sure about that accolade to Willow's character but she nodded in agreement. 'Sorry, what?'

'I said could you speak to the cops? See if they'll tell you anything?'

This was awkward. 'I could try, Cal, but it's getting late now, I'm not sure that I should–'

'Forget it, it was just an idea. Thanks for your help.' He stood up abruptly and walked back into the bar.

So much for the overture, and he must have just misunderstood Nick somehow.

Sighing, she finished her cigarette, threw back her wine, and went up to her room, wishing the morning would hurry and arrive so that she could test out some of her theories.

~

Rachel Goodwin breathed a sigh of relief. It had been a long night and yet another shock for all concerned. Worry about her job flooded her mind as she considered the uncertainties of Meadowvale's future. Two deaths. Two! Both of them murders, and now a third potentially fatal incident, quite possibly due to natural causes, but still... Maybe it was time for her to retire. Not just yet. She squared her shoulders. Come on girl, pull yourself together. There was time enough to worry about whether anyone would ever want to take a room at Meadowvale again, now that murder appeared to be included as part of the package, she had to focus on the practical for now, she had a long night and day ahead of her.

She ticked off items on her fingers: some kind of meal had been served to those who still felt able to eat after the terrible incident with Spencer; Mary had coped admirably under the circumstances; Albert and Elspeth had helped with clearing the table, and she herself had got a couple of the residents off to bed. She'd send Mary home, the poor woman must be exhausted, then she'd see who was still up in the lounge and see if she could encourage them to get to bed. There was Monty's memorial tomorrow afternoon still to think about, food to organise, and she hadn't even begun to write down a few words to say about him. The office phone rang and she picked it up, hoping it was good news about Spencer.

~

'Do you think he's alright?' Agatha asked no one in particular.

'Who, Spencer?' Albert eyed the sherry, wondering if he should pour himself another glass, he was still feeling a little shaky.

'Are you going to stare at it or pour us another glass?' Elizabeth's voice sounded loud in the quiet lounge.

'Of course, Spencer. Oh, Albert, your hands are shaking, here let me do it.' Agatha reached for the sherry, pouring them all another generous measure.

'You'd have thought we'd have heard something by now.' Elizabeth's eyes were troubled. 'Albert, why don't you go and ask Mrs Goodwin if there's any news, I, for one, don't think I'll be able to sleep until I know.'

'Can't you see he's struggling?' Davinia's eyes flashed dangerously. 'We've all had a terrible shock, as if it wasn't bad enough after what happened to Monty, and Dorothy, of course. It's a wonder we're all still holding things together.'

Albert shifted uncomfortably, not liking his manliness in a crisis to be called into question. 'I'm alright, there's not much that can shock me, I'm just tired, and the poor boy's not dead, is he? He's just had some kind of seizure, food poisoning probably, that's what it'll be, won't it?' He looked at Elizabeth as if she held all the answers. 'I expect he'll be right as rain and back at work in no time.' He reached for his glass, relieved to see that his trembling had finally calmed down. Taking a large mouthful of his drink, he leaned heavily on the arms of the chair and stood up. 'I'll pop along to Mrs Goodwin and see if there's news.'

'Food poisoning? What if it's something we all ate?' Agatha's face was worried as she ran through what she'd eaten that day, in her mind.

Elizabeth snorted. 'Well, if anyone's at risk it'll be you, Agatha, we can rest assured that you'll have eaten anything that was served here all day.'

'There's no need to be unkind, I can't help it if I have a healthy appetite.'

~

Rachel Goodwin replaced the handset in shock, having thanked P.C. Datta for letting her know. It was almost too much to cope with, how on earth had a young member of staff suddenly died, and after everything else that had happened? How was she going to tell the residents the news? All these terrible shocks they were enduring, and none of them young and strong but quite the opposite. She'd tell no one tonight, she decided, she'd make an announcement tomorrow once they'd all had their breakfast. She left her office, hoping that everyone had taken themselves off to bed by now.

'Ah, Mrs Goodwin, I was just coming to find you, the girls dispatched me for news. How is Spencer, have you heard?'

Groaning inwardly, Rachel Goodwin pasted a firm smile on her face, taking hold of Albert's arm, and steering him back towards the lounge.

'You really ought to be in bed, Albert, it's getting late.'

'We were just having a nightcap and wondering about the poor boy. Ah, here we are.' He lowered himself back into the armchair as the four of them looked expectantly at Mrs Goodwin.

'It's far too late for any news tonight, the best thing everyone can do is to get to bed, it's been a shock for you all.' She spoke firmly, hoping she'd meet with no resistance.

'But surely you can phone the hospital?' Elizabeth stared up at her. 'Aren't they open all the time?'

'Well, the last time I phoned they had no news and I was told to call in the morning.' It wasn't a lie, the nurse she'd spoken to earlier had said exactly that, no need to mention P.C. Datta's call to her. She had an idea. 'Let's get you all off to bed and if anyone wants hot milk I'll bring it to your room, how's that?' Agatha took the bait, as she'd hoped.

'That sounds wonderful, and perhaps a biscuit? Just to settle the stomach.'

'As long as it's not going to give us food poisoning.' Elizabeth had the grace to blush slightly as four pairs of eyes glared at her.

They drained their glasses and began to move.

'Where's my watch? I could have sworn I left it on the table here.' Albert looked around in confusion.

Groaning inwardly, Mrs Goodwin herded them along. 'Let's look for it in the morning, I expect we've all got ourselves in a bit of a muddle, it'll turn up.'

Davinia gripped her sister's arm, hissing something in her ear, and Agatha turned back, looking sheepish. 'Oh, I seem to have picked it up by mistake along with my glasses, sorry.' She handed Albert his watch and they made their way to their rooms.

Ten minutes later Mrs Goodwin delivered hot milk to their rooms, including a biscuit for Agatha, returning to the lounge to collect the empty glasses and the bottle of sherry, before making her way to the kitchen. She'd have a glass of sherry herself, she decided, for medicinal purposes.

SASHA CALLS IN REINFORCEMENTS

Sasha sat up slowly, quelling the slight feeling of nausea. Everything felt her sore, her stomach, her boobs, hell, even her shoulder. She hoped she wasn't coming down with anything. Climbing out of bed, she showered and left her room with her hair still wet.

'Morning, Jules, mind if I just grab a slice of toast to go? I'm keen to get on, it's going to be a busy day.'

'Help yourself, darling, and good luck with everything, I hope the memorial goes okay.'

'Thanks, have a good day.' She hurriedly buttered a slice of toast, spreading it with peanut butter, and ate it as she started her car, her mind running through all the things that she needed to do. Her first stop was Meadowvale, there was something she needed to find.

Entering, she skirted around a large box filled with what appeared to be bric-a-brac and made her way to the office where she found a tired-looking Mrs Goodwin.

'Morning, Sasha, you've heard the terrible news, I imagine? I told the residents this morning after their breakfast.'

'I have, I'm so sorry, how's everyone bearing up?'

'Surprisingly well in fact. Elizabeth galvanised everyone, much to my amazement, and suggested that we have a little charity drive in memory of Spencer, Monty, and Dorothy. It's done wonders for everyone's morale, taken their minds right off all the sadness as they've busied themselves sorting out things to donate. Elizabeth has been most generous, she's donated a handbag and I don't need to tell you that it's top quality, some kind of designer brand. I'll get the postman to take it all down to our local charity shop when he comes.'

It seemed the stern Elizabeth had a heart after all, Sasha thought to herself as she asked if it would be alright to check a few things and, given the okay, headed for the kitchen.

'Hi, Kirsty, I'm so sorry to hear about Spencer, how are you?'

'Thanks, Sasha, we're all still in disbelief, if I'm honest with you, he was so young, never seemed to get ill, and then just like that he's gone and dropped dead. What was wrong with him, do you know?' Kirsty cluttered around the kitchen as she spoke. 'There's no time to even think about it what with Monty's memorial this afternoon and sandwiches and cakes to prepare. Tanya should be in soon, and Mary, it's all hands on deck, the poor woman was here late last night, and Mrs Goodwin never even went home, she held the fort in place of Spencer.'

Finally, Sasha got a word in. 'We don't know what caused his death yet, I believe the coroner is doing an autopsy today. I'll try not to get in your way for long, but do you mind if I look around in here? Spencer was drinking a cup of tea and eating a slice of leftover cake, I understand, before he became ill, and his phone wasn't found on him.'

'Well, it's no secret that the boy liked his cake, real sweet tooth he had. That'll be Mary's cake, she'd made a Madeira and there was a piece left.' Kirsty hesitated. 'His phone, you say?' She whipped her phone out of her pocket and a moment later the sounds of someone screaming came from inside the pantry.

'What the hell?' Sasha looked around in surprise.

'He was always putting stupid ringtones on his phone.' Kirsty gave her a small smile. 'I just called it. It must have shot across the floor and into the pantry when the door was open, maybe he dropped it when he became unwell.' Pulling the door open, she bent down and retrieved the phone, handing it to Sasha.

'Now why didn't I think of calling it? Thank you, Kirsty.' She left the kitchen and went into the empty staff room, taking a seat and checking Spencer's call history before scrolling through the last few messages he'd sent, pausing at a message to Lucy, and reading it with interest.

You spoil me BaBe luvly cupcake But not as luvly as you xx

She checked the time of the message, noting that it had been sent the previous evening. What cupcake? Not Mary's Madeira cake, clearly, no, there must have been another cake from his girlfriend.

She read the last message, sent from his phone just a couple of minutes after the message was sent to Lucy, to a recipient saved as BigGee.

I just Got your Dosh it workeD Spence the Blackmailer haha But its too hot round here so I'll see you tomorrow.

So, Spencer had got hold of money during the evening, which he owed to BigGee, and she knew exactly who that was. More to the point, he'd got the money since he'd begun his shift, surely, which meant that someone who'd been at Meadowvale that evening had given it to him, or rather had been coerced into giving it to him, and she knew exactly what he'd been blackmailing them about. And too hot round here? Did he mean the fact that policemen were still stationed at both gates into and out of the property? Probably.

The use of capital letters was odd, she frowned, they were all in the wrong places. Something niggled in the back of her mind, something about Spencer, it had been when she was talking to Mrs Goodwin about the staff, but she couldn't remember what it was. Noticing an unopened message from Lucy in his inbox, she clicked on it, feeling sympathy for her niece's friend at the loss of her boyfriend. She sat up straight as she re-read the message.

What are you on about? I never gave you any cake today. Must have been your other girlfriend lol xx

Excitedly, Sasha considered the implications of those few words. Spencer had eaten a cupcake which he'd thought had come from his girlfriend…. except it hadn't… and within a short while he'd become ill, suffering some kind of seizure, a few hours after which he'd died. A poisoned cupcake? Seriously? It was the stuff of old crime novels, the kind she'd read as a girl. And how? How could someone have got hold of a cupcake, introduced some kind of poison to it, which had to be undetectable, and provided it to Spencer in such a way that he believed it to be from Lucy? For one thing how on earth had anyone been able to lay their hands on any kind of poison, and for another, how had they known about his penchant for cakes? Unless they had an intimate knowledge of Spencer and his sweet tooth…

She thought back to Chantelle's account of Spencer's words at the old motel. It was clear which day he'd delivered his demand, as well as which day his victim had handed over the five hundred pounds. And it was abundantly clear which day he'd been poisoned. And it had all taken place at Meadowvale. Unless she was barking up the wrong tree entirely and it turned out that Spencer had died of natural causes.

She was disturbed by the arrival of an ashen-faced Greg, who fell onto the cushion beside her on the sofa.

'I can't believe he's dead, Sasha, I really can't. He was fine last night when I knocked off, cheerful as anything. What happened? Was he ill?'

'No...' she said slowly. 'I don't believe he was. Greg, was anything delivered to Spencer yesterday? A package of any kind?'

Greg pondered her question. 'No, not that I know of, I think it was just post for Mrs Goodwin, envelopes, the usual stuff, no packages, although you'd have to ask her if anything was delivered earlier before I came on shift.'

'You didn't see him eating anything unusual by any chance? I believe he had a sweet tooth?'

Greg held his hands to his face. 'Oh my goodness, what am I like? I'd forget my head if it wasn't screwed on. The cupcake from Lucy, of course, but why–? You surely don't think–?' He clutched Sasha's arm, leaning in conspiratorially to ask in a stage whisper, 'Do you think he was poisoned? But dear Lucy would hardly poison her own boyfriend, would she?'

'I don't know anything for certain but something killed him out of the blue. So, Lucy dropped off a cupcake for him? When was this?'

'That's the funny thing, I found it in reception, poor little cupcake sitting there all on its lonesome. It must have been Miriam, Lucy will have asked her to bring it in for him, she must have left it there by mistake.'

'Are you sure it was from Lucy? Was it in a box? Did it have anything written on it?'

'Oh, wait, Agatha was caught red-handed by Albert, he said he saw her buying two in the patisserie – he might have just been teasing her of course. I think one was for Mrs Goodwin.'

Frustrated, Sasha tried again. 'So the other one might have been the one you found? But why did you think it was for Spencer? Did it have a card on it? Did it say it was from Lucy?'

'No... not exactly, I think it had Spencer's name on it, yes, that's it, just his name and nothing else. It must have been from Lucy, no one else would buy him a cake, we all knew that Lucy treated him to little gifts like that. I expect if Agatha bought an extra cake it was because she wanted to eat it herself, not give it away.'

'So, what did you do with it? This is important, Greg.'

'I took it through to him in the kitchen, I was about to knock off, he opened it straight up and took a big bite of it. Sasha, please tell me I didn't hand him a poisoned cupcake, I'll never forgive myself.' Greg shuddered theatrically.

'The autopsy will tell us, but you couldn't have known, even if it was poisoned. What did it look like? Do you have any idea where it was from? Did it look homemade or do you think it was from a bakery? Or the patisserie?'

'Definitely from the patisserie.' Greg nodded his head firmly. 'Their cakes come in lovely little boxes, those ones with the clear bit on top so you can see the cake. I didn't really study it, but it had some kind of topping on it, covered in little sprinkly things, hundreds and thousands, but not rainbow colours, these were black. A bit odd, now that I come to think of it, but maybe it was a goth cake, that would be right up Lucy's street.'

'Very interesting, thanks, Greg, you've been a huge help, but not a word to anyone about this, okay?'

'Mum's the word.' He mimed zipping his lips closed as Sasha asked him a final question.

'Greg, last question, I know you have to get on. Can you tell me if anything odd happened that caught your attention, any strange behaviour by anyone, no matter how small, on either Sunday or Monday?'

Greg giggled. 'Well, I don't know about odd or strange, half of them are odd and the other half strange as you like. Sorry.' He looked sheepish. 'It's just that they've all got their funny ways about them and half the time the goings-on here make me feel like I'm living in an alternative universe. Especially lately...' His eyes darkened. 'Right, let me think...' He leaned back, crossing his arms and legs.

'Just tell me everything that you can remember, who visited, anything at all...' she encouraged.

'Okay, Moira the queen bitch arrived and kidnapped Howard to take him home for Sunday lunch, very proprietorial, she was, wouldn't even let me fetch his slippers, had to do it herself.'

Sasha sighed inwardly, this was going to be slow progress, she needed to hurry him along. 'Go on,' she murmured encouragingly.

'So, okay, oh yes, David Bertram, mister high and mighty lord of the manor, he caused an absolute scene about the murders, you should have heard him, like it was all Mrs Goodwin's fault.' Greg's eyes widened, his arms, now unfolded, waving themselves around expressively. 'Anyway, Mrs Goodwin set him straight, round one to her I said to myself, so off they went, he and Judith, tails between their legs, taking Elizabeth with them off out to some fancy lunch venue.

So then after that, Kirsty had the cards to hand out from Mrs G for the memorial for Monty, which is today of course, and Spencer was on duty which I remember clearly because we both had the roast, which was very nice – poor Kirsty, she'd made heaps of food and only three residents ended up being there for lunch.' Greg pulled a sad face at Sasha, who tried to hide her impatience.

'Which three were there for lunch?'

'That would be the Lovewell sisters and our dear Lillian. And then things livened up a bit.' Greg sat up straighter, grinning. 'Elizabeth arrived back tipsy, nothing new there, weaving and wobbling her way to the lounge, oh, Richard brought Howard in at the same time but rushed straight off. For some reason Spencer rushed after him, not sure what that was about, I was too busy trying to stop things from getting out of hand with madam. Being malicious, she was, to Elspeth, who really wouldn't hurt a fly. Ah, that's what it was, Kirsty had asked Spencer to hand out the cards, that's what he was doing, he'd put them in all the residents' rooms – they'd had their names on the envelopes. The rest of them were for the relatives, so, Raymond got one, Mervyn too, of course, the dratted Moira had to turn up again, like a bad penny, returning Howard's slippers, so I took a card from Spencer and gave it to her, in case Richard's keeping any secrets from you and doesn't tell you, I said, you should have seen her face.' Greg's face had a spiteful expression on it, which he hastily removed. He sighed. 'So, then Spencer was all upset with me because he'd been asked to hand out the cards.' He spread his hands out as he finished, 'Like it mattered who delivered them.'

'So, pretty much everyone was here on Sunday, including all the relatives, by the sounds of it?'

'Yes, no, wait a minute, Mary was off, but she did call in and she took her card because I saw her holding it, plus another one, I'm not sure who that was for.'

'Willow, I can fill in that piece of the puzzle, I saw Mary at The Spotted Dog, she must have dropped Willow's memorial notice for her at the bar. So, basically, everyone received one from Spencer on Sunday.'

'Yes, I suppose so, should I carry on?'

There was more? She nodded, so far all she'd learned was that Spencer could have given his demand for money to just about anyone on Sunday, quite easily, using one of the memorial cards. Greg was a gossip, but he had plenty of information and within it, somewhere, was what she was looking for.

'And then you arrived – that's when you interviewed Elizabeth, although I'm not sure if you got any sense out of her after her boozing. I sent Spencer home at tea-time, which was just sandwiches and bits, everyone was quite excited about their trip to the village the next day so that was all they talked about – hair-dos, going to the bank, shopping, and lunch at the patisserie.' Greg pulled a face. 'I felt quite jealous, it all sounded great fun – how sad am I?' He clutched Sasha's arm. 'The patisserie – are you telling me that one of our lovely residents suggested lunch there with the sole purpose of buying a cupcake to poison Spencer with? They wouldn't, well, I mean, they couldn't... you've seen them, none of them would hurt a fly.'

Sasha didn't respond, she was wondering how to find out the movements of the residents and anyone else connected to Spencer, on Monday. She realised that Greg had spoken again. 'Sorry, what was that?'

'I said, as a matter of fact, I popped to the village myself yesterday to run a few errands.'

'I don't suppose you went to the bank as well?' She was still distracted, an idea forming in her mind.

'Well, yes, I did. Why?'

'And you didn't go into the patisserie, too, by any chance?'

Greg bristled. 'I popped my head round the door to have a bit of a giggle with everyone.' His eyes flashed. 'If you're suggesting that I bought a cupcake and poisoned Spencer, I can tell you that you're wrong. He had a lot to say, he rubbed people up the wrong way, said stupid things, like all his talk of blackmail that night, but he just loved stirring things up for no reason, and I was still fond of him, we all were.'

Hurriedly placating him, she was prevented from asking him anything further as he jumped up. 'Look at me chatting away and with so much to do, what with poor Monty's memorial. To think it would have been crafting with Willow this afternoon, and instead we're remembering another victim of murder.' He shuddered. 'Come and find me a bit later and I'll tell you what I can about yesterday, but I don't think I know anything that will help you nab your murderer.'

'Thanks, Greg, you've been a huge help, I'll find you in a while.'

Mollified, Greg pranced off and Sasha picked up her phone to call in reinforcements – she wasn't going to be able to do everything herself, she conceded – before heading out to the storeroom, reminded of something by Greg's comment.

~

Colin Hartley hovered awkwardly, waiting for Mrs Goodwin to notice him.

'Someone's been messing around with my garden waste, all disturbed it was, thrown all over the place. The thing is, well, I'm a bit worried...'

'Yes, yes, Colin.' Mrs Goodwin nodded distractedly as her phone rang for what felt like the umpteenth time. 'We'll sort that all out, now I really must answer this phone, it's been ringing itself off its hook today what with everything that's happened, and now we've got reporters all over us.'

'It's just, it wasn't safe, I shouldn't have left it there like that...'

'Hold on please.' Looking up at Colin, Mrs Goodwin frowned. 'Not now, Colin, please, we must all pull together and do whatever is needed.' She turned her attention back to her caller, Des Barnsley from the local paper. 'No comment, Des, I'm sorry, but I can't tell you anything.'

Des Barnsley put the phone down, not surprised by Mrs Goodwin's comment, or lack thereof. He'd pay a visit to

Pringle's Chemist, if anyone had the story it would be Dolly Pringle...

~

Sasha stood looking down at the cut pieces of fabric in the middle of the crafting fabric box. They shouldn't have missed this. Wildly patterned in vivid colours, she recognised them instantly as matching the piece from Kirsty's rag bag. Slipping her hand into a plastic bag, she gently laid the pieces out, nodding – this was the remains of Agatha's missing kaftan, and what's more, the pieces which made up the bottom hem were coated in mud. This was what Dorothy Newton's murderer was wearing when he or she drowned her in the pond by holding her head under the water with a walking stick. Could you describe a kaftan as a murder weapon, she mused? Agatha's kaftan... and Greg had mentioned that Agatha had bought cupcakes the day before – but Agatha as a murderer? She wasn't convinced, and then there was Monty – Agatha and Monty had been friends. And if, by some stretch of the imagination, Agatha was the murderer, why, then, make a fuss about her kaftan going missing? Why not keep quiet? Was it because she'd been spotted wearing it in the garden around the time of Dorothy's death?

Jane Weaver answered her call straightaway. 'Sasha, hi, I expect you're wondering about the results of Spencer Brent's autopsy? Pavani's still with Wilson Mwabila, I'll give you a call later once we know some details.'

'Thanks, Jane, I also need to tell you about the fabric I've found in the storeroom. I'm certain that it's Agatha Lovewell's missing kaftan – it's been cut into pieces and I'm pretty sure you'll find that the mud on the hem is from the pond where Dorothy was drowned. I found it in the middle of the fabric box in the storeroom so I guess we missed it before as we didn't know what we were looking for. I think Dorothy's murderer hid it there, hiding it in plain sight as it were. If it hadn't been for the piece they missed when they transferred it from Kirsty's rag bag the connection might never have been made. It's a pity that Ross hasn't been able to get the results back on the mud from that sample yet. Oh, was Willow able to help you at all? Cal seemed to think there was something else going on with her?'

There was a pause before Jane spoke again. 'Sasha, we're holding Willow – real name Norma Finch – it seems she's been doing the rounds of retirement and care homes for some time. She finds out about the residents, who has living relatives, who's alone, and gains their trust. She's already managed to benefit under a will from a deceased resident at another home.'

'So that's why she was going through the files at Meadowvale.' Her mouth wide in surprise, Sasha tried to make sense of it. 'I think she may have had the Lovewell sisters in her sights. That's awful.'

'Hmm, well, she was very practised at it that's for sure, and she would help herself to cash and valuables belonging to residents so we've caught ourselves a nice little common criminal.'

'So that could explain some of the thefts at Meadowvale, which I thought might have been Mary the kitchen assistant. It looks like I've got plenty wrong. I can't believe it though, Willow, well, Norma.' She shook her head in wonder, even as she guiltily acknowledged a tiny moment of gleefulness – little miss perfect wasn't so perfect after all.

'I have to go, I'll call you with the autopsy results, and don't worry about getting things wrong, there's so much going on at Meadowvale it'll be a wonder if we ever make sense of it all. We didn't find any stolen valuables in her room at the pub though, and not much in the way of personal belongings, apart from a box of old books, so I don't suppose she was planning on staying around here for too long.' Jane ended the call.

~

Mrs Pringle's face lit up as the bell jangled above the door and Maureen walked in holding Douglas. 'Hello, my dear, and here's darling Douglas, oh do pop him down, let's see if he remembers where the treats are. Sheila? We've got visitors, put the kettle on, I think we could all do with a cup of tea.'

'That would be wonderful.' Maureen smiled as they all watched Douglas make a beeline for the back of the chemist shop. The little sausage dog stopped, looked back at his adoring audience, tail wagging nineteen to the dozen, before staring up at the shelf containing his box of treats.

Torn between wanting to be the one to give Douglas his treat, and wanting to find out what Maureen's visit was all about, Mrs Pringle made a quick decision. 'Sheila, be a dear and give our little boy his treat, now, Maureen, what can we do for you? Terrible news about the young lad at Meadowvale, I expect you've heard?' As she spoke, she steered Maureen to a chair and sat down next to her, leaning forward, her nose quivering.

Grinning inwardly, Maureen nodded. 'I have, Sasha told me, it's awful, they've had such a terrible time there. In fact, the reason I'm here is because of something that Sasha's asked me to do and she wondered if you might be able to help...'

'Yes, dear?' Mrs Pringle leaned forward intently.

Maureen approached the matter delicately, not wanting to upset Mrs Pringle by insinuating anything. 'Sasha wondered, well, she knows that you have a good view of the street from the chemist, and she wondered if by chance you may have looked out of the window during the course of the day, and if you did that perhaps you might have noticed who was in the village yesterday, where they might have been, to the bank, for instance...' She dwindled off, not sure if she'd been clear enough.

The older woman was nodding slowly. 'Well, it's true, we can certainly see a good portion of the high street, and of course, if one happens to glance out there's a good chance one will notice who goes where. Not that one is *spying*, of course.' She gave a little cough. 'Er, was it the bank in particular that Sasha is interested in? I don't suppose you can tell me...?'

'I'm sorry, she didn't really explain it all to me, she just said that it was of the utmost importance and might help us concerning what's been happening at Meadowvale.' Maureen played her trump card. 'She was in here herself, as you will know, but she said that her powers of observation were nothing compared to yours. Thank you, Sheila, very kind.' Maureen took the cup of tea. 'She also mentioned the patisserie...'

Mrs Pringle tsked in frustration. 'We'd usually have a good view of it, but the minibus was parked a little in the way.' She glanced at Sheila who was making a fuss of a happy Douglas. 'Do you think perhaps...' She lowered her voice. 'Would you mind if Sheila took Douglas for a little walk? So that we can speak privately?'

Surprised, but not minding one bit, Maureen turned to Sheila. 'Do you know, Sheila, I think Douglas would love a little walk along the road. I don't suppose you would–?'

Sheila beamed, turning pink. 'I'd love to, I'll take good care of him. We'll walk along to Patricia's and say hello. Would you like that, Douglas?'

Douglas indicated that he would, indeed, love it, and the two of them left the chemist as Mrs Pringle shifted in her seat, reaching into her pocket for something. Pulling out a small notebook and popping her reading glasses on, she looked a little embarrassed.

'I don't make a habit of it, you'll understand, but ever since I was able to help Sasha over that man, Charles, on account of his visit to Pink's, which was out of keeping in the scheme of things, well, it occurred to me that one never knew when one might, quite naturally, observe something that might prove useful. And poor Sasha has her work cut out to find out who killed Dorothy Newton, not to mention poor Monty, and now the young lad, so I'd taken to jotting down the odd thing, just to jog my memory of course, in case Sasha should need to ask me anything.'

'Well, that's wonderful.' Maureen smiled encouragingly. 'Anything that you can tell us, anything at all.'

'Here we are, now, let's see... Albert Bird was the first to visit the bank, while Howard Norton went along to the supermarket with Lillian Springer. He went into the bank alone a little later and was followed by Davinia and Agatha Lovewell – that was after they'd been in here. Elizabeth Payton and Elspeth Parkhurst both had hair appointments at Patricia's and they went to the bank together after that. I didn't see Lillian go to the bank but I did see her son, Mervyn Springer, go in, and I also saw Richard and Moira Carding walking out at different times so I don't think they were in there together. Miriam Smithers rushed in looking harried, the poor woman's always in a hurry, and now, who's this? Oh yes, Gregory, he works up at Meadowvale, such a nice happy man, always smiling and cheerful. I've got a note here that he popped into the patisserie after the bank, but he didn't stay. And then it looks like Raymond Bird, that would be Albert's son – a shifty looking character, yes, he visited the bank. Goodness, it looks like just about everyone from Meadowvale was in the bank yesterday at some time or other. Now, I'm afraid I can't tell you exactly who lunched in the patisserie.' Mrs Pringle's face creased in vexation at this apparent inadequacy on her part. 'But it was around lunchtime that the young lady with the strange name went into the bank. You know the one, she does activities at Meadowvale?'

'Willow, isn't it?' Maureen was amazed at the information overload, Sasha would never believe this when she told her.

'That's right, and then Judith Bertram is my last entry, oh wait, there's a note here to say that she was in the bank earlier, before lunch.' Mrs Pringle stopped abruptly, drawing a breath, her face flushed with pleasure. 'That's all I have, I'm afraid.'

'You've been an enormous help, Mrs Pringle, truly.'

The door opened and Sheila walked in with Douglas just as Maureen was standing up. Mrs Pringle slipped her notebook into her pocket in a swift movement, bending down to pet the sausage dog who looked hopefully towards the box of treats. 'I don't suppose he could have just one more? You'll be wanting to pop into the patisserie, why don't you leave him with us while you make your enquiries?'

Crossing the road to the patisserie, Maureen entered, smiling at the girl behind the counter whose name badge declared her to be Judy.

'Judy, I wonder if you could help me? I'm here on behalf of–' She paused, wondering how to explain herself. 'On behalf of Meadowvale, the retirement home.' It was a bit of a stretch, but also kind of true. 'There was a little confusion yesterday when a group of residents lunched here, some kind of mix-up over cupcakes...'

The young woman's forehead furrowed. 'Not a problem is there? I wouldn't want to get anyone into trouble.'

Realising that she was on delicate ground, after all, a care worker had died after possibly consuming one of the patisserie's cupcakes if Sasha's hunch was correct, Maureen chose her words carefully. 'Not at all, it's more a question of who bought the cakes to take away, a kind of disagreement about whose they were...'

'Well, I don't know, I'm sure...' Judy's eyes darted from left to right, worriedly. 'It was a busy time...'

'Yes, of course, I believe that Agatha Lovewell bought extra cakes when she left, I don't suppose you could remember how many?'

'Agatha Lovewell…' Judy's face cleared. 'Ah, that would be the lady in the big dress, all colours of the rainbow it was, and then some. Good appetite, if I remember rightly. She said she was buying a gift for someone, now, was it two or three that she bought?' Her face screwed up in concentration as she tackled this difficult test of her memory. 'Three. Definitely three. I remember now because she asked for two and then changed her mind and said might as well make it three because you could never have too many cupcakes. I had to agree with her, they're quite small, barely a mouthful apiece.'

'That's so helpful, thank you, and no one else bought cakes to take away that you can recall? Anyone? Anyone at all? From Meadowvale or just someone who popped in, perhaps?'

'No… no, they all left then, I remember, because I went out the back to hang up my apron as it was my lunch break and I wanted to pop home and check on my mum. She's not been well and I said I'd take her something in for her lunch.'

'Alright, well, thank you, I won't keep you any longer.' Maureen turned to leave, holding the door open for someone as they walked in.

'Except for the other person.'

Not sure if she'd heard the girl correctly, Maureen turned back. 'Sorry?'

'Well, there was the other person who'd left something in the shop, but I couldn't say if they was from the home, bit bossy, they was, according to Theresa. She said they marched in and demanded a cake, all quick like, and put it in their bag and told her to keep the change. Theresa said she wasn't complaining as it was a brand-new fiver, straight from the bank she reckoned, and the cupcake only a pound. There's no accounting for folk, is there?'

'There certainly isn't, and I don't suppose you know if it was a man or a lady, or what they looked like?'

'Well, no, you could ask Theresa, only she's off for a few days now, gone to visit her sister and she doesn't use a mobile phone. She's in London, somewhere, I think if that helps?'

Not really, thought Maureen.

'She did make a joke, Theresa did, she's a bit like that, something about having to stop herself from curtseying. I'm not sure what she meant, like serving royalty, perhaps?'

Wondering if she'd found out anything that could help Sasha, Maureen expressed her thanks again and, having wrestled Douglas from his fan club, sat in her car and called Sasha to update her.

AGATHA MAKES A PHONE CALL

'Well, I don't know,' said Greg. 'I've got lots to do, Mrs Goodwin has got me making up Dorothy's old room for an incoming. A bit of a surprise for us all, what with all the scandal, you wouldn't think anyone would want to stay here, would you?'

'I could give you a hand while we chat?'

'You're a proper darling, Sasha, I'll get the linen. I was going to get Tanya to help me if I could drag her away from Lillian, I think she's made the poor dear her pet project, always with her, she is.'

Tucking the sheet tightly beneath the mattress, Sasha let Greg tell her what he could recall from the day before, her ears attuned for anything of significance.

'So, anyway, afternoon activity was a washout, they were all far too tired for Willow's literary discussion.' He giggled. 'Not that the girl knows much about anything if you ask me. She'd got some books from the library, but gave up when they all kept falling asleep, and then, before you knew it the visitors started rolling in and that was that. There was Judith, she's always here, her usual bossy self, like mother like daughter I always say, you can tell where she gets it from, and Raymond was hanging around, he and Mervyn are just the same, always lurking if you know what I mean – he was here too – and poor Miriam, Elspeth's daughter, rushing in and out in a fluster, but she does try, bless her heart. Oh, and her royal highness, Moira, had Richard on a tight leash, she doesn't let him out of her sight, I don't know how he puts up with it – scared of her probably, she is rather terrifyingly butch.' Expertly flapping the top sheet, Greg let it fall neatly over the bed as they began to tuck it in.

'Mary had made a Madeira cake for me to serve with afternoon tea – that's our Monday tradition – apart from dear Dorothy's day of demise, which was a Tuesday and when Kirsty made the lemon drizzle cake. I think that confused a few of them, they get used to routine otherwise they forget what day it is, poor dears.'

Straightening her back, Sasha considered Greg's comment, but Greg didn't stop speaking as he picked up a blanket and handed it to her to unfold.

'Anyway, a few of them stretched their legs before tea, taking walks in the garden, but Mervyn stayed with Lillian, she doesn't manage much of a walk. Elspeth headed off to catch up with Albert and Raymond and that's when I got royally ticked off by Judith. Mummy needs a walking stick, I was informed. Who does the woman think she is? I was despatched to the bench beside the greenhouse to help her back. Now the eiderdown, lots of work all these sheets and blankets but they're not so keen on duvets, a bit too modern for some of the old school. Howard was in the garden with his adoring fan club, poor things, if I didn't know better, I'd say they both harboured thoughts of romance. It's quite sweet, I suppose, anyway, I passed them when I took the stick to Elizabeth – not her usual hated one, although it's much better for her stability, especially when she's had one too many – I just grabbed one from the rack.' Greg passed Sasha a pillow protector and pillowcase and they wrestled with the pillows.

Sasha nudged Greg along. 'So, you helped Elizabeth back indoors?'

'That's right, and got myself ticked off all over again, they don't pay us enough, they really don't, but she was worried about her dignity if you ask me. Not a word, she said, and after I found her headfirst in the pile of weeds by the greenhouse. What on earth are you doing, I asked her? Have you lost something? She didn't take kindly to it, always so worried about anyone laughing at her. She'd never admit to falling over into the weed pile, too worried about looking foolish. So I helped her back, I insisted on it, I couldn't have her falling over again, it was probably all too much for her, what with the day out as well. We passed Richard, I thought he'd given Moira the slip but she was right behind him as always. Pop the towels in the bathroom would you? I'll just check the cupboards, and make sure we haven't left anything in here.

'Willow came in with the box from the storeroom, something about taking her work home. Just check those drawers for me, be a darling, and then I have to go and see what needs doing for the memorial tea.'

Doing as she was told, Sasha took the opportunity to draw things to a close. 'So when did you find the cupcake?'

'Well, that's when I did the rounds, it was quite a bit later by then, picking up bits and pieces, you'd be amazed at how much stuff is left lying around. I returned things to their homes, took a book back to the library and almost made Spencer jump out of his skin, you'd have thought I'd caught him robbing a bank. He was looking for a book, he said, although he didn't have one in his hand. I'd never have had him down for a reader, but I suppose we'll never know now.'

Nodding sympathetically, Sasha stood looking around the room, ready, now, for its new occupant. 'And that's when you found the cupcake?'

'Yes,' Greg sighed dramatically. 'I'll never forgive myself to my dying day. To think I delivered the poisoned chalice.' He shuddered. 'I just picked up the box in reception, saw Spencer's name on it and took it to him in the kitchen. He was eating it as I said goodbye and headed home.' Greg stood looking around the room, like Sasha.

'Makes me quite sad really, it feels like we're wiping away the last memories of Dorothy. This was her room, I'm not sure if you knew that? Poor dear, she was so happy with her garden view, always talking about the flowers looking pretty, but I don't think she realised this room has the worst view, what with it being the corner room and the only one looking out over the car park. There's not much of the garden to see, but still, it seemed to make her happy. Well, I must get on, thanks for helping me, I hope you figure it all out, Sasha, we could do with some closure. We'll see you at Monty's memorial service, I suppose?'

'You will, and thanks, Greg, this will all be over soon, you've helped me more than you know. Oh, one quick question, it's a bit of an odd one, it was something that Lillian said to me one day. I don't suppose you remember who dropped a fork at dinner one night, by any chance? Maybe you had a sort of memorial dinner for Monty?'

Greg frowned. 'Hmm, no, we've got the memorial today, oh wait, we did all have our dinner together and had some of his favourite food, but, Sasha my darling, they're always dropping their cutlery, poor lambs.'

She persisted. 'Maybe someone said something that upset someone? There was talk of blackmail?'

Snorting, Greg turned back at the door. 'Someone always said something to upset someone. Sorry, my love, if I think of anything I'll let you know.' He stepped into the corridor and paused. 'Blackmail, you say? That's funny.'

Sasha listened to what Greg told her with mounting excitement. She walked off, wandering into the entrance hall, mulling over everything that Greg had recounted to her, it could all make sense, everything tied in, but she had to be sure, after all, it was no small thing to declare someone a murderer...

Agatha stood up, her face flushing, as Sasha appeared. 'Such a lovely idea, don't you think? I was just popping a couple of things in the box, it's all in aid of the deaths.' She moved off rather hurriedly, gripping her expensive-looking handbag firmly in her hand, and Sasha headed through the library and out to the garden, encountering Colin Hartley, the gardener, as he walked straight into her, his mind clearly elsewhere.

'Sorry, Colin, are you alright? You look like you've got the weight of the world on your shoulders.'

'It's me should apologise, I walked right into you. It's that Devil's Weed, Thornapple as it's known, I tried to tell Mrs Goodwin about it but she's got too much on her mind. I should have got rid of it properly, I knew it was dangerous. I said not to touch it.'

In a flash of total clarity, Sasha pictured the scene the day she'd been with Monty in the garden, Willow taking everyone on a garden walk, various residents posing for their photographs with Charles Priestley, the gardener's voice sharp with concern. 'Why does it worry you, Colin? What is it?'

'Why, it's deadly, miss, you don't want to even touch it, let alone the seeds. And what with young Spencer's sudden death, well, I don't know, it's just worrying me is all.' He walked away, his face etched with concern.

A quick search of the internet told Sasha everything that she needed to know about Datura Stramonium, otherwise known as Thornapple or Devil's Weed. This was it, this must be what had killed Spencer, and she was pretty sure that she knew how it had been administered – she just needed the autopsy results to confirm it. Then, if she could tie the blackmail note to the killer, she'd be ready to reveal everything, but time was going fast and people would be arriving for Monty's memorial soon.

She called Pavani, hoping for news.

'Sorry, Sash, Wilson's still busy. He seems excited about something but won't tell me what, and I have to attend to some other matters. I told him I'd come back later.'

Frustration ripped through her – she needed to speak to Wilson. 'Can you give me his number?

Pacing, as she listened to the recorded message, she cancelled the call, rushing to her car – she could be in Rentham in about ten minutes.

Twelve minutes later she parked at the hospital entrance and rushed inside, glancing at the signboard before taking the stairs down to the mortuary.

'Wilson!' She banged on the door, pushing it open as Wilson Mwabila turned around in surprise.

'Can I help you?'

'Wilson, sorry for barging in, we've never met, I'm Sasha Blue and I'm working with the police to investigate the murders at Meadowvale. Can you tell me if you found seeds from a plant in the stomach of Spencer Brent?'

'Well, it's funny that you should ask that, I've just been examining them.'

Sasha listened to the man's excited voice as he explained his findings.

'Quite fascinating and not something I ever expected to experience here in England – back in my native Zambia, perhaps, and elsewhere in Africa, but here? Never. We often had cases there of people ingesting parts of the plant by mistake, not realising its toxicity. Similar to the Moonflower, of course, which was an attractive inclusion in any garden on account of its wonderful blooms and powerful evening scent, although a little less harmful, if you disregard its hallucinogenic properties – abused by some, hence the odd unfortunate mistake.' Wilson paused to draw a breath.

'Of course, they'll have to go off to the lab for analysis, but I know Datura Stramonium seeds when I see them. Quite deadly, how on earth did the boy end up eating so many of them? I found over a hundred seeds which is more than enough for a fatal dose. He'd been eating cake too, but not much to get excited about there. Datura is actually part of the nightshade family so we're basically saying that he died of atropine poisoning – unofficially of course until the lab report comes back.'

'That's great, Wilson, I had a hunch but needed your confirmation. Er, quick question, if the seeds were sprinkled on top of a cake, wouldn't he have tasted them and removed them? I'm guessing they don't taste very nice?'

'On the contrary.' Wilson chuckled. 'They have a sweetish taste so they probably just enhanced the taste of the cake. What a way to kill someone – you British and your eccentric murder methods – no wonder your crime stories are so popular.'

Her phone rang and, thanking Wilson, she hurried out. 'Hello?'

'Oh, Sasha dear, you said to call you if we thought of anything, and it was seeing the lemon drizzle cake on the table for the memorial tea that reminded me.'

'Agatha, is that you?'

'Yes, dear.' Agatha's troubled voice continued, 'As I said, it was seeing the cake, only she said that she ate it, but she didn't, I remembered, you see, I ate it when I found it still sitting there, such a shame to waste it. I just don't understand why she'd pretend, and when I asked her, she got upset with me and made me promise that I'd stop worrying and meddling and not say a word to anyone but, well, the thing is, I've remembered who was missing when Dorothy was killed. All that insistence about us not having cake, but we did. Kirsty made it because Mary had been off sick the day before and the trouble is that we were overheard by that very person, when we were talking and, oh dear, I know it sounds fanciful but I felt frightened all of a sudden, it was the look in their eyes... And Elspeth was wrong, it hadn't rained so I don't see how... it's all so odd, you see...' Her tone brightened. 'Oh, hello, dear, why how nice, but do we have time?'

'Hello? Agatha, are you there?' Sasha listened to the muffled sounds at the other end. 'Hello?' The line clicked and went dead. 'Dammit.' She called the Meadowvale number back, getting the engaged sound. All this cake talk was doing her head in, she thought as she raced back to Meadowvale, everything seemed to revolve around the damn things.

She tried to make sense of the woman's call. Did she know something, and if she did, was she in danger? Surely not with everyone gathering for Monty's memorial? But something had frightened Agatha, or rather, someone... A recollection of where she'd last seen Agatha appeared in her head – could that be where Spencer's blackmail note had been secreted?

All was quiet when she entered Meadowvale, and a glance out of the window confirmed that everyone was now gathered in the garden in memory of Monty. Hardly daring to breathe, Sasha hurried back inside and slipped inside the room, finding the object of her interest exactly where she'd suspected.

Retrieving the torn pieces of card, she pieced them together and read Spencer's blackmail note, his easily identifiable writing style proving beyond doubt that it was from him – something which the recipient would have easily known, it being common knowledge, if Mrs Goodwin's casual reference to it the day they talked about the staff, was anything to go by.

Five hunDreD quiD in an envelope in the library behinD the Lillian Books by MunDay evening or I tell the cops what you DiD to Monty.

Checking the reverse of the card, she found a number written in the corner, which told her nothing. There was one more missing piece of the puzzle which she was sure she would find in the same room and, after a little rummaging, she held the pair of grimy leather gloves in her hand.

Walking outside, Sasha stood quietly at the back of the gathering as Mrs Goodwin spoke about Monty, her mind racing as snippets of Agatha's call replayed in her head. *She said that she ate it. Why would she pretend? All that insistence about us not having cake. Elspeth was wrong.* The pieces fell into unimaginable place and she had to stop herself from gasping out loud – it was crazy, surely that couldn't be? She'd been so sure that she'd figured everything out, but she'd overlooked something about the diagram of the bruises on Dorothy's neck and torso...

Her eyes scanned the small group, seeking out Agatha, but there was no sign of the woman's flamboyant garb. Where was she? Her anxiety for Agatha's safety increased as she tried to work out who was missing, her eyes falling on someone's back – that was it, of course, Oz – the Australian connection.

Dorothy's new friend *from the Wizard of Oz* – the one who had lured her to her death. It stood to reason that no matter how careful you were you would make the odd slip in your speech. What was it that Elspeth had said? A gander. And when she herself had been looking for Mrs Goodwin, she'd been told that she'd gone walkabout. The interest in one resident in particular was the final confirmation – she'd found her home child. But had she found her murderer or just a piece of the puzzle? If she had then what had Agatha's call been about? Or could she still tie all the pieces together even with this new knowledge? Her wild theory gained momentum as her brain rapidly recalibrated all the pieces.

She needed to think it through again carefully, but of immediate concern was what had happened to Agatha. The group was dispersing, Monty's small memorial clearly over, and she pulled Greg aside.

'I need your help, Greg, I'm worried that something might have happened to Agatha. We need to search everywhere but I don't want to cause alarm, it may all be quite innocent.'

'Do you mean that she's been taken ill? We should tell Mrs Goodwin.'

'No, not ill, I'm concerned that someone's harmed her. She phoned me to tell me something important, but someone spoke to her and the call was cut off.'

I'll search the rooms, you search the garden, and I'll meet you in reception.' Greg strode off purposefully.

'Nothing.' They stared at each other grimly, a few minutes later.

'What do we do now?'

'Is anyone missing, Greg? Someone who was here earlier but has now gone?' Think quickly, I've got a bad feeling about this.'

'Let me check the car park, that'll be quickest.'

She hurried after him impatiently.

'Richard's car is missing, but, Richard would never...' Greg's anguished face turned to her. 'He wouldn't hurt a fly, I'm sure of it, only...'

'What is it? Talk to me.'

'It's just that, well, it was something he said to me once, that he'd made sure of something, oh, for goodness' sake, Sasha.' He shook his head. 'You've guessed about Richard and me, I know you have. We were talking about if his uncle found out about us, how it might affect him inheriting – you know what Howard's like, stuck in the dark ages and refusing to tolerate anything that doesn't meet with his rigid little way of looking at life. It just sounded so ominous, but I really don't think–'

'Greg–' Sasha interrupted. 'We need to hurry. So, Richard said he'd taken care of it, meaning he'd done something to make sure that Howard didn't find out about your relationship? Dorothy? Is that what you think? You think Richard murdered her?' She didn't want to believe it, what about her theory? And yet...

Her mind raced through the mentions of Richard in her interviews. He'd brought shortbread that day, very conveniently, and just about everyone had focused on that, but he'd been spotted in the garden and at least one person thought they'd seen him out there in the afternoon. Moira had also been spotted but they looked so similar that it was easy to confuse them...

'I don't, I can't believe it, but, oh, if only he hadn't come to see me that night.' Greg wrung his hands.

'What night? Help me out here, Greg.'

'The night that Monty was murdered.' He groaned, covering his face so that his next words were muffled, 'He slipped in through the side gate and then through the kitchen door, and surprised me. We had some wine and he stayed for a couple of hours, but...'

Was it possible? Had she been that way off track? Was Dorothy's new friend just coincidental? Richard had been at Meadowvale on Sunday – the right place and right time to receive a blackmail message – Greg had even told her that Spencer had rushed up to him with a memorial card before he drove off. Mrs Pringle had told Maureen that she'd seen him entering or leaving the bank, so he could have drawn cash. Could he have been the mystery person who bought the cake in the patisserie? Greg had passed Richard in the garden when he'd been helping Elizabeth back – had he been about to collect the seeds from the Datura Stramonium? But how had he known about them? Unless...

'Greg, can you remember whether Richard was visiting when Willow had everyone out in the garden to discuss plants, a few days ago? The photographer was there and they were all posing for him?'

He nodded slowly. 'Yes, I remember that, I'd popped in as it was my day off, and we met in the garden for a while, safe from the evil Moira. Richard had to go and have his picture taken with Howard and the Lovewells. Why? What does it mean?'

'It means that Richard could have murdered both Dorothy and Monty, that he could have been given the blackmail note from Spencer on Sunday, that he was seen at the bank on Monday so he could have drawn cash, and that he was in the garden the day that the gardener talked about the dangers of Datura Stramonium, so he would have known how deadly the seeds were. You told me earlier that he passed you and Elizabeth in the garden yesterday when you helped her after she almost fell into the garden waste pile – so he had the opportunity to collect the poisonous seeds, put them on the cupcake and leave it in reception for Spencer.'

Greg's mouth gaped as he stared at her. 'Poisonous seeds? From a plant here? On the cupcake which I gave to him...' His voice dropped to a whisper. 'Spencer saw us one night, as Richard was leaving through the side gate. Richard was horrified. He said he couldn't ever let him tell anyone...'

Another reason to want Spencer out of the way... but then how had the blackmail note ended up where she'd found it?

'Greg? Sasha? Is everything alright?

'Oh my God, Richard? You're still here?'

'Well of course I'm still here, I'm standing in front of you. What's the matter? I saw you both rush off. You look terrible.' He frowned. 'Where's my car?'

'Moira's taken Agatha somewhere in your car.' She ignored his surprised expression as she reassessed quickly – she was beginning to think that anyone and everyone could have committed every single murder – Moira Carding, the woman who Howard had described as manly looking, and who Monty had said was easy to mistake for Richard. She recalled the woman's strong handshake when she'd been introduced. A man had been seen in the garden on the day of Dorothy's murder by more than one person… had it been a man or had it been Moira? She'd certainly been in the village on Monday and could have purchased the cupcake in the patisserie, and Greg had referred to her as her royal highness, which could explain the comment made to Maureen when she'd made her enquiries. But could she place her at Meadowvale every time she needed to, even for Monty's murder? Irritably she shook her head, no, it didn't fit… which meant that she should still consider her crazy idea formed after Agatha's worried call… but should bear in mind that a degree of strength would have come in useful…

Jabbing at her phone, impatiently, she turned to Richard. 'I need you to speak to Sergeant Weaver.'

'Jane? I'm at Meadowvale and I'm concerned for the safety of Agatha Lovewell. I don't have time to explain now but I think she's been taken by Moira Carding and is in danger. They're in the husband's car, here he is, hold on. Richard, can you give Sergeant Weaver your car's details?'

Richard stared at Sasha in confusion as he took her phone, stuttering out the details before turning to her and Greg.

'But why do you think that Agatha is in danger from Moira?'

'There's no time to explain fully, you're going to have to trust me when I tell you that Moira may be planning to kill Agatha to stop her from disclosing details about the day of Dorothy Newton's murder which would implicate her.'

'Implicate her? In what?' Richard stared at Sasha as though she was mad.

'In Dorothy's murder,' Greg added helpfully, feeling much happier at this latest turn of events. 'I always said she was evil.'

'Where might she have taken her? Think quickly.'

Richard patted his pocket. 'My keys are gone, the keys to the shop. But Dorothy's murder?' He shook his head, filled with confusion.

'No.' Sasha shook her head. 'I need you to think of some place where she could harm her, on the river or something, maybe? I'll call Jane back and tell her to check along the river bank, it's got some pretty steep areas where it would be easy to push someone in. We've got to start looking somewhere.'

'No, wait.' His hand held her arm. 'My safe, my safe at the shop – there's a collection of military daggers. But what's that got to do with Moira? Surely you can't think...'

'Jane.' She spoke rapidly into her phone, 'Richard's shop, the military memorabilia at the end of the high street. There are knives there.' Nodding, Sasha turned as Davinia Lovewell appeared.

'Where's my sister? What's going on? I told her not to worry herself, not to say anything, oh dear, why couldn't she leave things be? She just gets confused. It's my job to protect her, I always try to protect her.'

'Come back inside.' Greg steered Davinia away, murmuring calming platitudes. 'Let's get you a nice cup of tea.'

~

'But I don't want to drink any more hot chocolate.' Agatha was tearful. 'And why are we in this shop? It's dark and cold in here. You said we were going to buy cakes.'

Moira took a deep breath as she stirred in another of her sleeping tablets to the hot drink. *Why would the woman not just fall asleep? She couldn't do it if she was conscious, she just couldn't.* 'This will warm you up, here, drink it. We'll go and collect the cakes in a minute, they're not quite ready yet. We'll get you one of those nice cupcakes, how's that? You can eat it on the way back to Meadowvale.'

Agatha brightened. 'Oh, that will be nice, I'm really quite peckish now. Alright, I'll drink the hot chocolate, but then we must get going, I don't want to miss the tea, Kirsty made lemon drizzle cake specially, it was my idea.' She drank down the hot chocolate and leaned back in the old armchair. 'I'll just close my eyes for a moment I'm feeling quite sleepy...'

Finally. Moira left the elderly woman and walked through to the back of the shop, opening the safe with Richard's key, and selecting one of the ancient daggers. Walking back, she stood over Agatha, her hand gripping the deadly weapon.

'Step back!' The door crashed open as police officers rushed towards her.

~

'Moira Carding is in custody and Agatha Lovewell is on her way to the hospital in Rentham. She'd been given sleeping tablets in hot chocolate but she's already waking up so hopefully the dose wasn't strong enough to cause her any ill effects. I'm heading to Meadowvale now so you can clue me in on everything. Well done, Sasha, it seems we've finally caught our murderer.' Jane Weaver rapidly updated Sasha.

'Not exactly...' Sasha grimaced. 'I think it's a little more complicated than that. Can you bring Ross and Pav with you? I'd like to speak to everyone with you all present.'

~

How much to expose of people's old lives? How many of their old lies should she uncover publicly? None was the answer, it wasn't her place, not really. And yet, so many of these seemingly innocent characters had kept secret something from their past that they were ashamed of and which, should it come out, would negatively affect their life going forward. Some of their lies were perhaps for a good reason, or an understandable one at least, but some were unfair to others and might affect their remaining future. It could also be argued that some of the actions taken, concerning past secrets, were criminal in their nature, even if they hadn't involved murder.

If Dorothy hadn't been murdered by someone wanting to protect their secret at all costs, Sasha would never have had cause to delve so deeply into everyone's past and find out the things that she had. It was a quandary and she mulled it over in her mind as she waited for the police to arrive.

She was distracted by the buzzing of her phone, and walked through to the games room, stepping inside as she spoke to Mrs Pringle, thanking her for her assistance with Maureen.

'But I've remembered something else, dear, you see, I told Maureen, when she was here with Douglas, and really, he truly is the sweetest dog, but I mustn't get distracted, I told her that I couldn't properly see the comings and goings at the patisserie, but I've found something out, it might be important. After Maureen left, I popped over the road and had a little chat with the young girl, Judy, who works there, she's inclined to be a bit slow, but I gather you're interested in who purchased cupcakes? Well, she wasn't sure who the other person was who bought one, but she said that Theresa had served them, and Theresa's away in London at her sister's and she doesn't use a mobile phone, not that I blame her, the curse of the modern ages, I call them, although I use one myself, just for the convenience, you know...'

Sasha tried to concentrate on Mrs Pringle's twitterings, as noises outside heralded the arrival of Jane Weaver and her officers. 'Dolly, I must go, like I said, you've been most helpful...'

Her eyes roamed over the pictures fixed to the wall, concoctions of wool and coloured card depicting residents – one of Willow's activities no doubt – she smiled, they weren't bad, she could even see who was supposed to be who.

'Yes, dear, I won't hold you up, you see, I've known Theresa's sister for years, we went to school together, so I gave her a call and spoke to Theresa and she described the person to me and I know exactly who it is. But is it true? Was a cake really used to poison young Spencer?'

'Dolly, you can't breathe a word of this, please, but yes, that's probably how it was done. Who was it? Who bought the cake?'

She listened to the name – it made perfect sense – as she stared at one of the pictures. It had been right here in plain sight, she realised, a clue she had overlooked which should have led her to Dorothy's murderer much earlier. The murder weapon was crudely drawn, but it explained the position of some of the bruises on Dorothy's back. The picture had been signed and she smiled sadly – poor Monty, he had unknowingly depicted not only Dorothy's killer but his own, too.

She looked at the image of Agatha holding a large piece of cake, wondering at the irony of it all – that cake had played such a role in these terrible crimes as well as in the solving of them. So many of the residents had mentioned the fact that Kirsty's homemade drizzle cake had been served on Tuesday instead of Monday but she'd paid no attention to such an arbitrary detail; Monty had given her valuable information in his interview, as had Agatha, but she'd paid no attention to their interest in cake; and Spencer, who, despite all his sins, hadn't deserved to die, had been killed with the help of a cake. Noticing the name signed in the corner of Agatha's picture, she allowed herself a moment of sadness, before squaring her shoulders – murder was murder and no one deserved to get away with it, no matter how sorry she might feel for anyone.

There was now no doubt in her mind as to how each of the murders had been carried out, and by who. Thanking Mrs Pringle, she headed through to speak rapidly with Jane Weaver, before turning to Mrs Goodwin.

'Well, I don't suppose Monty will mind now, will he? And if it's to bring to an end all these dreadful killings, although I can't imagine what it's got to do with anyone here, well then, yes, I suppose so.'

She had one more question for her. 'The numbers on the back of the memorial cards, what were they?'

'Oh, I jotted their room numbers on the back to make sure that each resident would receive their own card.' Mrs Goodwin clapped her hands and addressed the gathering.

~

'Preposterous.' Judith Bertram's face was flushed with indignation. 'I don't have time to sit around listening to a private investigator, certainly not. Various murmurs of assent joined her mutiny.

'I should go and clear up in the kitchen.' Tanya turned to go.

'I'm taking my mother to her room.' Mervyn Springer took Lillian's arm.

'Judith, I'd like to have a lie down please.' Elizabeth's voice sounded commanding as she addressed her daughter.

'Not sure that I want to listen to a rehash of everything, especially if it's all about who said what about who, come on, Ray, give me a hand.'

'Oh, do stay, Albert.' Elspeth's tone was imploring as she played with her ring.

'Have you heard about the bird? He lived in Norwich and ate porridge.' Sasha's voice rang out loudly and clearly, stopping everyone in their tracks.

'Please, take your seats, this won't take too long.' She waited for the dissenters to seat themselves before continuing.

'I saw him kissing the little dickie bird. Keys in the pot what have we got? Nobody likes a thief. All that glitters is not gold. The giggling little rich girl is a fake.'

There was a gasp from somewhere in the room as Richard anxiously whispered to Greg.

'Richard, quiet, my boy, Sasha's speaking.' Howard frowned at his nephew.

'You threw it away with the bathwater, your brave heart will never love you now.'

A face paled among her audience.

'Kissing in the cupboard, kissing in the garden, but it's all over if you kiss and tell.'

A chair was pushed back, scraping on the floor a little.

'Once upon a time there was a little boy and a little girl, but they didn't live happily ever after.'

'Sorry.' Tanya bent down to pick up the saucer she'd dropped.

'He got your keys and more while you were happy in the valley. The happily married liar just wants her money.'

'Judith,' Elizabeth hissed, 'I want to lie down.'

'Can you nose out the truth Mrs La de dah? Mummy was a naughty girl and the camera doesn't lie.'

About to help her mother out of the chair, Judith paused, lowering herself back into her seat as she stared at Sasha.

'You've all heard these cruel words before. Dorothy liked to find out secrets about people and when she did, she'd taunt them with cryptic comments which only made sense to the person themselves.' She looked around at the, now attentive, audience.

'To the casual observer, Dorothy's little snipes made no sense at all, but I reminded myself that she chose her words with great care – if something seemed meaningless then I should go back and look again – it would mean something. Of course, there was always the chance that she'd got something wrong, but most of the time her observations were extremely astute and predominantly correct.

Everybody lies, everybody. We may not mean to, or we may have the best of intentions, but we hide things that have happened in our lives, and someone wanted to protect their old lie no matter what it took.

'Where's Agatha? I need to know if she's alright.' Davinia's voice quavered as Kirsty sat down beside her, patting her arm.

It was time to get the show on the road. She drew a deep breath, looking around at her audience.

'Some of what I'm going to tell you today is going to affect the seemingly innocent, in as much as they aren't guilty of murder, but many of you have covered up secrets from your old lives, some of you are living a lie, or are guilty of a crime, and some of you, by your foolish behaviour, have played an unwitting role in the murder of Dorothy, and subsequently, of Monty and Spencer. I'm afraid that everything must come out as we unravel just how Dorothy's meddling caused these tragic events to unfold, and I'd like to apologise in advance for any distress–' She was interrupted by the loud boom of a man's voice as he rushed in.

'My wife called me, what exactly is going on here?'

'Our private investigator is accusing us of being a lying bunch of murderers.' Elizabeth's voice was mocking as she reached for her stick. 'Come on Judith, David can take us to yours, we've heard quite enough.'

Jane Weaver raised an eyebrow at Sasha, who shook her head.

'I'm sorry, Mr Bertram, I'm going to have to ask you to take a seat, no one is to leave.' She nodded at Ross, who moved to block the door.

'What? But that's ridiculous. I'm moving my mother-in-law to another home, and not before time. If she stays here she's likely to end up murdered by the cook or something equally absurd.' David Bertram's posturing fizzled out as he reluctantly joined his wife and mother-in-law.

'We'll begin with one woman's foolish lie – a pretence of wealth to get what she wanted. *All that glitters is not gold*, said Dorothy, as she taunted Elspeth about her fake jewellery.'

'Oh, Mum...' Miriam's despairing voice sounded loud in the quiet of the room. 'What have you done?'

'But I haven't done anything, really, this is all so silly,' Elspeth fluttered, blushing. 'Albie, say something, this is too unkind.'

'Now look here.' Albert made as if to rise from his chair, but Raymond held his arm.

'Hold on, Dad. Is it true, Elspeth? The jewellery's all fake? You were going to let Dad marry you believing you were loaded?' His laugh was bitter. 'What a waste of time, so much for our plan. The poor bugger who's been pinching it's in for a disappointment.'

'But we're getting married, we still are, aren't we, Albie? I only did it because I love you.'

'No one stole Elspeth's jewellery,' Sasha intervened. 'She panicked, concerned that Albert would find out that she wasn't wealthy and call the wedding off. It was a silly lie, made up by a woman who'd led a lonely life, widowed at a young age, raising her daughter alone, and just wanting to find love again.'

'You silly old thing, I've grown quite fond of you, you know.' Albert reached out for Elspeth's hand. 'We can still be married.'

'I don't think so, Albert,' Sasha said softly.

'I knew what Albert and Raymond were up to, but I didn't care. Don't you see? I just wanted to be romanced and to be a bride. I was worried that Albie might suggest selling some of my jewels to pay for our wedding, so I gave some of my rings to Agatha and told her not to tell anyone, I'd seen how much she liked them. I threw the other pieces away in the rubbish. But it hasn't done any harm...'

'The trouble is that it has, Elspeth. Dorothy taunted Albert with her clever words: *There once was a crook who cooked the books, he did his bird, but haven't you heard? They're plotting to take all the money.* Albert had been in prison for embezzlement at his place of work and he feared that if you discovered the truth about him, you'd call the wedding off.'

'Prison, Albie? But...'

'A jail bird, I knew it,' Elizabeth scoffed. 'I've got to hand it to Dorothy, she had a way with words.'

'Dorothy's murder silenced her, saving Elspeth's foolishness from exposure, and protecting Albert's old lie so that he could go ahead and marry his supposedly wealthy fiancée.'

'My dad might be a lot of things but he's no murderer,' Raymond exploded. 'Call yourself a detective? This is total rubbish. Dad, tell her she's got it all wrong.'

Sasha held her hand up, calling for quiet. 'Let's move along.

'Howard wasn't hiding any lies from his old life but his strict moral code and bigoted views put pressure on some of you with devastating consequences. Here are a few excerpts from Dorothy's notebook – *Kissing in the cupboard, kissing in the garden, but it's all over if you kiss and tell. A brave heart could never love a little magpie stealing all the shiny things. They're all lying dirty birdies. They've been naughty girls and the little dicky bird likes to sing to a different song. Poor brave heart.*'

'You found Dorothy's notebook?' Elizabeth leaned forward in her chair, staring at Sasha.

Sasha nodded. 'I did, and it was extremely enlightening. Here are two more notes: *The unhappily married liar just wants her money; you threw it away with the bathwater, your brave heart will never love you now.*

'The references to brave heart confused me until I conducted a quick search online and found out that the name Howard is possibly derived from German elements meaning brave and heart.

'Once I knew that, it made things clearer. There were four of you hoping for something from Howard, five actually, if we include Greg.'

'Five people wanted something from me? Who? And what's Greg got to do with it? What did I have that anyone wanted?' Howard blinked at Sasha in astonishment. 'And I'm not bigoted, I just like things to be right and proper, that's all.' He pursed his lips unhappily. 'You tell her, Davinia.'

Davinia kept her head down, her hands knotted in her lap, before looking up at Sasha, her eyes pleading. 'Is this all really necessary?'

'I'm afraid so, Davinia. Elspeth wasn't the only elderly resident hoping to find love, it seems that both Davinia and Agatha harboured hopes of romance with Howard.'

'Romance? With me?' Howard chuckled. 'Well, nothing wrong with admiration, the two sisters are fine upstanding women with impeccable characters.'

'And there we have the problem, Howard. Davinia was acutely aware of your views and knew that if you found out certain things about them you might change your opinion. She would do anything to protect her sister, Agatha, who had kleptomaniacal tendencies. Agatha couldn't help herself, she just liked *shiny things*, to use Dorothy's words.'

'Oh, this is priceless, we've been living with a liar, an ex-convict, and a kleptomaniac in our midst,' said Elizabeth, looking around for support as everyone avoided her eyes.

'I can think of worse things to be, Elizabeth.' Sasha fixed her eyes on her for a moment until Elizabeth looked away.

'And as for Davinia, she was blameless of nothing more than a young love affair which resulted in a pregnancy. In order to avoid a scandal, she was sent away by her parents, to return after the birth. *You threw it away with the bathwater, your brave heart will never love you now*, was Dorothy's taunt which told Davinia that she'd guessed, helped no doubt by Agatha's tendency to chat about the past quite innocently, with no knowledge of why her sister went away for a while.

'You had no need to live your life in shame, Davinia.' She looked sympathetically at the woman. 'The only mistake you made was to care about what Howard would think of you if he found out.'

Howard opened his mouth to speak, gaping like a fish, as Sasha continued.

'Richard and Moira had hopes of an inheritance from his uncle, and the financial pressure which they lived under due to Richard's struggling business meant that they had to keep him happy at all costs. Dorothy's comment, *the unhappily married liar just wants her money*, was a reference to Moira, who suffered an unhappy marriage to get what she saw as her due. Moira was aware of Richard and Greg's affair. Yes.' She nodded at Richard. 'A wife knows, and she, Richard, and Greg knew that Dorothy had guessed what was going on from her comments of *kissing in the cupboard, kissing in the garden*, and, *the little dicky bird likes to sing to a different song*. All three of them had a vested interest in making sure that Dorothy never gave the game away to Howard.'

'Richard?' Howard looked at his nephew in shock. 'What's she talking about? Clear this up, my boy, we can't have this kind of talk.'

'I'm sorry, Uncle Howie.' Richard shifted in his seat, refusing to meet his uncle's eye.

'And now we come to the next of Dorothy's taunts, *he just wants her to write two words, but she won't sign the contract*. She was referring to Lillian, but her target was Mervyn, who spent a lot of time here with his mother in his vain attempts to get her to change her will, under the guise of signing her new contract. But Mervyn wasn't working alone, as a note from Dorothy's notebook tells us. *Once upon a time there was a little boy and a little girl, but they didn't live happily ever after. It's time to come home children but she's already here. Why did you choose him?*

'This is a sad story of a young woman who, out of poverty, gave up her daughter when her husband left her, putting her into a home – The Sisters of Mercy. I had to choose, and he was such a poorly little thing, Lillian said to me one day. Her decision has clearly haunted her, possibly explaining why the little girl in her children's stories was named Emily, after her daughter.'

A gasp sounded and Sasha turned, nodding at Tanya. 'The words home children were a reference to the abominable child migration scheme, known as Home Children, where orphans were sent overseas, from the United Kingdom, to join new families. But many were sadly exploited for cheap labour.

'I don't know whether Lillian found out that her daughter, Emily, had been sent to Australia, but she mentioned it occasionally, so maybe she'd tried to find out what had happened to her. With no way of tracing her, she did the only thing that she could to try to make some kind of amends and left her wealth to The Sisters of Mercy, whose care she had entrusted her daughter to.

'Mervyn managed to trace his sister and embroiled her in his plan to make Lillian change her will, agreeing to share the inheritance if she could convince her to sign what they referred to as the contract. And this is where Tanya came in, recommended by Mervyn to Mrs Goodwin, to work as a carer and to gain Lillian's trust.

'Dorothy's comments convinced them both that their secret was at risk of being revealed and only they know why that would have been such a bad thing.'

'A bad thing?' Tanya's voice rasped. 'I hate her for what she did to me. She used to give interviews to magazines and say she only had one child. Mervyn found them and sent them to me. That's when I made my mind up – I never wanted her to know who I was. Do you think I wanted her fake apologies? Her explanations? A bit late now, isn't it? She ruined my life and she was going to give all her money to the place that sent me away. We just wanted what was ours, tell her, Mervyn.'

Mervyn ran his fingers through his thinning hair. 'It was stupid, I don't know why we ever started it, we were just being greedy. We could have talked to her, told her everything, maybe she would have–'

'She's not capable of understanding anything, look at her, she doesn't even know who you are. How would we get her to change her will for her son and daughter when she thinks you're her agent and that her daughter, who she discarded like rubbish, is far away, maybe even dead?'

'Well, we've mucked it all up now, haven't we? At least no real harm was done.' He looked across to Sasha. 'I'm ashamed of what we did if that makes things any better.'

'Sadly it's a bit late for that, Mervyn, harm has been done, I'm afraid, there have been three murders don't forget.'

'I told you that I always wanted to write a murder mystery.' Lillian's gentle voice filled the sudden silence as the others turned to look at her, sympathy in their eyes. 'The blackmailer always ends up dead. Now, is this meeting almost finished only I really must get on with my writing.'

At a nod from Mrs Goodwin, Kirsty moved to sit beside Lillian, holding her hand, as Sasha drew another breath. She was almost done.

'And now we come to the last person towards whom Dorothy directed her taunts – Elizabeth.'

'This is getting so boring. David, are you just going to sit there and let her blacken my name along with everyone else's?'

David Bertram and his wife exchanged a glance, as Judith put her hand on her mother's arm. 'We'll go as soon as she's finished, Mother.'

'But I want to go now. I don't want to listen to these lies.'

'Everyone else had to, old girl, reckon it's the least you can do, don't you?' Albert shrugged his shoulders as he gave her a long, inscrutable, look.

'*Keys in the pot what have we got*, was one of Dorothy's taunts directed towards Elizabeth. *He got your keys and more while you were happy in your little valley*, was another one, written in her notebook, and, finally, *Can you nose out the truth Mrs La de dah? The camera doesn't lie*. This last taunt, although addressing Judith Bertram, was intended to make Elizabeth aware that Dorothy had figured out her secret – her old lie, long buried, from her old life, which she would do anything to keep hidden.'

'Now, look here, this is all very well, but you're bringing my wife into it now and I won't have it.' David Bertram addressed Jane Weaver, 'Sergeant, I'd like to speak to your superior, this whole charade is insulting and demeaning to all concerned.'

'What's demeaning, Mr Bertram, is being shoved face down into a garden pond and held down until you drown.' Jane Weaver's eyes flashed. 'Or having your head bashed in with a marble vase, or suffering a painful hallucinogen-filled death from atropine poisoning. This charade, as you call it, concerns the murders of three people.'

'Sergeant Weaver is quite right, and not only were these deaths demeaning, they were a violation and an indignity to the victims. They were the cruellest of acts, planned and carried out by an evil, calculating mind, and any perpetrator of murder must and will be brought to justice. That's why we're here, and now, if you don't mind, I'll continue.

'To explain the history of Dorothy's taunts to Elizabeth, we must travel back to Africa, to Zimbabwe, then known as Rhodesia, where Elizabeth lived, where she married her husband, and where she gave birth to and raised her daughter, Judith.

'Happy Valley was in Kenya, where a group of party-loving wealthy British expats indulged in hedonistic partying including wife-swapping orgies. It is rumoured that ex-pats in many small towns throughout Africa have created their own Happy Valleys within their communities, thus perpetuating the hedonism, and to this day, there are stories of wife-swapping parties held in small towns across the continent. These days the term *keys in the pot* is used as a signal to begin the party, with spouses pairing off with whoever's keys they pick from the pot.'

Gasps were emitted around the room as eyes turned to Elizabeth in disbelief.

'During his interview, Albert made reference to Elizabeth's reminiscences, often after a few drinks, of her life in Africa, and her parties. He unknowingly gave me a clue when he referred to someone from his past who'd lived in Kenya and Rhodesia, who told him, and I quote this to the best of my memory – it still goes on, not just in the valley, in little mining towns in the middle of nowhere, in the big cities, all those places full of the settlers, all on account of the boredom, it's never changed.'

'You stupid fool, why couldn't you just keep your mouth shut?' Elizabeth spat her words at Albert, her eyes shining with fury.

'All of this explains Dorothy's taunts of Happy Valley and keys in the pot, but to explain her third taunt, we have some photographs which provide interesting suggestions to us. Elizabeth has her wedding photo in her room, and a photo of her blue-eyed husband holding Judith as a baby. But I found another photo which Dorothy had hidden, in which we see a group of young people gathered outside a club in Rhodesia. Elizabeth, who has blue eyes, is clearly identifiable, and a brown-eyed man with a prominent nose, has his arm around her shoulders.

'Mummy? Is this true? Is what she's saying true? How could you?'

'You never were that bright, Judith.' Elizabeth's tone was cruel. 'Where exactly did you think your brown eyes and beaky nose came from? It's just the way it was out there, everyone did it. We were young, we wanted to have fun, anything to alleviate the boredom of the endlessly perfect days in Africa. Of course, I couldn't tell Ernest, I let him believe you were his daughter, and

Ramsay never knew or cared.' Her laugh was bitter as she gazed off into the distance.

'I don't believe you. You're lying.' Judith looked desperately at her husband for support, but he sat forward, his head in his hands, seemingly robbed of words.

'I'm tired of lying.' Elizabeth sighed, looking directly at Sasha. 'Well, you've started, so you may as well finish this, don't you think?'

Giving Elizabeth a barely perceptible nod, Sasha continued. 'I'm sorry that you had to find out this way, Judith, but it's directly related to the events at Meadowvale these past weeks and therefore was inescapable.

'Dorothy's taunts about Judith threatened to expose Elizabeth's past lifestyle and the truth about Judith's father. She is married to a member of parliament and their daughter is getting married in a few weeks. Their whole meaning of life appears to be their social status, all Elizabeth talks about is the society wedding of the year, and she could not bear the thought of the scandal if her old lie was revealed. And so, just as for those of you already mentioned, Dorothy's death conveniently silenced her forever, saving Elizabeth from the shame and humiliation she dreaded.'

Pausing to gaze at the silent group, Sasha quelled the sadness within her.

'The cruel murder of Dorothy brought relief to a number of you. Your old lies were safely buried in the past again and life could go on. But with so many of you benefitting from her silence, how do we even begin to fathom out who actually murdered her?'

All eyes were fixed on Sasha.

'Once we know who murdered Dorothy, we can move on to who murdered Monty and Spencer. These are the points of interest, derived from my interviews with you all, which led me to the answer.

'The sounds heard in Dorothy's room before lunchtime; the sighting from someone's room of Mervyn Springer leaving in his car before lunch; the library door to the garden left swinging open; Albert caught in the drizzle; Agatha heading off into the garden shortly before the crafting session ended; a missing walking stick rubber; a stained handkerchief; an unknown man seen in the garden before tea; red for danger; Kirsty's homemade lemon drizzle cake; a missing pink pen; a new friend; the art displayed on the wall in the games room; a book by Agatha Christie.

'It was the mention of this last point, the title of Agatha Lovewell's favourite book, which finally set me in the right direction, and so we begin Dorothy's last, fateful day.'

OLD LIES

'Dorothy spent the morning of the day of her murder, taunting people in the lounge and writing notes in her notebook, which she then took to her room after coffee, before returning to fall asleep in her chair in the lounge until lunchtime. Elizabeth Payton, in one last attempt to get hold of Dorothy's notebook and destroy it, took the opportunity to search her room, overheard by Davinia in the room next door – she had gone to her room just after Dorothy returned to the lounge, to rest. As Elizabeth searched, she glanced out of the window and saw Mervyn Springer leaving – a point which she later informed me of, forgetting that Dorothy's room has the only view of the car park – she then changed her story to say that she'd seen him leaving in the afternoon, around the time of Dorothy's murder, although not one person mentions having seen him in the afternoon.'

'You conniving old bag.' Mervyn pushed himself up from his chair.

'Sit down please, Mr Springer.' Jane Weaver's voice brooked no argument.

'Dorothy wrote one more note in her notebook, which I haven't mentioned until now. This time it's not about anyone else, but about herself. *I've got a new friend from the Wizard of Oz. Shh, she's going to tell me a secret this afternoon.* Tanya was Dorothy's new friend, the odd slip in her accent or choice of words having been picked up on by Dorothy. And so, tragically, Dorothy had an appointment with her own death that afternoon.

'No one remembers seeing Dorothy after lunch, so at some point, she headed off to meet her new friend, and Willow gathered everyone for a crafting session. By now, the plan to murder Dorothy was underway.

'Albert didn't participate in the crafting session, but headed to the pond, to be joined by Moira, who had returned in trousers in hopes of not being recognised should anyone see her in the distance. They were joined by Davinia, who was not to know that her sister would place a slice of cake in her room for her, as well as Elizabeth, who had rushed off from the crafting session, slipped on a kaftan she'd stolen from Agatha's room, and left via the library, leaving the door swinging, as was her habit – something which annoyed Albert so much that he couldn't refrain from mentioning it to me.'

'Albie? What's she talking about? I don't understand,' said Elspeth fretfully.

'But what on earth were you doing, Elizabeth, wearing one of Agatha's kaftans? And Moira? Davinia?' Howard's face was bewildered. 'Why was everyone at the pond?'

'Oh, do be quiet, Howard, this ridiculous story is far too entertaining to spoil it by interrupting.'

'Mother, for the last time, will you please be quiet?' Judith glared at Elizabeth, before nodding to Sasha to continue.

'Anyone who looked out at the garden would have assumed that it was Agatha, as indeed they did, although each time it was mentioned to me, I picked up an air of puzzlement. The reason for this became clear as we discovered that Agatha had spent the time with Lillian, had helped her look for her pink pen in the library, the door of which had been left swinging by Elizabeth, and had sat at the table threading beads with both Lillian and Howard until the end of the session. Howard had even made a joke about Agatha staying there until dinner was served. But back to Dorothy's appointment with murder.

'With everyone assembled, Tanya met Dorothy beside the pond, where Moira, having the most strength, pushed Dorothy over so that she lay face down in the water. It was then down to Elizabeth, with her tripod walking stick, Davinia, with her walking stick with the pimpled rubber, and Albert, with his walking stick, to hold her head beneath the water until she drowned.'

Gasps of shock were emitted around the room and Sasha waited for everyone to settle before continuing.

'Once the deed was done, Dorothy's handbag was hooked from the water in the hopes of finding her notebook and destroying all evidence concerning their secrets. But they didn't find her notes, for Dorothy had torn the pages out and hidden them in her dolls, who looked after her secrets, as she'd once said to me.

'Albert hurried back, not realising that his handkerchief, stained with his hair dye, had fallen from his pocket at the scene, hearing Elspeth calling him and needing to keep her away, explaining his damp clothing away with mention of being caught in the drizzle, and his absence as his attempt to search for her missing bracelet. He commented unthinkingly on the fact that Elizabeth had left the library door swinging again. While he changed his wet clothes, Elspeth went to tea, saving him a piece of cake. Davinia made her way to tea, unaware that her sister had left her a piece of cake in her room – a point which she covered up quickly in our interview when Agatha mentioned it – her face flushed from the exertion, and commented on by Howard as matching her red blouse. Unbeknown to Davinia, the rubber tip from her walking stick had dislodged while they were holding Dorothy's head under the water, some of the bruises on her neck and back clearly showing groupings of small dots from the pimples. I have no doubt that it is sitting at the bottom of the pond still.

'Moira left by the side path to return home, while Elizabeth removed the kaftan, now muddied on the hem, and gave it to Tanya, who rushed back inside, hurriedly cut it into pieces, and hid it in the bottom of Kirsty's ragbag in the kitchen, before clearing away the cake plates – not stopping to wash her hands, a point noticed by Monty. Elizabeth then entered the conservatory, in her red blouse, where Monty tripped over her tripod stick, which explains his comment to me of red for danger. By now all signs of there having been cake were gone and Elizabeth drank a cup of tea.

'Of all the residents, Elizabeth was the only one unaware that homemade lemon drizzle cake had been served, it being a Tuesday and not the regular Monday, and of all the residents, Elizabeth is the only one who uses a tripod walking stick, its three feet having left clear, equidistant bruises on Dorothy's back.

'And there it may have ended, with no clue, at the time, as to who murdered Dorothy, thanks to muddled, unreliable accounts of the day. The murderers had got away with it, they'd protected their old lies and secrets, and thanks to their plan to each play their part in Dorothy's murder – just like those characters in Agatha's favourite Agatha Christie book – they had ensured their collective silence.'

'An extremely clever plot.' Lillian nodded approvingly. 'Murder on the Orient Express, such an enjoyable story, don't you think? But I don't remember anyone drowning in a pond in that one, it must have been another of her books. Of course, it was the famous Belgian detective, now, what was his name...' She looked up at Sasha, momentarily confused. 'But you're not from Belgium, are you, dear?'

Sympathetic looks were directed towards Lillian as Mrs Goodwin moved across the room to sit beside her, taking her hand.

'Following Dorothy's murder, the residents involved, Elizabeth, Albert, and Davinia, went to great lengths to express their dislike for one another – something which Mrs Goodwin mentioned to me, since they used to be friendly. But then everything changed when I arrived to help the police – memories were stirred, new details were emerging, and I mentioned that I would be searching the premises. Unbeknown to me this was the catalyst for the next murder – that of Monty Mallowan.

'The hiding of the pieces of kaftan in the rag bag was a temporary measure, but one which Elizabeth had not panicked about as it seemed unlikely to be discovered for a long time, until she was galvanised into action with the threat of another search of Meadowvale. And so, last Thursday night, once everyone was sleeping, she removed the pieces of kaftan from their hiding place in the kitchen and made her way out to the garden via the conservatory, where, fatefully, Monty had fallen asleep.

'At the same time, Spencer arrived at the side gate to enter the grounds and retrieve his drugs from their hiding place in the greenhouse, leaving the two girls, Lucy and Chantelle, in the car.

'Elizabeth and Spencer crossed paths when she hid the pieces of fabric in the craft box in the storeroom. Spencer, perhaps attracted by torchlight, stood outside the storeroom, wiped the glass, and watched Elizabeth.

'Elizabeth's activities must have disturbed Monty – maybe he saw the pieces of Agatha's kaftan and realised what had happened on the day of Dorothy's murder. Perhaps he even guessed what Dorothy's taunts to her had been about. He tackled Elizabeth about it on her return from the garden and, suddenly, Elizabeth is back to square one – but this time she is not just at risk of her old lie being revealed, she is at risk of being exposed as a murderer.

'She was wearing her black leather gloves – these ones right here, which she later cleverly hid in among Agatha's misappropriated bits and pieces – and she picked up the marble vase, hitting Monty over the head with it, not once but three times, before placing the vase on the floor and making her way to bed.

'We'll never know how Spencer came to follow her back to the conservatory, but we do know that he bragged to his girlfriend and friends on Sunday evening that he knew who had killed Monty and that he planned to use his knowledge to make money, indeed, he'd already delivered a blackmail note to the person concerned, that very day.

'Spencer entered the conservatory and helped himself to Monty's wallet, holding Monty's head and using tissues to wipe his bloodied hands, before returning to his car where he wiped his fingers on Lucy's jeans, transferring blood to them.'

'And it all happened on my watch, I'll never forgive myself to my dying day.' Greg's horrified face looked around pleadingly at the group.

'None of us will, Greg,' said Mrs Goodwin despairingly.

Sasha waited a moment for the murmurings to die down.

'It was a terrible, undignified end to Monty's life, but he'd left us a valuable clue regarding Dorothy's murder, in his depiction of Elizabeth, displayed on the wall in the games room with everyone else's from a recent crafting session, complete with her tripod walking stick. The groupings of some of the bruises will now be able to be matched to Elizabeth's tripod stick – the only one of its kind used at Meadowvale.

'On Friday evening, Mrs Goodwin gathered everyone together for dinner, to chat fondly about Monty, but Spencer stirred things up by suggesting that someone may have seen who killed Monty and might try their hand at blackmail, in essence, suggesting to Elizabeth that he may have seen her.

'Lillian, unknowingly, suggested that in that case, if it were in a book, the next murder would be of the blackmailer, and somewhere during this discussion, Elizabeth, in her anxiety, dropped her fork, a detail noticed by Lillian – who informed me, telling me that it was a clue – unaware that all these small points were helping me to build a picture of our murderer.

'And so we come to Sunday when Spencer is tasked with distributing the memorial cards for Monty's service. He writes his demand on the bottom of one of the cards, leaving it in Elizabeth's room, where she opens it in my presence when I accompanied her to her room after our interview. I attributed her white face to sadness about Monty, whereas it was, in fact, due to the words scrawled in Spencer's identifiable writing style – a product of his dyslexia, where he often mixed up his capital letters and used phonetic spelling.

'Five hunDreD quiD in an envelope in the library behind the Lillian Books by MunDay evening or I tell the cops.

'Elizabeth knew the demand was from Spencer and she agreed to join the others on a trip to the village the next day so that she could withdraw cash from the bank and make him his payment, thus buying herself some time. In the meantime, she had to figure out a way to silence him as soon as possible.

'Our group of residents convened in the Parva Patisserie for lunch, where Agatha purchased an extra cupcake for Mrs Goodwin, plus a couple for herself, to take back to Meadowvale. It was as they were getting into the minibus that Elizabeth went back into the patisserie and bought a cupcake, hiding it in her bag. She still needed to get her hands on some poison and had a plan.

'Colin Hartley, the gardener, unknowingly gave me the information I sought when he expressed his concern, earlier today, about the Datura Stramonium which he'd removed from the garden and disposed of on his garden waste pile.

'Some of you may recall the day you had your photos taken in the garden when Elizabeth referred to a plant called the Moonflower Vine which she recognised from her days in Africa. Colin had stopped her from touching it, warning her of its deadliness, and had removed it there and then, such is its toxicity. It had probably seeded itself from an errant seed in the birdseed from the bird table.

'Desperate to silence Spencer as soon as possible, Elizabeth took a walk in the garden with Judith, feigning tiredness when they reached the greenhouse, and asking her daughter to return and fetch her walking stick.

'While she was alone, Elizabeth took a seed pod, filled with enough seeds to poison an adult fatally, from the toxic plant, just as Greg arrived, who mistakenly believed that she had fallen over. Greg, believing her to be embarrassed, promised not to say a word to anyone, and helped her back indoors.

'All that was left to do was to sprinkle the seeds over the cupcake topping, write Spencer's name on the box and leave it in reception, where she hoped it would be found and given to Spencer. It was known that he had a sweet tooth, loved his cake, and that his girlfriend often dropped him off a treat as a surprise.

'A while later, Greg was collecting bits and pieces left lying around, and returned a book to the library where he bumped into Spencer who, I'm guessing, had just retrieved his first blackmail payment, placed behind the Lillian Springer books as he'd instructed, by Elizabeth.

'Greg, as correctly guessed by Elizabeth, found the cupcake and took it to Spencer in the kitchen, before saying goodbye and leaving for the day, as Spencer began to eat the small cake.'

'I watched him bite into it.' Greg shuddered, looking at Sasha apologetically. 'Sorry.'

'Each seed of Datura Stramonium contains a small amount of atropine, a hundred seeds contain approximately enough for a fatal dose, and the tiny, black seeds have a sweetish taste so Spencer would have found nothing unusual about the sprinkled seeds on the cake. The poison would have taken effect within the hour, which is when Spencer began overheating and hallucinating, making his way to the lounge before collapsing and later dying at the hospital.'

The room was completely silent as Sasha looked around at the shocked faces.

Slowly, Elizabeth began to clap. 'Bravo. What a fantastic story. You've no proof of any of it, of course.'

Sasha nodded. 'You're forgetting about Spencer's blackmail demand, written on your memorial invitation, with your room number on the reverse. Yes,' she acknowledged Elizabeth's surprised expression. 'You didn't realise that Mrs Goodwin used your room numbers to keep track of things. You tore it up and disposed of it in a handbag which you put in the charity box – your suggestion, supposedly in memory of the deceased – but you didn't factor in Agatha's penchant for pretty things. It's thanks to Agatha that we have this valuable evidence. You should have thought of that, after all, you hid your gloves in one of her boxes in her room.

'Perhaps we should move on to Agatha's phone call to me earlier, in which she was distressed after seeing the lemon drizzle cake on the table. It had reminded her of the day of Dorothy's murder, and some inconsistencies which were bothering her – the fact that Davinia had pretended that she ate the cake left in her room; the fact that Elizabeth had insisted that no cake had been served; and the fact that Albert's clothes had been wet even though it had not drizzled with rain.

'Unfortunately, Agatha had earlier expressed her concern to Davinia, in earshot of Elizabeth who, desperate to prevent Agatha from telling anyone what she'd remembered, instructed Moira to take her somewhere and stop her from talking.'

'To stop her from talking, to kill her do you mean?'

'Where is Agatha?'

'Has she been killed?'

'Oh no, not Agatha. How could you, Elizabeth? My own sister, who wouldn't harm a fly.' Davinia's sobs rose above the others' voices. 'All these deaths, why oh why did we ever listen to you? It was bad enough that you wore her kaftan, but to have Moira kill her...'

'Be quiet, Davinia, control yourself. Don't you see? This is all just supposition, our little super sleuth has been playing a very enjoyable guessing game. The whole thing is absurd, there's not an ounce of proof.'

'That's where you're wrong, Elizabeth. I rue the day you roped us in to help you kill Dorothy.' Davinia stood up shakily. 'Everything that Sasha has said is true. We wanted to stop Dorothy from exposing our old lies. I feel so ashamed, I don't know what came over us. Albert? Tanya? Aren't you going to say anything? And now we find out that she murdered Monty and that poor young boy, and now she and Moira have killed my sister.' She turned to Sergeant Weaver. 'I'm prepared to make a full statement, please arrest me.' She walked slowly towards the officer as all eyes followed her.

'I'm sorry, old girl.' Albert smiled sadly at Elspeth before standing up and joining Davinia. 'Tanya?'

Tanya removed her tunic, laying it over a chair, and joined them.

Jane Weaver nodded to her officers, who guided the three from the room, before moving to stand in front of Elizabeth to caution her. 'Elizabeth Payton, you are under arrest on suspicion of murder...'

'Judith, we're leaving.' David Bertram pulled his wife up from her chair. 'I'm never going to live this down.'

'Goodbye, Mother.' Judith's eyes were cold as she gave her mother one last look and left with her husband.

Sasha felt a touch on her arm and turned to find Greg smiling sadly at her.

'Here's a cup of tea, why don't you sit down?'

Sinking into the nearest chair, she took the tea gratefully, sipping it as she looked around at the residue of what had been Monty's memorial, filled with remorse at what she'd done, at the heartache she'd caused in exposing so many old lies.

Mervyn sat close to Lillian, stroking her hand as he murmured something to her gently which made her smile, before kissing her gently and telling her he'd be back to visit soon.

Howard moved to sit beside Elspeth, handing her his handkerchief and patting her arm. Elspeth reached a hand to touch her hair, smiling prettily as she thanked him, a small flush rising in her cheeks.

Miriam sat quietly, thanking the powers that be that Lucy had not been involved in anything violent after all, and grateful that she hadn't destroyed the tenuous trust between them by speaking to the police about her fears, before whispering something to her mother and leaving. She'd collect Lucy from that nice friend of hers, Chantelle, who'd been so kind to her in her grief at losing her boyfriend, and they'd spend some quality mother and daughter time together. She'd ask Dr Singh for some time off, perhaps they could go away for a short trip...

Raymond stood awkwardly, clearing his throat and sidling out of the room, avoiding everyone's eyes.

Greg served cups of tea, his demeanour quiet and reserved, before taking the last cup to Richard. 'Here, I expect you need this. I'm sorry about Moira.' He touched Richard's arm in solidarity.

Howard looked across, catching Richard's eye, excusing himself to Elspeth. He stood up, leaning heavily on his stick, and walked across the room to his nephew.

'It seems I've got some soul searching to do, my boy.' He cleared his throat. 'I don't condone all this skulking around, mind you, but I fear I may have been somewhat, ah, narrow in my way of thinking.'

Richard looked sheepish. 'No, I'm the one who must apologise, Uncle Howie, I'm ashamed that I focused on inheriting from you rather than making a success of my business. Will you forgive me?'

'Nothing to forgive, now give your uncle a hug and we'll say no more about it.'

Rachel Goodwin looked around at her diminished residents and staff, still reeling from the shock of Sasha's disclosures and Sergeant Weaver's information regarding Willow. 'Kirsty, Mary, let's see if anyone wants a piece of cake, and, Greg, our new arrival is due any minute, perhaps you could wait at the entrance for him.' The show must go on.

The sound of voices preceded the opening of the lounge door as Agatha was wheeled in.

'Really, I'm quite alright, there's no need to fuss.'

Surprised faces stared at her as Elspeth stated the obvious. 'Agatha, you're alive.'

'Well, of course I am. What did I miss? Where's my sister? Oh goodie, there's still some cake.'

Quietly, Sasha took her leave, feeling drained of emotion.

~

Des Barnsley thanked Mrs Pringle for the tea. 'Nothing like proper tea in a teapot, I always say. Now, you're sure you can't tell me anything about the goings-on at Meadowvale? It's not like you not to have your finger on the pulse.'

'I'm not saying I can't tell you, but I always say to Sheila it doesn't do to gossip, don't I, Sheila? I'm sure the police will release a statement soon. In the meantime, you might like to pay a visit to the military memorabilia shop tomorrow, I have a feeling that business may pick up for the owner.'

Mystified, Des took his leave, as Mrs Pringle fingered the notebook in her pocket. She was beginning to feel a little tired of murder. She dropped it quietly into the waste bin, before pausing and retrieving it. Perhaps she'd keep it, for now, you never knew when something important might happen. She slipped the notebook back into her pocket and turned to Sheila with a smile. 'Let's go home.'

~

Sasha locked her car and walked across to the door of the pub. Depression washed over her. She felt tired... she felt... old... Maybe she'd spent too much time at an elderly care home. She'd done what she came here to do, found out who murdered Dorothy Newton and helped bring justice for her death, together with Monty's and Spencer's. She'd pack up and head home tomorrow, back to... well, nothing, she thought bleakly, pushing the door open.

The bar was quite busy, but Jules caught her eye, waving her over. 'What d'you need, love?'

'To forget about today, Jules.' She smiled sadly. 'It wasn't a good one.'

Feeling a little better after a chat with Jules, she took her second glass of wine outside, lighting a cigarette and staring out at the Black River. Someone had left a book on the table and it sparked something in her head. Did it matter? She felt so weary of everything. A figure slipped onto the bench seat opposite her and she looked up into Cal's eyes.

'If you're here to have another go at me, forget it, Cal. I just want to have my drink and smoke in peace and then I'm going to bed. It's been a long day.'

'I'm here to apologise, will you let me?'

Nodding, she listened to Cal telling her how wrong he'd been, how badly he'd treated her, how he wished he could turn back the clock. He explained about his marriage, how she'd needed a passport, how her brothers had involved him in something and held it over his head, and how she'd then left him, taking all his savings and possessions, and how he'd tried to track her down to get a divorce, only to have her turn up in Parva Crossing, pregnant from her new boyfriend, who was in prison, along with her brothers.

'That's when you met her. I told her I'd help her if she gave me a divorce, so I packed up and took her to London. I got a job, rented a flat, and supported her until her boyfriend was out of jail six months later. I got my divorce and came back here.' He spread out his hands, his eyes sad. 'I never meant to hurt you, Sash.'

When he'd finished, she stood up. 'It's fine, Cal, really, forget all about it, I'm sorry about what happened to you. We've all said and done things we regret. I'm off to bed now, before I fall asleep at this table.'

'See you tomorrow? I've got to clear out Willow's stuff now that the police have finished with her room, but maybe we could have lunch or something? Try again?'

'Lunch sounds nice, let's see tomorrow, and Cal, if you find a box of Lillian Springer first editions in Willow's room, will you take them back to Meadowvale? They're pretty valuable and they belong in the library there. Goodnight, Cal.' With the last loose end tied up, she dropped her empty glass at the bar and headed to her room, and sleep.

EPILOGUE

Her head had barely touched the pillow, it seemed, when her phone's ringing woke her.

'Hello?' Groggily she checked the time on her watch – three-thirty in the morning. 'Hello?'

'Sash? Oh, thank God. I need your help, I've, well, I've done something stupid... there's so much blood. It's everywhere. She's dead, Sash, but I didn't kill her, I swear. You've got to help me. There's so much blood...'

'Eric?' She sat up, wide awake. 'Where are you? What's happened? Tell me everything.'

She listened to Eric's story, thinking rapidly. 'Stay there and don't touch anything. You're going to have to trust me, okay? I'm calling D.S. Palmer, he's a friend of mine. He'll be with you shortly and I'm on my way. We'll sort this out.'

Half an hour later she tiptoed down the stairs, dropping her bag on the floor while she scrawled a quick note to Jules, which she left on the bar, before quietly closing the door to the Spotted Dog behind her.

DON'T MISS THE NEXT SASHA BLUE MYSTERY

Nocturnal Lies

'There's so much blood... it's everywhere... you've got to help me...'

Eric Latimer's frantic phone call to Sasha in the early hours of the morning prompts her to rush back to London to his aid, leaving Parva Crossing and some unfinished personal business behind.

All the evidence points to Eric having killed the woman, identified as a high-class escort, but he swears that he is innocent.

As Sasha delves deeper into the case, she discovers puzzling similarities between the woman's murder and other cases, but the police aren't convinced and her investigation is being hampered by factors beyond her control.

Battling her personal problems, she turns to her friend Zoe for help and refuge, but Zoe is concerned at just how far Sasha might be prepared to go to prove Eric's innocence.

London's night life has a dark and deadly side and it seems that high-class call girls are in danger from a ruthless killer. Or are things not quite as they seem?

Has the killer come up with the perfect plan to get away with murder? Or can Sasha find her way through the smoke and mirrors to get to the truth... and save the man she once planned to marry?

Nocturnal Lies is the fourth book in the Sasha Blue Mystery Series. Although each book may be read as a standalone there are ongoing connections between the stories which make them more enjoyable when read as a series.

Follow me on your favoured social media platform for book release date info.

ABOUT THE AUTHOR

Linzi Carlisle grew up in Dartford, Kent, in the UK, before moving to South Africa where she met her husband. They lived in Zambia and England, before returning to South Africa to live in the beautiful town of George, part of the Garden Route, nestled between the Outeniqua Mountains and the Indian Ocean – the perfect spot for writing. They share their home with their two beautiful cats.
Old Lies is book three in the Sasha Blue Mystery Series and is preceded by Village Lies and Graphic Lies.
She is also the author of Skipping Christmas in Holly Crescent – a heart-warming winter tale.

A MESSAGE FROM LINZI

Thank you so much for choosing to read Old Lies, the third book in the Sasha Blue Mystery Series - I hope you enjoyed it!
To stay in touch, and keep up to date with new releases, you can just click on 'follow the author' on any of my book detail pages on Amazon, or see the list below.
I love seeing your photos of my books on social media and if you can take a moment to review Old Lies anywhere that would be fabulous!
Sharing book recommendations is one of the ways I've been able to enjoy and share many great books over the years.
Nothing beats word of mouth - sharing your thoughts is a great way for readers to find out about my books.
Thank you.

Blogger: www.linzicarlisle.blogspot.com
Instagram: @linzicarlisleauthor
Facebook: www.facebook.com/linzicarlisleauthor
Goodreads: goodreads.com/linzicarlisle
Twitter: @linzicauthor